WHO PUT BELLA IN THE WYCH ELM?

Blake Myers

Coffin & Nails Publishing

ISBN 979-8-9921451-0-6 (hardback)
ISBN 979-8-9921451-1-3 (paperback)
ISBN 979-8-9921451-2-0 (ebook)
Library of Congress Control Number: 2025930437

Edited by Kathryn Hall – www.cjhall.co.uk
Cover art by Faye Lane – www.faylane.com

Printed in the United States of America
10 9 8 7 6 5 4 3 2 1

Published by Coffin & Nails Publishing 2025
www.coffinandnailspublishing.com

*To my mother who tirelessly helped me
become a lover of books*

My heart was fashioned to be susceptible of love and sympathy, and when wrenched by misery to vice and hatred, it did not endure the violence of the change without torture such as you cannot even imagine.

~ *Mary Shelley*
Frankenstein: The 1818 Text

Forward

To those from the parish of Hagley, UK, this is my retelling, though I know many of you may take grievance with my narrative direction and artistic license. I mean no offense to you or Bella's memory. To rectify any misconceptions and misrepresentations, I have appended this story with an Afterword. In the meantime, please enjoy the story for what it is, a ghost story of the most fantastical nature, and after the Epilogue, remain a little longer as I pay appropriate homage to the woman who haunts your hearts more than your town.

To those wandering into this tale without so much as an inkling as to who Bella is, enjoy the tapestry of fact and fiction woven onto these pages. I have taken much care into preserving historical accuracy within the scope of fantasy. As mentioned in my note to the denizens of Hagley, I will attempt to make a brief dissemination of such facts, for Bella has haunted my heart as much as she has my mind these past two years.

There are inevitable spoilers in the Afterword, so I beg of you, do not read ahead. Let the suspense of the narrative lead to its conclusion, before you venture into the veracity of her story.

Prelude

Pearl slumped over her porridge, drifting into a deep slumber that providence marked as her last. Tears trickled down Thomas' weathered cheeks as he reached across the table and dabbed the corner of her mouth with his napkin. "It'll all be over soon enough, my love."

Puffy and red-eyed, Thomas scanned the quaint kitchen that had hosted nearly every meal in their 50-year marriage. His eyes hovered on a photo of their wedding day, he and his bride standing in the June sun outside St. Michael's Church. To Thomas, the photo never did Pearl justice. She was exquisite. Across the room, his eyes caught the chipped dishware, the first purchase they made as a couple, nestled in the antique glass cupboard they inherited from his parents. On the wall next to the cupboard, a photo of their last holiday to Malta, wearing their matching raffia hats, hung tilted on a crooked nail. Thomas strove in vain to preserve these sweet memories, but they retreated like waves on a shore, supplanted by the terrible act he had just committed—even if it were inevitable.

Thomas pushed himself from the table and cleared the dishes one last time. He set them in the sink and stared as the water washed over the bowl, rinsing away the evidence down the drain. Not that he cared anymore; he didn't intend to cover up his deed.

As he dried the bowl and returned it to the cupboard, the whispers of the *other woman* floated through the lips and voice of Pearl. An occurrence all too common these days, even when Pearl slept. Thomas leaned forward on the counter, squeezing his eyes shut, and prayed, wishing away Pearl's torment in her last moments. He thought back to the unattended kitchen knife and the carving of *those words* Pearl had gouged into the table—and the cuts into her wrists. Shallow and hesitant, but there had been blood. Oh god, so much blood. Thomas grimaced at the memory, using it to excuse his evil act and blame the *other woman*—she gave them no recourse.

But the act was done. It wouldn't matter any longer, at least for him and Pearl.

Thomas hung the towel on the rack and closed the cupboard door. He sat back on the counter, wiping his tears with his sleeve, and marshaled his strength for what followed next. He took a deep breath, then shifted his attention back to his wife, whose sleep deepened bit by bit. He sulked behind her and ran his fingers through her short brown hair and down her shoulders, tenderly straightening her blouse and flattening the wrinkles.

Had he made the right decision? Doubt festered in his thoughts, which swiftly vanished as Pearl sleep-whispered again, pleading more intensely. Nothing could satiate that question; Thomas conceded defeat years ago.

"Come, my dear, let's get you off to bed," said Thomas

as he slid his arm under Pearl's and then scooped up her legs. Her frail body slid against his chest as he lifted her from the kitchen chair. She rested her head in the nook of his neck; her weak and tepid breath sweeping over his skin as she continued whispering.

As he lifted her and staggered away, his eye caught the words Pearl had carved into the table. He had planned on sanding it out before it all ended, but what use would that serve now? They weren't Pearl's words after all, but the ever present, desperate plea of the *other woman*.

"Shush, my dear. Just rest. There's no need to worry about that answer any longer," he said, tears trickling into a full stream.

Thomas lumbered out of the kitchen, past the sitting room, and up the staircase. Cumbersomely, he navigated each step while he bore his sweet Pearl in his arms. One last time, they'd make the journey together to retire to their room. Pearl's end would be peaceful—that he made sure of—but he expected his own fate to be far less fortunate. The *other woman* wouldn't allow it.

Soon *those words* no longer came from Pearl's sweet lips, but from the ether and air surrounding them. *Her* voice swirled and engulfed Thomas as he struggled the last few steps toward his bedroom. Rage consumed her pleas as they manifested into demands and threats. Thomas pushed forward, reassuring himself. *It's almost over. It's almost finished,* he thought.

His arms burned from the weight of his wife, despite her meek size. His knees buckled as he reached the bed and leaned over to set her down.

Ignoring the *other woman* the best he could, he tended to his wife. He changed her into her pajamas and slid her under the comforter, placing her favorite book on her lap as if she were reading. *Fallen asleep amidst Mr Darcy wooing Lizzy. A fitting way to close out your chapter, my love.* His trembling hands held hers one last time before he kissed her breathless lips. Pearl was gone.

While his time to solve the *other woman's* plea had ended, he knew it would soon be passed onto another. It's how it always worked; it's how it always would. April 18th, after all, was in two days. Thomas pitied the soul who'd bear this mantle, though not enough to spare them of it—if it were indeed possible.

Scurrying to the desk that overlooked the garden, he reached in a side drawer and withdrew a black and white marbled composition notebook. In the pencil drawer over the chair, he fetched a key and placed it along with the notebook atop the desk for whomever found him and Pearl. *Taylor will know what to do*, he thought.

A creak from the upstairs landing floated into the bedroom. He listened to the horror of the *thump-shush* meandering down the hall toward him. *Is she here?* Thomas thought in a panic. He fumbled his things, knocking the key off the desk, as he hastily set them down, before rushing to the closet door.

Fingers sweaty and twitchy, he grabbed a bedsheet from the closet and fastened one end to the outer doorknob and the other end to a belt. He tossed the linked pair over the door, letting them droop down the opposite side. Thomas knelt, fidgeting with the noose in his hands, and looped it around his neck. He glanced at his wife and tried to eke out a final goodbye, but the *woman* wouldn't let him; *Bella* wouldn't let him.

Thump-shush, thump-shush.

She had entered the room.

Screwing his eyes shut, he let his legs go limp and fell forward, cinching the noose tight. His pulse thundered under the pressure of the belt. Blood swooshed through his constricted arteries, weakening with each passing second.

Thump-shush, thump-shush.

The sheet stretched taut and the closet knob bent under his body's full weight. Thomas' lungs burned, his final breaths gurgling, as he struggled against instinct, resisting the urge to stand. His eyes bulged like two tiny balloons clenched in a fist, trying to burst from his sockets.

Thump-shush.

Bella, unnaturally twisting her joints, contorted and snapped herself to the ground, facing Thomas. Filthy, dark hair framed her dead eyes as she pressed against him. Her spectral hand, gnarled and rotten, clutched him by the hair and wrestled his ear to her cracked and putrid lips, tormenting him for the last time with *those words*. *Those words* which haunted him and the parish of Hagley:

Who put me in the wych elm?

Chapter 1
One's End Is Another's Beginning

"Liam, Liam, where's my phone?" Emma Lloyd peeked through the sleep in her eyes to read one-thirty on the clock, her hands fumbling on the nightstand to locate her phone. "Liam?" She reached over to find an empty pillow—something she'd never grow accustomed to.

Sweeping her shoulder-length, brown hair out of her face, Emma searched the bed, flipping the sheets all around. She sent a book flying across the room as well as the TV remote before eventually finding her phone and picking up. "CSI Lloyd," she answered, not yet fully coherent. "No, I'm not on call tonight." And nor did she want to be convinced otherwise. After a short chewing out, she grunted, "Belbroughton, you say? No, no, no, don't tell me the directions. Message me the address; I'll never remember how to get there."

Emma slunk out of bed and changed from yesterday's clothes she still wore into something semi-clean she found tossed over the chair. She sniffed it and gave it a pass. *It's one in the morning... no one's clothes will be pressed and clean,* she thought. Scuffling into the kitchen, she snatched a banana from the fruit basket and scribbled a quick note:

> *Penelope,*
> *Got called in. Have to cancel brunch.*

Running toward the door, she opened the fridge and grabbed a Red Bull for the road. She paused and then snagged another—make that two more—before continuing out.

The satnav led her to a brown-bricked cottage in a village unaccustomed to flashing blue lights in the middle of the night. The curious sight of the police this early in the morning attracted bystanders still in their bathrobes, gawking at the officers coming in and out of the house. Most of whom were likely contaminating Emma's crime scene. She parked up and then grabbed her ID badge hanging by a lanyard over the rearview mirror.

Before she could reach for her kit and camera on the passenger side floor, a young, uniformed constable tapped on the glass. "Are you the crime scene investigator?"

"Yes, I'm CSI Emma Lloyd," she replied, as she rolled down the window.

"I'm PC Louis McArthur. The Superintendent sent me to fetch you. Need any help with anything?"

Emma pulled her bag strap over her shoulder and replied, "No, thank you. I've got it."

"Yes, ma'am. Follow me." McArthur led Emma up the driveway, into the house and to the living room, where several other officers had gathered. The decor looked untouched from the mid-1980s, which, despite the lack of fashion, fostered sentimental memories of her grandparents. Wholesome and welcoming.

McArthur, looking smitten with Emma by his side, nervously introduced the officers, starting on his left. Detective Inspector Alfred Wright, a portly, jovial-looking fellow, long past his retirement, instantly endeared her to him. Something about him reminded Emma of her father—she couldn't help but smile. Towering next to Wright, Detective Sergeant George Edwards, whose smug glare befittingly complemented his Magnum PI mustache, fared far less in his first impression after looking her up and down and licking his lip. If Wright wanted to make her smile, then Edwards wanted to make her recoil. Finally, around the circle and to Emma's right, stood Superintendent John Taylor. His somber demeanor had worn heavily on his features over the years, yet it gave him the appearance of a wise, mentorlike chap.

Unease fell on Emma as their eyes sized her up. She had always thought that being slim and attractive had its advantages in life. This was not one of them. The sense that it somehow reflected on her capability—or the lack thereof—emanated from the others and set her teeth on edge.

Superintendent Taylor outstretched his hand and spoke with a wavering voice. "Thank you for coming at such short notice. This case is an emotional one for us, as it's one of our own. Dr Thomas Evans was our CSI."

Emma swallowed the knot in her throat, which included a little pride, as she had completely misread the room. "My condolences. I can't imagine the difficulty. Can you bring me up to speed?"

"Apparent suicide. Nothing has been touched except for the note a neighbor found taped to the front door. They discovered it when checking in on them after both Dr and Mrs Evans missed a dinner date on Friday and multiple unanswered calls over the weekend." Taylor escorted Emma to the kitchen. "The two main areas of interest are here and the bedroom where the—where Dr Evans and Pearl were found."

"There are two deaths?"

"Ahem… yes. Dr Evans, as I mentioned, initial observation points to suicide. Mrs Evans is less clear; possible natural causes. I'll leave you to it." He dabbed his eye and abruptly left the room.

Shrugging off the anxiety of her first crime scene investigation—solo to boot—Emma pulled out her pocket spiral-notebook and jotted down her first notes: Monday, April 17th 2023, 2.33am. Victims — Dr Thomas and Pearl Evans. *This is a whole different world from forensic collision,* she thought. Taking a quick scan around the room, she scribbled a few more notes of her first impressions. The kitchen, much like the living room, bore the markings of meticulous care, but needed dire modernization. A chair leaning precariously on one leg sat wedged underneath the kitchen table. Emma checked her camera for an empty SD card and then snapped a few overview shots.

Click, click.

A pot of porridge sitting on the cooker across the room drew her attention. Their last meal, she presumed. She inspected it, as well as the bits of leftover porridge sitting in the sink strainer.

How many meals had they shared here? How many holidays had they planned together at this table? How many 'I love you'*s exchanged before walking out the door to work?* These were the things robbed of her and Liam.

In a half-opened utensils drawer toward the other end of the counter, a pill bottle conspicuously jutted outward and prevented the drawer from closing. "Not where you should be," she said. The bottle was turned with its label out of view. Emma photographed it from several angles before placing it in an evidence bag. Once lifted, she could read the label: Zolpidem. The prescription from Clark's Pharmacy bore Friday's date and was issued to Dr Thomas Evans. Oddly, the chemist filled the prescription two days prior, but the bottle was already empty. *Note: contact the pharmacy regarding the prescription.*

As Emma finished logging the bottle into evidence, she noticed a marbled crucible tucked behind a jar of biscuits on the countertop. A white powdery substance lined the mortar and pestle. "And what were you used for?" She made a note to test the crucible, porridge, and the contents of Dr and Mrs Evans' stomachs for Zolpidem, a common sleeping aid.

Click.

Emma took swabs of both the leftover porridge in the pot, the sink drain, and the mortar before fingerprinting and bagging it and the pestle. She didn't want to make any assumptions prematurely, but evidence now leaned to a possibility of a murder-suicide—pending a toxicology report and fingerprint analysis. Handing off the evidence bags to PC McArthur, who so graciously volunteered to assist her, she made a last sweep of the kitchen. Emma collected fingerprints from all the remaining items of interest—the drawer, pot, chair, and table —*interesting*. One placemat sat on the table, but two chairs were pulled back, indicating two had been seated. Peering out from underneath the side of the mat, deep gouges had been scratched into the wood. Emma photographed the mat before removing it and revealing more deep gashes as if something was scratched away.

"Do you know anything about this? What was here or when it was made? Scratches look recent and it appears something was underneath," she asked of Taylor. He pursed his lips and shook his head, refusing to make eye contact.

Click.

Other than the tilted chair and the rug leading to the staircase having been disturbed, no other signs indicated a struggle anywhere else on the ground floor. She snapped photos of the living room and entry hall and then turned to Taylor. "Are Dr and Mrs Evans upstairs?"

Choking back a few tears, Taylor replied, "Yes, she's carefully tucked in bed, and he's... he's in the room as well."

"Can you show me?"

Superintendent Taylor led Emma upstairs and down the hall toward the master bedroom. As they walked, Emma snapped shots along the way, keeping track of anything that might be out of place or suspicious. She saw the tension in Taylor as they entered into the bedroom, his shoulders pulled tight and his head hung low. Edwards and McArthur followed behind them, both looking equally downtrodden.

Despite not knowing either Dr or Mrs Evans, heartbreak welled up inside as she took in the sight of the two in their last moments. Mrs Evans laid in bed, just as Taylor had described. Dr Evans, partially kneeling, hung from the closet door, frozen in a twisted position and clawing at the belt around his neck.

On the floor, in the middle of the room, laid a single scrap of paper. Emma snapped a photo before placing it in an evidence bag.

> *John, I'll never be free from her—free from that damn question.*
> *~ Thomas*

"You said a neighbor found the note?"

"Yes, they pulled it down from the front door and still had it with them when they came inside to discover the Evanses. They dropped it here before calling 999," replied Taylor.

"I'll need their fingerprints to help cross-reference," she said. Without being asked, McArthur sprang into action and made his way back downstairs to collect them from the witness. "Who is John?"

"I'm assuming that'd be me," said Taylor. "My given name is John. I, uh—I was the closest thing he had to a best friend. We worked together for nearly twenty-five years." Taylor fought back the tears the best he could.

"Do you know who he's referring to here? Who *she* is? A family member? Mrs Evans? A friend? Perhaps a case he's working on?"

"No, they had no children and no family nearby, and they were both well-loved in the community and at work. But it could be any number of cases—there were dozens involving female vics. As far as him saying anything, he made no comment to me about anyone causing problems." Emma looked over at Edwards, who nodded in agreement.

Emma surveyed the room. "We should make a list of cases where the vic involves a woman. Rape, murder, or maybe even a domestic abuse case. Anything that could shed—"

Out of the corner of her eye, Emma spied Edwards pick up a black and white marbled notebook from the desk and hide it behind his back. "I haven't processed that yet. You shouldn't touch anything until I've given the all-clear."

"My apologies," replied Edwards. "It's just a personal diary of the Doctor. Considering the nature of the situation, I thought I'd give it to family relatives. No need to have their laundry aired out in the station, right?"

Emma held out her hand and waited for Edwards to give her the book. "Which I fully respect, and I promise you, the contents of the journal will only be used to determine his state of mind. Details of the personal nature, not related to their deaths, will remain confidential, I promise."

Taylor and Edwards exchanged a concerned look before the superintendent nodded for Edwards to turn over the journal to Emma. Reluctantly, he conceded, but scoffed and flashed contempt toward her.

Promptly bagging the notebook, Emma labelled the evidence bag and noticed the title on the front cover: *April 18th Evidence.* "Personal diary, huh?" As she logged it, she wondered why Edwards concealed the item. She shrugged it off. *Not my station; not my problem,* and then photographed the desk where he had found it.

Turning her attention to the deceased, she processed Mrs Evans first, photographing her and checking for any signs of a cause of death beyond her suspicions. Mrs Evans laid in repose in bed in her flannel pajamas and under a tattered quilt, with her hands folded over her waist. Her face relaxed and calm, as if caught in a blissful dream. Carefully positioned on her lap, a copy of *Pride and Prejudice* laid open to chapter 34. The bandages around both her wrists drew Emma's attention. She slid back the gauze with the end of her stylus and photographed the incisions. At first glance, Emma estimated three-, four-days-old at the most—based on redness surrounding the wound—probably self-inflicted due to angle and depth. *Was Mrs Evans suicidal?*

Click.

Emma pulled down the comforter and lifted Mrs Evans'

shirt to reveal her midsection. She made a slight incision in her upper right abdomen and inserted a thermometer. *83.6°, so that's about 10 hours, give or take.* She looked at her watch. *That would be a window around 4-6pm the day before, Sunday.*

While Mrs Evans died peacefully, Dr Evans, on the other hand, had met his end in anguish. Emma had never seen a hanging in person, only photographs from case studies. Most of the time, they quietly passed and simply looked asleep, no different from Mrs Evans' appearance. However, the Doctor wasn't so fortunate in his death. The signs of a struggle were quite clear. *Did he have a change of mind?* she thought. His eyes displayed petechial hemorrhaging, as to be expected, but he had also severed his tongue—more than likely from biting down during the tussle. Dr Evans' right hand, positioned behind his head, still held the belt while his left hand grasped the noose.

Click, click.

As with Pearl, Emma checked his liver temp—they matched, indicating same estimated time of death. Unfortunately, in cases of murder-suicide, the times of death are generally coinciding. In and of itself, that's not conclusive evidence to support that theory, but not a good sign in Dr Evans' favor.

Emma came back to his eyes, as something seemed off. The Doctor wasn't looking forward, as expected, but to his left, toward the doorway of the room, as if he saw something at the moment of death and couldn't look away. *What terrible thoughts plagued him so deeply he'd murder his wife and then kill himself?* Emma questioned. She ran a litany of queries through her mind, trying to piece it all together. The missing motive boggled her the most—assuming Taylor's description of the couple was accurate. One question above the others kept nagging her, which she couldn't even put into words. It never fully manifested in her mind. Like a word on the tip of her tongue, it sat taunting her to utter the question aloud, but left her incapable of doing so.

Shaking off the odd feeling, she finished the final set of photos, jotted down her observations in her pocket notebook, and did a final rundown on her checklist. "The coroners can come and collect the bodies now. I'm finished." Emma looked up at Edwards and Taylor—their mouths drawn downward and brows furrowed. Taylor's eyes were swollen and red, as if a floodgate was about to burst at any moment. Edwards' jaw clenched tight, and he squeezed his notepad in his hand like he was wringing water from a towel. *Grief affects everyone so differently,* she thought.

As Emma waited for the coroners to arrive, Taylor stepped out and made a phone call. Based on his body language, he appeared agitated with the individual on the other end and at one point raised his voice, demanding some term to be met. Normally, Emma wouldn't have given the call much notice, except for the fact that Taylor returned to the room and hand-ed her the phone. "You need to take this."

"CSI Lloyd speaking."

A familiar voice spoke on the other end, the head of West Mercia Police, Chief Constable Harris—a man of few words.

"Thank you, sir. I—" Emma paused as he cut her off. "It's 5:30 now. I can finish my preliminary report and be at Hindlip Hall by nine. Will—" Again, she waited until he finished speaking. "Eight it is, sir." Harris hung up and left Emma wondering what was going on.

Chapter 2

The Interview

Emma dashed up the stairs of Hindlip Hall, the head-quarters for all of West Mercia Police. Little beads of sweat trickled down the side of her temples. Sweat was the least of her worries compared to being forty-five minutes late to her meeting with the Chief Constable. And that was sec-onded by her inability to keep her eyes open. She knew once the adrenaline wore off, she would need a serious boost. Snag-ging the third Red Bull as she ran out the door this morning looked to be a smart move.

She reached the top floor and caught her breath before cracking open the can and chugging it as quickly as she could. After finishing it, she tossed it in the bin and collected herself. Emma took a couple of slow deep breaths, whisked the sweat from her brow, and then flipped her hair to neaten it up and lay it right. She stood up tall—as tall as five-three could—and straightened her shirt. Her heart raced, but not from the run. Emma had no idea what the Chief Constable wanted, and that wreaked havoc on her nerves.

As calmly as she could muster, she opened the door to the office and greeted the receptionist. "CSI Emma Lloyd here to see Chief Constable Noah Harris."

"Please take a seat, Dr Lloyd. He'll be with you shortly."

The receptionist clacked away at the keyboard and flipped between several binders and folders on her desk. Emma sat impatiently, her foot fidgeting all the while. She scrolled through her emails and opened up BBC news to pass the time—anything to stay awake. If he didn't call her in soon, that caffeine was going to burn itself out.

A few minutes later, and not a minute too soon, the receptionist's phone buzzed gently on the table. She looked up at Emma and put her hand over the speaker. "He'll see you now."

Emma stood and straightened out her shirt and slacks one last time, then walked to the door. As she reached for the handle, Chief Constable Noah Harris opened the door and greeted her. "Thank you for coming. I know you had an unexpectedly long night." He motioned to a chair opposite of his modern glass desk, which contrasted starkly with the stone, Jacobean style of the office and building. The desk befitted Harris nonetheless, since they both shared a smooth, shiny surface on top. He was slim and well-built for his age, having kept up with active-duty standards by running ten kilometers every day and frequenting the weight room—denoted by the gym bag sitting in the corner.

Feeling her eyes grow heavy, she sat in a slightly uncomfortable position to keep herself alert—a trick she learned in uni. Harris sat down and immediately picked up her file and started flipping through the pages, periodically stopping to read something. Emma couldn't guess what he could glean from a file that he didn't already know, being that they were hardly strangers.

"I see you've gone back to your maiden name," he said.

"I never got round to legally changing it after the wedding because… well… it seems a little moot now."

Harris flipped through her file again. "Graduated early—A-levels at seventeen. Eleven years in medical school before becoming a medical examiner. You were a coroner's pathologist for two years before changing careers and going into police forensics. Why?" he asked.

You know that answer, Noah, she thought as her mind wandered back to that day. If it hadn't been for Liam's death two days' prior, it would have been just another Tuesday at Gloucestershire Coroner's Court. Emma needed out of the house; she needed normalcy—something she hadn't felt in months…

She wiped the running mascara from the bags under her eyes as she plodded up the steps and through the main doors of the coroner's office. She kept her eyes down, refusing to engage in any sympathetic stares from the receptionists, and just subtly waved her hand and feigned a smile in response to their greetings.

After dropping her things off in the locker room and changing, Emma headed to the prep room to scrub up and put on her mask and gloves. As she did, a colleague, Sarah Greene, backed through the two-way swinging doors, rolling off her gloves and tossing them in the biohazard bin. Sarah, wide-eyed and stammering, locked gazes with Emma and froze.

"What are you doing here?" asked Sarah, her eyes fluttering back and forth between the door and Emma.

"Hey. I needed out of the house. I wanted a distraction."
Emma pulled up her mask, wiggled her gloves on, and stepped
toward the doors.

Sarah casually countered Emma and remained between
her and the doorway. "That's bollocks. Work is the last place
you need to be. How about we both clock out and go grab
brunch somewhere. You eaten yet?" Sarah put her hand on
Emma and gently nudged her to follow.

"I'm not particularly hungry. I already had a banana and
a Red Bull. Work distraction is all I need." Emma brushed
Sarah's hand away and tried to step around.

"No, come on, let's go get coffee. I promise I'll be a bet-
ter distraction than boring work." This time, Sarah was more
forceful when she took Emma by the elbow and guided her
away from the morgue.

Emma eyed Sarah's hand and pulled her arm away. "What
are you doing? Leave me be. I just want to go to work." Emma
shoved Sarah out of the way and reached for the door.

"Stop! You don't want to go in there! Just come with me. I
promise it'll be okay," replied Sarah.

"Why are you keeping me out of the morgue? What's your
problem? I'm fine. I can work."

"Emma, listen," Sarah aggressively blocked the doors,
"you don't want to go in there. We had no choice. The drug
trial legally required us. Please, just come with me." Sarah's
plea went ignored.

"What are you talking about? Legally required what?
What's going on?" Emma, tears welling up, refused to admit
what she already knew. "Let me in!"

"No! Stop, don't go…" But it was too late. Emma had
pushed passed Sarah and flung the doors open.

A wave crashed down on her and sent her reeling to the floor, weeping at what laid before her. She threw her face in her hands as she sobbed. Her throat tightened; her cries cracking underneath the pressure as she swallowed between breaths. How had she not known?

A colleague, standing over the autopsy table holding a scalpel in his hands, stood aghast as Sarah rushed to Emma to help her out of the room. "I'm so sorry, Emma. You weren't supposed to be here today. You weren't supposed to see this." But Emma was there that day; she had seen it: Liam, on the table, cut open like a lab rat.

"Emma?" Harris asked, bringing her out of her rumination. "Do you want to answer the question?"

She looked at her hands tightly folded on her lap. "I... I just couldn't look at another autopsy table after that. Being there, in that room, day after day... I couldn't. With my education and experience, scene of crime forensics made the most sense. Keep me away from a morgue; away from hospitals."

Harris shifted uncomfortably in his seat and cleared his throat. "And why did you move into collision forensics instead of scene of crime forensics? That seems like a move in the wrong direction."

"At the time of my initial application, there wasn't a position available. I took what I could get in the hope I could transfer over at a later date. In hindsight, it was a poor choice. I have a transfer request in currently."

"Yes, I see you've requested to be transferred to Scenes of Crime unit... three times. And denied twice?"

"Correct. I regularly applied for the transfer even if there wasn't a position open. I know there still isn't an opening now, but I was hoping with my qualifications they'd make—"

"And other than today, how many crime scenes have you worked during the last eighteen months?"

"None, sir, at least not outside of the classroom. Just collision investigations and my two years as a coroner." She hated calling *him* sir.

"How has your work-slash-personal life balance been since..." Harris cleared his throat, "since Liam's passing?" His eyes glistened at the question. He knew full well how she was holding up—and it was no better than how he was doing.

"I did several months of therapy as recommended and took some time off. Getting back to work helped set a routine and make things feel normal again. I still—"

"What did you make of the Hagley team? Did you get along?"

"Overall, they were professional and courteous. I wasn't so impressed with DS Edw—"

"Tell me about the case."

Sure, if you would let me finish a sentence! Emma calmed herself down and coaxed a respectful tone. "Initial findings, based on scene, indicate a murder-suicide. Waiting on toxicology results and the autopsy reports to confirm."

"Initial findings," he scoffed. "Your *initial* findings here state a *possible* murder-suicide. Something change during that time?"

"No, sir. I—"

"Because if I'm going to approve your transfer to the SOCO position at the Hagley station, I'm going to need some assurance that your work is going to be above reproach. Especially with appearances and all."

"I'm sorry, transfer?" Emma stammered in surprise. "I don't understand."

"Yes, as you probably realized last night, there is now a vacancy in their station for an in-house Scene of Crimes Officer. Honestly, you're not my first choice here, as there are CSIs with more experience and seniority. Don't get me wrong. Your work in Collision is exemplary—your record is spotless and your supervisor speaks highly of you. Yet, most experienced CSIs wouldn't have allowed a detective to disturb evidence prior to documentation."

"That—"

Harris held up his hand for her to shut up. "On top of it, you were clearly biased and too presumptive regarding murder-suicide. I expect more objectivity from an investigator."

"Yes, I understand. I'll do my best. But, I'm not sure why me."

"As much as I'm opposed to the idea, *they* chose you. On paper, you are a qualified candidate. However, my hands are awkwardly tied here due to an unusual set of circumstances."

"I'm surprised they need their own CSI. It's a tiny parish police station. Don't they use West Mercia Forensics here at Hindlip for cases?"

"They do for the majority of their work. That is ultimately left up to Superintendent Taylor to decide on a case-by-case scenario. Due to an annual private donation that is too big to say no to, which oddly includes an earmarked requirement for Hagley, that station has maintained its own CSI unit for quite some time—albeit a unit of *one*.

"However, most of the duties in Hagley involve cold cases for West Mercia Forensics, so you'll primarily deal with back-logged paperwork and analysis. There won't be many actual on-scene investigations until October—it's Hagley after all.

It's not glamorous, but it's a foot in the door to get you out of Collision."

"I'm a little taken aback. I'm not gonna lie," replied Emma.

"All I need is a yes or no, *Lloyd*." He said her name with a hint of disdain.

Holding back her excitement, she answered, "Yes, I accept. When do I start?"

"Immediately. Today, in fact."

"I'm sorry, what?"

"According to Superintendent Taylor, there is some urgent business that you are needed with—starting this week. No details given, but it was a factor in my rash decision to approve their request. The earmark donation gives the Superintendent full say over the position—it's a thorn in my side. Once we conclude here, you'll need to turn right back around and report to Hagley."

Emma sat stunned, burning a hole through Harris' head. *I start today?*

"My secretary will make accommodation arrangements for you until you find a place more suitable. I can't imagine you'd want to commute from Tewkesbury every day. Here's the address for your satnav—I know how you are with directions. Any questions?"

"No, sir."

"Don't make me regret this, Lloyd. Welcome to SOCO. You're dismissed."

Chapter 3
The Letter & Journal

Professor James Webster
69 Kidderminster Rd,
Hagley DY9 0PZ
Monday, November 7th, 1955

To whom it may concern,

> *Those who cannot remember the past*
> *are condemned to repeat it.*
> *~ George Santayana, 1905*

While our great statesman Winston Churchill immortalised his rendering of this truth in the annals of history only a few short years ago, for the sake of both literary accuracy and word selection, I shall use George Santayana's original sentiment unabridged. No exhortation in your future duties I am about to chronicle could serve you better than the above adage.

It is verily impossible to convey to you the events of the

last few years than simply to give you the pertinent excerpts of my diary—raw, unfiltered, and unedited. Each entry directly subsequent to its correlating event in question. Therefore, I shall, as logic best dictates, provide the entries in chronological order as I experienced and recorded them. They will, over time, tell as much of the story as is humanly possible.

Please, for the sake of the veracity of the events that have transpired—and for your own edification—suspend any disbelief you may have as you read these pages. While I was limited to scientific observation and documented the events as such, what you will inevitably discover is they are something *more*. And so, as promised, let us start at the beginning:

*

Monday, 19th April, 1943

Today I was summoned to inspect quite a peculiar case in Hagley, specifically the wooded area adjacent to Hagley Hall and under its purview. A person, deceased, unknown time of death, unknown sex, unknown age, was discovered in the most bizarre location: inside the rotten hollow of a wych elm tree.

Four local boys, Robert Hart, Tom Willetts, Fred Payne, and Bob Farmer, crossed paths with the skeletonised remains on the day prior, April 18th, while out poaching bird eggs and rabbits in Hagley Wood. Though the quartet had initially promised to conceal the discovery out of fear, the young Willetts boy could not keep the secret and confided in his parents. Subsequently, they contacted the local authorities to report the discovery. Detective Superintendent Sidney Inight was then assigned the case, who in turn contacted me for forensic study.

The site of the discovery laid approximately 100 yards into the woods from a dirt road just off the A456. Just past a small grove of silver birch trees, a small grassy glade opened up with several wych elm trees lining the far side.

The tree in question stood curiously in centre view upon entering the clearing. Its branches and boughs had been coppiced so many times over the years, as had many of the trees in Hagley Wood, that it had grown wild and misshapen. Low boughs twisted and mangled together to form what appeared to be the trunk of the tree—in fact, they had fused and knotted together. In doing so, they formed abnormal voids and hollows, especially when a bough rotted out. The gnarled mess appeared as a single tree trunk from afar, about two yards in diameter and a little over two yards tall. The current regrowth of branches protruded out in every which direction, extending the height of the tree another twelve, fifteen yards. The hundreds of leafless branches that jutted out of the peculiarly shaped trunk invoked something otherworldly, likened to a Lovecraftian horror. Even without the events to follow, it conveyed a sinister feeling that emanated about the grove.

When I first arrived on scene, a local constable, PC Jack Pound, was interviewing the four boys. DS Inight stood at the tree, peering into the hollow and jotting down measurements. All about the wooded floor, amongst the leaves and grass, a few rudimentary markers had been placed, indicating items of interest—specimens that awaited collection and analysis.

Without instruction, I proceeded to set up my Speed Graphic camera on its tripod to photograph both the tree and the surrounding area.

Afterwards, I methodically scanned the underbrush for more items. All in all, the items discovered in the underbrush were:

1. A woman's leather crepe soled shoe (left foot), 4.5 to 6.5 in size
2. Fragments of clothing (later to match that of fragments found in the hollow)
3. 1 tibia bone
4. Several, various bone fragments

After finishing my assessment of the surrounding area, I joined DS Inight at the tree to assist in the removal of the skeletal remains inside the hollow. The opening was approximately 24 inches wide and about 12 inches in height. On the right side, the opening swung upwards to give the overall shape of an L lying on its back. The remains could not be properly extracted without first cutting away a large bough obstructing the opening as well as removing an overhang of the hollow, which then finally exposed the three-and-a-half-foot deep void behind. From there, the extraction of the remains—a complete skeleton at first glance—became less cumbersome.

I will not be able to determine the sex and age of the individual until I complete my anthropological autopsy later this week. However, upon initial observation, simply holding the femur in hand and guessing its length, the individual was very short in stature. Either indicating a woman or child.

What brought this poor soul into this state may not be discernible. A best-case scenario, the victim was murdered prior to being wedged into the hollow; a worst-case scenario was that the individual was still alive. It takes three to four days to die of thirst, depending on weather, general health, as well as their physical exertion. Science can study and factor those conditions, but it cannot tell me how long the victim clawed at that opening until relinquishing their fate and accepting their death.

Chapter 4
A New Job in a New Town

Emma got out of her car and took in the unassuming building that would be her new station. The two-story, Neo-Gregorian style building fit in perfectly with the surrounding red bricked semi-detached homes flanking either side. Emma was no stranger to small towns. Her home of Tewkesbury was small by British standards after all, but the parish of Hagley hardly eked out a speckle on the map, which made it feel more like a ghost town than a lively village.

Emma dragged herself up the entrance ramp and through the front entrance, fighting off the exhaustion of the late night. A uniformed front counter officer greeted her as she entered. "Good morning! How may I be of assistance to you today?"

"Good morning. I'm CSI Emma—"

"Dr Emma Lloyd! Very nice to meet you. I'm Victoria Brown. Everyone calls me Vickie, though, but my grandmother called me Vee. Perhaps that might be too personal. So, you can stick with Vickie or Victoria... or Vee, whatever you prefer." Vickie had a very plain appearance about her, quite bland to be honest, and the generic police uniform didn't help. Her personality, on the other hand, shone like a lighthouse, which just naturally drew Emma to her. Emma couldn't help but think she was the type of colleague that everyone just loved and adored.

"Thank you, Vickie. It's a pleasure to meet you. And you don't have to call me Doctor. To be honest, I hate the formality." Emma leaned her elbows on the counter. "So, being my first day and all, down to business. I know absolutely *nothing* about this station. Total virgin here. I have no idea where my desk is or the evidence locker... well, anything really. Mind helping a girl out?"

"Oh, absolutely! It'd be my pleasure! Through the security door here is a short hallway where the loos are. That'll lead you right to the main bullpen. Everyone's offices are to the left or right of that. Kitchen and break room are on the left as well as the supply room. On the far side of the bullpen, you'll see Otis. Just take him down and Bob's your uncle—you'll see your lab straight ahead. The evidence locker is also on the lower level, just to the right. I'd show you around, but there's no one to man the desk for me. Any questions?"

"Okay... uh... who is Otis?"

"Oh dear, I'm sorry. Otis... as in the lift. You know, Otis Elevator Company?"

Emma laughed. "I'm daft this morning... I should've guessed."

"No problem. Just a little humorous nickname around here," said Vickie.

"No, no, no, no, it's my bad. I'm just knackered—and I'm a tad nervous since it's my first day and all."

Vickie fell somber. "Love, we're just glad you're here."

She reached across the countertop and took Emma's hand. "Losing the Doc so suddenly and under those circumstances has taken its toll around here. We haven't fully wrapped our heads around it. Some people are just now finding out." Vickie sniffled and dabbed the corner of her eye. "He loved his job and his duty, and he'd be pleased that a capable lassie like yourself has come to fill his shoes. No one is expecting you to solve all his cases in one day. Not even the Doc could do that."

"Well, if that's the case, I'll do my best to honor his work and do him proud." Emma offered a comforting smile.

Attempting to compose herself, Vickie handed Emma a keycard. "You'll need this to access the laboratory. It's restricted access for only you and Superintendent Taylor. It's a temporary card until you get your new ID made. Unfortunately, it doesn't work on this entrance door, so I'll still have to buzz you in. Whisper carefully."

"Thanks," replied Emma, puzzled at Vickie's odd farewell.

Emma made her way down the hall toward the bullpen. Photos of past and present officers, detectives, and notable station staff lined the walls on either side. She stopped at a photo of Professor James Webster, a forefather of modern forensic science in Britain. He was a rotund fellow with a glass eye and a monocle—and a genius beyond his years. He made his fame in this area for several high-profile cases, one in particular—the Hagley Wood murder.

"Great, another giant set of shoes to fill," muttered Emma.

She continued to the bullpen, which opened up to a large area fitted with desks and rolling notice boards scattered about. Crime scene photos and case notes, as well as officer assignments and shift schedules, adorned the boards. In the front corner, a corkboard was plastered with pictures of Hagley's infamous graffiti involving Prof. Webster's unsolved case in Hagley Wood. For eighty years, residents had been vandalizing local establishments and monuments with the same phrase: *Who put Bella in the wych elm?*

Emma approached the board and studied the photos. *Why do they keep tagging this same phrase? Is it a prank or something else?* She took one down and studied it. Tingles ran up her back and down her arm, raising the hair on her neck. "I hope to never have a case as bewildering as this."

Pinning the photo back onto the board, she turned and continued on her way. As she passed another corkboard, this one dedicated to a series of unsolved cases over the years, Emma abruptly stopped to read the board's title: *Death Week.*

Splash.

"Cor, blimey! I'm so sorry," said Emma as she recoiled from the coffee sloshing from the cup.

"No worries, that was going to be your coffee anyhow," replied the man, shaking the hot brew off his sleeve.

"Yes, but that's *your* shirt. I'm such an oaf. I just stopped and didn't know anyone was behind me." Emma scrambled and grabbed some tissues off the desk next to her and patted the hot coffee off his sleeve.

"It's okay, really. I was planning on spilling coffee on this shirt later anyway, so it's all good." He held his hand out to shake Emma's. "I just wanted to come and introduce myself. Hi, I'm DCI Oliver Bennett."

Blushing, she took his hand. "I'm CSI Emma Lloyd. Nice to meet you."

Oliver grinned at his sleeves and proceeded to roll them up to hide the brown splotches setting in on his white shirt.

Out from underneath the rolled cuff on his left arm, a deep burn scar peeked out and caught Emma's attention. "I wanted to give you a proper welcome," said Oliver, "but coffee was the only thing of value here as a gift. So, my handshake will have to suffice for now."

Leaning in and pretending as if she was telling a big secret, Emma whispered, "For future reference, I'm not a coffee drinker… I know, shocker. I think I'm the only person in all of West Mercia Police not to drink coffee. I'm a Red Bull kinda girl."

"You're in luck! We have it in the vending machine down the hall."

"Oh, thank God! I'm gonna need a lot today."

Oliver's phone buzzed and dinged. "I'm sorry, please excuse me… I'm going to be late for a deposition. I've got to run. It was really nice to meet you. If you have questions or need help with anything, just let me know. My office is just over there. Whisper carefully." With that, he darted for the door.

Emma watched as he ran for the exit, unsure why her eyes lingered. She just stood there, locked in place. When she snapped to, she realized she also had somewhere to be— except she hadn't the foggiest idea where that was. *The lab, yes, that's right. Where's that lift?*

At the end of the room, tucked into the wall, just as Vickie stated, nestled Otis; an early-century cage lift with an art-deco bronze analog floor dial above. Clearly, the lift was original to the building. Emma opened the door and slid the black metal cage to the left, stepped in, and closed it. The worn-out analog buttons had lost their labels over the years, but she assumed with only three buttons, the bottom one had to be correct. The lift jerked as it started lowering; the cables twanged under its own weight. Emma wondered if she needed to take the stairs next time.

The lift stopped with a clank and a thud. Emma sighed; she had made it down in one piece. When she opened the gate and door, she was greeted with blackness, save a sliver of light from the lift. The light failed to reveal a wall switch until she used her phone's torch to locate it just to the right of the lift call button. She flipped it to find a dank hallway with a cold tile floor in an alternating black and white diamond pattern. Green subway tiles plastered the walls waist high, with peeling white paint continuing up and across the ceiling. Bare pipes and conduits ran the length of the corridor and disappeared into either end of the hall. A single florescent light dimly illuminated the steel laboratory doors across from her.

She tapped her keycard on the sensor pad, which was arguably the only item in the hallway from this century. After the locks clicked and buzzed, she entered and found, much to her dismay, a pre-world war mortuary retrofitted into a lab. Upon further observation, the room looked to have been twice renovated, the first being a coal room—evident by the overly rusted coal chute on the far side. The room bore other hallmarks of this: no windows and the telltale brick-arched ceiling that spanned the entire width of the room. She needed a tetanus shot just to stand in the doorway.

The green wall tiles and patterned floor continued in from the hall, but the upper wall and ceiling were bare maroon bricks with black speckles, sporadically littered with cobwebs in the darkest corners. Emma wondered if the bricks had ever been painted or if they had completely peeled over the years.

Her eyes were drawn to the antique porcelain-coated

cast iron autopsy table—littered with rust spots and chips—situated in the center of the room. Its water hose and nozzle dangled from the ceiling and drooped over the drain at one end. A dialed mortuary crane scale hung above at the foot of the autopsy table. A single pendant light, directly over the table, lit the room insufficiently, leaving the corners of the lab shrouded in murky shadows. She stood distraught, throat tight, eyes fixated on the autopsy table—not what she hoped to see in her new *office*.

Moments passed and Emma finally stirred to finish her assessment of the room. To the left sat a wooden worktable with several microscopes, a fume hood, a spectral reflectance scanner, and a chemical cabinet. To her relief, these items were fairly new. Next to the workstation sat an antique wooden desk and office chair—more items straight from the 1940s. How Dr Evans could have sat in that chair for hours on end was beyond her. She scanned the other side of the room to find several more vintage cabinets clustered together and four in-wall, refrigerated cadaver units, wooden framed with tarnished metal doors, each baring a McCray Refrigerator and Cold Storage Co. logo dated 1910. *Do they expect me to perform autopsies or keep cadavers?* Emma wasn't prepared for that answer yet.

Slinging her laptop bag onto the desk, Emma went about settling in. She checked the desk drawers and took stock of what supplies she needed—all the while haunted by the autopsy table behind her, looming like a specter. Emma tugged on the small cabinet drawer to her right to discover it locked. She checked the desk for a key but found nothing that fit. She added it to her to-do list in her pocket notebook, noting that Dr Evans might have had the key in his personal possessions.

A knock rapped and tinged on the steel doors to her left.

Emma was surprised that she hadn't heard Otis clanging and thumping, alerting her to someone's arrival. "Come in," she answered, forgetting that only one other person had a designated keycard.

The door buzzed and Superintendent John Taylor entered and leaned up against the autopsy table in the middle of the room, at ease like he was the master of this domain. "We haven't had a chance to discuss your duties properly, with the whirlwind of events in the last 12 hours. This isn't exactly how I foresaw Dr Evans' replacement, that's for certain."

"Again, my condolences for your loss. I know it can't be easy."

He held his hand up, fighting back tears in the process, and waved it off. "It is what it is now. There's no amount of mourning that will bring him back. We just have to keep moving forward. With that said, I know Chief Constable Harris explained to you briefly about the position, no?"

Emma nodded. "He said mostly cold case processing? With some active cases from time to time, is that right?"

"To put it simply, yes, that's about right. This is a local parish station after all. But, as Hagley police is under my jurisdiction, I'll call you out to cases in neighboring towns from time to time. No need to let your skills go to waste down here all day. For now, familiarize yourself with your laboratory. There's a stack of cases in Evans' inbox there for you to review—obviously, no rush on them. Take your time. Here are your van keys. Any questions?"

"Van?"

"Yes, you get your own forensics van. This will save you time from having to requisition and pick one up from

Kidderminster vehicle depot."

"Okay, that's fair enough." Emma pocketed the keys. "Oh, and is there a stairwell around here? That elevator is dreadful."

"Unfortunately, no. For reasons unknown to me, the stairs leading up to the bullpen were sealed off decades ago. However, there is an emergency exit that leads directly outside next to the evidence locker down the hall. It's not alarmed, so feel free to use it."

"Better than nothing, I guess. And one more question. More curiosity than anything else. CC Harris didn't mention *why* Hagley needs its own forensics department. I'm sure cold cases could easily be processed at Hindlip with the rest of the active cases. Just not sure why Hagley, I guess."

"Curiosity can be a bitch. There's not an easy explanation. To be frank, it's above your pay grade... for now. Understand?"

"Yes, sir."

"Take tomorrow off and get yourself settled in a little. There are several quaint communities and towns nearby with some flats to rent—or a house to buy, if that's what you want. Don't worry about a time frame. We can float your hotel costs for a while until you find a place." Taylor handed her a small scrap of paper with an address on it. "We'll get started with your first crime scene on Wednesday. Meet me here around 9am. Bring the van."

Since when do we get advance notice of a crime scene? thought Emma.

Chapter 5

A Theft of Desperation

Despite Timothy Burrow's enormous frame, he tucked himself tight between the hedgerow and the fence, waiting for Mr and Mrs Hughes to finish packing their car and leave. He had been casing their house for a week ever since he overheard them talking of their holiday in London to visit their great-grandkids, and it would soon be time to make his move.

After busting out the flood light with a rock the previous week, Timothy knew their security was lax. Anyone more concerned with it would have replaced the light right away, especially before making an out-of-town trip. They were prime for the pickings. Not to mention they made no real effort to hide the spare key under the flowerpot on their back terrace. Yes, prime for the pickings and none too soon—Timothy's food supply had run out.

As he spied through the leaves, his ears tingled, metastasizing into a ring. Timothy struck the side of his head several times, banging and banging with the heel of his hand, as he counted down. *Ten, nine, eight.* He couldn't afford this, not now. *Seven.* He needed this haul; he needed to do this. *Six, five. Come on, go away. Four, three, two.* The ringing and pounding subsided as he reached *one* and steadied his breathing, allowing him to return his focus back to the Hughes.

Which came just in time as the house lights turned off and car doors slammed shut. Timothy waited a few more minutes as he listened to their car start up and pull away. He needed to hurry before any of the neighbors awoke and before the ringing returned.

Don't touch anything you don't plan to wipe down or take with you. Be smart. Be smart. You can do this, he thought as he traipsed through the garden to the back door. Timothy snatched the spare key from under the pot and unlocked the house.

He did a quick survey of the first floor, noting where people liked to hide valuables, though in truth that was mostly guess work since this was his first time. Everything Timothy knew, he had learned from the movies and internet. The freezer, jars and cans in the kitchen, envelopes taped behind paintings, in books and desks, and, of course, the proverbial 'under the mattress'.

Timothy refocused, first things first: food. He crept into the kitchen and rifled through the cabinets, tossing any non-perishables he found into his rucksack, filling it till it overflowed. A jar of Marmite, six cans of tuna, two cans of mixed nuts, several cans of beans, and a load of bread. The next two cabinets yielded similar scores.

Food, though, regardless of how much he found, would run out. Timothy needed money or something he could pawn. Just enough to get back on his feet. *Upstairs. They would keep all the good stuff upstairs, right?* He turned his attention on their master bedroom.

As Timothy entered the room, the stench of *old people* rushed his nostrils. He buried his nose in the crook of his elbow—it reeked. The odor conjured memories of visiting his grandmother when he was a kid; memories he'd like to forget. It was almost more than he could bear, but he couldn't leave until he found something of value.

He prowled to the vanity, still covering his nose, and checked if anything was taped to the back of the mirror. No score. A family photo of their grandson and his kids sat on the edge of a neighboring chest of drawers. Timothy played rugby with him back in school—a real pompous arse. If anyone deserved to have their house burgled, it was him. Well, his grandparents, at least. Same difference as he'd inherit it all anyway. Timothy punched the frame, shattering the glass. Moving to the jewelry box, he flipped the lid open to discover a few trinkets and earrings, but nothing of value.

"I'll just be a second, dear, don't worry. I'll just run up and grab it," said a woman's voice from the downstairs hallway. Had they returned to get something they forgot? Timothy panicked as he knew Mrs Hughes was headed his way. He bolted for the closet behind him and tried to hide amongst her dresses, hoping that's not what she came for.

As he pulled her gowns to conceal himself and scooted to the back of the closet, he felt the handle of an old cricket bat. No doubt Mr Hughes' idea of in-home security. He wrapped his fingers around the handle and squeezed tight. *Only if I have to.* Mrs Hughes shuffled into the room, moving like those speed walkers you see in neighborhoods—all that effort in their arms, but no actual speed.

While he listened to Mrs Hughes search for something in the vanity, the ringing in his ear returned. *No, not again! Ten, nine...* Soon, the ringing mutated into *those words*—his jaw tightened as he winced. *Eight, seven.* He squeezed his eyes tight and held his hands over his ears, still gripping the bat in his hand. *Go away. Six, five, four.* But *those words* didn't go away. They swelled in his mind until they manifested audibly, deep in his ear. *Those words* never stopped. Shapes swirled under his eyelids until dark, pen needle dots arose and consumed his vision, turning his mind black before he reached *two.*

*

Timothy awoke standing on the edge of the staircase, squeezing the bat so tight his knuckles turned white. Sweat dripped down his cheeks and off his scruffy chin. He teetered forward and stopped himself before plunging headlong down the stairs. In a panic, he checked the bat. Blood dripped down the edge. "Oh, God no..." He turned and looked back into the master bedroom. Out from behind the bed peeked a pair of men's tennis shoes—still worn by its owner. "What did I do?" His heart pounded against his chest.

He looked at his watch. Four hours lost. He needed to go before the police came—or the Hughes' came to.

Not thinking straight, he dropped the bat at the top of the landing and bolted down the stairs. He skipped every other step as he flew. At the bottom, he grabbed the newel post to swing his momentum around the other direction and toward the back exit. His rucksack, overflowing with food, rocked back and forth against his weight. As he neared the door, he lost control and slid into a wooden coat rack. It toppled over him, spilling out the contents of the hidden compartment in the upper hutch. There, strewn out on the floor next to Timothy, laid a bolt action hunting rifle and two boxes of ammunition.

Chapter 6
Closing a Chapter

Emma reclined in her car parked outside her semi-detached house in Tewkesbury, waiting for Penelope Collins to arrive. She had known Penelope since primary school when Penelope's parents moved to London from Seville. Penelope didn't know a lick of English upon arrival, so her parents put her in every club imaginable to force her to learn, which is where fortune brought her and Emma together. They played football on the same team for ten years right up until they left for uni. Penelope had a wicked left leg.

A black Mercedes C-class, belonging to Penelope's husband, pulled up behind Emma's Mini Cooper. Emma got out to greet her. "Hey, Pina-lope." Emma never pronounced her name properly—a long running joke from their favorite movie.

"Hey, love," she replied in her fading Spanish accent. Penelope's platinum blonde, tightly curled hair tickled Emma's cheeks as they hugged.

Emma leaned in through the open door to speak to Chris,

Penelope's husband. "Thanks for letting me borrow your missus for the day."

"No problem. Anything that will help you move out of our guest room is fine by me," he said with a chuckle.

"Oh, sod off, you git," replied Penelope. "Come on, Emmy, don't listen to his guff." She gave Chris a wink and then took Emma by the arm as they walked up the front steps.

"So, when was the last time you were here?" asked Penelope.

"I don't know. A day or two after the wake? I came to pack a few more bags and let the cleaners in to deal with all the rubbish. The company that manages all the Airbnb rentals take care of everything else."

"Almost two years? It's been that long?" Penelope pulled Emma in closer as they walked through the door, tilting her head against Emma's. "I'm just glad you're finally selling it. You've been talking about it for months."

Not a thing had changed from Emma's memory of the flat, minus Liam. A flood of memories of life together in the home broke the dam of denial in Emma's heart. Their engagement party, intimate candlelit dinners of takeaway Chinese on the floor in front of the TV, countless birthday parties, the call from the doctor, the at-home hospice, the wake. Emma couldn't bear it on a daily basis.

Liam insisted, like any loving spouse on their deathbed, for her to move on and live a happy life, but it wasn't a switch Emma could just flip. It would take time, and two years felt like the tip of the iceberg. However, this new job, this new opportunity, could be exactly what she needed—exactly what Liam would want. To close this beautiful chapter of her life and to start anew, full of hope and potential. Emma didn't consider herself religious, she was agnostic at minimum, but she liked to believe he was smiling down on her as she took these first steps.

"Alright, sister, where do you want to start?" asked Penelope.

"Why not right here in the front sitting room? You got the sticky-notes?"

"I have," replied Penelope. "Here's a set for you. Let's just do four categories: keep, sell, give-away, and rubbish. What d'you think?"

"Sounds good to me." They went about quietly labeling everything in the house for the removers, a task which Emma thought would be much easier than it really was. The atrocious pleater sofa Liam's grandparents gifted them should have been an easy *give-away*, but when Emma placed the sticky note onto the cushion, she found that it said *keep*. As she moved around the room labeling other items, she kept walking past it thinking she would change it, but as they progressed into the dining room it still said *keep*.

Penelope broke the silence first. "So, you've got to spill the beans on this new job. It seemed to come from nowhere."

"It did… and to be honest, I'm still kind of surprised by it. One minute I'm being called in off duty to process a scene and the next I'm being offered a job. The real kicker—I'm replacing the guy whose scene I processed. Feels strange."

"When did you find the time to knock him off?" Penelope giggled. Emma scrunched up a piece of paper and threw it at her. "Fine, fine, so you didn't kill him. But it is odd."

"No, the odd thing is where I'm assigned. I'm at this tiny police station that covers a couple of parishes in the middle of nowhere."

"I thought you were going to Kidderminster?"

"I'm under its jurisdiction—that's where my superintendent works from. However, for some odd reason, which no one has explained yet, this station gets a grant or something each year that requires their own independent CSI. Noah said the donation is too big to turn down."

"Ugh… Noah… that ass." Penelope rolled her eyes and made a foul face. "Do you have an entire team under you?"

"No, it's a solo job. But it's a foot in the door for SOCO. Do some decent work and I could be transferred back to Hindlip or to a bigger station. It pads out the resume and gets me out of the collision unit."

"Is it a temp job?"

"No. Permanent position. I was expecting something temporary since it's on such short notice and the position was literally open less than twelve hours."

"So, what do you do, then? I can't imagine a parish having any high demand for a crime scene investigator."

"Cold cases, apparently. I have a stack that I'm already going through. If it wasn't weird enough already, my superintendent gave me an address and said, 'Meet me here Wednesday at 9.'"

"Ooh, cryptic. Perhaps you're really working for Home Office and MI6!"

Emma shook her head. "Oh, yeah, I totally forgot to tell you I have double-O status… which now that I've told you, I'm gonna have to kill you."

"I'm shaking in my boots," Penelope said, laughing. "Is the pay at least good?"

"Meh… there was a little rise, but not much. But I've got a van."

"A van? Wow, that's a perk everyone wants to have. Five quid says you have to pay for the insurance." Penelope sat on the edge of an armchair and brushed her curls behind her ear. "But seriously, I'm proud of you and excited to see how this turns out. It'll be good—I know it."

"Thanks. I *am* excited, but I'm not going to lie and say I'm not nervous either."

"How are the new colleagues? Nice?"

"Yeah, I think so. I've only met a few. The front desk officer, Vickie, she's a hoot. Reminds me of Caroline from uni, remember her? Then there's a young PC called McArthur who's nice and an older Detective Inspector called Wright. DS Edwards seems like a real git, though. Comes off arrogant and cocky. Then there's Oliver."

"Oliver... first name basis on that one. Huh, Oliver. I'm assuming he's the cute one, then?"

"Stop." Emma gave a little side glare in Penelope's direction, yet she didn't deny the statement.

"It's just a question. You're the one that chose to use his first name. Not my problem my best friend is a slag and trying to snog someone on the first day."

"Seriously, not now. Not here."

"Fine, fine, I'll play nice. Just promise me that as you give this new job and new city a chance, that you also give your heart a chance, too."

Emma groaned. She knew Penelope was right but admitting it out loud made it all too real.

After finishing the last room, Emma made one last scan around the house, making sure nothing was missed. She didn't want to come back if she didn't have to. Her eyes hovered on the sofa and she bent over to pick up the sticky note. She scratched it out and paused, waiting to write another instruction. She made up her mind and stuck it back on the cushion. It still read *keep*.

The girls then walked to the front hall and put on their jackets. A dust covered frame caught Emma's eye sitting on the hall table next to the key tray—her wedding photo. She blew off the dust, snuck it in her bag, and left, locking the door for the last time.

Chapter 7
Hagley Wood Murder

Emma wondered if she had entered the address into the satnav properly as she had driven out to the middle of nowhere, which said a lot when your parish was already in the sticks of the Black Country. Thankfully, within a few moments, she spotted two cars parked in a lay-by up ahead—one of them bearing police markings.

She pulled the van into the lay-by and parked next to Superintendent John Taylor and Detective Sergeant George Edwards. They were leaning up against their vehicles awaiting her, their breath still visible in the cool spring air as they chatted and sipped their coffee. *Great, Edwards… I wonder what evidence he'll contaminate at this scene.*

"Good morning, Lloyd," greeted Taylor. He reached behind, picked up an extra coffee, and offered it to her as she got out.

"No, thank you. I appreciate it, but coffee and I don't mix."

"Suit yourself." He set the coffee back on the hood of the

car and looked at his watch as if he were waiting for an alarm. A few more moments passed of silently watching the seconds tick by, and then he finally spoke. "Alright, it's time. Let's get this over with."

"I'm not exactly sure what we are doing here. Do we have a case?" asked Emma.

"Let's just say, this one pays your bills and leave it at that." Taylor grabbed a map, some red twine, and marker flags from the back of his car and handed them to Edwards. "In the rear of your van, there is a box labeled 'April 18th'—grab it. You won't need anything else except your camera."

How do you know what I'll need and not need? she thought. Emma circled around the van to the double rear doors and opened them. Below a shelf of supplies, tucked away on the floor, she saw a plastic container with April 18th written in large letters across the top. She cracked it open and checked under the lid where a supply list had been affixed. *What the hell is this?* She grabbed the box, her camera, and a forensic coverall suit.

"You won't need the coveralls," said Edwards. "Matter of fact, it might make things worse."

Emma flashed him a puzzled look and slipped them on anyway. *It's procedure and they should wear them too, Emma thought. How can they be so careless and not worry about contaminating a scene?*

Taylor and Edwards had already disappeared into the tree line when Emma finished suiting up. She hustled to close ground and nearly tripped several times doing so. *Where are they going?*

They trekked about a football field's length into the woods, past a small grove of silver birch trees, and finally to a tiny glade in the woods. There, before her, just as she had seen in dozens of news articles and documentaries, stood *the* wych elm—completely unchanged after all these years.

Emma laughed out loud. "Well played!" *An initiation joke... no creativity if you ask me.* She turned and started her walk back when she noticed they weren't laughing and had begun to mark out a grid with the red twine. *Wow... they are really trying to sell this joke. Alright, I'll play along.*

As Taylor finished up the grid, Edwards followed behind with flags and marked items according to the map Taylor had handed him earlier. Each flag marked numerically. Emma tromped over to the closest flag and examined its item: a tibia bone.

Somberly, Edwards spoke up. "You have to go in order of the flags."

Emma ruffled her brows. She located flag number one and started processing. An old-fashioned woman's crepe soled shoe, circa early 1900s. *What is going on? This shoe looks authentic. If it's not a prank, what is this?*

She photographed the footwear and slipped it into an evidence bag after logging it in her notes. Emma then moved on to the next flag. Meanwhile, Edwards walked to the right side of the tree line while Taylor stood at the wych elm measuring the hollow.

Speaking to no one, Edwards began to ask a series of questions as if he were taking a witness statement. "Why were you boys in the wood? What time was that approximately? Which of you found the skull?" So on and so on.

Emma stopped her task and watched Edwards conduct his eerie interview. What was he playing at? This didn't feel like a prank at all. It couldn't be a test, could it? An exercise to gauge Emma's acuity and skills in the field. No, they observed her work at a scene solo not three days ago. If they doubted her ability, why hire her in the first place? *Perhaps this is a case study?* The 'what if's' occupied her thoughts as she worked the scene.

After the last flagged item was collected and processed, Emma backtracked to the start of the grid. The conundrum of their activity clouded her judgement; she had no idea if she missed anything.

"Don't worry about double checking. Everything was flagged that needed collecting," said Taylor. "Let's process the tree."

She joined Taylor and Edwards by the wych elm and took the procedural photos required before extracting the contents in the hollow. As she peered into the hole, a most frightening intrusive thought reared its head: What if this *is* a real crime? Something off the books—a cover up. Emma toyed with the thought. They hire an eager outsider desperate to change her lot in life—someone desperate enough not to ask too many questions. It made sense. She couldn't imagine Harris would deliberately do this to her, even with their history. Even he wouldn't stoop that low. Yet, nothing about this seemed right.

As Edwards pulled out a handsaw to cut away the branch obstructing the hollow, Emma attempted to suss out what exactly they were doing here. The bough eventually fell away, giving them access to its secrets within. She peeked inside the void—its shadows concealing the skeletal remains. She reached in, wrapping her gloved fingers around the detached skull, and retrieved it. Emma cleaned away the debris and was careful not to disturb evidence nor the clumps of hair clinging to the last fragments of desiccated scalp. She hesitated and studied it before placing it in a protective box.

"Is something wrong?" asked Taylor.

Emma examined it for smooth textures and mold lines created from casting; inaccurate density and weight. All indicators of composite resin—signs the skull was a replica. She traced her fingers along the surface and inside the orbital sockets, even up under the soft pallet of the mouth. If it were a replica, Emma could dismiss her intrusive thought as paranoia. Her conclusion sent her stomach tumbling downward.

"No, sir," she responded.

Chapter 8

The Autopsy

How many laws did I just break? thought Emma as she entered the lab and sorted the evidence for processing.

She leaned forward in her chair and put her head in her hands. They failed to observe at least a dozen forensic procedures at the Hagley Wood scene, not including chain of custody violations. She ran her fingers through her hair and then massaged the back of her neck. What exactly were they doing there? Taylor gave no indication if it was a prank, a case study, or a *real* crime scene—the latter being the most bewildering. If these remains were from a murder victim, how did he have two days' notice in advance? How did he and Edwards have a map to evidence location? And that interview? Nothing made sense. If this were indeed an actual crime, then she'd have no choice but to go up the chain of command to report it. Who is above Superintendent Taylor? Harris? IOPC? Her stomach twisted. *Do I really want to be a rat? The girl who turns her colleagues into internal affairs after one day?*

It all hinged on a single fact: is this the famous Bella of

the Hagley Wood murder or a *new* victim? Solve that conundrum and a clearer course of action would present itself. There was no room for error. The answer, or so Emma hoped, lay in evidence bags on an autopsy table—somewhere she hadn't wanted to be in a very long time.

She paced the room, circling the table, gathering up the courage. *It's just bones, no flesh to cut into,* she reminded herself. *It's just a table, and just some bones… it's not Liam.* The backs of her eyes tightened, pushing tears to the front. She swallowed hard and forced herself to the cold porcelain surface where all the remains had already been pre-sorted and meticulously organized in evidence bags.

All the hard work had been done on scene. The skull was wrapped and placed in a protective box; the vertebra separated out and placed in bags according to their vertebra groups; ribs, sternum, and other torso bones bagged together; and finally, each limb with what appeared to be their respective appendages. Emma only needed to piece it together like a jigsaw puzzle.

Beginning the slow and monotonous job, she laid out a long sheet of paper over the autopsy table. Next, she placed each grouped bag in the approximate area corresponding to anatomical location. She carefully lifted the skull and mandible from the box and placed them on the table first—careful not to disturb the last remaining clump of hair attached to the left side of the skull. The smell of putrefied wood still lingered as she sorted the remains. The more she committed to the task, the more her *muscle memory* kicked in.

A chill swept over her as the HVAC unit spun up, humming gently in the background and sending a gentle wisp of sterile air across the room. Emma gazed into the skull, much like Hamlet, pondering the person now bereft of flesh laying before her. Hamlet knew Yorick and remarked he had *kissed I know not how oft. But who knew you? Who kissed your lips? Who reminisced about their days together or mourned your absence? Somewhere, there was a loved one who never learned of your fate—whoever you are.*

Emma's lecturer of anthropology, Professor Jennings, harped on the importance of bones—the stories they could reveal. She championed the notion that through them, the life of the person could speak to you. Of course, she spoke anthropologically about culture, broader historical facts, diet, gender, and so forth—not intimate life details. But with these remains, something differed. Each touch pierced the barrier between flesh and essence. As she picked up the hyoid and placed it under the mandible, she could almost *hear* the victim, like a faint cry that whispered from far away.

The cries unsettled Emma—their woeful pleas bearing undertones of malice. With each bone fragment, the malice burned, like a trapped animal that nipped your hand as you set it free.

Undaunted and dismissing it as nonsense, she identified each cervical vertebrae and laid them in order. Because of the spinous process, she had to lay them backwards on their anterior side as opposed to how they would be positioned if the skeleton had connective tissue remaining. She tediously repeated this process for the thoracic vertebrae, then the lumbar vertebrae, and finally the sacrum and coccyx. One by one the bones urged and berated her in equal sums—should she stop or continue? Emma had to know; she couldn't stop.

The whisper, which cried from a distance at first, crept closer. For whatever reason, be it a subconscious trigger related to the original case or something else, Bella's infamous question coalesced, rumbling amongst her thoughts.

Emma, redoubling her efforts, progressed to the legs. The left and right femur, both patellae, two fibulas, and one tibia. *Wait, where's the other tibia?* Emma consulted the logs from the scene—one tibia recovered. Had she missed it? Was it laying somewhere in the underbrush? Taylor was very clear. "Only process the flagged items." She wondered if that bone was missing in the 1943 case file and marked it down in her pocket notebook to confirm with original autopsy reports. She returned to the table and continued with the meticulous task of identifying the small bones of the feet.

Emma looked over her process thus far. "You were short!" Normally, coroners took measurements of the femur to estimate body height, which she fully intended to do, but it was quite clear at eyeshot that this vic was easily under five foot. That meant the vic was either a woman or child.

Rolling her shoulders back and stretching a bit, she succumbed to the yawn she had been fighting for the last forty-five minutes. The hotel bed did nothing to alleviate the exhaustion of the previous forty-eight hours. Rest seemed a foreign concept at this point. She needed a pick-me-up and went in search of the vending machine.

Walking out the steel doors of the lab, something nagged and pulled at Emma's mind not to abandon the remains. The *question* repeated louder in her mind like a desperate cry, begging her to return. With each step, it continued to manifest physically, weighing on her feet. Emma dismissed it as fatigue and continued on.

She shuffled out of Otis and into the bullpen, looking down the hallway either direction for signs of the kitchen.

Edwards stuck his head out of his office. "You need something, Lloyd? You look lost."

"Lost is an understatement. It's my lot in life." She cringed for over sharing. "DCI Bennett said there's a vending machine around here somewhere. I need caffeine to finish this reconstruction."

"I'm surprised she let you out." Edwards pointed to Emma's right. "Down the hall on the left. You'll see it in the kitchen."

"Thanks."

The station was tiny enough that even Emma couldn't get lost—at least not for long. Small blessings. The vending machine, tucked neatly between the fridge and the wall, stuck out just far enough for her to spot it immediately. "Yes!"

Emma felt inside her pockets, looking for some loose change, and snagged two quid. Searching the rows for Red Bull, she found her choice empty. *Son of a b...* She scanned for something else and reluctantly settled for a Coke. She leaned back against the wall, cracked open the tab, and took a deep swig. Closing her eyes, she rested her head on the cold brick wall and hoped she didn't fall asleep standing.

No sooner had she relaxed her shoulders than the pull to return to the lab began tugging. Gently at first, then progressively stronger. It started in her stomach, yanking, twisting, like a hand had reached in her gut and wanted to disembowel her. Emma's heart raced and a tightness fell on her chest. The more she fought, the worse it got. *I just want to rest for one minute.* Frustrated, she pushed away from the wall and slunk back to the laboratory. Each step became lighter and lighter until she faced the steel doors and the panic subsided.

Emma returned to her task—barely revived from her

break. She took stock of the next step and picked up the humerus bones, putting them into place. The radius and ulna were set on the table, respective to the left and right alignment.

As she came to the final stage, the hands, a wandering thought entered Emma's consciousness—more of a curiosity really. How had Bella come to her fate? How had the real Bella famously come to lose her hand? Emma picked up a bone of the wrist, inspecting it carefully, but not quite able to determine left or right side. *Was it an accident? Premortem and unrelated to her death?* Emma placed the bone down on the right side, but in a small fit, she jerked and scattered the remaining pile of bones across the paper. *Had the hand been taken to hide her identity? Somehow able to reveal her name to anyone who discovered her?* She straightened the pile and picked up the previous bone she had misplaced—exhaustion had clearly taken hold. She reached to align it on the right once more, only to find her hand jerked again. *Had her hand been taken in malice for a more sinister act?*

A dark void emerged in Emma's mind. Images flashed back to that morning in Hagley Wood as she stared into the hollow of the wych elm. The darkness of the hollow washed over her and enclosed around her. It constricted her, entrapping her in its nothingness. She pushed back at the dark, but it didn't budge. Soon, Emma's arms and legs fell dead, rendering her incapable of escape. Her fate reduced to her mind alone in the blackness of the hollow, squeezing tight around her, choking her off from the world outside. Her eyes looked up at the opening, helplessly out of reach, and watched as day broke, flooding the hollow with slivers of light, illuminating the rotten coffin within. As quickly as the sun rose, it set, plunging her back into the dark, its cold nothingness embracing her. The sun rose and fell over the hollow day after day until Emma had lost all memory of the world outside. Only the hollow existed. The days and nights merged—time lost meaning in the hollow. Day and night ticked like an endless metronome back and forth. Back and forth; back and forth.

She blinked from the flickering pendant light swaying above her. She shook off the dread; such an odd and specific thought to have. It vanished as quickly as it came, but the sensation of claustrophobia in the hollow lingered in its place. She looked down at the bone she still held between her fingers, analyzing it a second time. "It's the left hand?"

Hovering over the left side and shaking, Emma hesitantly set the bone down. *Yes, that's correct—it is the left hand.* Bone after bone, she arranged the metacarpals and phalanges until the pile was empty. *Done.* She leaned forward, arms crossed, with her elbows against the cold antique table, and analyzed her work. The remains looked like Bella, but vague recollections weren't the concrete evidence she needed for identification.

"So, who are you and what were you doing in that wych elm?" she said to the reconstructed skeleton laying before her.

The steel doors popped open, and Emma jumped. "Blimey, you made me jump, Pete!"

"I'm sorry. I didn't mean to startle you," replied Taylor. He slowly stepped toward the table and gave the remains a once over before backing away to her desk, distancing himself as far away from the autopsy table as possible, as if the skeleton could leap up and grasp him. Emma detected a quiver in his voice as he spoke. "You finished her, I see. That might be a record for a first attempt."

"Possibly a *her*. I still need to check the sub-pubic angle and the sciatic notch first, then I can make a clearer determination of sex."

Taylor scrunched his brows, looking confused why Emma doubted the sex of the remains.

"Other than that, I need to check for any fractures and trauma, healing patterns, et cetera to determine the cause of death. I'll also have to send some bone scrapings to Hindlip for testing—DNA and whatnot."

Taylor waved her off. "No. Don't send any samples to Hindlip. Matter of fact, nothing of the Hagley Wood case leaves this laboratory. No bone samples, no fiber samples, no nothing. Everything you'll need is in this lab."

Everything I need is not *in this lab,* she thought. "I can't sequence mitochondrial DNA here. Only Hindlip has that. And it's the best way to trace familial relations for an ID."

"Lloyd, I will ask for your complete discretion and obedience on this case. No questions asked—literally." Taylor handed Emma a file he had tucked under his arm. "Dr Evans and I drew up a very specific protocol for this project."

Emma scanned it and thought the tasks were quite antiquated and lacking—no mention of DNA, radiographic examination, or any other modern analysis. "Stick to it—word for word—down to the date and times stated. Do not deviate. It's a little incomplete, but it'll hold you over in the meantime until I can amend it with the final steps," said Taylor.

"You want me to follow this word for word?" Emma quoted the protocol. "'Leave the remnants of clothing on the worktable. Do *not* place in an evidence bag.' That breaks chain of custody!" She flipped to another page. "It calls for a mock press conference? There's even a script? What the hell is this?"

"Don't screw with me on this, Lloyd. I'm serious. If you know what's best for you, you'll do as you're told. You were hired because I thought you were a competent and obedient tech. If I was wrong, let me know and I'll hire a replacement."

Emma furled her brows, unsure of the necessity of such restrictions, and only deepened her concern over what she had stumbled into. "I'll comply, but there's no long-term storage appropriate for skeletal remains in this lab. Only the morgue drawers."

Taylor started to answer and then stopped, as if to collect his thoughts. "You won't need it."

Chapter 9
News Clippings

Hartlepool Northern Daily Mail
Saturday 24 April 1943

HAGLEY WOOD MURDER

Further details have been released today to help identify the woman whose skeletal remains were found in the hollow of a wych elm tree earlier this week near Stourbridge in Hagley Wood. Portions of her clothing were still attached. The woman aged between 25 and 40, thought to be nearer 35, and approximately 5ft tall with light brown hair, was dressed in a dark blue and mustard striped cardigan and mustard skirt. Blue crepe soled Gibson style shoes, size 5 1/2, were found in the vicinity and thought to belong to the victim. All garments appear to be secondhand. In addition to the clothing, a wedding ring made from rolled gold, probably worth two shillings and sixpence, was found on the woman. All evidence at this point in time indicates the woman had been dead for at least 18 months.

*

Birmingham Daily Gazette
Tuesday 04 May 1943

PLEA TO DENTISTS TO HELP IDENTIFY WOMAN
POLICE NEED HELP IN HAGLEY WOOD MURDER MYSTERY

Police are seeking a different line of inquiry regarding the Hagley Wood murder after a recent conference attended by Professor J. M. Webster, Director of the West Midland Forensic Science Laboratory.

While Worcestershire constabulary have sought assistance from neighbouring police stations, the difficulty of identifying the woman recently discovered in the hollow of a wych elm tree on Sunday 18 April has been problematic, to say the least.

Recent efforts have focused on the clothing and shoes of the deceased, but a renewed effort will now shift towards physical traits of the woman herself, specifically her potentially unique dental records.

CROOKED TEETH

Forensic evidence points to one missing tooth in the lower right jaw as being removed premortem, possibly within one year prior to death. The extraction was most likely via a dental procedure and could help police identify the woman. Local dentists are being asked to review their records.

There are no other identifying markers such as fillings. However, the misalignment of her frontal teeth, both top and bottom, adds to her unique dental structure.

If anyone has any information pertaining to the potential identity of the woman, please contact the Chief Constable of Worcestershire or your local police station.

Chapter 10
Stacey

Mostly cold cases, huh? No "on scene" cases until October, huh? I call BS, Noah Harris, thought Emma.

The call came into Vickie around 6am from Bert Haggard, who took his dog for a morning run around Bartley Reservoir every day. With the water level lower than usual, it wasn't hard for him to spot the tip of the car booth breaching the water's surface. Emma arrived on scene at 7.15am, right around the time they were fishing the car out of the reservoir and Edwards was wrapping up Haggard's statement.

Water poured out from under the doors, soaking the grass all around. Mud, mixed with algae and weeds, covered the car and made it difficult to identify model, make, and color at first glance. The flat tires dragged across the embankment, digging into the soil, as the recovery truck struggled to pull it out, most likely due to the weight of the water and mud inside the car adding an extra two to three tons. The cable, stretched out to the road where the lorry could better anchor, twanged under the tension as it reeled it in, inch by inch.

Emma got out of her forensics van and walked around to the side door to grab her gear and slip into her coverall suit. She looked around at those gathered in the early hours: Oliver Bennet and George Edwards stood inspecting the vehicle while Alfred Wright assisted the recovery truck pulling the car from the murky waters. Everyone's breath floating as a fog in the cool morning air.

Local news crews had already gathered, which kept Louis McArthur busy maintaining the police barrier. As Emma scanned the crowd, there were a few new faces on her side of the crime scene tape, one of whom was making a B-Line toward her. He had a little jog to his step.

"Dr Emma Lloyd?" He waved as he walked, trying to gain Emma's attention. "Hello, I'm Mayor Otto Parry. Pleased to meet you!" His gray hair swept from the left and awkwardly flopped over the top, not so subtly covering his baldness. His weathered features were pleasant enough, but something seemed *off*. Like the age of his face didn't quite match that of his eyes. She couldn't place how old he was. Sixty, maybe? Seventy? Even eighty didn't seem out of the picture. He could give a carnival guesser a real run for their money.

"Hi, yes, I'm CSI Emma Lloyd. And likewise, pleased to meet you, sir." She finished pulling the coveralls up over her shoulders and then reached out to shake his hand. Emma went to let go and continue her prep work, but Parry held tight and pulled her in a little closer, awkwardly still shaking her hand as he spoke—typical politician's power move.

"I hope you don't mind my interruption, being your first case and all." He gestured with his other hand toward the muddy car. "I just wanted to meet our city's newest civil servant."

"Oh, it's not a problem. I'm just getting started. You

haven't interrupted anything at all," Emma replied.

"I just like to know everyone working under my purview—make sure everyone meshes together. Everyone should feel right at home in Hagley. Like a part of a big family. I know it's a little corny—the fact that it's my campaign slogan and all—but we really are 'In it together'. And there's no unity like family, right?" His smile popped, baring his perfectly straight veneers, but not wrinkling his crow's feet.

"I absolutely agree. Well, it was—"

"Listen, if there's anything you need, just let me or the superintendent know and I'll make sure it happens. I believe in giving my fellow functionaries all the tools they need for success."

"Thank you. I really appreciate that. It was really nice to meet you, Mayor Parry."

"Likewise. Good luck on the case. Whisper carefully." He finally let go of her hand and then waved to Supt. Taylor, jovially greeting him like an old friend, as he bounded away.

Emma—puzzled again by the odd farewell—snapped her nitrile gloves over her fingers, grabbed her camera and kit, and trod over to the vehicle to join Oliver on scene.

Oliver chuckled as she approached. "Parry should consider himself lucky he didn't have any coffee for you."

Emma blushed. "I was reserving my clumsiness for you, but as you are covered in mud, I think you saved me the effort."

"Touché," replied Oliver.

"Is it normal for the Mayor to come to crime scenes, especially this early in the morning?" Emma walked over to the window and attempted to peer in through the thick encasement.

"Did he really call himself *mayor*?" Oliver belted out a laugh. "Grant it, he is the chairman of the parish council, but mayor, he is not. But yes, to answer your question, he's always floating around somewhere—station, crime scenes, etc. He's independently wealthy, which funds his campaigns and gives him the freedom to be *intimately* involved in as much of the ongoings of the parish as possible."

Edwards butted in as he inspected the car. "He could give some old Italian grandmas a run for their money on local gossip. Just be glad you didn't meet the wife, she's literally certifiable—a total nutter."

Mud and algae caked the number plate. Oliver knelt down and splashed water on it, washing away the gunk, and then ran the now exposed number through Number Plate Recognition. "Plate number A122 XYT. Registered to Stacey Inight, 31, of Rubery."

"Is this an old All-aggro?" asked Edwards. "Haven't seen one of these in years. I would've dumped it in the lake and claimed the insurance on it, too. Hell, I'm surprised it's not fully rusted out."

"Registration says it's a 1983 Austin Allegro. Good eye, Edwards. However…"Emma didn't like the way that sounded,"…both the car and owner were reported missing last October."

Emma finished up her cursory photos of the location, the condition of the car after pulling it out, and other environmental measurements for her report, recording everything in her pocket notebook. "Alright, let's check and see if there are any occupants," she said.

Edwards, who was already standing by the driver's side door, reached over to check if the door was locked. Before

Emma could warn him, he had pulled on the handle, releasing a torrent of water and mud from inside and throwing the door into him. The muddy water swept Edwards off his feet and sent him to his hands and knees.

"No, don't do that!" she said, too late. Emma watched in horror as unknown amounts of evidence washed back into the reservoir. "I have a pump and filter for the water…" Her voice trailed off, knowing that it was useless information at this point. *What will Harris say when he hears about this?*

She stepped around Edwards to assess what evidence might still remain in the passenger compartment. Her heart sank. A partially decomposed body sat belted into the driver's seat.

"Do you think that's the car owner?" asked Oliver.

"Tough to say. There's significant bloating, but the clothes, jewelry and hair indicate female at first glance. Obviously, we'll need to send the remains to the coroner's and get a full run-up. Let's see if there's any ID in the bag on the passenger floor."

Emma walked around the other side, took more photos of the interior and then removed the waterlogged handbag from the car. She carefully removed its contents: one woman's wallet, a set of keys (probably house keys), an iPhone, a soggy bag of marijuana, a lighter, a smoking bowl, lipstick (NYX shade Prague Red), a makeup compact (also NYX brand), and an empty, nondescript pill bottle. She handed the wallet to Oliver.

"Well, unless we find another ID in the car, this says Stacey Inight. How long do you think the car has been submerged?" he asked.

"Decomp and bloating suggest an extended period. Inight disappeared in October of last year, right? Average water temperatures would be quite cold starting in October and through winter. While there was significant water in the car, all the windows were sealed, keeping fish and other critters from feasting. Both factors could easily suggest 6-8 months—give or take. That puts it square within an October timeline."

"Inight. Why does that name sound familiar?" asked Edwards, still cleaning himself up from the flood.

Taylor walked over and answered. "Because you walk past her great-grandfather's photo every morning at the station. Sidney Inight was Detective Superintendent during World War II at Hagley. Very influential man. His son, Stacey's grandfather, also served on the force in Hagley for a short stint."

"Once Lloyd confirms ID, we'll need to inform the family," said Oliver.

"No need. She doesn't have any—not anymore, at least. Poor girl was on her own at sixteen."

"Does she have a partner or anyone to notify?"

"Her boyfriend reported her missing at the time," replied Taylor. "It was Wright's case—he could fill you in more when he gets down here."

"Emma, what are the chances you can get that iPhone to work?" asked Oliver.

"Well, there's no home button, making it at least an iPhone X. Apple's first water resistant phone was the 7 or 8, I forget which. I've heard loads of stories of people losing their phones on the river and divers find it a year later and power it up. So, as long as there isn't any damage to the phone casing compromising the seal, it's quite possible. The real question is what security does she have. Face ID will be tough due to the late-stage condition of the vic, making it unlikely it would recognize them. Assuming that it is Ms Inight, and this is her phone."

"Can you hack it?"

"Not to sound all Dr McCoy, but I'm a doctor, not a hacker. Apple is notorious about refusing to help law enforcement access phone data, citing US personal privacy laws. But, there are some forensic software and devices that could help—model dependent, of course. Give me a day or two."

"Fair enough. Keep me appraised. First thoughts? Accident? Foul play?"

"Well, I don't see anything off-hand to suggest foul play. No visible gunshot or knife wound, but again, the condition of the body is hard to judge. Not to be a broken record, but I'll know more after the autopsy. There is this empty pill bottle that raises a few questions. Could be accidental or a deliberate overdose. Car rolled in on its own or another passenger pushed it in to cover it up. I've got more questions and hypotheses than answers for you at this point. Everything is on the table."

Emma looked over her shoulder to see if Wright was coming over to shed any light on the case when she noticed an unexpected face on the inside of the police barrier talking with Parry. "Is that Bryant Jones, the reporter from the *Daily Mail*?"

Oliver groaned. "Unfortunately, yes. I wonder what his grimy tentacles are groping at now."

"Why is he even allowed behind the police barrier? I'd expect after his little exposé that he'd be banned from every police station and crime scene in the country, much less here."

"It's exactly *because* of that exposé that he's here. Not long after that scandal, which hit our station particularly hard, the IOPC recruited him as a special investigator. That alone gives him certain privileges. The higher ups figured giving him access would be good PR."

"More like 'keep your friends close and your enemies closer' if you ask me," replied Edwards, still recovering from his mishap.

Emma hated to agree with Edwards, but truth was truth, regardless of the source.

"Keep your eye on him… you're fresh blood and he'll find a way to weasel a story out of you really quickly," said Oliver. Edwards gave a nod of agreement.

*

Emma wrapped up the on-scene evidence collection and ordered the car to be towed to the compound until she could process the vehicle at a later date. As for the corpse, Taylor requested she perform the autopsy in-house. If it were indeed Stacey Inight, he considered it a sign of respect to a family who served Hagley well. Emma didn't understand the need as Stacey had no living family, but she respected the order and had the vic bagged and loaded into her van to be transported back to Hagley.

To her relief, the emergency back exit had a stair lift that allowed her to lower the gurney to the cellar and not have to parade it through the bullpen and down Otis. Emma didn't even think it would fit in the lift—much less support its weight and hers at the same time. She rolled the body into the lab and moved Bella from the autopsy table to one of the drawers and closed her inside. *I'll deal with you later.*

Stacey Inight wasn't the first autopsy Emma had ever

performed, not even close, but was the first since Liam passed—excluding the Hagley Wood reconstruction. Her hands shook as she wheeled out the mayo table and prepared the sheers, forceps, retractors, and bone saw. Sweat formed on her brow, despite the coolness of the room, and ran down into her eye. The pounding in her chest swelled and her skin tightened. She closed her eyes and took a deep breath, exhaling long and slow. Flashes of Liam on the autopsy table ripped through her thoughts. The brightly lit, gleaming white tiled walls and shiny steel autopsy table faded to the background, leaving Liam afloat on a sea of light, chest open and his heart resting on the scale. Emma puffed her cheeks and blew out, opening her eyes and wiping away a tear.

What her eyes beheld contrasted starkly with her recollections. The memory of the modern facility of Gloucestershire Coroner's Court vanished as her sight adjusted back to the dismal lighting of Hagley's coal cellar converted laboratory. The lab consisted of a disproportionate mix of post WWII museum pieces and recycled mid-century furniture housing a scant number of modern technology. Even her bone saw was corded and needed an extension cable to reach the autopsy table. At least it wasn't a hand saw. Emma questioned just how big this donation was that "couldn't be said no to". The morgue refrigerator units and autopsy table had to be original pieces, as were all the wiring and lighting. Where did the money go?

Before beginning the autopsy, Emma wanted to dry out the iPhone, as that process required a few days. She selected a plastic box and retrieved a bucket of silica gel beads from the cabinet. She placed the iPhone on a bed of beads and then poured the rest of the silica overtop.

A latch behind her clicked.

Whirling around, Emma caught the door to Bella's cadaver unit creaking open, gently swinging amongst the shadows of the room. She walked over and closed it, but it refused to latch. This side of the room was impossibly cold—open refrigerator unit or not. Emma pulled her lab coat tighter to her neck and then pushed with her hip against the door. When she released it, the door naturally swung open. She fiddled with the handle and then pushed with her full weight against the door until it clicked. She looked for the drop pin used to secure the latch, but it had been ripped off—the metal cord severed and frayed. Emma snatched a pencil off her desk and crammed it into the sleeve of the latch. *Why is it so cold?*

She then returned to her worktable and sealed the iPhone inside the box with the silica.

The doors to her lab, adjacent to her desk, buzzed and swung open. John Taylor traipsed in, munching on a sweet pastry. Emma's stomach growled—she still hadn't eaten breakfast yet. "Good morning, Lloyd." He perched one leg on the corner of her desk, leaving her unsure if the vintage piece of furniture could support his weight.

"Good morning, Superintendent," said Emma.

"I know we just chatted at the Inight scene, but I thought this conversation would be better if we did it in private. There's a lot we still need to discuss about your transition here." Taylor stuffed a heaping bite in his mouth. "How's the Badger's Sett treating you? I know you were supposed to stay at the Premier Inn next door, but the long-term nature of your stay became problematic."

"It's a little strange staying over the top of a restaurant, but the flat is nice—private and well looked after. I do hope to find time this weekend and search for something more permanent."

"Good, good." Taylor's eyes flicked about the room. "I see you're making yourself at home in the lab. I can tell you've reorganized."

"Is that okay? I just thought it was a better set up this way."

"Oh yes, it's not a problem at all. Whatever allows you to be more efficient. It doesn't affect me any." Taylor seemed off—distracted and miles away.

"I do have one question." Emma tugged on the locked drawer next to her desk. "There isn't a key anywhere that I can find. Do you have one or know where it is?"

"I'll have to check. I think those are Dr Evans' personal files. I'm not a hundred percent sure. I'll have someone come by, change the locks, and clear it out when I get a free moment. If there's anything in there you need, I'll leave them on your desk."

Why not just give me a key?

Taylor fumbled with his words as he pulled on the Hagley Wood protocol papers peeking out from underneath some other files. "Listen, uh, I want to—" He cleared his throat and shifted his weight uncomfortably. "I want to apologize for the other day. I was way too harsh. The Hagley Wood project was something that Evans and I planned to do together—it's a *special* project. I know it's strange, unusual, whatever, but I just need you to humor me. Just extend me this one courtesy. You have full rein of this lab and all its cases. Hell, on active cases, you have lab testing priority at Hindlip—another perk of working here. I'll never question nor challenge you on anything except the Hagley Wood murder. It's my one request.

Just follow the protocol to the letter, please."

Emma appreciated the apology, but it didn't exactly explain away the oddity of the protocol's strict regimen.

Across the room, the pencil shoved in the morgue lock snapped and tumbled to the floor. Bella's door crept open, garnering Taylor's attention. He flinched and stood to his feet. "Did you put Bella in the morgue drawer?" He nervously took a step away from the refrigerators.

"Yes, I thought it best until I finished the Inight examination," replied Emma.

"I wouldn't keep her in there too long. She doesn't like dark, cramped places. It's in the protocol." He tapped the Hagley Wood papers, accentuating his point.

Chapter 11
Scrawlings, Scribbles, and Insanity

Emma retrieved the iPhone from the Stacey Inight case and finished preparing it for examination. It had sat drying out all weekend—more than enough time for the beads to do their work. She flipped it around, inspecting the charging port, and looking for any other defect, before cleaning off the last bit of grime and plugging it in. Immediately, the charging icon appeared and moments later, the Apple icon and home screen popped up—no passcode required.

While Stacey hadn't been smart enough to use a passcode, she had added an ICE contact, but no name to go along with it. Emma tried the number, but it was disconnected. She made a note in her pocketbook to track down Stacey's phone records and any contacts she had stored. Next, she launched the messages app. There were only a few message threads saved, but all the names were initials with emojis, leaving no indication of their identities. The most frequently messaged contact was *TB*. Clearly someone of the romantic nature based off the heart and kissy-face emojis littering in the message thread.

The last text from Stacey simply read:

> *I'm sorry*

The next message had failed, indicated by a *could not send video file* system alert. No other context given, but both messages were dated the same day as Stacey's disappearance.

Emma started the cloning process to her computer and perused the phone's contents in the meantime. Since the system message mentioned an unsent video file, she started there. Queasy butterflies fluttered in her stomach. Although she was only trying to solve the mystery surrounding Stacey's death, her actions felt invasive. Like a voyeur peeping through a bedroom window. But she had no choice; it was her job after all.

Much like the message app, most of the pictures and videos contained just one other individual. He was around Stacey's age, brown-haired and clean shaven except for a tiny soul patch on his lower lip. Emma could only assume he was *TB*. They looked very much in love.

The last video, again dated the same day as the last message, had a thumbnail preview of Stacey teary eyed sitting in her car. Emma prepared herself for an unpleasant replay.

> *Hey, Teddy Bear.* *sniff* *I just want you to know how much I love you. I wish it didn't have to come to this. But you know as well as I do that whatever curse I have, you now have too. I hate myself for letting you in and passing it on. I do this hoping somehow it frees you from her.* *sniff* *I just can't take it anymore. And I can't bear to see you suffer because of me. It's—it's her fault and there's nothing I can do about it. I'll never be free from her; I'll never be able to answer her. I'm sorry. I love you.* *sniff*

The last frame froze on Stacey, tossing back a mouth full of pills. It wasn't likely Emma could test for drugs in Stacey's system, though the cold water preserved her quite well. Since the autopsy revealed no water present in the lungs, it would add up that she had overdosed before the car slipped into the reservoir. Yet, it wouldn't hurt to at least try and test for opioids for confirmation, nonetheless. Emma scribbled another note in her pocketbook.

She played the video again—something felt familiar about it. She did so several times, trying to nail it down until she came to the end on the fifth playback: *I'll never be free from her; I'll never be able to answer her.* Where had Emma heard that before? Who said it? She swiveled in her chair until a thought popped into her head from nowhere. *Evans' suicide note.*

Nah, that couldn't be it. Or could it? It nagged Emma enough that she sprung from her chair and marched down to the evidence locker to see if his suicide note had been forwarded to Hindlip or if it remained in Hagley. Sure enough, it sat on top of his journal. Emma snagged the evidence box with both items and dipped back into her office. Both cases were hers, so she had every legal right to re-examine the evidence, especially since both were open cases, but it felt wrong somehow—insubordinate, invasive.

She pulled the evidence bag with the note out of the box and flipped it over to read:

> *John, I'll never be free from her—free from that damn question.*
> *~ Thomas*

Emma's thoughts raced between the two suicides, trying

desperately to find an answer… *Free from who? The text wasn't the same word for word, but close enough to be uncanny. Is it the same woman? What connection do two suicides separated by six months have? Other than cryptic suicide messages. Weak connections—her grandfather and great-grandfather worked at Hagley; Evans worked at Hagley. Decades apart at that. One used pills; one hanged themself. No family or direct social connections. Nothing—nothing connects these two together except their peculiar suicide notes about a woman.*

Who is the woman? What question and answer? The Toxicology report for Evans, which arrived earlier in the morning, confirmed sleeping aids in the porridge, on the pestle, and in Mrs Evans' system—3,000mg of Zolpidem and o.15mg/l of oxycodone. A lethal combination. The fingerprints lifted off the mortar, pot, and pill bottle matched Dr Evans. All evidence now pointed to murder-suicide. Emma hadn't considered how she'd break the news to Taylor, but knew it was coming.

But why did Stacey kill herself? Guilt maybe? Why did Evans kill himself and his wife? Stacey mentioned passing it on to Teddy Bear—whatever *it* was. *Did Evans feel that he had passed something on to his wife? Is that why he killed her? To spare her? No, too many assumptions.* Mrs Evans had wounds on her wrists that were consistent with suicide, but there were no hospital or doctor's records indicating an attempt nor the wounds themselves. *There was no indication in his note, but did he mention it in the journal?* Emma had been so preoccupied from the previous week's transition and the odd Hagley Wood cold case that she hadn't read the journal to glean any insight into Evans' motivation. Better late than never.

At first glance, the journal contained nothing of a personal nature. It solely pertained to the Hagley Wood case; matter of fact, it looked exactly like the protocol Taylor gave her—only more detailed. Emma flipped to the front and read the first entry:

> *Friday, February 3rd, 2023*
> *Dear unfortunate soul,*
>
> *It's with a heavy heart that I pass this on to you. I pity the burden you are about to undertake, but it is time I retire. That means you have been selected as my successor and with it, this case.*
>
> *Taylor will fill you in on the day-to-day responsibilities of your "other" duties, but this journal will guide you in the only important case you will ever work on during your tenure at Hagley.*
>
> *There has been an unwritten tradition that each predecessor writes a letter of guidance to prepare their successor for this journey. I received one, as did my predecessor before me. I pray that this is the last such letter, but I fear it will not be.*
>
> *If you have questions beyond what this journal records, which undoubtedly will occur, Taylor will do his best to assist. Do not attempt to contact me. I will be reclining on a front porch of a cabin on the edge of a beautiful mountain lake while my wife and I enjoy a hot cup of tea, soaking in the mountain fresh air.*
> *Farewell and Godspeed,*
> *Dr Thomas Evans*

So, he planned to retire? she thought. *What happened in the last two months to change his mind?*

Emma thumbed back through the journal and paused on

a page of wild scribbles, incoherent at first, and then revealed itself to be page after page of *those words*. Littered all over each leaf, along with that question, were dark spirals, coiling inwards until each formed a deep black hollow, which in some instances had bled and torn through the paper.

She flipped back to the section containing the protocol and realized it ended, quite incomplete, around July's instructions involving an Ethelinda Wood, whoever she might be. The sentence started on the bottom of one page and when the leaf turned to the next, the words transmuted into mad scrawlings. A light switch had turned off for Evans and what crept up to the pages were the nightmares of E.A. Poe. For nearly half the journal, spilling over the edges of the page, one phrase repeated, *those words*—Who put Bella in the wych elm?

The last page of the journal, which tore as she turned to it, revealed a sprawling sketch of the wych elm tree. Its black, leafless branches and boughs bled from the margins off the edge while the massive trunk spanned the gutter down the spine. The hollow swirled outward from the middle. It beckoned Emma. She stared into its abyss as clouded thoughts billowed in her mind. Indiscernible whispers resounded with familiarity but eluded her.

She slammed the notebook shut and tossed it on the table. She spun around in the chair several times, attempting to clear her mind. The air in the room constricted around her like she were the one entombed in the tree. That black hollow of nothingness—had Evans' mind been as entrapped as Bella? Had… Stacey's? The photos on her phone…

The first time Emma had examined the photos, she only saw Stacey and *Teddy Bear*. But there, on the walls behind her, taped amongst posters of *Oysterhead* and *Phish* were dozens of sketches of the wych elm and its spiraling empty void—just like Evans' journal.

A knock thumped on the door. Emma, composing herself, got up to answer, and before she could see who it was, they flung the door open, knocking her back.

It was Bryant Jones.

"So you're the new mysterious Hagley forensics tech, huh?"

Annoyed by his rude entrance (and just about everything else about him), she refused to answer.

"I'll take that as a yes. I hope you don't mind my intrusion, but I always find it best to ask for forgiveness than to ask for permission. It comes with the job after all." Bryant barely made eye contact with Emma as he spoke. His eyes were too busy spying everything in the room, unquestionably taking mental notes.

You didn't actually ask for forgiveness, you git! "Is there something I can help you with?" she asked with gritted teeth.

"Let's cut to the chase. I like that about you already! Question one: Why did Dr Evans kill himself?"

"You know I can't answer that. It's an ongoing investigation and I plan to hand it off to Hindlip due to conflict of interest."

"And yet his journal is on your desk and it looks like you've been reading it." He snagged it up in a flash and started to thumb through the pages before Emma could snatch it from him.

"*That* is not yours to read. It's still evidence in a case and it's his personal, private journal." She put it back in its evidence bag and set it face down on the table. Bryant mockingly gestured his hands up in defense of himself.

"April 18th evidence. Riveting, I'm sure. And obviously oh so personal and private. Would it happen to be related to our friend over there?" Bryant motioned to the skeletal remains in the open morgue drawer.

"Again, no comment." He was wiggling under her skin like a maggot.

"Odd, though, isn't it? There are no pending cases in this jurisdiction that involve skeletal remains. What are you working on?"

Damn, this guy doesn't miss a beat. "I'm sorry, but you know I can't answer *any* of these questions. Matter of fact, I prefer you leave. This is a lab with strict environmental controls, thus the need for the security doors. I can't have you here as it breaks protocol."

Bryant eyed the cobwebs in the corner and smirked. "Come now, I'm just doing my job. Keeping civil servants honest suits both my occupations." Bryant's sneer made Emma's skin crawl. "I'll play nice, though, if that's what you want. Can you at least tell me how it is that you got Dr Evans' post so soon after his demise?"

"I was called in to process his scene. I must have made an impression on Supt. Taylor as he requested my transfer."

"And you weren't on call that evening, am I right?"

"No, I wasn't."

Still scanning the room, he continued his grilling. "And you used to be in Collision Investigations, correct?"

"Yes."

"There's a big difference between traffic accident scenes and crime scenes. Why do you think *you* were called, then?"

"I don't know, and it doesn't matter. You'll have to ask the Chief Constable."

"Oh, I did," he replied, avoiding how Harris had responded.

"If you already have your answer, then I guess we are finished. I have work to return to."

"One more question: What *urgent* matter necessitated your immediate transfer? This post has never been one to process many active cases until mid-October during 'Death Week'." He glowed with pride at its mention. "I can't imagine anything being urgent here at the moment."

"I think you're blowing this all out of proportion. There was a position that needed filling, and I filled it. End of story. Now, if you don't mind, please leave."

Bryant moved to the door and pulled it open, turning back at the last second. "Darling, you are the *only* CSI tech assigned to a local parish police station in the entire West Mercia Police force and you were transferred under extremely unusual circumstances… that's not the end of the story."

Chapter 12
Going off Protocol

Both Stacey Inight and Dr Evans had an obsession with Bella—a cold case that was already surrounded by more oddities than a circus freak show. What drew these two individuals to the Hagley Wood murder, Emma hadn't the foggiest, but there had to be a connection. Before Emma took anything to Oliver and Taylor, she needed to research more about the original case—help clear up some mystery and organize the facts. Something more than just internet sleuthing would satisfy. Answers best found in the forensics archives at Hindlip, the West Mercia Police Headquarters.

Emma rapped on the window to get the attention of the desk clerk who was scanning a pile of documents and listening to his earphones full blast—she could hear it through the glass. The clerk swiveled round, took his AirPods out, and came to the window. "Good afternoon. Sorry about that. Digitalizing these old files is boring—got to stay entertained somehow. How may I be of assistance?"

"I need to see an old case file—reference number 010:18

BA14908," she said as she pressed her ID badge to the window.

"Let me see if we have those digitally in the system. If so, I can throw them on a flash drive for you." He clicked away on the computer and then grimaced. "Let me guess, you're a Hagley tech?"

"Yes, how did you figure?"

"Three types of people come looking for those files: amateur crime detectives, journalists… and Hagley CSIs. Which leads me to a little bad news."

"Spill it. It'd be par for the course at this point."

"These haven't been digitalized yet. You're going to have to physically go downstairs to the archive for them. Closed cases are last on our list to process, especially ones that old. I'm still in the '70s over here and working backwards." He pointed back at the stack of files he was working on when she arrived. "Sign here and I'll buzz you in. Again, it's downstairs, row 4."

Emma signed and proceeded through the heavy security door, leaving behind the brightly lit modern facility. As she descended the stairwell of the 400-year-old building, the archives rolled back time, delving into Hindlip's history. She fiddled in the dark along the wall closest to the stairs for the lights and discovered an old timer switch. She cranked it all the way up and waited for the lights to flicker on. The time label had peeled off, leaving Emma guessing how long they'd stay on. Fifteen, twenty minutes? She had no idea.

Exposed electrical conduits ran along the baseboards and led her into an expansive network of chambers separated by their stone columns, conveniently hidden by the array of wooden shelves. Ragged and worn carpet runners overlayed the smooth stone floor and held back the cold. Steel frames spanned each chambered arch and suspended antiquated florescent lighting above her head.

The stacks meandered like a maze around the columns, seemingly in no discernible order. The closest row read 254 and ran along the outer wall disappearing into the flickering abyss of florescent light swallowed by the centuries old cellar as she looked down the end of the aisle. As Emma searched, she came across several chambers where square trestle tables replaced shelving sections and offered themselves for research to the unfortunate visitor. One of those tables would soon be her friend for the afternoon.

Emma spotted row four and started searching the stacks for the reference number. The majority of the archived cases were a single, small box containing a file or two—most likely the initial incident report and a few witness statements. When she eventually stumbled on Bella's case files, she found three overflowing cardboard boxes clumped together by masking tape, bursting at the seams. "Well, this should be fun."

Lugging them one by one to a table, Emma ran through the litany of questions she needed answers to. None more pertinent than Bella's location and anything that might connect Stacey and Evans. She set out her notepad, pen, and laptop, cracked open a Red Bull—surprisingly the first one of the day—and then dug into the trove of documents and reports.

Click.

Emma checked her phone. *Only fifteen minutes?* She fumbled from the desk and guided herself by the faint light squeaking through the obstructed hopper windows behind the shelving running along the far wall. She grabbed her phone from her pocket, used its torch to scan the walls for a light switch, and spotted one three rows down. Emma cranked it all the way around and returned to her work.

The intense frequency of the antiquated florescent tubes strained her eyes, setting off a wicked headache and tinnitus. The florescent hum intertwined with the squeal in her ear and pushed the headache behind her eyes. She didn't look forward to all the reading ahead.

Emma cracked open the first box and sent a page fluttering toward the floor. She caught it mid-air and added it back with the others. The page, frayed and yellowed over the years, recorded the first of many Freedom of Information requests. The clerk had been right. The list contained a who's who of journalists and documentary filmmakers, some of whom Emma recognized as their works gained semi-notoriety within her field.

She tossed the top stack to the side and rummaged through the rest of the box's contents, focusing on locating chain of custody documents, autopsy reports, and evidence logs. Anything that confirmed Bella's last known whereabouts. Was she in an evidence locker or in her cadaver drawer?

Click.

"What? Fifteen minutes already? I'm gonna spend more time turning on the lights than researching." Before Emma got up to turn them back on, someone cranked the dial and the lights flashed on, humming their dull song. *Someone else must be here.* She returned to the box and stared at the immense disaster before her. She picked up a stack of papers and thumbed through them. All intermingled together, Emma found witness statements, missing person reports, incidence reports, various warrants, transcripts, and a single page of an autopsy report. That was just what she held in her hand. No telling how the rest of the three boxes fared.

"Excuse me," said a voice from down the aisle. "Every-thing okay? Need any help?" It was the archives clerk, still wearing his AirPods and pushing around a cart.

"I'm just trying to make head nor tail over these boxes. It's a disaster. Have you seen this?" asked Emma.

"Unfortunately, yes. You saw the list on top. Everyone and their brother have been in that box. It's like the village bicycle."

"I thought that meant... never mind. It's gonna take me hours to sort through it all."

"Would you like some help? I need to take a break from the scanner and would love the change of pace."

"You know what? I'd love the help. I'm Emma." She reached out to shake his hand.

"I'm Rory. Nice to meet you. So, is there anything in par-ticular you're looking for?"

"Yes, actually. A couple of different items would come in handy. A complete autopsy report, or something that would say where the remains are currently."

"That last one I can tell you right off the bat. FYI, I've been in this box a time or two cleaning up after others. It's a fascinating case, after all. That last question is answered here—" He rummaged through the first box and pulled out a file near the top. "Here's the case closing report from 2005. Page two, it says that the remains were lost around the '50s. They had shuffled around from museum to museum for sev-eral years and then just vanished. The officer who wrote the report said they're probably in a pauper's grave somewhere."

"Well, that kind of helps. Not the definitive answer I wanted, but beggars can't be choosers, right?" Emma huffed as she scanned the three boxes. "Let's try to make a little sense out of all this. Can we start grouping in piles? That way we'll know what we're looking at."

"Sounds like a plan," replied Rory.

The two set out quietly organizing everything into multiple categories until Rory broke the silence. "So, which theory do you back?"

"Which what?" asked Emma.

"Theory on her death?" Rory handed her a document to read. "Domestic dispute gone wild, Nazi spy ring, or witchcraft? OooOooOoo—" Rory comically made a ghost sound and waved his arms around like he was floating.

"Domestic abuse," she answered without hesitation. "Occam's Razor says it's the simplest answer."

"Ah, spoken like a true forensic scientist. Sorry, but that's boring. You need a little more imagination."

Emma, tired of bending over the table and sorting files, sat down and crossed her arms. "Okay, smarty pants. Enlighten me with your *imagination*."

Rory, wide eyed and perky, took a seat next to her, leaning forward with his elbows on his knees and gesticulating. "Witchcraft. Easy. You've got her missing hand *and* the strange murder of Charles Walton in 1945, not far from Hagley."

"No, what you've got is a lot of circumstantial evidence and outlandish conjecture."

"Okay, then you tell me why every single bone of her right hand is missing. Outside of that one leg bone—"

"The tibia."

"Yeah, that one. Anyway, outside of that, everything was recovered."

"Dogs probably? Any carrion animal could have carted off with it."

"How many dogs can climb trees like that? None I know."

"Okay, fine. Suppose it was taken by someone for nefarious reasons. Why was the hand taken? For what purpose?"

"Easy peasy." Rory rifled through the documents until he found what he wanted and passed it to Emma. "Here, the *Hand of Glory*."

Click.

"Seriously, how can you work like this every day?"

"You get used to it. I'll go turn it on."

Rory got up and disappeared into the stacks as Emma picked up the file he was looking at and started reading in the light of her phone's torch.

Several rows away, she overheard another group discussing a case. Their whispers indiscernibly floated down their row and through the aisle. Something crawled down her back and made her shiver. Where they were, Emma couldn't see, but she wondered why they hadn't turned on the lights themselves.

A few moments later, the lights flickered back on and Rory bounded back to his seat, picking up where he left off. "Okay, so the *Hand of Glory*. That's as creepy as it gets. Read that right there." He leaned out of his seat and pointed to the section of page Emma was holding:

> *The Hand of Glory is a relic of an executed criminal, hanged for their crimes, and used to bestow the owner of the hand with great power. According to folklore, the macabre artifact aided thieves and evil doers in a myriad of ways such as unlocking doors and safes.*

"That's a lot of malarkey, if you ask me. Do you really think that's why someone killed her and took her hand?"

"Yeah, why not? People do some weird stuff out there. Look at John Wayne Gacy or Ed Gein or Elizabeth Báthory. Hell, Báthory killed 600 girls and bathed in their blood to gain youth and beauty. That's messed up. But it just goes to show that people will do some sick and twisted things."

"Okay, I'll give you that. All three of them were demented murderers. But that still doesn't show that *this* case, *this* murder, was motivated by witchcraft."

"But it makes you think." Rory picked up another stack of papers and started sorting them. "Until a theory is definitively disproven, you can't dismiss it."

Emma shook her head. "I could just as equally say it was aliens, but with no actual evidence to support it, it just becomes wild speculation. It's always best to focus on the most likely scenario and explanation, especially if evidence points in that direction."

"Aliens… agreed… right out. *But*, let's look at the other evidence. What is there to support a Nazi Spy ring or even domestic violence?"

Emma sat in silence as she sorted more papers and pondered his question. "None. There's nothing here to support *any* theory."

"*Precisely!* And until you get any evidence to prove or disprove a theory, they all have to remain on the table. Now, aliens. That's total BS. There's *never* been any verified case of alien life despite the rubbish the US government is now admitting. There have been centuries, nay, millennia, worth of real examples of human sacrifice and torture because of witchcraft. So it is far more plausible."

"You make a good point. However, I'm not sold." Emma thumbed through a new set of files and tossed them in their respective stack until she stumbled upon an autopsy report. "Yes! Okay, one item down." She set it aside and continued.

Click.

"Oh, come on!" she said.

Rory again volunteered to turn on the light and dashed down the row to the switch along the right-side wall.

The voices of the other group bellowed louder as she sat in the darkness, awaiting him to turn the dial. She still couldn't make out what they were saying, but it felt familiar somehow. She pushed the intrusive thought to the side as the lights came on.

As she waited for Rory to return, she read the autopsy report. Rory was right. Just like the skeleton laying on her autopsy table, the original report stated only her right hand and left tibia were missing. *It is a little odd, I guess, that not one bone of her hand was ever found in the clearing with the shoe and clothing.*

Rory plopped down and grabbed a stack of files. "Hey, you wanted an autopsy report, but do you need photos? I have a bunch here."

"Yes, perfect!"

"See, look, no right hand." He pointed to the full skeletal reconstruction photo and to the spot where Bella's right hand should be. Sarcastically mumbling between his teeth, he play-fully taunted Emma. "I'm tellin' ya, it's witchcraft."

Emma thumbed through the photos Rory found, specifically looking for close-up details of the skull and dental markers. She laid them out on the table and compared them to the high-resolution photos on her computer as Rory worked through other files. Identical, down to every little bone defect and the clumps of hair remaining on the skull. Bella was indeed in her laboratory. *Odd. Why keep her remains a secret?*

There was no cover up; no murder scene off the books. Taylor had told the truth, even if it was masked behind secrecy. This answered one question, but not the connection between Stacey and Evans. Emma needed to keep digging.

The other group's chatter intensified, yet remained indiscernible, irritating Emma and setting her nerves on edge. She rolled her neck and stretched her muscles as she tried to block out their whispers, now drilling into the back of her eyes, magnifying the headache she already had.

Click.

"It has NOT been fifteen minutes!" Emma jumped up and headed to the light switch.

As she neared it, the voices grew louder. They had to be sitting nearby.

She twisted the dial and went in search of the other group to ask politely for them to keep it down. When she entered the main aisle, she looked to her left and saw Rory diligently sorting through the third box. She turned to her right, in the direction of the whispers, but no one sat at the two tables in the main aisle. They must be somewhere.

She scurried into another row and followed the voices. They were behind this next stack, but she still couldn't make out what they were saying. When she came to the end and peered around the corner, she expected to see a group of officers huddled around a box of files. Yet, the row was empty.

The voices now drifted from the main aisle where Emma had just checked moments earlier. She tip-toed down the row hoping to catch what they were discussing, but when she reached the main aisle, the table was bare of any occupants. The whispers, however, had swelled and encircled Emma. Their muffled conversation escaped her, but it felt familiar somehow—like she knew what they were discussing.

She stood at the end of the row and closed her eyes, trying to locate where the group was hiding in the stacks.

"Emma? Emma? Are you okay?"

She opened her eyes to Rory, standing next to her. "No," she replied. "I mean, yes. Sorry, yes, I'm fine. It's just a migraine."

"I have some Paracetamol back at my desk if you need some. I know how those migraines can really wreak havoc."

"No, thank you. I'll be fine, really. I just need some rest."

"Suit yourself. Anyway, I just realized what time it was. I have to close up in 30 minutes."

"Much appreciated," said Emma. "I'll pack everything up. Thank you again for all your help."

"No problem. Glad to be of service. If you're ever back here again, don't hesitate to ask for help."

As he walked back to the reception desk and the scanner, the voices swirled gently in her ear. "Hey, Rory, you might want to remind the other group down here that you're closing up. They're around here somewhere."

"I'm sorry? Other group? We're the only ones down here." He turned and disappeared down the main aisle. The whispers faded into the recesses of her mind. It was all in her head, implanted by the silly talk of witchcraft—or so she hoped.

Emma returned to the table and tidied up the clutter. Her face was flushed with embarrassment—how foolish of her to get worked up. She collected the photos and placed the files back into the boxes, this time in much better organization than she found it. *Thank you, Rory*. As she gathered up the stack of autopsy photos, a post-it note fell and fluttered to the table. Emma picked it up and read: "Ethelinda Wood, Worcestershire - Hand of Glory." She scrunched her brows, remembering the name from Evans' journal. "Who the hell is Ethelinda?"

Chapter 13
A Cuppa in a Wagon

The last legible notes from Dr Evans' journal mentioned Ethelinda Wood. A name Emma saw cryptically written in the case files at Hindlip archives. Why? Who was she and what connection did she have to Bella? Emma had yet to discover a link between Stacey and Evans, so Ethelinda became the next, and only, lead to chase.

Tracking down Ethelinda posed a greater challenge than Emma expected. State records returned a birth year, 1924, but gave zero results on current address—not uncommon for those in the Roma community. Several previous addresses popped up on court summary reports, listing localities as far away as Doncaster and Norfolk. The note from the archives mentioned Worcestershire, which was as good as any city to check first—and much closer.

Worcestershire was a beautiful town, with timbered and stucco Tudor buildings, a large, beautiful cathedral, and a sleepy river bisecting the city. Unfortunately, a place none too welcoming to gypsies, making Emma's search far more difficult than it was already.

She stopped at The Bridge Inn, an old Tudor and stone building, and slipped inside for a quick dinner and to ask around for local Romani campsites. She took a seat at the bar and ordered fish and chips, making sure the bottle of malt vinegar was full before ordering.

After her meal, she stopped the barman in the middle of feverishly wiping down the bar. "Excuse me, I'm looking for someone that might be in a traveler's campsite, an Ethelinda Wood. Do you know of her or know of a campsite nearby where I could find her?"

The bartender scrunched his brows and scratched his burly beard. "Good question. I know there are a few places in the area they frequent. Some farms and the like on the outskirts of town. But unfortunately I don't know anyone by that name. They do keep to themselves most often, not surprising considering how some folks feel about them."

A patron at the other end of the bar interrupted. "Why, in God's green Earth, do you want to talk to them? Nothin' but a bunch of criminals, if you ask me."

"We didn't ask you, Tom," replied the bartender. He turned back to Emma. "I think there are a few pitches up the A449, there at the roundabout. Not sure if they've moved on or not. You could also try out Martley Road before you get to Peachley."

"I'm telling you, it's a waste of time. They have no right being here and need deporting," said Tom.

"And just where would they go?" asked the barman in frustration. "Just ignore him, miss. He's had a bit too much to drink, and it looks like I might need to cut him off."

"Thank you," replied Emma. "Appreciate the help." She put a twenty-pound note on the table and left.

As she walked out into the evening sun, casting long shadows down the street, a waiter from the pub ran out and stopped her. "Excuse me, but I might be able to help. My best friend from school is a gypsy... her surname is Wood. Maybe they're related?"

"It's possible," said Emma. "I'm not sure if she has extended family or not, but it's worth a try. Can you tell me where I might find your friend?"

"They're a fairly private family, they don't like outsiders. It might be best if I take you there myself. I get off in thirty minutes. You could follow me. Would that be alright?"

"That'd be perfect. Thank you. I'll wait right over there in the dark grey Mini."

The boy rushed back inside, and Emma walked to her car to wait. She got in and leaned the seat back to get a little shut eye. She must have dozed off pretty quickly, as the next thing she recalled was the boy rapping on the glass. She sat up and rolled down the window.

"My scooter is there—the red one. Just follow me. It's about ten minutes away."

Emma nodded, and the boy trotted off to his scooter and then started down the road. He weaved in and out of traffic, slowing down occasionally for her to catch up and led her out of town, toward Peachley, as the bartender had suggested. Finally, the boy turned onto a gravel road and headed toward a settlement of trailers and campervans.

Pulling up to a trailer, the boy got off his scooter and motioned for Emma to stay in her car. He knocked on the door and a beautiful young girl about his age, smiling ear to ear, answered. They spoke for a few minutes, and then he pointed at Emma. The girl gave her a stern look; Emma waved courteously and smiled. The young couple argued for a moment or two before the girl finally nodded and the boy motioned for Emma to get out and follow them.

"This is Rosella, Ethelinda's great-granddaughter," the boy said.

"What do you want with my nan?" she asked as they walked along the gravel path across the encampment. She was barefoot except for beaded anklets on both feet, and she wore a long, colorful skirt that flapped in the spring wind. Emma could tell why the boy liked her, despite the fact that their *friendship* was more than likely shunned by both their families.

"I have a few questions I need to ask her about a case I'm working on."

"Wait, you're police? Marc, you didn't tell me she was a copper!" She smacked him on the arm.

"I didn't know," he replied sheepishly.

"I'm not a cop... well, I work for the police. That is true. I'm a crime scene investigator, and my predecessor had your great-grandmother's name written down as a source for some information, but he didn't say what that was in his notes."

She looked at Emma sideways. "Why don't you just ask him?"

"I would, but he passed away last week. She isn't in any trouble, I promise you that. I just need a little clarification."

"I'm sorry for your loss," said Marc.

"I never met him, sadly. Which is why it's all the more difficult picking up where he left off in this case. Again, thank you so much for allowing me to speak with your nan."

Rosella walked up to an old wooden bow top caravan, painted in bright, beautiful colors. Nearby, a horse grazed on the grass, dragging his reins behind him. The young girl climbed up the small wooden staircase and knocked. "Nan, I have someone who would like to see you. Are you home?"

An elderly woman, looking every bit of her 100 years, came to the door, dressed in traditional clothes that looked so stereotypical gypsy that Emma thought she looked like a performer more than someone wearing their everyday attire.

"Nan, this is a crime scene investigator from the police. She said you spoke with her former colleague and she needs to follow up."

The old lady sized up Emma and grumbled something under her breath. "Yes, that'd be fine. Hello, miss, I'm Ethelinda. How can I help you?"

Emma stepped up and shook her hand. "Thank you, I appreciate it. I'm CSI Emma Lloyd."

"Nice to meet you, lassie. Come on in. Would you like a cuppa?"

"Yes, please, that'd be great," replied Emma.

"Nan, do you want us to come in with you?" asked Rosella.

"No, my love, I think it might be best I talk with this young lady alone. I doubt this will be an appropriate conversation for you. Now, you two go off and whisper sweet nothings to one another."

Marc blushed and Rosella bashfully brushed her hair behind her ear as they turned and walked away.

The spacious inside of the Vardo caravan surprised Emma as Mrs Wood seemed to have efficiently managed to put a whole flat into the available area—minus a bathroom. In the back, sliding French doors separated the large, raised bed from the living area. Immediately to the left, a kitchenette with a cast-iron stove tucked up against the wall. On the opposite side, a bench and chest of drawers ran the length of the Vardo to the French doors. Nestled between the kitchenette and bed, another small bench and coffee table resided. Every item, from the woodwork to curtains, was adorned in bright maroons, greens, and golds; gaudy in Emma's opinion, yet still beautiful.

"Pardon my granddaughter's caution in introducing us. She, like many, is still weary around strangers whose intentions are not clear. Even at her age, she's become a little jaded and skeptical."

"I totally understand. I know general sentiment towards Roma are less than cordial nowadays—well, not that they have ever really been."

"Let's not be coy, you can say gypsy. I can't help who we are, even if the notion we are from Egypt is historically and factually inaccurate."

"Has sentiment always been like this?"

"Oh, it comes and goes. It's really about the people. You get folks like young Marc there who see us for who we are— gentle people trying to live according to our traditions. Then there are those who see us as vagabonds and criminals. Sadly, there is a little truth to both perceptions. Do you want sugar with your tea?"

"Yes, please. Two."

Ethelinda poured the steaming tea from an antique porcelain pot into a mismatched, chipped teacup which reminded Emma of the Disney movie *Beauty and the Beast*. She added two sugars, served herself, and then gingerly reclined on the opposite bench.

"I was sad to hear the news of Dr Evans." Ethelinda crossed herself and whispered a prayer. "I'm assuming that's the colleague Rosella spoke of. Had you worked with him long?"

"I never actually met him—I was called in to process his scene and then asked to replace him shortly afterwards. So, you remember Dr Evans, then?"

"Oh yes. We met about thirty years ago, through a friend of a friend type thing. But it was another ten years before he inquired about what you have come to ask me."

"I'm sorry, what?" Emma got the feeling that everyone around her knew more than she did.

"I told you, let's not be coy. You said that you are his replacement, which means you have inherited all his cases as well as... his *other* project. And there is nothing that would drive a young lady like yourself out into the sticks and to a gypsy camp like the question on the tip of your tongue, driving you mad with curiosity. So, go ahead, ask your question."

Emma didn't know how to respond—a part of her wanted to ask *the question* from the vandalism but thought it nonsense. "Okay... erm... I've seen your name in his notes as well as someone else's notes regarding an unsolved case. Why?"

"Oh, my dear." Ethelinda clasped her hands together. "You don't even know the right question yet. I bet she's not happy with you at all. Well, sweetie, I am an expert on things of a less than scientific nature. Not because I practice them, mind you, but because I have seen many things in my life and I've kept my eyes and ears open. That has allowed me to learn a great deal about things I sometimes wish I didn't."

"What things? I'm sorry, I'm very lost here." Emma took a sip of her tea, which was still too bitter even with the sugar.

"I know the unsolved case of which you speak. Most people do. However, there are only a few that actually understand it as we do. You, my sweet child, are here about Bella. And let me be very clear, Proverbs 9:10, 'The fear of the Lord is the beginning of wisdom.' Those words will serve you well if applied to Bella. Don't cross her." Ethelinda took a sip of her tea and continued. "Now, to the question you don't even know yet: What is the Hand of Glory?"

Why does everyone refer to Bella in the present tense? Emma dismissed the notion and continued. "All I know is the Hand was a prominent theory related to Bella's case, as the public in the UK and US got swept up in the Satanism frenzy that sidetracked cases all throughout the '70s and '80s. Just speculation and fantasies," said Emma.

"But are they just fantasies? You see, the Hand of Glory, very much an ancient practice in witchcraft, is like all things supernatural. There are two ways we can view it: it's not real, or it is real. But what *you and I* believe doesn't matter. It's what the practitioner believes that matters, because it's their belief that motivates their actions, and those actions which have real-life consequences. Whether it is infused with supernatural power doesn't matter in the end, only their actions wrought by their beliefs. Because of this, we cannot discredit a theory just because we ourselves don't believe in it." Ethelinda's voice quivered from age.

"Okay, then, so what is the Hand of Glory?"

"I'm glad you asked," Ethelinda replied with a chuckle. "The Hand of Glory is both a punishment and a reward. It is a punishment to the victim and a reward to the recipient of the hand."

"Punishment? How so?"

"The common understanding is that the hand would be that of a criminal who was hanged and executed for their crimes. But what constitutes a crime? What law? Many occultists *assume* it applies to our modern Judeo-Christian laws that form the basis of our governmental systems, but they fail to remember those laws don't govern those who practice witchcraft. Laws of the coven are far more important. So, one could say, betray or offend one's family, and it would justify the execution."

"And what did they do? To make the Hand of Glory, that is."

"It's simple. After the individual was executed, their hand would be severed and fat would be removed from the deceased. The fat would be rendered as a candle; the hand would be mummified and used as a candle stick."

"For what purpose?" Emma's stomach turned.

"That's a bit more mysterious, as many gifts have been attributed to the owner of the hand. One in particular that occultists agree on is that when the candle is lit, anyone within reach of its light would be held powerless to move, except for the owner of the hand who could move freely and remain hidden from its illumination like one still in the shadows. And let's not forget that over the years, the gift of extended life has also been attributed as well, but it's highly debated by experts and practitioners alike."

"Do you actually believe any of that?"

"I'm a God-fearing woman." Ethelinda crossed herself. "I've been following the path of the Carpenter since I was about Rosella's age. But anyone who believes in the miracles of God, by default, must also believe in the curses, Satan, and his legion."

"So you think the Hand of Glory is real?"

"As I said earlier, I've seen many things. And all that matters is that there are those out there, those even in this gypsy community, who do. People like my uncle who don't fear God."

"So why did Dr Evans contact you?"

"He wanted to know about *the hand*; he wanted to know if it were conceivable that someone from the gypsy community would have been willing to kill to create a Hand of Glory. If perhaps someone from the Romani community could have killed Bella."

"What was your answer?"

"Unfortunately, my answer was yes."

"Did he have a suspect list?"

"If he did, he never showed it to me. I wouldn't have any clue."

"Do you have any suspicions?"

"I was a little girl at the time of Bella's death and my parents had moved us away several years before. So not only do I have no idea who might have killed Bella, I also don't have any idea who she might be."

"Thank you for your time, Mrs Wood. It's much appreciated."

"You are more than welcome."

Emma finished her tea and got up to leave before Ethelinda reached up and took her hand. "Emma, you need to know, 'We wrestle not against flesh and blood, but against principalities, against powers, against the rulers of the darkness of this world, against spiritual wickedness in high places.' Ephesians 6:12. Guard your mind and heart—set your spirit on Him to protect you."

Chapter 14
Drakelow

Timothy flopped down on the worn-out mattress, sliding his sleeping bag out of the way so he didn't spill tuna juice all over it. He cracked open the tin and dove in. His filthy fingers shook as he lifted each bite to his mouth.

The yellow floor lamp he stole from a construction site shone on the opposite wall of the small half-brick and stone room he called home. Home, because here no one bothered him. It was a security blanket from the world outside, save *her*.

As he ate in the cold tunnels, *those words* returned. He wiggled his finger in his ear and belted out nonsense words to drown them out. They subsided and were replaced by the comforting drips of water on the stone floor. A cold draft swooped through his torn mittens, over his knuckles, and down his sleeve, sending shivers down his back. The hundred feet of sandstone above his head withheld the warmth of the early spring, so he took a risk and plugged in his small space heater. Timothy set the tuna down and stretched over to the extension cord to plug it in.

The light zapped and darkness engulfed his cell. The breakers blew again. He would have to venture back up one level and check the fuse box.

Timothy didn't mind walking through the tunnels in the dark. In the pitch black, you can't see the shadows leap and jump, nor see *her*. He hated *that woman*, but he didn't have a choice, now, did he? She followed him wherever he moved— from home to home.

Turning right out of his room, he ran his fingertips along the wall to the first intersection and turned right. He had it all memorized. 30 steps to the T-junction then left, 200 steps to avoid the cave-in, another 150 paces to the big chip in the stone wall, indicating the staircase on the opposite side.

The stairs were steep and narrow, with no railing and uneven steps. The walls crumbled here, as the sandstone was softer than the tunnels above—perhaps why they sealed it off and never completed the work. As he reached the top, the stairwell ceiling dropped low, so that he had to almost crawl out of the entrance to the upper level. Timothy pitied any fat construction worker who had to squeeze down there. He picked up the can of WD-40 he kept at the top of the stairs and gave the hinges a good spritz. If he didn't, the machine used to conceal the tunnel would squeak and wake the dead—he had to keep it constantly greased to remain hidden from security.

Once on the upper level, movement was easier, with fewer obstructions and more light. More light was a relative term. Not all the lights worked and even then, only some had functioning bulbs. Occasionally, a stream of light traveled down a corridor and bounced off the white sandstone, turning a corner, but in the end, darkness ruled supreme in Drakelow.

Those words returned as he continued his weaving path through the darkness of Drakelow. "Shhh, go away… go AWAY." He muttered under his breath, swatting at thin air as if it would make the voice stop. He crept a little faster and hoped the hum of the technical room would drown out the noise, though he knew nothing would make it stop. It grew more intense with each step. Holding his hands over his ears, he crouched down in the dark and rocked back and forth. *Ten, nine, eight, seven, six.* His hot tears wet his cheeks. Timothy scrunched his eyes tight. *Three, two, one.* The ringing subsided and *those words* faded to the recesses of his mind.

He wiped the tears with the back of his hand, got up, and ducked into the technical room. Security never locked the door, but that wasn't the issue—finding spare fuses was.

He gave the old metal hinges a quick spray with lubricant and waited for it to settle. Timothy needed to be fast. He cranked the knob and opened the door and headed straight to the supply fuse box in the corner. *Bloody hell, empty.*

Timothy opened the upper fuse box door and fiddled around the lower inside edge to locate the release latch. A secret panel below popped open. He couldn't recall how many times he had done this, but he did remember the first. It was late spring and he had ridden his bike past the entrance gate, all the way to the outer steel doors, and waited as instructed. His new boss, Mr Chapman, told him someone from the company would arrive at 10am for an orientation and a tour of the tunnels. He set his bike down in the grass and lit up a joint while he waited.

A few minutes later, a brown '83 All Aggro puttered through the gate and pulled up next to him. He didn't know if the car had originally been brown, or if it had just completely rusted over. A young girl, about Timothy's age, got out and greeted him. "You Timothy Burrow?"

"Yeah."

"Great. I'm Stacey Inight. I'm here to give you a tour—all the ins and outs of the job." Stacey rustled through her bag to fetch the keys to the large metal door labeled adit A in large block letters above the casing. Timothy followed her to the door, watching her walk the whole way. She was a bigger girl but had curves in all the places he liked.

Stacey tugged the door open, releasing a rush of cold air from within its blackness. Timothy stepped forward to follow her in, but bumped into her as she stood, staring into the empty corridor beyond. Stacey stood motionless for several moments before he interceded. "Stacey? Stacey, are you all right?" *She's having a seizure,* he thought. *What do I do?* "Stacey?"

She shook it off and replied, "Yes?"

"Hey, are you alright?"

"No… um… I just get these blackouts sometimes. Just give me a minute." She sat down and leaned her head against the tunnel doors, massaging her temples with her fingers. "Do you have any more weed?"

"I, uh, I don't smoke."

"I saw you flick that J when I drove up… and you reek of skunk. Besides, we both know who we work for."

Timothy pulled out another blunt from his jacket and lit up, handing it to Stacey after he took a hit. She took a deep drag and held it for a few moments before exhaling. "Thanks, I just need to level off."

"No problem." He waited in silence as she composed herself.

"Alright, you ready for your *orientation*?" Stacey air quoted.

"Sure."

"Do you want the standard tour or the bonus tour with all the nasty details?" She pushed herself up from the ground, taking another hit, and dusting herself off.

"Bonus tour."

"You got it, big fella." Stacey entered the door and used the torch on her phone to find the large breaker switch on the wall. When she flipped it, the lights flickered on in sequence down the tunnel. "Here we go. Drakelow tunnels began construction in 1941 as a secret facility to build airplane parts for Hercules, Pegasus, Centaur, and Mercury engines. It took approximately eight months to complete the three and a half miles of tunnels covering 285,000 square feet." Stacey guided Timothy through the sprawling facility. "During the Cold War, there was extensive reconstruction to the tunnel layout to convert the facility to a nuclear fallout shelter for the government. The costs became too great and the work was never finished, so they eventually dropped the project and abandoned the tunnels altogether. After decommissioning the tunnels in 1993, it underwent more reconstruction." Stacey finished off the joint and threw it to the ground, squishing it under foot.

"You sure know a lot about this place," said Timothy.

"I think that's the most you've said to me all morning. You're the quiet type. Just a big ole gentle teddy bear, ain't ya? I like that." She gave him a wink before continuing. "I give tours occasionally, in between the duties Chapman has me doing." Stacey stepped into a technical room lined with shelves, electrical conduits, and breaker boxes. "So, one of your jobs, besides helping with the airsoft competitions and paranormal night tours, is dealing with this hunk of junk."

"What is it?"

"This controls the whole electrical grid down here. In another tunnel, near adit B, there are two backup generators, but this still houses all the breakers. Some of them have been updated to use modern breakers. Others, like this one here, still use WW2 tech."

"Why do I need to know all this?"

"Quite often, the fuses blow during events and we have to change them out. The new ones are easy to replace, but the older ones are a pain in the arse. Sometimes we have to swap them out from an unused area until replacements come in. They're specially made. Just make sure these here are always running. They operate *the farm*."

"So it's true? Chapman grows weed down here?"

"I'll show you that when we get to the *bonus* part of the tour a little later. But first, I wanna let you in on a little secret." Stacey reached into the bottom of the panel, and Timothy heard a click. Below the unit where she stood, a door popped open, revealing more 1940's circuit breakers. "So these here… we have no idea what they control. Chapman found them a couple months ago, but we can't track what and where they control."

"That's wild. What do you think?"

"I mean, this was an underground, top secret military facility for 50 years. It could literally control anything or nothing at all," said Stacey.

Timothy, tear forming on the lower edge of his eye, shoved the painful memory aside. He removed the fuse, which controlled the lower tunnels, and then selected a working fuse in the panel above that operated an unused section. To do that, he had to flip off the power to the entire upper-level tunnels to prevent electrocuting himself.

The outage would alert the guards, so he had to be swift. Even if the guard walked, they'd arrive within minutes and there was nowhere to hide if they arrived faster than expected.

Timothy held the burnt fuse in his mouth, placed his left hand on the switch and his right over the good fuse. Taking a slow deep breath, he threw the power, plunging the entire facility into darkness. The fuse was frozen in place and he couldn't unscrew it. He had to choose another. He ran his fingers over the other switches to find an active fuse. He didn't know what area it controlled, as he couldn't read the label in the dark. He just had to risk it. Furiously unscrewing the fuse, Timothy swapped the old one in, twisting it into place as quickly as possible.

Disgruntled voices floated down the corridor, arguing over who would check the technical room. Time was running short.

He finished screwing in the burnt fuse and threw the power back on. The lights flickered above and hummed their typical resonance. Timothy quietly closed the upper panel with one hand as the other hand screwed the good fuse into the secret panel. He flipped his breaker on and closed its panel door.

Rushing as fast as he could, he hugged against the wall as he moved to the closest junction, ducking behind the corner before being seen. He peered around the corner to catch a guard head into the technical room, scratching his head and arguing with himself over how the power came back on.

Timothy needed to take a different route *home*. Slinking through the corridors and counting the different junctions, he arrived at the entrance to the lower levels.

His ears started ringing again, nagging his mind. Timothy hit the side of his head to push it out. "Ten, nine, eight, seven…" *Those words* soon followed. "Six, five—" His mind fell dark.

*

When he awoke, he was scrawling *those words* onto the wall with chalk. How and where he got the chalk, he couldn't recall. It was always that way. No matter how often he emptied his pockets, there would always be more, like a perpetual curse of Elisha's oil jar.

Timothy looked at the graffiti; the last few letters were bloodied. He held his hand up and realized the chalk had run so low that his fingertips scraped against the stone and ripped open as he wrote, leaving the last word *elm* pinkish-red. One nail had ripped back to the quick, the torn part hanging on by a bit of flesh. His blackouts were getting worse, and he was helpless to do anything about it. *Why can't anyone answer the question? Someone has to know, right?*

With the lights back on, he made it back with ease. Unlike the upper level, the original permanent ceiling lights no longer worked even with functioning bulbs, so Timothy had strung up some fairy lights down the corridors that he had stolen from a Christmas tree in the city park. They were bright enough to light the way, but not strong enough to hurt his eyes.

His rucksack had a few medical items, nothing much, just some disinfectant and bandages. As he dumped the full contents of the bag onto the floor, the newspaper he had collected fell out. His heart sank when he picked it up and saw the obituary again.

Poor Dr Evans. Timothy remembered hearing him speak in school about police forensics during a career fair once. He even mentioned her case in his presentation. It was the first time he had ever heard *those words*. Of course, back then he read them on the projection screen; now he heard them in his mind. He believed if anyone could answer her, Dr Evans could. He felt lost now. *The police have to know, right? This is their job. They have to know that answer! Dr Evans couldn't have died without telling them. No, no, he did! Why haven't they shared it? Maybe the new woman knows. She replaced him. She knows, she has to know!* he thought.

Down the corridor, somewhere in the vast darkness of Drakelow, rats scurried and squealed. They always did when *she* returned. Her footsteps drudged across the grit and stones out in the deeper corridors. *Why didn't she ever come down the stairwell?* His heart raced—he'd rather blackout than see her.

Thump-shush.

He threw his things in his rucksack, tearing off his boots as quickly as he could at the same time. The half-eaten can of tuna somersaulted off the mattress, sending fish and juice flying across the room, as he swatted it out of his way.

Thump-shush.

Timothy huddled up in his sleeping bag with it pulled up as far over his head as possible. Forgetting the lamp was still on, he wiggled out just enough to pull its plug from its socket, letting the darkness swallow the room.

Thump-shush.

Her shuffling grew louder as she neared the doorway. Timothy again pulled the sleeping bag high over his head and turned his back to the entrance. He preferred facing the darkness of the wall than facing her. He screwed his eyes up and prayed. *No, no, no, no, no, please God, no…*

Thump-shush.

Each scrape of her foot across gravel preceded a whimper as his tears mixed with his bubbling snot. She stopped at the foot of his bed before kneeling down and lying next to him. Her arm, cold and intangible, wrapped around him and gripped tight. She stank of rotten wood. Nuzzling up close to him, he could sense her ghostly lips on his ear as she whispered her unsatiated question.

Chapter 15
The Scandal

Daily Mail
Wednesday 30 September 2009
By Bryant Jones

DEATH WEEK: DEATH BETS EXPOSED IN HAGLEY POLICE STATION

A local community is reeling in response to a leaked internal police memo which unearthed a macabre betting pool conducted by the officers in the Hagley police station in eastern West Mercia Police Authority. The wager: predicting the annual murder, suicide, and incidental death rates within their jurisdiction, which covers Hagley, Stourbridge, Dudley, and Rubery, during the middle weeks of October.

The memo in question, authored by Superintendent Charles Burton of Kidderminster and addressed to all employees of the Hagley station, provides a chilling insight into the distasteful competition that had become an annual ritual.

In one incriminating section, Superintendent Burton writes, "Congrats to Constable Morris for his impressive prediction last year: 3 murders, 8 suicides, and 11 non-suspicious deaths. Get ready to ante up, gents. This year there will be a £75 minimum to participate." His casual tone raises questions about the level of insensitivity within the force, pointing to a troubling culture that glorifies tragedies.

The scandal is bound to induce outrage from locals and families of victims, raising questions about the integrity of those entrusted with maintaining public safety. Is it possible that, in their callousness, some officers are hoping for higher casualty rates to win the pot? Or worse, might they be influenced to manipulate the figures?

Over the years, rumours of an internal pool had circulated within social circles surrounding station employees. Local residents had long suspected such improprieties, but there had never been any substantial proof beyond the urban legend that had developed in its wake. However, one whistleblower, PC George Edwards, brought the scandal to light after contacting the Daily Mail.

Sources within the station, some who asked to remain anonymous, have confirmed that this grim competition has been going on for at least a decade. This indicates a deep-rooted issue that goes beyond an individual or group of officers, suggesting systemic moral decay within the station.

The local community, which has regularly suffered from staggering above average deaths rates every October, is now confronted with a new reality that has sown distrust and anger. Traditionally, officers had always been sympathetic to the plight affecting the eastern jurisdiction, but it appears to have all been a ruse to cover a perverse, profit-driven game.

West Mercia Police and the Independent Office for Police Conduct (IOPC) have both been alerted to the situation. In response, they promised immediate action. "This is a matter of utmost seriousness," commented IOPC Director Matthew Whitmore. "We'll conduct a comprehensive investigation to ensure all involved are held accountable. This deeply disturbing behaviour has no place in our police force."

Superintendent Charles Burton, a police officer with over 30 years of experience, has been placed on administrative leave pending both an internal Police Authority investigation and an independent IOPC investigation. Chief Inspector John Taylor, from the neighbouring station of Kidderminster, will serve as interim superintendent until said time the investigations are completed.

Hagley Parish Council Chair Otto Parry has gone on record saying, "To restore faith in our community, there must be transparency throughout the investigation, swift action against the culprits, and measures to prevent such incidents in the future. Anything less would leave a lingering dark cloud over our parish, already pained by the circumstances."

This scandal serves as a stark reminder that integrity should never be compromised, not even in jest. Those in law enforcement must remember that they are the protectors of society, its well-being, and peace.

West Mercia Police did not respond to the Daily Mail's request for comment by press time.

Chapter 16
The Cottage and the Key

Emma barely eked out a hello as she strolled past Vickie on the way into the station Monday morning. Vickie, giggling from something she read, cheerfully greeted Emma and buzzed her in without so much as looking up from her tabloid.

Emma lumbered into the laboratory to find the morgue refrigerator door open—again. She plopped down at her desk and zoned out for a moment, lost in her thoughts of yesterday's interview with Ethelinda. She reared back in the chair and stared at the ceiling. The cobwebs needed cleaning again and a curious crack in the ceiling arch had begun to spider its way across several bricks. Ethelinda's words, reverberating in her head as she made a note to call maintenance, "for our struggle is not against flesh and blood" creeped her out. Exposure to human violence was not uncommon for a CSI, but that quote made Emma think twice about Bella. She shuttered and futilely pushed the thought to the recesses of her mind.

Bella plagued Dr Evans—his journal confirmed that—and Emma refused to succumb to her as he did. Rule one: use work as a distraction. She picked up a stack of paperwork and started from the top, selecting cases with the most probability of solving. The desk lamp dismally illuminated her desk much less the room, aiding the nagging feeling of darkness creeping around her as she worked. She rolled her neck and brushed off the unsettling sensation that Bella lurked behind her.

Emma tossed a file to the side with a DNA request attached and picked up the next file for review. To her surprise, Evans' journal had found its way into the pile, leering at her. "What are you doing in here?" she said. Without thinking or deliberate intent, Emma started reading. She couldn't fathom why, as she had already gleaned everything lucid from within its pages—yet, she felt compelled. She was about to close the book when she noticed a page with a trace of black ink peering out from underneath the incoherent blue inked scribblings. *What's hiding under here?* she thought.

She powered up the spectral reflectance scanner and opened ImageJ on her mac. After scanning the page, Emma adjusted the color threshold, hue, and saturation to isolate the obscured text. To her surprise, the page contained a new series of lucid notes hidden underneath.

> *Bella's 2017 facial reconstruction image by Anthropologist Caroline Wilkinson of Face Lab, Liverpool UK, while limited by the original extant skull photos, is impressively close, but not completely accurate. I applaud Ms Wilkinson's efforts and feel her accolades are well deserved. Any inaccuracy in the reconstruction is no way reflective of her skill, but solely on that of the publicly available evidence with which to use.*

"How did he know her reconstruction was wrong?"

The notes continued across the bottom of the page and to the next, requiring Emma to shift the scan right. Repeating the process:

> *I've locked her secrets away… no one should see them.*
> *I've locked her away, too.*

Unfortunately, it didn't take long to discover the obscured notes had delved back into insanity. The only other phrase on the page possible to discern read:

> *I've locked her away, I've locked her away! I put Bella*
> *in the cabinet!*

"What?" Confused, Emma swiveled around and looked at Bella laying on the morgue drawer. *What do you mean you locked her away?* She swiveled back to the computer and accidentally kicked the drawer on her right. "Huh… did you mean *that* cabinet?"

What was it that Taylor said about curiosity? Emma didn't care. Picking up the phone, she called McArthur.

"PC McArthur, Hagley."

"Hey, it's Lloyd. I've got a quick question for you. Did you find the cabinet key Taylor requested you locate?" *That lie might catch me in the arse later.*

"What key? Superintendent never asked me to find anything. Should I have?"

"Well, I have a locked cabinet here in the laboratory and there isn't a matching key anywhere. Do you know if Dr Evans had any keys on his person and processed into evidence?" Emma could've looked too, but the digital trail would've tipped off Taylor.

"Let me check." Emma heard the click clack of the

keyboard over the phone. "Just his house and car keys. Nothing else."

"I have a second favor I need to ask. Do you have access to his house? I'd like to drive over there and see if we can find anything."

McArthur couldn't hide his excitement over the phone. "Absolutely! I'm here in the station and I could take you there right now."

"Give me five minutes," she replied.

When Emma came up to the bullpen, McArthur's face hung forlorn. He swung his uniformed jacket on and snagged a set of keys off the desk. "Bad news. I just got called out to the Shaw's. Apparently, there's a huge row after Mrs Shaw accused the Darby kid of vandalizing her house with a 'who put Bella' graffiti. If I give you the keys to Dr Evans' place, will you be able to manage? Do you want to wait until I come back?"

Emma considered the offer, but impatience won out. "No, I think I can manage. I still have the address in my satnav—I hope."

"If you're back before me, just put the keys on my desk and I'll take care of the rest. Whisper carefully."

*

Emma shook her jacket, sending droplets of rain onto the entryway floor of Evans' small cottage. Strands of hair stuck to the side of her cheeks as she ran her fingers over her head, squeezing out the rain. The last time she'd graced this doorway, the atmosphere was somber—and for a very good reason. She expected, under the circumstances of this visit, that the house would feel differently. Just your average home eagerly awaiting its occupants to return from an extended holiday. Yet, nothing had changed. The air hung heavy and cool, exuding loneliness as if it knew no one would be returning.

Out of habit, Emma flipped the light switch and found that the power to the house had been disconnected. Understandably, the house sat vacant and would remain so indefinitely—at least until the courts determined who the deed would pass to. Faint flashes from the storm outside streamed through the windows, revealing the home otherwise shrouded in darkness. Emma took out her torch and started her search.

The key could be anywhere. There was no telling if it would be on a ring with others or by itself. Without any distinctive markings, she'd have to collect any key that looked the right size. She puffed her cheeks and blew out—this was going to take a while.

"If you were a lost key, where would you be?" Scratch that. It wouldn't take a while, it was going to take forever. Emma's stomach dropped at the daunting task ahead.

She let logic pick where she'd begin. *Where do people leave keys? At the front door.* Emma checked the wooden stand beside the entrance, rifling through the drawer and sifting through the clutter it had collected over the years. Next, she moved to the hall tree nestled in the corner on the opposite wall. The Evans' had left several jackets hanging, but the pockets only produced a variety of coins, a package of tissues, some old receipts, and copious amounts of lint. No luck.

Emma stepped into the living room. The cooler air sent goosebumps down her rain drenched skin; her hairs stood on end. She rubbed her hands over her arms to warm up as she scanned the room for the next possible location for the key.

The coffee table drawers offered little hope, revealing only drink coasters and the remote to the TV. Likewise, the knick-knack bowls on the bookshelves turned up empty.

Emma's breath floated out into the room like a foggy mist, prompting her to check her smartwatch—15 degrees outside. Why was it so cold in here? She pulled the collar of her shirt tighter against her neck.

The sitting room was a bust, no better than the hallway, so she headed to the kitchen. The drawer where Dr Evans stashed the sleeping pills immediately drew her eyes. It hadn't even been two weeks since she was last here, but it felt like a long, forgotten memory.

A floorboard creaked upstairs. Emma stopped mid-search and stood quietly. A few moments later, another creak floated down and into the kitchen. She wondered if she was alone in the house. She had the only house key that she was aware of and there was no indication any of the Evans' distant relatives had come up from London.

Emma brushed it off as the house settling and continued her search. Both junk drawers were empty. She checked her watch—two hours and nothing to show for it.

The floorboard creaked again. This time, without thinking, she called out. "Hello? Is anyone here?"

Yes.

Emma's haunches pricked up. Had she imagined that? Emma could have sworn she heard it.

"This is CSI Emma Lloyd of West Mercia Police. If anyone is here, make yourself known." She waited for a response. "This is West Mercia Police. Anyone there?" Emma chewed her bottom lip and shook it off, reluctantly setting out on her quest once more.

The whole downstairs had been searched top to bottom. Every nook and cranny, under every seat cushion. Even under the couch. If there was a key in this house, it wasn't on the ground floor. Emma set her focus on the upstairs. As she placed her foot on the upper landing, the board beneath her creaked—a familiar sound.

The creak sent her imagination into a frenzy. Had someone else been upstairs earlier? She stood at the edge of the landing and waited for any other sign of another person. Again, only silence. She crept deeper into the first floor, this time sliding swiftly into the bathroom.

With no lights and a tiny bathroom window with drawn curtains, darkness quickly enveloped her. Only her torch aided her amidst the blackness. She checked the drawers and under the sink. Nothing again. As she left the bathroom, she avoided looking into the mirror. She had had enough of the eerie sensations; she didn't need her eyes playing tricks on her either. Unfortunately, that didn't stop her mind from conjuring someone standing behind her in her faint reflection, sending goose-pimples rippling down her spine.

Making her way back to the hall and toward the guest bedroom, a faint sound came from the master suite. A gentle *thump-shush* drifted out. She took a step toward the room before she heard it again. Emma wanted to call out, but her throat tightened. She waited, hoping the sound would go away much like the creaking floorboard. The cold continued to send chills over her shoulders—it was obviously dropping in temperature.

Thump-shush.

Emma's ears perked. Her heart thumped against her chest, rushing pulses of blood past her ears. She reached for the door to the master bedroom and pulled it toward her, careful not to alert anyone who might be on the other side.

The room was dark, and Emma knew she'd have to risk giving away her presence by shining her light inside. As she did, she heard the *thump-shush* again.

The torch failed to light the room, but instead only revealed the specific area Emma shined it. The bed, where she found Pearl the previous week, laid empty—sheets still pulled down from when the coroners took her away. Emma inched forward, now standing fully in the door frame, and moved the light toward the desk and chair.

Thump-shush pounded louder, followed by a rush of cold air over her. Emma swung the torch to the right, shining her pale beam across the other side of the room. Movement caught her eye, *thump-shush*.

The closet door where Dr Evans had hanged himself, thrust open and banged against the wall, slowly swinging back across the carpet. Next to it, glass lay strewn on the floor along with a raven, bloodied and lifeless. A breeze ripped through the gapping remains of the broken window, smashing the closet door into the wall again.

Relieved, Emma closed the door, securing it in place after kicking glass out of the way. As for the window and raven, there was nothing she could do but let someone at Hagley know, so it could be tended to later.

She rolled her neck and massaged her shoulders, attempting to relieve the tension. She had uncovered the mundane source of the *thump-shush*, but the memory of the *yes* she heard in the kitchen still lingered. She wanted out of the house, but refused to leave empty-handed, either.

Emma was out of options until her eyes caught the desk

where Edwards violated protocol and lifted the notebook. It was as good as any place to resume her search. She rifled through the drawers and looked all around but found nothing. Defeated, she flopped onto the antique chair, ready to give up. Something poked her in the rear. Emma sprang up and reached out to see what had jabbed her. Her fingers fiddled in the crack of the cushion, the tips just grazing something metal.

Chapter 17
Webster's Journal

Monday, 27ᵗʰ March, 1944

At this juncture, there isn't much about this case that shocks me. As we approach the anniversary of the poor woman murdered in Hagley Wood and stowed away in the hollow of that tree, we are no closer to discovering who she was, nor the identity of the perpetrator. We are caught like one swept away by rising waters, at the mercy of fate and flailing against all hope.

Early in this AM, Inspector Inight received a disturbing phone call regarding vandalism in the Hagley area. No theory as to who the culprit might be, as there were no witnesses to the act. The handwriting was distinct but written in such a way that it could have easily been disguised as a ruse.

The words recorded mocked my colleagues who have been diligent all these months to ascertain the full facts of the Hagley Wood murder. However, after further review, I strongly feel the tone appears more sympathetic to their plight than a taunt. It has also given us a possible clue to her identity, a name.

The vandalism read: WHO PUT BELLA IN THE WYCH ELM?

Bella. Is that your name? Is that a name ascribed to you at birth by your family or a name a stranger has given in hopes that personifying you beyond that of a faceless skeleton will aid in your vindication?

Nonetheless, Bella is now the name the community has embraced and one we are gladly willing to bestow upon her, whether it be true or not. I much prefer to speak of her as *Bella* than as *that woman.*

I cannot venture to state the veracity of the claim, as there is too little evidence with which to follow. There are those in the department who state the author of the chalk message knew *Bella* personally. If so, why not come forward? Why not speak to the police and aid our endeavour? Are they the murderer, overcome by guilt, speaking to the police in hopes they will be caught in order to ease their conscience? Or are they a witness, hesitant to come forward out of fear that the killer they know will take retribution upon them?

There are more questions than answers. Therefore, we have resigned that we may never solve the mystery. Inight has stated, quite emphatically, that perhaps we should close the case.

Thursday, March 30th, 1944

I can still barely process the series of events that has taken place today, and thankfully, much to my relief, the general public is unaware of the acts and I pray to God above, it remains that way.

However, one conundrum is answered to some extent:

Who was the author of the chalk message?

We were called out again to yet another series of chalk messages scrawled upon public property.

As I processed the scene, taking samples of the chalk and photos of the message, a report of another message came to Insp. Inight. This time, the culprit had been seen and identified. Richard Bailey, a local farmer, was seen by a passerby writing the message on a fence post and gate out on Hassel Lane. Constable Ward had been sent to fetch Mr Bailey and take him into custody.

Though I was not privy to all the events thereafter, PC Ward was quite forthcoming in his testimony after the initial shock wore off and he awoke in the recovery room. The relevant gaps of my knowledge, as provided by PC Ward, are quoted verbatim below via his official police report:

> On March 30th, 1944, at approximately 9am, I, Constable Harold Ward, of Worcestershire Constabulary, responded to a reported incident on Hassel Lane. Upon arrival, I observed Mr Bailey wandering aimlessly in some mental fit—completely unresponsive to any verbal commands. There were clear chalk markings on the fence post and gate. At the time of my arrival, he still had the chalk in hand. I proceeded to assess the situation and took the following actions: As Mr Bailey showed no signs of violence and had no history of such, I placed him in the back of the car unrestrained. Afterwards, I took a witness statement from Mr Henry Pugh. I then proceeded to drive to White's on Pershore Street to rendezvous with Insp. Inight and drive the two back to Hagley station.
>
> During the course of my transportation of Mr Bai-

ley, he roused and became quite agitated. In the begin-
ning, he simply mumbled to himself and rocked to and
fro in his seat. Within a few minutes, he had grown bel-
ligerent, screaming obscenities and the phrase "who
put Bella in the wych elm". The more I told him that I
did not know, the more aggressive he became. At some
point, he began striking me in the head with his fists.
Before I could appropriately respond and stop the car,
I blacked out. The next thing I remember was waking
up in the hospital.

This statement is a true and accurate account of
the incident to the best of my knowledge and recol-
lection.

The point at which I was able to observe the events, the
situation had grown to great peril. The car was careening out
of control and heading toward us. When the squad car crashed
into the side of the storefront, it was apparent that Mr Bailey
had attacked PC Ward and probably would have killed PC
Ward if not for the accident.

The crash stunned both driver and passenger, but as we
rushed to give aid, Mr Bailey regained consciousness. He
began to thrash violently about in the backseat of the car,
screaming only *those words* he had written in chalk. Before
we could restrain him, he bashed his head into the door window, sending shards of glass everywhere.

Insp. Inight attempted to calm Mr Bailey but was unable
to do so before Mr Bailey commandeered PC Ward's sidearm and took his own life. His death was instantaneous. Insp.
Inight was within close proximity of Mr Bailey at the time and
was thus covered in copious amounts of brain matter.

PC Ward will be in need of long-term recovery as his left eye is no longer viable after the damage sustained by Mr Bailey's attack. As a monophthalmic myself, I empathise with his situation. However, I am also an example of the successes you can have in life with only one eye.

On a personal note, I have come to experience two unusual phenomena. Firstly, since this event, I have been unable to stop thinking about the query Mr Bailey wrote in chalk. That question runs over and over in my mind and there are times in which I think I hear it audibly whispered in my ear. It is often accompanied by a serious case of tinnitus, for which I cannot find a medical cause. Secondly, unbeknownst to me, I have begun doodling dark spirals throughout my journal and paperwork. I was completely unaware of my actions until Insp. Inight pointed them out to me. It is a subconscious tick I cannot control. All in all, both are quite unsettling, to say the least.

It should also be noted that there are a few in the station who have adopted a superstitious opinion of the aforementioned events related to the graffiti and Mr Bailey. Several officers have voiced their feelings that the writings are a direct result of trying to shut down the investigation. When pressed for details, the men expressed that 'something' (of which they could not describe) was not allowing the station to put the case to rest—the more we try to close the case the more 'something' pushes back. While Insp. Inight and I do not share these beliefs, it is important to note that the atmosphere in the station has changed and much of it is in direct response to these opinions.

Chapter 18
Blackouts

Timothy's eyes opened to darkness. He reached up with his frail hands and rubbed his sunken sockets, hoping his sight would return. He barely recognized his gaunt fingers upon his skin, knobby and rough.

Slowly, his eyes adjusted enough to realize he was down in the lower depths of Drakelow. But where? His head reeled; he slapped his hand on the wall to catch his balance, trying to keep his knees underneath him.

How long had he been out? He felt as if he hadn't eaten or slept in days. Stomach pangs seized and growled, confirming his hunch. Timothy lifted his hand to check the time, but his watch spun and dangled loosely on his wrist. He reached with his other hand, held it straight, and pressed the backlight button. May 17th. 5:45 am. *Two days? I've been out for two days?*

He leaned with his head against the wall, hands in his face, weeping. A part of him just wanted to collapse and give up. Never to move again. Just lay there until death took him. Another part, driven by something else, said no. After a few moments of self-pity, Timothy succumbed to survival and pushed himself from the wall, wiping away the tears and smearing the filth on his face.

Despite being lost, the way back to his room wouldn't be an issue. Just remember Stacey's instructions: always go to the end of the corridor and turn right and you'll find your bearings eventually. The real issue would be fortitude—did he have the strength? His feet shuffled amongst the uneven, stony floor, unable to lift them off the ground.

As he meandered in the pitch black, a buzz tingled in his ears. Timothy hadn't the will to count from ten. He let it whelm up and take him under like a ship in a maelstrom.

*

Timothy awoke, still in the tunnels, but this time the flickering lights of his guided path lay just ahead. The fairy lights blurred in and out of focus, but hope sprung up ever so lightly— his water and food were nearby. And none too soon. This time, when he checked his watch, it read May 18th, 8:01 pm.

He leaned forward and let his frame pull himself home. His fingertips brushed the wall, keeping him steady as he stumbled along. Timothy only thought of water. His tongue, as dry as the sandstone underfoot, stuck to the roof of his mouth.

As he rounded the corner, light from his room crept out into the hall. He drove himself forward, mustering every ounce of strength. When he entered the room, he flinched at the light that now swallowed him. Timothy covered his eyes and blindly stumbled to his mattress before collapsing upon it. It reeked of piss.

His rucksack, with all his food stores, lay just out of reach. Timothy dragged himself the final few feet to snag his bottle and find relief. He popped the cap off and thrust it upwards, dousing himself in its cool waters. It splashed across his face and washed away the remainder of the dirt-stained tears. After chugging its full contents, he gasped and caught his breath. With his thirst temporarily quenched, he turned to satisfy his hunger.

Half a jar of Marmite rolled out of the bag first, and then he rummaged until he found the bread, tore a chunk off, and dipped it into the jar. Timothy devoured it before cracking open a can of tuna and downing it as fast as possible.

Laying back on his pillow, he closed his eyes. Perhaps he could get some *real* sleep. Obviously, he had no recollection of the time spent when he blacked out, but this one truth had become quite apparent: it didn't involve sleeping. Every time he came to, he was fatigued and hungry. His body relaxed and his mind drifted, slowly giving way to dreams that didn't involve *her*.

*

Horns blared and cars whizzed by, sending torrents of dust into Timothy's face. He found himself standing in the middle of a road, unaware of how he got there or even where *there* was. Drivers yelled from their windows as they sped by. "Get out of the road, you bloody fool!"

The same feeling of defeat he had in the depths of the tunnels returned. Should he just take a step into traffic? Let it all end. Timothy lifted a foot as a lorry approached—it'd be quick. Before he knew it, the truck had blown by and he was standing on the pavement. He knew *she* wouldn't allow it.

He looked up and down the street but didn't recognize any buildings or street signs. The morning sun, already hot, sent trickles of sweat down his temple. His watch said May 19th, 7:36 am. Another day lost.

Beyond a thorny hedgerow where he stood, an elderly couple tended to their well-manicured garden. Being seven foot one had its advantages, so he didn't have to strain too much to speak over the tops of the bushes. "Excuse me, madam, sir, can you tell me what city this is?"

The old woman's eyes widened as she gasped and scurried behind her husband. The man held his hand up, still holding the spade. "We don't want any trouble, young man. Please, just leave us be." After another moment, he turned to his wife and whispered. "Martha, get in the house."

Timothy scrunched his brows, grimaced, and flipped the old man the bird. This was nothing new. Even at the shelters, the workers feared him. What he tried to explain—and what they couldn't understand—was that it wasn't him they feared, but what *she* made him do. They never believed him. They just pumped him full of drugs, giving *her* a stronger foothold.

Weary and forlorn, he trod along the roadside and checked the street signs along the way in hopes of figuring out where the hell he was. Nothing looked familiar; he was truly lost. Timothy's size sixteen feet thumped the pavement as he lumbered along, looking for anything to help him find *home*.

He must have walked for fifteen minutes before another set of footsteps joined the shuffling of his feet. A more labored *thump-shush* drudged behind him. He turned around and saw, much to his dismay, *that woman* trailing behind along the pavement. Her leg, bent and twisted under her mustard-colored skirt, flopped and dragged along.

Up ahead, just around the corner, he spotted a SPAR convenience store. If he hurried, he could duck inside and lose her. He scoffed at his own thinking. *Lose her.* A silly notion; more like a futile act.

Timothy picked up the pace and ran around the corner, darting across the tiny car park and into the storefront. A bell dinged as he entered the cool, air-conditioned shop. He spun around, walking backwards away from the door, and checked if she had followed him. There was no sign of *her*, but that didn't mean anything.

Dashing into one of the aisles, his bulky rucksack, which he was unaware of wearing until now, knocked over a few jars of pickles. They crashed to the floor, sending gherkins, juice, and shattered glass all around his feet. Timothy crouched down and scooted a little further away from the door. He held his knees and buried his face, only peeking under the crook of his elbow.

A trembling voice called out from down the aisle. "Sir, we don't want any trouble. Just, please move on and leave, that's all we ask." A fat, pimple-nosed teenager, wearing a green corporate polo shirt, stood next to the broken pickle jars.

"I'm not here to cause trouble—I'm just hiding. I'm just trying to get away from her," said Timothy.

Still shaking when he spoke, the boy replied, "Who? Who are you hiding from? There isn't anyone here but us."

"She's always here. She's always with me." Timothy buried his head deeper between his arms and knees.

The bell at the front door dinged.

Timothy tightened his fetal position and rocked to and fro at the sound of shuffling feet. "She always finds me."

"Sir, is there someone I can call for you? Do you need a doctor or social services?"

"They can't help me. Useless charlatans, they can't stop her," he cried.

"Sir, I don't understand." The boy looked around. "There is no one else here. There's no woman."

Timothy looked up at him, tears in his eyes. "That's where you're wrong." Peeking out from behind the boy, a filthy yellow skirt flapped. Timothy's eyes widened as he saw the twisted leg, its bare foot covered in dirt and leaves, slide just out of view. He shot up from the floor, towering over the boy, and crashed into the shelves behind him. "That's where you're wrong! *She's* here now!"

Confused, the boy swiveled his head, blinking his eyes as he shrugged his shoulders. "What? There is literally no one but you and me. Sir, please, let me call someone for you." As the boy shifted his body, looking around the store, he revealed more of the wicked woman behind him. Crushed leaves matted against her blue and yellow striped cardigan which hung torn over her narrow shoulders. A few buttons dangled by a thread, barely holding the sweater up. She leaned in tight, pressing her face to his shoulder and sliding her arms around his plump waist, embracing him like a lost lover.

A shiny glint, refracting from the florescent light above them, caught Timothy's eye—glass. The *woman* held a shard of the pickle jar in her hand. Her fingers flexed and tightened around it; her knuckles white from the grip. He looked back at the boy, who was saying something, gesticulating and pointing toward the door. But Timothy couldn't hear him. The whispers of the woman and her infernal question drowned everything out.

It happened so quickly that Timothy couldn't open his mouth in time to warn the boy. He lunged forward to pull him away, but it was too late. The shard of glass slid effortlessly across his fat throat, revealing the bright pink flesh below his freckled skin. Before the boy understood what happened, glistened claret flowed freely down his belly.

Timothy caught him as his knees buckled and his body fell limp. Gently setting him on the ground, Timothy dropped the bloodied, glass shard and placed his hands over the wound. Blood spurted from between his filthy fingers. The boy's eyes stared off into an abyss over Timothy's shoulders. Timothy couldn't distinguish his own screams from that of the *woman's*, still standing in a pool of blood and pickle juice a step away. He turned his face from her as dark speckles circled in his peripheral vision, closing in until everything turned black.

*

Timothy's eyes focused as he blinked away the darkness. He held a piece of chalk against a red bricked façade. *Those words*, written by his hand, scrawled in blood-soaked chalk, spanned the whole wall. Blood, sticky and cool, dripped down his sleeve and from his fingertips. *The boy! Oh my god, what happened to the boy,* he thought as he stumbled backwards from the wall. He tossed the chalk onto the ground, or so he thought. In the slightest of movements, unaware of his own actions, he slipped the slender white stick into his front pocket.

He shook his head and rubbed his eyes with the heal of his hands, trying to process the events of what had happened and where he was now. He circled away and looked across the car park toward the street. It wasn't the convenience store.

Where was he? Timothy swung back around and looked at the building, eyes drawing to the marquee: Hagley Police Station.

Tears welled up once more and trickled down his cheeks. Quickly, the thoughts of the boy fell to the side and memories of Dr Evans and his replacement flooded in. *Do you know her answer?* he thought. "Can you help me—"

Timothy stumbled through the front door and was immediately greeted by a plain-looking desk clerk, round of face and quite forgettable. "Please help me—is she here?"

"Sir, it's going to be okay," replied the woman, who was fumbling with a button under the countertop.

"NO! It's *not* going to be okay! Where is she? She has to know! She has to know *who put Bella in the wych elm!*"

The desk clerk stepped back from the counter, away from Timothy, holding her hands up and trembling. "Sir, I promise you. It's going to be okay—just put the gun down."

Frustrated she wasn't listening, Timothy yelled louder. "Where is she? Is she here?" Unaware why the desk clerk was so frightened, he looked down at his hands to see the stolen rifle aimed at her. When he looked back up, everything turned black.

Chapter 19
Who Put Bella…

Cold cases: the substance of nightmares that haunt officers for years, keeping them up at nights, filling them with regret. Murders, rapes, violent acts fraught with unknowns and mysteries. Evidence withers and fails, and officers are left just as lost as they were at the start. That same disheartening reality fell on Emma as she scanned the contents of the locked drawer for the hundredth time. A month had passed since she found the key at Dr Evans' and she was no nearer to unearthing the secrets of the skeletal woman laying on her autopsy table then the day she walked into the wood.

Much of what she found in the drawer was unrelated to Bella, save one file in particular. A file that she had hoped would explain Dr Evans' ramblings in his journal. They ended up revealing more questions than answers.

As she did every morning since unlocking the drawer and finding the folder, she perused its contents. Baffled each and every time she looked at the photos within.

Emma picked up the top photo, which was exactly what

she expected based on the lucid reports from the journal—a famous reconstruction photo from 2017. Bella's face was square jawed, with puffy cheeks, and a slightly pudgy nose. Her teeth jutted subtly outward from her constructed smile. Light brown hair, with hints of wavy-curls, puffed around her face and stopped just before her shoulders. Bella's complexion, complete guess work on behalf of those involved in the reconstruction, looked no different than Emma's.

The following several photos showed the reconstruction process in different phases, ranging from skull wireframes to musculature overlays and mockup sketches. All these photos, including the first one, bore a sticker in the lower right corner that read:

2017 Hagley Wood Murder / Bella Reconstruction
Face Lab of Liverpool John Moores University
Caroline M. Wilkinson FRSE

That's where the banal and expected ended and the enigma began. Emma flipped the next photo over and inspected it for the umpteenth time. The image, faded with a slight tint to it, revealed a *different* Bella. The eyes, brows, and bridge of the nose remained identical—even the crooked teeth subtly protruding from behind the lips. This photo, however, was markedly different in other features. The jaw line drew more effeminately, as did the nose and cheeks. Her hair, darker, almost black, laid fairly flat with only a hint of waves. Even her skin tone took a darker complexion. Extensive bruising and swelling covered her neck and face. The bottom of the image bore a simpler label with no artist ascribed. Just *Bella 1944*.

What really drew Emma's curiosity was the pose between the two images. In the 2017 image, Bella's eyes were open, with her hair naturally falling down as if sitting up, whereas in the 1944 photo she was laying down on a porcelain table with her eyes shut.

This conundrum deepened as she flipped through the remaining photos. The rest all appeared exactly the same as the 1944 image. They dated 1947, 1948, 1949, and continued all the way to 2022. Why were there so many facial reconstructions and why hadn't they been released in 1944? Or perhaps, was this not Bella?

As she placed them back into the folder, she caught a final glimpse of the 1944 photo as it slid in between the others. Bella's ashen eyes opened and rolled toward Emma. Emma shrieked and dropped the stack, scattering the photos across the floor and under the desk. Her heart skipped a beat as she threw her hand over her mouth. A whiff of decay floated in the air. She had been studying these photos for far too long and now her mind played tricks on her. She slid off her chair to one knee and picked up the photos, spying the 1944 photo overturned and near the autopsy table. Emma crawled over and carefully added it with the others, relieved Bella's dead eyes were closed.

Stupid imagination on an empty stomach made her feel she needed to eat something to set her head straight. She kept a fresh stock of bananas in the lab, but she wanted something stronger—something jelly filled. Time to raid Oliver's donut stash and get a Red Bull.

Putting her silly behavior behind her and blaming it on hunger, Emma strutted out of the lab and took Otis up. As soon as the door opened and she reached for the gate, Oliver rounded the corner and walked straight to the lift.

"Hey! Just the CSI tech I wanted to see. I come bearing

gifts." He must have been a mind reader as his *gifts* included a donut and a Red Bull.

"Exactly what I was looking for!" She exited Otis, slid a few papers to the side of the meeting table, and hopped up, cracking open the Red Bull and diving into the sweet American treat. A bad habit Oliver picked up from a former US colleague; a habit that Emma could get used to.

Oliver leaned against the table opposite Emma. "So, rumor has it that you've taken up the old Hagley CSI mystery."

"The what?" she asked.

Oliver chuckled. "Dr Evans' little hobby—Bella."

With a mouth full of sugary donut, she replied, "Hobby? More like obsession. He couldn't let it go. And neither can Taylor, if you ask me." She ungracefully brushed a little powdered sugar off her nose.

"And you? Hobby or obsession?" He leaned relaxed, arms crossed, eyes attentive to her.

She chose her words carefully. "Just an itch that needs scratching."

With a flirtatious smirk on his face, Oliver asked, "You want help scratching?"

Emma laughed. "In the words of Taylor, 'I don't think she'd like that'." She took another healthy bite of donut.

"No, seriously, why not? Maybe you just need a set of fresh eyes. I've never really followed the case, so I'd be totally unbiased."

Emma avoided accepting or rejecting his offer. "Out of curiosity, did Dr Evans ever talk about it? Or Taylor or Edwards?"

"Taylor and Edwards? No, not that I ever noticed. Evans, well, everyone knew it was his pet project. Of course, who can blame him? That case has been a pet project of this station and every CSI assigned here ever since she was first discovered. Hagley is haunted by it for sure. People talk about it, never in polite society, just in pubs and around campfires or the like—all the typical urban legend stuff. Of course, then there's the perpetual graffiti—the 'curse of Hagley'. But did Evans actually discuss the details of the case? No. He just always carried her case file with him and you saw him reading it all the time. Making notes and whatnot. Why?"

"Taylor is all mysterious about it. The whole thing just feels off, if you—"

A red light on the ceiling flickered on and rotated around, sending pulses of crimson light into the bullpen. A moment later, a klaxon blared.

"Is that the fire alarm?" Emma asked, jumping off the table and to her feet, dropping her access card in the process.

Before Oliver had a chance to answer, shouting traveled down the hall and into the bullpen. Emma couldn't quite make out what the man was yelling. A few constables came running from the back of the station. Oliver peeked down the hall and Emma froze like a deer in headlights.

Again, more shouting belted down the hall. This time it was audible as the front security door was open.

"Who put Bella in the wych elm?" an unknown voice yelled.

A panicked woman's voice replied, "Put down the gun, sir!" Emma couldn't make out who spoke.

Bang!

Gunfire rang out. A different officer yelled, repeating the same command. A gunshot silenced him.

"Who put Bella in the wych elm?"

Bang!

Reload.

"WHO PUT BELLA IN THE WYCH ELM?!"

Emma heard Edwards yell, "Go, go, go!" And then a volley of gunfire returned. Oliver sprang into action and ducked into his office to snag his PAVA spray—the only deterrent he had at his desk. Emma flinched at the gunshots, unaware she hadn't moved yet to take cover.

A brief silence fell over the station before Edwards came staggering into the bullpen, collapsing on the floor. Emma finally snapped to and rushed over to give him aid. The top right quarter of his skull was missing, and he was bleeding profusely. She grabbed anything within reach to stop the blood flow, but it was too late. He convulsed and then exhaled.

Oliver ran over to Emma and pulled her back from the hallway into the bullpen. He ripped off his Kevlar and gave it to her. "Put it on, now."

The assailant kept yelling the same question over and over again as his voice grew closer. Each question followed by gunfire. Emma didn't know if it was indiscriminate fire or aimed at someone. She peered around the desk and down the hall—the security door was jammed open by a body laying prone. He stepped through.

Emma scurried back under the desk. "He's coming into the bullpen," she whispered to Oliver. He peeked over the top of the desk and then dropped down.

"Where is she?" the assailant screamed. "She knows! She *knows*!"

Emma squeezed tighter underneath the table, pushing back with her hands on the floor. She nudged something cold with her fingers; something too pliable to be metal. She glanced over and saw a woman's bare foot—pale skinned with black putrid spots and covered in soil and crumpled leaves. The ankle caved inward, forcing the foot to twist unnaturally. Emma jerked her hand away, bumping her head against the underside of the desk. When she looked back, the woman was gone.

The assailant fired a shot across the room. "Who? Who did it? I know you know!" He reloaded.

Oliver grabbed Emma's chin and forced eye contact. "Take Otis to the basement and keep the cage open at the bottom. He won't be able to call it up. You hear me?"

Emma just stared at him, unable to respond.

"Do you hear me?" Oliver repeated.

This time, she nodded.

"Stay low, go now."

Another shot rang out across the room from the assailant's rifle. Reload. Outside, Emma could hear police sirens as the officers from other stations were responding to the call.

Oliver crawled in the opposite direction of the lift to distract the shooter. Emma, staying low as instructed, made her way toward Otis. As she crept, she heard something behind her, *thump-shush... thump-shush*. She looked back—nothing was there.

When Emma neared the lift, Oliver leapt out from behind a desk and sprayed the assailant in the face with the PAVA. He flinched and shot his rifle toward Oliver, striking him in the chest.

In tears, realizing Oliver had been hit, Emma bolted for Otis. She knew it would take him longer to reload after getting sprayed; it was her only chance.

Pistol fire came from another direction. The assailant regained composure and reloaded, returning fire and hitting someone.

Emma slammed her hand against the call button on the wall. Twisted metal cut into her fingers. Where the call button had been previously, a bullet hole now resided.

"You! You know!" His eyes seethed under the flickering florescent light. "WHO PUT ME IN THE WYCH ELM?" The words came from the assailant's lips, but the voice had changed; darker, full of terror. He loaded another round and took aim.

For a glimmer of a moment, as he pulled the trigger, a woman blinked in and out of view, limping across the bullpen. She appeared in such a flash that Emma didn't see any particulars about her, save one. Rage—wild, unadulterated rage.

The rifle misfired. He ejected the round and loaded another. Emma ran to the hallway in the other direction as he fired the second shot; the bullet whizzed by her head.

His demands burgeoned, refusing to be ignored.

Behind her, following her down the hall, she heard two sets of footsteps. The pounding of the assailant's massive frame and a softer *thump-shush*. Emma didn't look back, but instead darted into a storage room, looking for cover. Cabinets and shelving units lined the walls of the tiny room, each filled with office and cleaning supplies. She opened one and discovered it had an empty lower shelf. Before he could track her, she climbed in and shut the doors. Emma pulled her knees as tight to her chest as she could, barely stuffing herself into the cramped unit. She grabbed the exposed door mechanics and pulled it shut, driving the locking rod into place.

Images of the wych elm hollow flashed before her. Bella stowed away, bleeding to death, holding her knees tight to her chest just like Emma was in that moment. Adrenaline surged as she hid in the darkness, unable to catch her breath and silence herself. She clasped both hands over her mouth to muffle her panting and remain concealed.

Emma peeked through a tiny hole and watched in horror as the door to the utility room burst open. His voice grew hoarse as he yelled obscenities. Cleaning bottles and cans ricocheted off the cabinets and floor as the assailant thrashed about the room. The smell of ammonia drifted into the cabinet and choked Emma—she tried to suppress a cough, but it was too strong. She muffled it as much as possible in the crook of her elbow.

All movement outside stopped. One by one, he rattled the handles of the cabinet doors. Metal hinges creaked open. Then the next cabinet beside hers. Same. He came to Emma's and jiggled the handle. Locked.

Bang!

A stream of light followed the bullet into her cabinet just next to her shoulder. He reloaded again.

Pssst

A squib—the barrel was lodged. He reloaded.

BOOM!

Catastrophic rifle failure; her chance neared. The assailant started kicking the door until the latch fell off and he could pry it open. Emma had to run; she released the lock. When the doors flung opened, she thrust with both legs as hard as she could against his knees. His legs flew out from underneath him, sending him flying chin first into the upper shelves, striking his jaw.

She kicked furiously until he moved far enough out of the way that she could wriggle out. Emma rushed for the door and was about to turn the corner when he snagged her foot, tripping her up. Grasping her by the ankle, he pulled her back into the room and crawled over the top of her.

The assailant took the rifle—shattered at the receiver—and held it down over her neck. Despite the rifle's condition, he leaned his full weight into it. Emma kicked and thrashed with all her strength to get free but couldn't. Her lungs pulled hard, gasping for air. Her hand frantically searched for anything to strike him with. Her fingers found a box cutter.

She fumbled with it, trying to snag it with the tips of her fingers, but the attacker kept shifting his weight, knocking it back out of reach. It spun in place—around and around, with each desperate attempt. Finally, he shifted his weight again during their struggle, and Emma grabbed it.

She slid the blade all the way out and thrust it into his side, twisting and snapping it off between his ribs. He barely reacted except to pull the rifle up and bash her head with the stock.

Reeling from the blow, Emma tried punching him in the side where she stabbed him, but she couldn't muster the strength to inflict any pain. Her head grew light as dark speckles enclosed around.

He pulled the rifle back over his head once more and was about to drive it down again when a rush of bodies flew through the doorway, tackling the assailant.

Chapter 20
Aftermath

Emma adjusted the rear-view mirror and tugged back her collar to inspect the extensive bruising on her throat. Pain radiated with every movement and speaking hurt as well. There would be no need to check the purple goose egg just below her hairline—that was obvious from across any room. When the paramedics initially tended to her, they suggested she visit the hospital for further care, but she refused. They responded with a plea to at least rest at home for a few days. However, that wasn't happening, either. Why should she stay home when several of her colleagues would never return home again?

She turned the mirror back up and stared out across the station parking lot at the circus gathering. The media had already descended on Hagley like carrion birds, ready to feast on the tragedy. Not surprising, Bryant Jones scurried among them, flashing his smug smile and his IOPC badge, giving him access inside the station while the other news crews and journalists had to stay behind the police tape.

Any officer who arrived had to wade through the masses, dodging microphones and questions. Emma knew she was fodder, and she didn't have the wherewithal to deal with the bombardment. In hopes of avoiding it all, she picked up her phone and sent McArthur a text message. *Would you mind coming to the car park to get me?* Emma gingerly leaned her head back and waited.

A few minutes later, Louis McArthur came bounding down the steps, splitting the crowd like Moses. Seconds later, he tapped her window. "Good morning, Lloyd."

Assisting her out of the car, he held his arm around Emma as he escorted her through the journalists, all yelling questions over each other.

"Ms Lloyd, Ms Lloyd, why did the assailant target you?"

"Ms Lloyd, is it true you hid while your fellow officers were slain?"

As he lifted the police tape over Emma, McArthur leaned in tight and whispered, "Just ignore them, Emma. They don't know the truth." He had never called her Emma before.

Free from the jostling barrier of reporters, Emma walked past *those words* scrawled on the brick façade and continued toward the entrance. No doubt a procedural argument raged internally on when it should be washed off. As she reached for the door, something unsettling about the graffiti caught her attention, but she couldn't put her finger on it—something peculiarly familiar. She paused, took out her phone, and snapped a pic before proceeding inside and leaving the frenzied media behind her.

Inside the foyer, the reminders of the previous day's horrid event hit hard. An unknown face greeted McArthur and Emma from behind the counter where Vickie had been smiling twenty-four hours earlier—a smile that no one would ever see again. On the wall behind the counter, CSI techs had removed a section where the bullet had passed through Vickie's neck and imbedded in the sheetrock. The blood splatter had yet to be painted over.

"Excuse me," said the counter officer, "are you Dr Lloyd?"

Not wanting to speak, Emma held her hand toward her throat and nodded.

"This was sitting here with your name. I believe it's your new ID badge." The officer handed her an envelope with Emma's name on it—written in Vickie's hand. "There were instructions to collect your temporary card. Do you have it?"

Emma looked in her bag and scrunched her brows. Looking back at the woman, she shook her head no.

"It's ok. Once you find it, please return it. With everything that's happened, I'm sure it just got lost in the hubbub of yesterday."

Hubbub is not *how I'd describe it,* thought Emma. She suppressed the urge to slap the clerk.

Walking through the security door and into the hallway, Emma was affronted with more realities. The blood where Edwards perished hadn't been cleaned, only cordoned off with small evidence cones. Taylor had informed Emma that there was nothing she could have done to save Edwards, but that didn't ease her guilt any. He breathed his last in her arms and that would haunt her.

The other officers that died Emma had only met occasionally during her short time in Hagley, but that didn't affect her any less. The sting of all four deaths, regardless of her relationship with them, left her with the desire to both vomit and punch a hole in the wall—order didn't matter.

As she trudged into the bullpen toward Otis, she spied CC Noah Harris speaking with Bryant Jones, and Councilman Parry. She eavesdropped as she passed by, but they ceased their conversation when she was within ear shot. Emma could only imagine what they were discussing. Harris gave a sympathetic nod, and Bryant smirked. Parry, on the other hand, wore a cold expression on his face, completely void. It sent goose-pimples down her back. Emma rushed away, but she could still feel his glare as she left their view.

The graffiti on the station bothered her. Why, though? It was hardly a rare occurrence in these parts. The assailant had clearly lost his mind, so it was likely to be symptomatic of his insanity than to have any meaning or relevance. Still, it's odd, right? Emma passed Otis and circled around the bullpen to the corkboard with all the *Who put Bella* vandalism photos. As she stood, blankly staring at the pictures, she couldn't help but notice the handwriting on the outside of the station matched many of the photos on the board. Which couldn't be right. Some of them were older than Emma, much less the assailant.

McArthur wandered over and stood next to her, setting down an armful of casefiles. "This guy is certifiable, don't you think?"

Raspy, Emma replied, "You literally just read my mind." She reached for her throat as she spoke. "Have you been here long? Assigned to Hagley station, that is?"

"Yeah, I grew up in Hagley, actually. Only station assignment I've ever had. Why?"

"Do they ever catch any of these graffiti 'artists'?" she asked, air-quoting the word *artists* as she gestured toward the board.

"Well, the town surprisingly puts up with it. Most of the

time it goes unreported and people just wash the chalk off themselves. The obelisk is the only time paint has ever been used. Just another part of the town curse they can't control."

Emma ignored the *town curse* comment—she didn't believe in curses. "If you don't catch any of them, then could it be one person?"

"I didn't say we don't catch *any*. There are always a few that get caught around Death Week—which is when this happens the most."

Emma leaned back on a table. "Death Week. Interesting. What is their state of mind when you catch them? What's their excuse?"

"Well, some are just teens on a dare. So about what you'd expect—embarrassed they got caught. But there are some who get caught that are complete nutters—full-on mental breakdowns. As my grandmother always said, *So heed this tale, to not fall prey, or in her nightmares you will stay.*"

"That's not creepy at all. Do you have a dossier on the shooter yet?"

"Yeah, they just sent it over a little while ago. Do you want to see it?"

"If you don't mind, thanks."

McArthur stretched over a table to grab the top file off the stack he set down moments earlier. "Here you go."

Emma opened the file and found herself staring into the same dark eyes of the man who had attacked her. "I've seen him before—"

"Yeah, in the supply closet attempting to murder you."

"No… that's not it. From another case." Emma pulled out her phone and logged into the VPN to access her case files. "Here. This guy. What do you think?"

"Give the guy a haircut and a shave... I think so. Yeah, yeah, definitely, that's him. Just leave the soul patch." McArthur handed the phone back to Emma. "What case is that?"

"The Stacey Inight case—the one we fished out of the reservoir. They were dating. When do they plan to interrogate this guy?"

"They already started. Taylor and Wright have been at Kidderminster station with him for hours. Apparently, the guy won't crack. Last I heard, not a single word yet."

Emma had an idea. A very, very bad idea. She just needed a few items from her lab.

*

Every eye in the Kidderminster station gawked as Emma marched through the halls to the interrogation room. She slipped into the observation area where two other inspectors had gathered around a monitor watching the CCTV of the interview.

"Morning, Lloyd," replied one.

Emma saved her voice and nodded in response.

"I'm surprised you even want to be at work today, much less in this room."

"Curiosity, I guess," she squeaked out. "It felt personal. I want to get a feel for the man who tried to kill me."

"Well, you're not in luck, unfortunately. The guy is catatonic. If it weren't for the fact he had been heard yelling yesterday, we'd have thought him a mute. Taylor and Wright can't get a peep out of him."

"Do we have *anything* on the guy?" Every word felt like knives in her throat.

"Timothy Burrow, 32." The officer handed Emma a small rap sheet on the assailant. She had previously read it at Hagley, but she humored the other officer and pretended to read. "A local from Hagley. No record except two summary convictions for shoplifting. The rifle he used is connected to a B&E and assault earlier last month in Wolverley. His parents said they kicked him out several months ago after a string of *bad incidents*—he's been a street sleeper ever since. Oddly, the CCTV in Hagley showed he had blood all over his hands and clothes when he entered the station. It's being cross-referenced to see if it's related to another murder at a SPAR supermarket on Worcester Road yesterday early morning."

Emma faked perusing the file as she casually made her way toward the door to the interrogation room, occasionally watching the CCTV monitor. She waited to seize her opportunity which came when DI Alfred Wright stood up and exited the interrogation room and joined Emma and the two officers in observation.

Emma pulled Wright to the side and lowered her voice. "I need to get in there. I have to interview him."

"What? No, dearie, I can't let you do that." Wright was the only man who could call her dearie outside her father and not irk her. "Taylor would have both our hides."

"Please, I *need* to do this. I know I can break him. The perp won't expect me in there."

Wright studied Emma. She could see the wheels turning in his head as he considered her request. "You really think you can get him to talk?"

"Yes, I do."

"Then I guess I need to go for some tea and biscuits. Good luck, dearie." The old man gave her a timid smile and gently squeezed her hand as he waddled away. Emma burst through the door and took a seat next to the superintendent.

Taylor's eyes popped, and his mouth dropped open. He hadn't even had a chance to process what was happening before Emma started interrogating Timothy.

"Good morning, Supt. Taylor. Sorry for my delay. Mr Burrow, I'm CSI Lloyd. You may remember me from yesterday's events." She swallowed hard suppressing the pain.

Timothy didn't look up. His eyes were locked on his shackles.

"I have a few questions I'd like to ask, if you don't mind." Emma pushed through the pain. "Is that alright, Timothy? Can I call you Timothy or do you prefer Teddy Bear?" He twitched.

Taylor leaned over to Emma and whispered, "What in God's name are you doing in here, Lloyd?" She sensed his fury.

Emma ignored him and pushed her line of questioning. "What is your relationship with Stacey Inight? Is she your girlfriend?"

Grabbing Emma by the arm, Taylor pulled on her to follow him.

Timothy reached up with his bearish hands and wiped away a tear. "This isn't about her—" He muttered so low that Emma almost missed it. Taylor let go of her arm and slowly sat back down, shocked that Timothy finally spoke.

"It's not about Stacey? Cause to me it looks like it's *all* about her. Looks like you went looking for vengeance and had nowhere to go, so you came looking for it in Hagley." Each syllable was a razor blade in her throat.

"No, no, it wasn't about her."

"Okay, okay, it's not about Stacey. Let's set her aside for a moment." Emma squared her shoulders and leaned forward, knowing the next line of inquiry was about to get rough. "Would you like to tell me why you wrote this?" Emma slid a printout of his graffiti on the station under his gaze.

Timothy flinched and turned his head.

"Did you write this?"

"Yes."

"Would you like to tell me why?" He didn't respond. "Okay, that's fine. How about these? Did you write these?" Emma slid a few more photographs of graffiti taken earlier in the year onto the table. "Cause it's the same handwriting and they aren't far from where your parents live."

Taylor leaned in and questioned her, but Emma didn't acknowledge him and continued. "How about this one? Was this you?" She put the 1994 photo of the Wychbury Obelisk on the table next to the others.

Burrow grunted in discomfort, rocking back and forth.

"How about these? Did you write these too? They all share the same handwriting." Emma then placed the remaining photos on the table from 1944 and 1954. Taylor uncomfortably shifted his weight in his chair and pursed his lips as he looked at the camera.

"Emma," whispered Timothy, "do you know who put Bella in the wych elm?"

He knows my first name… how does he know my name? she thought.

Taylor again looked at the CCTV camera and mouthed something that Emma couldn't see. She collected all the graffiti pics and put them in a stack next to Timothy.

"Timothy, why did you write these? Can you tell me why this is important for you to find the answer?"

He stopped rocking, and a tear trickled down his cheek. "She made me do it."

"Who? Who made you do it? Who is *she*?" He didn't reply. Emma pulled out her phone, set it on the table, and played Stacey's final video. "Is it the same woman Stacey talks about here?"

Timothy clenched his eyes shut as tears streamed down. Emma wondered if it was the first time he had seen it. "Is it Timothy?"

"Yes."

The proverbial shit was about to hit the fan and Emma didn't care. She reached in another file and pulled out the famous 2017 Face Lab reconstruction photo of Bella and put it right under his gaze. "Is this her?"

Taylor choked and nearly spit out the water he was drinking.

"Answer me, Timothy. Did she tell you to do it?" Emma then put another of the 2017 images on the table.

"No."

Taylor's shoulders relaxed at the answer, but his face was still bleach white.

"Okay, if not her, how about this woman? Did she tell you?" This time Emma put the 1945 photo of Bella from Dr Evans' secret files on the table.

Timothy leapt from his seat, falling to the floor from his restraints, and sent his chair sliding across the room. He screamed at the top of his lungs. "No, no, no, no… make her go away!"

Emma pushed more intensely, leaning over the top of the

table, holding the photo up in front of his face. "Did she make you do it, *Teddy Bear*?"

His voice changed and filled with fury. Timothy charged the table, his restraints preventing him from reaching Emma. His massive frame towered over both her and Taylor. "WHO PUT ME IN THE WYCH ELM, EMMA?!"

Taylor grabbed all the photos off the table and yanked Emma by the arm, forcing her to leave the room.

Timothy continued to thrash and yell as Emma resisted Taylor, shouting in return, her voice cracking. "Who is that, Timothy? Tell me her name!"

"You know who it is!" replied Timothy. "You've seen her, Emma! You know who it is!"

Dragging Emma by the waist, Taylor forced her out of the interrogation room and back into the observation area, now filled with the faces of half a dozen shocked police officers. As Taylor slammed the door behind him, they all heard Timothy yell once more:

"Who put Bella in the wych elm, Emma?"

Chapter 21
The Hopeful Pitch

Bryant Jones slipped into an unoccupied office and secured the door behind him. He needed privacy for this call, especially with the prying eyes and nosey officers nearby. With the shooting now gaining national attention, his story wouldn't stay buried for long. Others would catch on soon enough. He had to get his editor, Kirk Schmidt, on board asap—and that would not be an easy task.

Bryant pushed the papers off the desk to make room for his laptop, knocking them to the floor and nudging the occupant's name plate teetering on the edge. He snatched the plate off the desk, saving it at the last second. *DS Edwards* it read. He had always been a quality source—what a shame to lose that contact now.

Edwards' first meeting with Bryant turned out as fortuitous as anything Bryant could have hoped for. A simple anonymous email with promises to expose police corruption piqued his curiosity. How could it not?

A run-down pub on the outskirts of London hosted their

meet up—chosen by Edwards himself. Bryant thought it far too cloak and dagger for such a mundane parish police station and the promises of drama that came with it. If Bryant hadn't known better, based on the level of secrecy Edwards took to conceal himself as a source, he would've thought this scandal went all the way to the crown. It did not. Yet, Bryant wasn't one to take an opportunity for granted—he could, after all, weave a tale to be so much more if the base elements existed in the story from the get-go. A little exaggeration never hurt anyone, certainly not Bryant.

He spotted Edwards immediately, not because he was only one of two patrons in the establishment, but because of the two, he was the only one dressed like a 1980s police trope straight from the TV. Bryant took a seat across from him. "You Constable Edwards?" At least he hadn't picked code names.

"Yes, I'm assuming you are—"

"Bryant Jones, at your service. So, tell me what's got you so worked up?"

Edwards slid a memo across the table. Bryant picked it up and scanned it, shocked at the lack of decorum. "This legit?"

"Yes."

"And anyone else willing to go on record to collaborate your story?"

"There might be a few, DI Wright, perhaps."

The two of them discussed the particulars of the story, detailing the scope of the scandal. Bryant offered anonymity, but hadn't planned on following through, as he'd need to publish at least one source on record to lend credibility.

At the time of publication, Edwards received backlash from the constabulary for being a snitch. If it weren't for the IOPC and the incoming superintendent, Taylor, Edwards would have been shamed out of the force.

Bryant tossed the name plate back onto the desk and opened up Microsoft Teams, dialing up his editor. A few rings later and up popped Kirk. "Bryant. The online staff meeting isn't for another hour. You're early."

He didn't care. Bryant had to pitch the story—strike while it was hot and no one else was on the trail. "Listen, I'm here in Hagley—"

"Hagley? What in the bloody hell are you doing out there? I thought you were in Birmingham. We already have someone assigned to the Hagley shooting." Kirk's walrus mustache still had a wisp of coffee foam frosting the tip.

"I am... I was... doesn't matter. I'm here at Hagley station and I've got a lead on another scandal brewing." Bryant had that fiery glint in his eye, one that Kirk knew all too well.

"Let me stop you right there. Grant it, the *Death Week* article was a massive boost in sales and shook up all of West Mercia Police, but lightning doesn't strike twice in an inconsequential parish like Hagley. The readers will get bored with it—plus, no one is that lucky. Not even you."

"Hear me out!"

"No, no, you need to come back—" The conversation wasn't even two minutes in and Bryant's editor wasn't having it.

Bryant disregarded Kirk and dove in any way. "The CSI technician stationed in Hagley died in a murder/suicide a month ago—"

"What did I say? No!" he replied as he waved his hands in front of himself.

Bryant ignored him and continued. "—and the tech brought in to investigate the murder/suicide, CSI Emma

Lloyd, was hired as his replacement the next day."

Getting perturbed, Kirk yelled, "Stop!"

Bryant didn't give a crap what Kirk said. He was gonna finish this pitch. "The technician hired the next day *just* so happens to be Chief Constable Harris' sister-in-law."

Kirk put his head in his hand as he reluctantly listened, conceding the battle to Bryant. He rubbed his face and then massaged his temples with his thumb and middle finger as his other hand fidgeted with a pen against the desk.

"On top of it, they have skeletal remains in their laboratory. *But*, there's no active case in Hagley involving skeletal remains. The corpse, who might they be? Well, the 'toe tag' says: *Bella*."

Kirk hung his head and pulled his hair as he shook it in disbelief. "You're worse than Flat-Earthers," he mumbled. "There's no way you can connect these events—it's a ridiculous theory. It's not even circumstantial. Just stop."

Bryant paid no attention to the insult; he had the key here. "And now the pièce de résistance: the Hagley station shooter was reported to have been yelling over and over again 'who put Bella in the wych elm?' *And*—wait for it—*specifically* targeted the new CSI tech, Emma Lloyd." Bryant leaned back in the chair and crossed his arms in complete satisfaction with himself.

Kirk opened a bottle of anti-acids and popped three, his mustache flopping as he chewed. "I don't need this headache right now. Why can't you just be a normal reporter and investigate Trump or Harry and Meghan? Something that *sells*."

"You love me and you know it! Look, I have a copy of the marriage license and the wedding announcement from the local Tewkesbury paper, so the relationship between the

Chief Constable and the CSI tech is rock solid. I also have the Chief's secretary on record discussing the circumstances of her hiring."

"Okay, but you have to make the other connections with the shooter and the body in the lab. What's your angle here? Have you seen the security footage or have any other proof?"

"I can finagle a copy of the Hagley security video, so don't worry about that."

His editor, rearing back in his seat, replied, "I can't believe I'm saying this. How much time do you need?"

"Two weeks, tops."

Looking at the camera, Kirk gave Bryant a deadly stare. "Two weeks? No. One week. No one wants to hear about an eighty-year-old cold case and nepotism, regardless of how you twist the two together. It's boring and nonsensical—an absolute stretch of the imagination. One week and if you don't have anything substantial by then or you haven't convinced me it's gold, then it's dead. I mean it—*dead*. Oh, and I want this 100% above board. No 'fast and loose' with the facts. Double—no—triple check your sources. I want a copy of the police report for the human remains *and* a coroner's report. Use your IOPC connections if you have to. I don't want this blowing up in my face and coming back to haunt me."

Bryant slammed the computer lid down and did a little fist pump. The only thought on his mind was how that byline was gonna look in the newspapers.

Reaching in his bag, he pushed aside his car keys and pulled out a security key card. Bryant spun it between his fingers and inspected the single label printed on its face: Hagley Police Laboratory. Spotting this gem under a table before anyone noticed it after the ensuing chaos of the shooting was the exact type of *luck* Bryant needed—it also meant he didn't have to risk pinching it off Lloyd.

"You, my plastic little friend, are my saving grace."

Chapter 22

The Answers She's Been Awaiting

If the force at which Taylor slammed his door shut failed to indicate his degree of anger, then the tomato red complexion that consumed his face was the next dead giveaway.

"I don't know where in God's name I should begin!" he yelled. "Should I start with the fact that you barged into an interrogation where you don't belong? Or perhaps that you took these out of the laboratory?" Taylor held up the file of facial reconstructions.

Emma opened her mouth and vaguely remembered something about foolishness and removing doubt. "I know—"

"Shut that God damn mouth right now! They were rhetorical questions. I distinctly remember giving you a direct order—" He strangely lowered his voice to a furious whisper, clenching his jaw as the words seethed through his teeth. "—that *nothing* of Bella's case should ever leave that lab. You have no idea what you're dealing with, Lloyd. You are putting *everything* at risk!"

"You're right—I have no idea what I'm dealing with

cause you actually haven't told me anything." This was destined not to end well. "You give me the most outlandish set of protocols, none of which makes any sense, and then don't give me any explanation. You just expect me to *process* the evidence as instructed. You think *you* don't know where to begin? Step in *my* shoes. I'm in the dark here."

Taylor fumed as he listened, waiting for Emma to stop. "I *have* been in your shoes. So don't assume otherwise! I wish—I wish beyond all that is holy that I could satisfy all your curiosities in one fell swoop. I can't do it." He leaned with his hands on his desk, head lowered.

"You can't do it? Or you won't do it? Because where I'm sitting, it looks like the latter!"

In one motion, Taylor swept the contents of his desk against the wall, sending papers flying in the air and his laptop smashing into bits. When he looked at Emma, finger wagging in her face, tears had welled up in his eyes. "You don't have the right to judge me on this, but I'll give you a pass due to your ignorance, which isn't your fault. After yesterday, it's apparent things have changed and I don't know how to correct it. I don't know if it's because of what Evans did or if it's something you did, but we are in for a world of hurt. More than you can imagine—yesterday was just the beginning." Again, he lowered to a whisper. "And your stunt in there, bringing in the photos of Bella like that? We have no idea what flood gates you've opened up."

What is he talking about? Has he completely lost it? thought Emma. "Enlighten me, sir! Because I feel like we are having two different conversations right now."

Shaking his head, Emma sensed his reluctance to give in to her request. "Listen, the IOPC is already all over this shooting. Now, with that stunt you just pulled, they're going to start looking deeper into you, which I can't have. We can't risk it." He raised his fists up slightly and punched the table. Emma saw trickles of blood on his knuckles. "I have no idea how to pull the IOPC off you. I can't explain why you were there, why you asked about the graffiti, nor why you showed him photos that no one is supposed to know exist! I can't even destroy the interview recording because half of Kidderminster station was in the observation room, gawking at you and Burrow!"

How serious is this that he'd consider destroying evidence to cover things up? What is going on?

A knock on the door interrupted him, followed by a timid voice speaking through the frosted glass. "Sir, they are ready for the transfer."

Taylor paused for a moment, holding back his fury. "Thank you. I'll be out in a minute." Looking up at Emma, he continued, "I'm transferring that disaster of a perp out of Kidderminster and away from you. For *your* protection. When I'm back in an hour, we're gonna have that conversation that you want. You're gonna *sit* in that chair and hang on *every word* that comes out of my mouth as if your life depends on it. And don't doubt for a second that I'm not being literal." And with that, he punched the table once more, swearing incoherently, and then left the room.

Emma slunk into her chair. Taylor was right about two things. There was no way he'd be able to explain why she'd brought up the writings and the photos. Emma barely understood it herself. She could hear it now. *You're not a handwriting expert.* And that was true. And the photos? She didn't even know for certain who they were until Burrow recognized them—even then something felt off. And how would she explain that to anyone? How did she get these photos? The unanswerable questions piled on Emma's conscience.

Sitting in that chair until Taylor returned wasn't going to solve anything. She needed fresh air—and some caffeine. As the officers transferred Burrow, Emma had time to spare, so she pushed up from the chair and headed anywhere but Taylor's office. She snagged the last Red Bull from the vending machine and headed to the side entrance, where people took their smoke breaks. Emma hoped no one would be there; she needed peace and quiet. The doors opened to a burst of early summer sunshine and empty concrete steps to collect her thoughts on.

Taylor was justified regarding her actions during the interrogation—she had no place in that room. His secrecy regarding the Bella case, on the other hand, was *not*. Soon enough, Emma would have her answers.

A few moments later, the rumble of a prisoner transport van broke her concentration as it arrived at the side security exit. It backed in and two guards got out, waited a few minutes, and then banged on the steel doors. Emma would see Burrow one last time; one time too many, in her opinion.

*

Supt. John Taylor spied Burrow through the porthole in the jail door, brooding on the edge of the bench. His disheveled hair flopped over his face and blended into his scraggly beard. Burrow's gigantic build tensed, rocking back and forth. John doubted Burrow would ever open up again. The opportunity to get answers had passed.

What a cockup. Lloyd really screwed the pooch on this with her tirade during the interrogation. It didn't matter that she *was* right; it only mattered that no judge would *believe* Lloyd—or John, for that matter.

Hell, when John first assumed command from disgraced Superintendent Burton fifteen years ago, he hadn't believed it either. Burton and Dr Evans couldn't convince him of the truth, regardless of the copious evidence. John had to see a full cycle firsthand, beginning to end before he accepted it. Edwards reacted in the same disbelief—he needed to see it, to believe it.

John assumed Lloyd would need to see it firsthand as well. Perhaps that was his mistake; perhaps Emma would believe it all. He had held her medical background against her, thinking it would sow too much doubt, but the connections she'd made already screamed differently. Nonetheless, John promised her an explanation and before the day would be over, she'd have her answers. He had to trust she was indeed ready for the raw truth.

How does one start that conversation? Evans had simply asked, "Do you believe in ghosts?" John remembered laughing, but Evans had remained stoic—unfazed by his skeptical chuckle. He guessed he'd know what to say when he was looking Emma in the eye.

"You know the drill: stand up, walk to the door, turn around, and slide your hands through the slot," said John. Burrow didn't budge. "*Stand up,* walk to the door, turn around, and slide your hands through the slot, *now!*"

John didn't want to do this the hard way. It would only add to the debacle if he and the others burst in with batons, forcing him to the ground and cuffing him. He wanted this transfer to go smooth—no, he *needed* this transfer to go smooth. Get Burrow out of this station and let him be some-one else's problem.

Burrow finally stirred, staggering to his feet, and shuffled to the door. As he walked, he dragged his left foot across the floor like he was hurt. But he hadn't been, which was unre-al considering the beating he received when originally taken into custody. Even the six-inch razor blade Lloyd snapped off like a prison shiv in his ribs looked like a scratch when the paramedics finally removed it. *Smart girl—probably saved her life,* he thought.

Foul body odor drifted through the port as Burrow neared, even though he had changed from his homeless rags and into a prison uniform yesterday. John peered through the port, bare-ly able to see the top of the back of Burrow's head. Without looking away, John slipped one cuff onto Burrow's dainty, almost feminine left hand—quite odd, really. As he slapped the other cuff over the right wrist, it slid down and fell against the door, clanking gently as it swung.

John looked down to see only one hand and a bloody stump. Black, putrid marks covered the pale flesh; its black veins spidering under the skin.

Flinching backwards, John checked the view port. Burrow was nowhere to be seen. Instead, dark, mangled clumps of hair, soiled in dirt and leaves, peeked over the lower lip of the port window.

John screwed his eyes tight and clenched his jaw. *She's not here—it's just in your head.* He hesitated, not wanting to confront reality yet. To his relief, when he opened his eyes, two burly hands, filth caked under the nails, jutted through the slot.

"Sir? You okay there? You look jumpy," asked an officer, awaiting him at the end of the hall.

"Yes, erm, I had something in my eye. I'm good," replied John. He latched the other cuff onto Burrow and proceeded to unlock the cell door.

"You see her too, don't you?" said the gravelly voice behind the door. "I see her every day."

John didn't reply, yet he couldn't help but reluctantly feel a flash of sympathy for Burrow in that moment—he was, after all, a victim too.

He opened the door and escorted Burrow down the hall to join the other officer. They proceeded through another set of security doors before arriving at the exit where the transport van was parked on the other side. John pounded on the door and waited for a response.

Two knocks banged back and John opened the door, revealing the rear of the transport van and two other guards. He handed off Burrow, took a clipboard from a guard, and signed the transfer papers. Out of habit, John slid the ball-point pen into his breast pocket. He hung the clipboard in a secure slot on the back door and looked over at Emma sitting on the step. She didn't see him as she was too busy staring at her feet, which was probably for the better.

The guards took Burrow by the arms and assisted him into the van, forcing him down on a bench. Each took a seat on either side of Burrow and waited for him to be restrained. John knelt and fished the shackles through a steel ring on the floor as the third officer sat down across from everyone. Taking the ankle cuffs, John lifted the pant leg to secure Burrow. As he pulled the hem up, he saw slender, bare legs—pale and rotten. The odor of decay filled the van.

*

Emma finished off her drink and turned to walk up the steps when she heard a commotion coming from the transport van. The van swayed gently for a few moments before three quick pops echoed against the building.

It took her an instant to recognize the gunshots, but it felt like an eternity before she could move. Her mind froze at the memory of Burrow in Hagley station the day prior. After shaking it off, she rushed to the door she had propped open with a rock. She cupped her hands around her mouth and tried to yell, but her voice cracked from the stress of her injury. She swallowed hard and tried again. "*Shots fired! Shots fired! Shots fired,*" belted down the corridor and into the station.

Emma didn't wait for a response. She pulled her phone from her pocket and ran toward the van, dialing 999 in the process.

Before she arrived, Burrow's hulking shape stepped out of the van, still shackled and covered in blood. His sneer unnaturally curled ear-to-ear as he gestured to her—beckoning her to follow. In a flash, he had turned and run toward the back parking lot, away from Emma.

She pursued, but stopped when she neared the open doors of the transport van and saw the carnage inside. She leapt in, trying not to slip on the pool of blood already coalescing.

The first officer took two bullets, one to the neck and the other to the face. The third exited out the roof without hitting anyone. The guard next to him laid crumpled over the lap of the first—his head twisted backwards 180 degrees. The officer behind her leaned back against the wall with a ball-point pen shoved into his eye socket so deep the cap was barely visible. His hand, still holding the gun, twitched.

Emma threw her phone on the bench and took the gun out of the officer's hand, switching the safety on in the process. She could barely make out the voice of the operator over the gurgles of a fourth victim—a survivor—laying on the floor. As she rolled him over, Emma yelled at the phone, "Four officers down! Four officers down! Kidderminster police station, prisoner transfer van!"

To her horror, Emma immediately recognized the man staring up at her. His hand grasping at his neck. She ripped the bottom of her shirt and placed it over Taylor's gushing wound. His skin had been peeled back as if a wolf had gnashed down and torn it to shreds.

His eyes locked to hers as he tried to speak, "B, B, B—."

"Don't talk. Just lay still, sir! Help is on the way." Emma didn't know if she was lying or not, as she still couldn't hear the operator on the phone. "Help! I need immediate medical assistance! Officers down!"

Taylor lifted his hand and tried to point as he spoke his last word. "Bella—".

A chill swept over her as fingers wrapped around her shoulders and tightened their grip. They tugged on her, pulling her backwards, forcing her to let go of Taylor. Emma's feet slipped out from underneath her and she lost her balance. Out of the corner of her eye, a yellow blur flashed past her and swarmed Taylor. The first paramedic, still holding on to Emma, yelled instructions to the others as his colleagues attempted to resuscitate Taylor.

Emma sat in blood and watched with futility as they attempted to save the Superintendent. She knew it was too late. Scanning the chaos, her mind drifted to the grin Burrow flashed as he ran off. Emma couldn't save Taylor, but she could catch Burrow. She scrambled to her feet, pushed past the other paramedics attending to the guards, and jumped out of the van, slipping and falling into the doors.

Burrow had run toward the back car park, which led to an adjacent neighborhood, but he was still in shackles. Emma could catch up. She bolted for the back gate and looked either way for him. Nothing. As she randomly chose a direction, her feet kicked something, tripping her up. When she looked down, it was a bloody set of keys still attached to unlocked shackles strewn on the ground. Burrow was in the wind.

Chapter 23
The Vigil

Visitor chairs in hospital rooms were just as uncomfortable as Emma remembered. However, she had also perfected the precise placement of pillows and blankets to make them tolerable enough to sleep in. A skill she didn't think she'd use again.

"Excuse me—" A nurse gently touched Emma's shoulder, "Mr Bennett will be in shortly from recovery."

Emma rubbed her eyes and sat up. "Thank you." The smell of mylar balloons and flowers mingled with sterile air and disinfectants.

"Emma? Emma Harris?" asked the nurse.

Emma blinked and focused her eyes on the young nurse standing next to her. A familiar face soon appeared. "Bethany? Hey." Emma's voice cracked, still raspy and sore from the attack last week.

"Wow! I didn't recognize you at first. You cut your hair. How are you?"

"Having flashbacks, apparently," Emma replied. "What

are you doing here? I thought you worked in Oncology?"

"I did. I transferred to trauma about two years ago. Not long after—" Bethany hesitated before continuing, "—Liam passed. My condolences… I never got to see you afterwards. We nurses often never do once you go into a hospice. For reasons you can imagine, Oncology just got too dark. I needed a change of pace. So, here I am. Are you and Mr Bennett…?" Bethany, not so inconspicuously, glanced down at Emma's left hand.

"No, no, no." Emma waved off the notion. "He's a co-worker I'm indebted to. Just checking in on a friend."

A frail voice, still groggy from anesthesia, interjected. "Am I interrupting anything important? I can come back later." It was Oliver, as an orderly wheeled his bed into the room.

Emma shot up, fluffing her hair and straightening her shirt. "Hey, how ya feeling?"

Bethany smiled at the two of them and then whispered to Emma, "He's cute. Good choice."

Blushing and unable to hide a smile, Emma stood stupefied until Bethany saved her. "It's good to see you again, Emma." The nurse turned to Oliver. "The doctor will be in shortly to give you an update on the surgery. If you need anything, just buzz. Okay?" Bethany glanced back at Emma. "Make sure he drinks plenty of water." Bethany pulled the blanket a little higher over Oliver, covering extensive burn scars and grafts—faded with age—that ran up his left arm and disappeared under his hospital gown. She checked his IV bag, adjusted his meds, and then left, giving a too-da-loo finger wave to Emma.

"You make one visit and you're already on a first name basis with the hospital staff? You don't already have the doctor's home number, do you? Should I be jealous?" asked Oliver.

"Second visit, thank you very much. The first time you were drooling whilst you slept. I shagged the doctor in your bathroom—twice." Emma approached his bed and brushed her hair behind her ear. "How's the shoulder? In much pain?"

"I don't feel anything right now. I'm sure I'll have an up-date on that once the room stops spinning. Whatever this is, you need to try it."

"I'm pretty sure it's the anesthesia, so I'll pass. I do have to drive back to work shortly."

Oliver sobered up a little, but still slurred his speech. "Howz everyone at the station?"

"Making do as best as we can. About what you'd expect. McArthur is stepping up to the plate, though. He's covered quite a few extra shifts on top of his own and has even done some administrative work to help out Wright as interim su-perintendent. I think Wright's taking it the hardest out of ev-eryone."

"He's been at the station the longest. I'd be surprised if he wasn't," replied Oliver. "Now, how are *you* holding up?"

Emma hesitated. She didn't want to burden him with her own troubles during his recovery—it felt unfair. That, and ad-mitting she was considering making an appointment with the therapist who helped her through Liam's death wasn't exactly something she wanted to announce to anyone, even if it were Oliver. "I'm fine. Not great, but fine. Dealing with it in my own way, I guess."

"Just don't push yourself too hard. I know you're like a dog with a bone when you get something in your head. Promise me that after the vigil tonight, you'll take a couple of days off. You won't do anyone any good if you're burning the candle at both ends."

"How d'you hear about the vigil?"

"Your favorite person stopped in yesterday, unannounced, pretending to be my brother." His tongue stuck to the roof of his mouth as he spoke.

"Wait, what? Who?"

"Bryant Jones," replied Oliver.

Emma scoffed. "My favorite? *Clearly* you know me so well. What the hell was he doing here?"

"His typical mischief. Sticking his nose where it doesn't belong. He did have quite a few questions about you. Be careful. I think he's developing a crush."

Just another issue on her laundry list of problems. Exactly what Emma wanted. "Well, he can eat—wait, no, even that's too good for him." She shook her head in dismay.

"Don't feel bad. He's like this with everyone. You're just his new *flavor of the month*. Now, about the vigil. Jones had that *oozing* voice when he spoke about it. Gave me the feeling something was up."

"That depends on who you're asking. In short, children from the school across the street from the Kidderminster station brought some flowers and teddy bears on Monday and set them by the marquee. That kinda got a makeshift memorial going. It was fairly grassroots until Parry got hold of it."

"Oh, Parry got involved. Color me shocked."

"He really ran with it, that's for sure. Feels like a campaign event, if you ask me."

"Again, totally not surprised."

"I have to be honest, though, in his defense, the community was already getting behind the memorial. I think there's even a GoFundMe fundraiser for the families that someone started. So, when Parry said, 'let's hold a vigil', everyone was ready to jump on board."

"Okay, but that sounds pretty standard. Not sure why Jones made it sound *different*."

"I hadn't got to that part yet. He may have caught wind of Harris' plan. Which, if he did, may put a spanner in the works. Harris is hedging a bet Burrow might come back."

"That's a long shot bet."

"Yeah, well, it's all anyone has. Burrow is holed up somewhere, and no one has the foggiest. His parents and friends are clean. So are his best friends from school. He has no money, and no means to travel—his parents had his passport. Not to mention his face is plastered absolutely everywhere. I'm surprised the hospital hasn't hung one up in here. I passed three in the car park and lobby coming in today. They also put up extra surveillance around the memorial and there's gonna be some undercover officers intermingled in the crowd tonight."

"Are you going?" asked Oliver.

"Unfortunately—yours truly is the bait. Harris thinks he might actually try to make a second attempt. I've had a security guard at my hotel all week."

"We're gonna get him, Emma. I promise."

"*You're* not going to do anything except *rest*. If he shows up, there will be plenty of officers to get him." Emma glanced down at the text message notification on her watch. "Damn. Listen, I wish I could stay longer, but I need to get going. We have a briefing before the vigil and I'm already late."

"Thanks for visiting. I appreciate it more than you know."

Emma lingered for a moment, unsure what to do. She leaned in and kissed his forehead.

*

Emma dawdled about backstage, watching McArthur and a few other officers set up the podium and finish the lighting. Where she really wanted to be was in the crowd, searching for Burrow, but she had been relegated to other duties which boiled down to *nothing*. Be the bait. Total BS in her mind.

Harris refused to take any more risks than needed, which Emma understood, but standing on stage, being made a spectacle, felt wrong. Yet, there was no convincing him otherwise. She would be on the podium along with Mrs Taylor and Mr Brown, Vickie's husband, as the other officers did actual police work.

Mrs Taylor exuded composure and steadfastness despite her grief. She patiently awaited instructions and tenderly held her speech, as if it were a treasured item. Everything Mrs Taylor was, Mr Brown wasn't. He looked lost, like his anchor in life had been cut and he was left adrift. Mr Brown, disheveled and unkempt, wandered the backstage area, seeking reassurance from anyone who walked that he was indeed in the right place. His speech notes, crumpled and disorganized, precariously stuck out of his coat pocket, ready to fall to the ground at any moment.

Councilman Parry, who had again introduced himself as Mayor to several individuals already gathered, poorly masked his excitement. If he beheld any sorrow or grief at all, then it resided somewhere unassociated with his desire to be reelected. Lingering behind Parry, a frail, gray-haired woman, looking many years older than him, followed closely wherever he went. She nervously twitched at any sudden movement or sound and chewed her lower lip, leaving a little raw spot on the right side. Emma had heard the stories about Mrs Parry, and now seeing her in person confirmed the rumors. Clinical psychiatry wasn't Emma's forte—it held little relevance in crime scene forensics—but she had all the hallmarks of paranoid schizophrenia.

Slowly but surely, as the sun crept below the horizon, the empty car park at Kidderminster station transformed into a somber crowd. Traffic had to be diverted around the neighborhood to accommodate everyone gathered, most of whom had spilled out past the pedestrian walk and into the street. Harris, already nervous Burrow would slip through undetected, spouted new orders over the radio to cover sections the cameras weren't set up to observe.

Eventually, the time came for Emma, Harris, Parry, Mrs Taylor, and Mr Brown to take their seats on the small makeshift stage. Emma was grateful she wouldn't have to speak, not necessarily because it was still painful, but because she was an outsider—too new to give any words of solace that would come off sincere. She felt the loss. She'd have to be heartless not to, but she had no anecdotes, no stories, no shared moments of years past to speak of.

Nevertheless, her role was on the stage with the others. As the lone survivor of both attacks, her job to draw Burrow out was paramount to Harris' plan.

As they took their seats, Parry poised himself at the podium, ready to commence the vigil. So far, no sign of Burrow. Councilman Parry introduced everyone on stage and thanked the crowd for coming. He listed off a few others in the community who helped make the vigil possible, and he did so with a hint of compassion in his voice. But Emma didn't fall for it.

She gazed into the crowd and hoped she'd see signs of

Burrow, but all she saw were faceless shadows. The stage lights shined bright in her face, preventing her from seeing clearly.

Mrs Taylor took the mic first, sharing from her heart. During her speech, her graceful composure devolved into tears. Harris had to come and comfort her, placing his arm around her until she finished.

Mr Brown was a blubbering mess from the get-go. Despite stammering through his speech, even getting lost here and there, his words were masterfully crafted and painted a picture of Vickie as beautiful as any Rembrandt.

The time came for Emma's lone task in the vigil that didn't involve being a lamb to the slaughter. As they lowered the stage lights and prepared for the moment of silence, Emma lit her candle and shared her flame with those at the front of the crowd. Her candle flickered and danced in the darkness as she first passed her flame with those on stage and then those closest to the steps.

Little by little, as Harris read the names of the eight fallen men and women, a tiny sea of lights engulfed the crowd. Faces danced from flickering flames, gently illuminating them. For the first time during the vigil, people emerged from the shadows, even if the dim candles offered little light.

Emma scoured the mass for Burrow and failed to see anyone resembling him, but her eyes were drawn to a peculiar unlit section toward the back. She squinted her eyes, focusing her vision on the one person still shrouded in darkness amongst the ocean of lights. She checked if any other officers had also seen it, but no one seemed to be responding. When Emma looked back, the dark area had moved forward.

It meandered through the crowd, parting it like a predator

stalking in tall grass. Emma fixated on it, unable to move. As it neared, the darkness took shape. Not the brooding hulk that one expected of Burrow, but a small frame, not much larger than a child.

Harris, now having finished paying his respects to the eight fallen heroes, asked the crowd for a moment of silence. He motioned Emma to return to her seat. She couldn't. Something held her in place.

The shadow grew closer and as it did, it nudged those it passed. Each one it touched changed, as if in a trance, and started whispering. Emma couldn't make it out, as the ringing in her ear intensified and consumed her mind. *How is no one else seeing or hearing this?* she thought. Not even Harris responded to the murmuring crowd, disrupting the moment of silence.

The form now stepped out from the throng, standing at the foot of the steps just feet away from Emma. As it did, Mrs Parry, hissing and pointing, barged her way from backstage and stumbled to the front of the crowd where the shadow stood, making a fuss about whoever or whatever it was. Emma didn't hear Harris close the moment of silence as her attention was fixated on Mrs Parry's handlers strong-arming her away from the crowd. Whatever had slithered through the crowd had slipped away in Mrs Parry's commotion, but a lingering odor of rotten flesh remained as a reminder of its presence. Before her eyes could adjust to the stage lights bursting through the candle lights, her head spun and darkness enclosed around her vision.

"Emma? Emma, are you okay?" Harris crouched down in front of her as she sat in her seat on the podium. "Hey, there you are. You looked to be in your own world there for a few minutes."

"What? I'm sorry. Is the vigil over?" she asked, looking out at the dispersing crowd.

"Yes, has been for ten minutes. Are you feeling okay?"

The answer to that question was an unequivocal *no*, but she wasn't about to tell Harris that. "Yes, I'm fine. Just knackered."

Chapter 24
Crossing Lines

Bryant smirked as he waltzed through the dimly lit, empty halls. Everyone with a pulse was at Kidderminster, working the vigil, leaving Hagley station a ghost town. That gave Bryant free rein. He pulled the keycard from his back pocket and tapped it on the laboratory door-lock sensor. As expected, the door buzzed open.

He shuddered from the rush of frigid air escaping the old morgue. *Had it been that cold the last time?* he asked himself. Bryant flipped the switch and waited for the lone light over the autopsy table to flicker on. Not only had he forgotten how cold it was, but he had also forgotten how run down the lab was. Despite a few modern pieces of equipment, it looked unchanged from the 1930s. Rusted morgue refrigerators, stained and chipped autopsy table, and cobwebs resting in the corners. *I guess Lloyd isn't one for housekeeping.*

With everyone occupied for the next several hours, Bryant needn't rush. He sauntered to the autopsy table and ran his fingers gently over the rusted edges. He thought perhaps the skeletal remains would be on the table, but that'd make the game too easy. He relished the challenge.

To his delight, three morgue drawers sat empty and only one remained closed—minus a tiny issue. A zip tie, cinched tightly through the drop pen hole, with a handwritten label, secured the latch shut. Bryant couldn't cut and replace it without tipping off Lloyd. He'd have to revisit this issue last. He pondered on a solution as he searched the rest of the lab.

Lloyd's desk offered the most potential, then perhaps the file cabinets after that. Bryant reclined in her chair and leaned back, scanning potential sources of dirt. He rifled through the files in the desk trays, but they were only boring cold cases offering little interest. The pen drawer and left side filing cabinet yielded similar results. The right side drawer on the other hand jerked and held firm when he pulled on it. "What do we have here? Oh, a generic, pickable lock. How convenient."

Bryant took out his pick and torque wrench from his back pocket and inserted them into the locking mechanism. He fiddled with the pick until the tumblers aligned and the core loosened. As soon as he tried turning the lock, the pins fell out of position, locking the mechanism. Bryant tried again, getting all the tumblers in place and turning the core. Still locked. "Come on, you son of—." As he attempted a third try, a bang of metal on metal clanged behind him.

The morgue fridge door, previously secured with the zip tie, now swung freely, revealing a white sheet lain overtop something. That *something* better be the skeleton. Bryant didn't waste any more time on the cabinet lock and inspected the morgue drawer's contents. Curiously, the zip tie was still intact. *Had it been like this previously and I've not noticed?* he thought.

Sliding the drawer out and slipping back the sheet, Bryant revealed the skeletal remains he hoped to find. He took a series of photos from different angles and zoomed in on the skull— the source of the most unique identifying features. Temptation beckoned for him to take a small wrist bone, knowing there was a solid chance at a DNA result, but he couldn't risk it. He speculated Lloyd would notice. She might be corrupt and dirty, but she was still competent. Although, she'd never notice a hair. Bryant carefully used a pair of tweezers to extract a few strands attached to the skull and placed them in a bag.

He didn't care his editor rejected the story earlier that day. He was going to break this story on his own terms, regardless of what anyone said. The plastic bag, shoved in his pocket, held the key. *Now I'm going to get some answers.*

Chapter 25

Burn

Otis thumped as it stopped on the lower level. Emma threw the cage open and didn't even bother turning the light on as she buzzed herself into her lab. She stomped in, threw herself into her chair, and leaned back, letting her mind drift. Her eyes caught the crack growing in the ceiling, stretching across the brick arch. Specks of dust fluttered from the fissure and landed on the autopsy table behind her. A snap and ting stole Emma's attention and brought her back to the moment. Looking in the direction of the sound, she saw the cadaver door swinging open, despite having zip tied it closed. She marched over to the refrigerator units and slammed it shut, sending flecks of rusted paint to the floor. She then flipped it the bird after she secured it in place again. "I hope it feels like the wych elm."

Emma flopped back down in her chair and opened up FaceTime on her mac. She knew she'd wake Penelope, but she needed to vent.

"Hey, love," said Penelope as she brushed the sleep from

her eyes. "How did the vigil go?"

"Hey, Penelope," replied Emma.

"Cor, blimey! You said my name right. What happened? Spill it."

"What hasn't happened? Ugh—." Emma dabbed the corners of her eyes with a tissue. "One, Burrow *didn't* show up. So there's that. Noah is livid."

"You knew it was a slim chance. But you had to try, right? I'm sure they'll catch him eventually. They have to."

"Not before I lose my mind, though."

"Listen, we know between the two of us, I'm the crazy one. You have nothing to worry about. Besides, crazy people don't know they are going crazy when it happens. So you've got that going for you." Penelope paused and wrinkled her brows. "However, at the risk of me sounding overly concerned, what makes you think you're going bonkers?"

"Do you remember the one cold case I told you about last month?"

"Which one? Oh! You mean the famous one—with the girl in the tree. Yeah, what about it?"

"I feel like—I feel like there's something else going on with it. Something that Taylor couldn't tell me before—before he died."

"Like what?"

"Oh God, you wouldn't believe me if I told you! You'll definitely think I'm nuts."

"Try me."

"So, tonight, at the vigil. I swear I saw her."

"Saw who?"

"The woman from the cold case, Bella."

"What? Where?"

"At the vigil, walking in the crowd. God, even I think I'm crazy saying it out loud."

"Okay... you're right. You're a loony. I'm calling Bedlam Asylum."

"Oh, shut it. I'm being serious. It's just one thing after another with that case. I mean, come on, Burrow was clearly obsessed with it. You can't tell me that's a coincidence. Hell, the day Taylor died, he was frustrated about it, going on about how 'something changed' and it's only gonna get worse. What the hell am I supposed to do with that?"

As Emma spoke, the morgue drawer popped open. "See? That's what I'm talking about. Just nonstop," she said.

"I don't see how you could work in that place so late at night all alone. It's like Frankenstein's lab in there." Penelope shivered. "You want to know what I think? What you should do? Nothing—do nothing. Literally. Just... walk away from it."

"I can't just walk away from a case."

"You said it yourself, right? That case isn't open anymore. It's officially closed. No one will know. Taylor is gone. He was the one obsessed with it. That was his pet project, not yours. No one will know if you just *stop* investigating."

"How am I gonna go about that?"

"Honestly, if I were you, I'd burn it all. Every damn file and piece of evidence—*including* Bella. Take it all to a field somewhere and pour a crap ton of petrol on it and roast some marshmallows as it goes up in flames."

"I can't just up and destroy evidence."

"Yes. Yes, you can. Who is gonna come asking about it? No one. If you don't do it, I will."

Emma huffed and blew a strand of hair out of her face.

"Maybe you're right, Pena-lope. Maybe I should."

"Of course I'm right. Just don't let your colleague back there see you do it." Before Emma could respond, Penelope interrupted. "Bollocks, I'm waking up Chris. Gotta go. Laters, babes."

"Wait, what, who?" But it was too late; Penelope had ended the call. Emma swiveled around, but no one else was there; no one else *should* be there. She sent a text message to Penelope, but it just said *delivered*. Penelope must have switched her phone to silent. Emma closed FaceTime and rolled her shoulders—pricks of goosebumps rippled under her fingers and she couldn't shake the feeling she wasn't alone.

She reclined in her chair and stared at the crack in the ceiling, running across the brick arch and to the green subway tiles. *Did it just grow bigger?* Penelope was right; no one would come asking questions. No one would ever know. All that would remain, would be ash in a field. It'd get blamed on kids and be ignored. If Emma was gonna do it, she was gonna do it right. She was gonna burn *all* the evidence. Not just Bella—the tree, too.

She had everything she needed right here. There were half a dozen, if not more, highly flammable substances in the lab. Notably acetone, isopropyl alcohol, and the big one, diethyl ether. Not to mention she could syphon some petrol from the van. The hollow of the wych elm would create a nice incinerator effect if she fed it the right amount of oxygen. Getting it hot enough to burn Bella's remains wasn't out of the question.

Could she do it? Did Emma have the courage? Before she answered that question, she had already picked up the April 18th box, dumping all the related files into it. She paused as she pulled back the sheet from Bella—her memories of that first day at the tree welled up. The curiosity she once felt had been replaced by frustration and anger. While she wanted nothing more than to get this over with, she couldn't help but place Bella's remains carefully in the box—bone by bone with undeserving care. The pendent light flickered overhead. Emma looked up as it blinked, popped, and burnt out with a burst. Her mac screensaver glowed from her desk in the corner, casting faint shadows across the dark laboratory.

Emma, ignoring the hindering dark, set the box down for a moment and started collecting all the flammable liquids from around the lab, emptying out the wooden cabinet next to her desk. When she returned to the box, she found several items had been taken out and placed back on her desk. Had she done that and not realized it? Emma pushed on and placed the accelerants in the crate and then returned the misplaced files back into the box.

As she rode Otis upstairs, the familiar chill from the lab followed, as if attached to the crate in her arms. Emma ignored it. Tonight would be Bella's last.

She threw Bella and the evidence into the back of her van and snatched a spare jerry can and hose from the vehicle depot. If it could burn, she was gonna use it.

Hagley Wood lay a ten-minute drive from the station: promising a quick jaunt across town. The walk into the woods to the wych elm would take the longest, considering Emma had to find it in the dark and she had only been there once before.

She pulled up to the street and then left onto Hagley Causeway in the direction of the wood. She came to the first roundabout and instead of continuing on straight past her hotel and toward Hagley Wood, she found herself doing a 180 and returning to the station. Confused, she pulled back out and headed toward Hagley Wood once more. This time, she caught herself trying to do another 180 and forced herself to complete the roundabout and head straight through. The tug to return to the station bellowed within, making it difficult to focus on her task.

Determined, Emma pinched herself several times to keep alert. This time, she managed to make it to the tiny lay-by where she'd met Taylor and Edwards several months earlier. A hundred yards away, the wych elm awaited.

Emma hopped out and gathered the April 18th box full of files, accelerants, and that bloody corpse, and set them on the ground next to the back tire. She grabbed the jerry can and hose from the van and unscrewed the petrol tank cap. She needed to drive back, so she didn't syphon everything out of the tank. Just enough that when combined with the other accelerants, the fire would burn long and hot. She stacked the jerry can onto the box and started her trudge through the woods.

The trailhead laid dark and difficult to find, something that had kept many curious parties from finding the wych elm over the years. The silver birches creaked as they swayed in the warm night breeze, casting shadows that moved about almost consciously under the waning moon. Leaves rustled beneath her as she struggled to stay on the path and keep hold of the box with Bella's remains. The thick underbrush snapped and cut as she trod through the wood. *Where is that damn tree?* she thought as she scanned through the mist surrounding the Hawthorn trees, realizing she had lost the trail. Emma turned back around to retrace her steps, but she couldn't find the path. Stumbling through the underbrush, the moonlight

failed to light her way, leaving her to guess the direction toward the glade. Twice she crisscrossed the silver birch grove
in her hunt to locate the trail.

A breeze danced between the trees, stirring the surrounding leaves. Her senses piqued at the sound of the rustling fo-
liage, swaying almost rhythmically. *Thump-shush. Thump-
shush.*

Emma stopped and composed herself. The moon shone
to her back when she entered the woods. If she kept it to her
back, starting in the silver birch grove, she would find the tree.
When she crossed the grove again, she set the moon behind
her and trekked forward. After a few moments, the woods
opened up to a glade.

Across from her, twisted and disfigured, the wych elm
loomed. Its branches as gnarled as witch's fingers, knobby
and thin, swayed in the breeze. Amongst the shadows, festooned by dead leaves and dark soil, stood Bella, staring
motionless into the hollow. Her hair, as mangled as the tree,
brushed the edge of her dark and yellow striped sweater. The
yellow skirt, torn and stained, flapped as the wind blew. Once
Emma stepped into the opening, she twisted around and gave
the same smile Burrow flashed when he leapt from the van.

Emma clenched her eyes shut and wished her away. *She's
not really there. It's just your imagination.* Before she opened
them, a hand swept over her chest and across her shoulders,
sliding down her arm and twisting its ethereal fingers between
Emma's. A warmthless body pressed tight against her—tiny,
even in comparison to Emma's short stature. An arm wrapped
under the April 18th box and around Emma's waist, pulling
her closer. She couldn't breathe, but not from the stench of
rotten wood and flesh emanating from the embracing figure.

She's not there, she thought. Bella rested her head on Emma's shoulder and nestled in tightly. Emma could feel her whispering, her jaw and mouth rustling against her clothes, her frigid breath penetrating deep and prickling her skin, but Emma couldn't make out the words amongst the wind.

A knot formed in her throat and she swallowed hard. "What?" Everything within Emma told her not to speak. It was too late.

The fingers intertwining with Emma's squeezed, ragged nails pinching tight against her flesh. The arm around her constricted tighter. Bella's body tensed as she moaned. *Who put me in the wych elm?*

Emma wrestled herself free and blindly stumbled toward the tree, whipping herself around before opening her eyes to an empty glade.

She clutched the box tight to her side. The leaves rustled in the distance, the same *thump-shush* as the breeze turned cold, sending goose bumps over her arms. *It's in your head, Emma. It's all in your head,* she reminded herself.

Before she changed her mind, Emma rushed to the tree and opened the box with Bella and all the evidence. She tossed the files and photos in as tinder at the bottom of the hollow and then she dumped Bella bone by bone into the tree. All that remained were the bottles of accelerants. Emma snagged the diethyl ether and popped off the cap. It would all be over soon. No sooner had she lifted her hand to dispense the ether, the cold breeze returned and swept over her shoulder, bringing with it the whisper, *Who put me in the wych elm?* before darkness enveloped her.

*

Emma jerked awake, face planted on her desk, sitting in her chair in the lab. Checking her watch, it was Saturday morning. When did she come back? Had she been so exhausted she forgot it all? She stretched and rubbed her eyes, grabbing her car keys off the desk, when she saw the April 18th box sitting empty next to her and the bottles of accelerant on top.

As she picked them up to place them back in the cabinet, she noticed they were full. Hadn't she used them all? Behind her, metal banged and hinges squeaked. When Emma spun around, the morgue drawer swayed and banged again. She tiptoed around the autopsy table, toward the refrigerator and peered inside. Resting on the drawer, as if undisturbed from the previous night's events, laid Bella.

Chapter 26
A Hero Comes Home

Emma hid the welcome-back cake under a box, and then plopped down at her temporary desk in the bullpen. The lab had become *complicated* and isolated from the rest of the station, at least that's what she told everyone. The truth of it, even if she didn't fully admit it to herself, was Bella—Emma had to get away from that bloody skeleton, along with everything that came with it: the increasing blackouts, the morgue doors opening and closing, and that incessant unanswerable question.

Getting rid of her hadn't been as easy as Penelope had proposed, and being subjected to *that woman's* presence everyday wasn't boding well for Emma's mental health. She had no choice but to ignore her—consequences be damned. It's not like she could do anything about the case, anyway. Taylor's incomplete protocol had exhausted its timeline, leaving Emma at a standstill. Well, except for Bella's DNA she'd submitted as her own to Ancestry.

Emma opened her mac and launched the mail app as she

waited for Oliver's return. He was expected any minute now and she needed a non-engrossing activity. She hoped the Ancestry results had arrived overnight, but she was out of luck—something too common these days. What Emma did find, was the same message thread of bad news of those in the station: a spouse lost their job, a cancer diagnosis, another death in the family. She never thought herself superstitious, but the timing of these events and their frequency tripled since the shooting. The other emails didn't fare any better: more Bella vandalism to document, toxicology results from last week's suicide, fingerprint analysis in the Byrd murder case, and nothing on Burrow's whereabouts.

Oliver needed to hurry up and bring a little joy back to the station. Emma peaked over the top of her computer of those gathered for the soiree. Judging by their faces, she thought it resembled a funeral more than welcome-back festivities. McArthur moped like a dejected lover, Wright wore melancholy like a cheap suit, and everyone else looked like their dog had died. Emma hadn't been at the station long, three and a half months since Dr Evans died, but she knew everyone well enough to know something was amiss. She might have been a little jaded for personal reasons, but she blamed Bella. Something about her had an effect, not just on her, but anyone within proximity—the town included.

Kicking her feet up on her desk, Emma leaned back in her chair and spied the cork boards in the bullpen. Case after case littered the board closest to her, all of them unsolved *Death Week* cases over the last few years. She returned to her emails and the back log of active cases, now outnumbering her cold cases—it seemed October had arrived early.

"Get ready, he just pulled into the car park," yelled

McArthur down the hall and into the bullpen. Everyone rushed to take a position as he turned out the lights. Emma supposed she should be excited in this moment, but it escaped her.

On the surface, as they all yelled *surprise* when Oliver walked in, joy flashed and radiated in the room at his return. Yet, dead faces had consumed the atmosphere, like masks of happiness pulled down to conceal the truth. Laughter shrouded in sorrow fell flat in her ears.

Oliver weaved through the officers, each offering their congratulations and giving him a pat on the back for his return. He spotted Emma and headed her way.

"Welcome back, *Superintendent* Bennett." Emma blew a noise maker, wondering if her words sounded as hollow as they felt.

"I'll never get used to that title, that's for sure." Oliver reached over and gave her a hug; Emma stood on her toes and nuzzled her cheek against his chest. He looked down at her desk at the other *surprise* she had waiting for him. "Oh, a bowl full of *jelly*. How... nice?"

"The nurses kept talking about how much you just loved the hospital food, so I figured I'd pick you something *really* nice." She clicked her tongue and held up an *okay* hand gesture.

"Absolutely, totally my favorite. No doubt I'll have both seconds and thirds," he jested.

Emma leaned back over the desk and retrieved the cake, pulling off the box cover.

"Now we're talking!" said Oliver. "Who wants cake?" The officers feigned excitement as they gathered around.

A recognizable face weaseled his way to the front of the line. "Superintendent Oliver Bennett. Welcome back and congratulations!" Councilman Parry took Oliver by the hand before he even had the chance to offer the handshake. Parry gave the long, awkward, double-handed shake that people hated from politicians. "Listen, I think it's fantastic that Chief Constable Harris named you the next superintendent after Taylor's passing. One of our own from Hagley running all of North Worcestershire LPU—as it should be. And as I told your beautiful colleague, Dr Lloyd here, on her first day: if there is anything you need, and I mean anything at all, you reach out and ask. I'll make sure you get it."

"Thank you, sir. It's good to be back and see everyone again. To be honest, I'm still in shock Chief Constable Harris selected me for the position."

"Don't be so modest, Bennett. You're a decorated officer. You selflessly risked life and limb in that building fire in 2014. There's a whole family alive today because of your valiant efforts—you know, that little boy is all grown up and just passed his A-levels. And let's not forget what you did for Dr Lloyd—taking one in the chest and still apprehending the assailant. You're a bona fide hero in my book, Bennett. Capped off with your credentials, experience, and work ethic, there was no one else on the force in all of West Mercia more deserving." Still shaking Oliver's hand, Parry yanked him closer. "And between you and Emma here, Hagley—parish and station—needed the moral victory. Promoting you to the job was precisely what everyone needed." He released the handshake and slapped Oliver on the bad shoulder, causing him to wince ever so slightly. Parry shifted his gaze to Emma. "Now, how have you settled in?"

Emma didn't like Parry's unnatural smile—unsettling, to say the least. "About as good as anyone could, considering the events. Still trying to get my feet wet around here."

"Oh, I'm sure you're doing magnificent. But, I am curious, how is *our girl* doing?"

"I'm sorry? *Our girl?*"

"Well, *Bella,* of course. Taylor and Dr Evans always kept me appraised on that case. More of a courtesy to the town's Mayor—nothing compromising to the investigation, I assure you. But, she does keep our pubs and hotels full with all that tourism, so her mythos is well appreciated by the Parish Council."

"More like *dark tourism,*" said Oliver.

Parry side-eyed Oliver for a moment. "Yes, quite right. Dark tourism might be closer to the truth. Either way, Bella is what we have. Why else have I ordered the Wychbury Obelisk *not* to be cleaned of the graffiti. People come from all around to see it. You know, I have a cottage just a stone's throw from Hagley Wood. Not a week goes by in good weather that I don't see someone wander in looking for that tree."

"Does anyone ever find it?" asked Emma.

Parry shrugged his shoulders and exhaled. "Who knows. I'm sure some have. If they do, they never boast about it—at least that I've ever heard. But, as I was saying, you need to take good care of her. See to it she gets what she needs. Don't want to make her feel neglected." Parry chuckled, but Emma wasn't sure what the joke was. "Anyhow, I'll let you two get back to the shindig. Whisper carefully." And like a wisp of foul air in a breeze, he vanished into the gathering.

Emma wrinkled her brows and inquired on the expression. "You said that to me on my first day. What the *hell* does it mean?"

"What does *what* mean?" replied Oliver.

"*Whisper carefully.* I hear it all the time."

"It's a line from a local children's rhyme. *Whisper carefully, her tale of sorrow.* It's kind of tradition in Hagley to say goodbye with it. Small towns and all. How *does* that poem go?" Oliver glanced upward, trying to remember it.

A voice behind Emma chimed in,

> "*In Hagley Wood, in shadow's grip,*
>   *Fair Bella lies, in death's long slip.*
> *Just beyond the silver birch glade,*
>   *Underneath that wicked tree's shade.*
> *Who put her there in the wych elm's hole?*
>   *Who took her life, but left her soul?*
> *She slumbers in the wych elm's hollow,*
>   *Vengeance seething in bone and marrow.*
> *In Death Week's end, will Bella doth stand,*
>   *Searching, yearning for her lost hand.*
> *Seeking what the thief has taken,*
>   *Perhaps your hand so she might awaken.*
> *So heed this tale, to not fall prey,*
>   *Or in her nightmares you will stay.*
> *And from today until the morrow,*
>   *Whisper carefully, her tale of sorrow.*"

Emma twisted round to hear the last verse from McArthur, who had undoubtedly eavesdropped on the conversation. "And I thought *Ring Around the Rosie* was dark. Do parents really say that to kids?"

"You know, campfire stories and stuff. Dads try to scare the kids while the uncle comes creeping out of the forest with one hand tucked in his sleeve, yelling, *'Who put me in the wych elm?'* Then you have the grandparents telling kids if they don't behave and go to bed on time, Bella will come and take their hand for her own."

"How serious do people around here take all this?"

"A few... depends on who you ask," replied Oliver.

McArthur interrupted again. "I'd say that's an understatement. Superintendent Bennett didn't grow up here—I did. And I'd say it's a safe bet just about anyone who has lived here for any significant amount of time believes it on some level. Hell, ask anyone who's ever worked at the Gypsy's Tent, and you'll hear numerous opinions on the matter."

"The Gypsy's Tent?" asked Oliver.

"It's called the Badger's Sett now. It's where Lloyd's rental is."

"So you think there's more to Bella than just a cold case?" asked Emma.

McArthur didn't respond right away. "I'd say there are too many coincidences. *Especially,* around Death Week. I've said it before. My grandmother was convinced Bella haunted this town. She would go on and on about how she once saw Bella one autumn walking into Hagley Wood when she was a little girl. She always crossed herself every time she told the story. For me, I'll leave it like this: every April 19th I get chills going down to the evidence locker and going past your lab. And it grows—intensely I might add—until the end of Death Week. So yeah, I think there's more to it."

Emma pondered how much McArthur knew. "That's oddly specific. Why would my lab creep you out?"

"This building has serviced Hagley since the '30s. She was brought here—to your lab—in '43. The stairwell leading up to the bullpen was sealed up in '45 with no explanation. I think a part of her never left this place. I've never gone into your lab and never will if I can help it. And before you call me crazy, I'm not the only officer around here who feels that way."

Emma looked at Oliver. "What about you? Are you superstitious? Do you agree with McArthur?"

Oliver clicked his tongue. "I mean—I don't know. I grew up in the church, so I'm a firm believer in God, Satan, Heaven, and Hell. But ghosts or hauntings per se, that's a tough sell. But I'm not gonna lie and say Death Week isn't a compelling argument for *something*. I just don't know how it would actually apply to Bella."

"Oh come on, sir. You know as well as I do every couple of years there's a report during Death Week of a cadaver at a local morgue missing a hand—just like Bella. And you have that murder in October '51, where the homeless woman had her hand amputated and she bled out. She was reported to have been screaming 'Bella did it, Bella did it' before she died. I call that *compelling*."

"Crazy people doing crazy things doesn't mean the ghost of Bella is walking the streets of Hagley looking for a hand to steal. This is the stuff of urban legends."

Emma contemplated saying something, sharing her experiences over the last few months since joining Hagley. McArthur would believe her, but would Oliver? Would she actually want to drag them into all this? Risk passing it along like Stacey did to Burrow?

Before Emma had the chance, the desk clerk squeezed through the gathering and whispered something in Oliver's ear, handing him a folded note in the process. His jovial smile dropped from his face and his shoulders tensed after he opened and read it. He wadded up the paper, tossed it in the bin, and locked eyes with Emma and McArthur. "Burrow has been spotted."

Chapter 27
The Siege

All West Mercia police force had assembled outside Drakelow Tunnels and the heads of the five Local Policing Units gathered inside the makeshift command center set up near adit A. Before them laid a map of Drakelow, all entrances and exit points circled in red. The technical room and other points of interest were marked in blue. Finally, other various colors crisscrossed and ran the length of every corridor and room—each representing an armed response unit. Oliver and Harris stood at the head of the group, presenting the plan.

"Listen up," said Harris. "We have three-point-five miles of known tunnels covering an area of 285,000 square feet. This includes numerous rooms, smaller connective corridors, ventilation shafts, built-in structures, and large, abandoned machinery. Currently, there is no power. Objective A is to restore power. We will send a tactical team in with a maintenance worker to restore electricity to the main breakers located in the old Rover offices.

"Each LPU and their respective assault teams are assigned a number of corridors and rooms to clear and apprehend the target. This is objective B. Maps marking your areas will be distributed shortly. Due to the grid nature of the tunnels and the different rooms splitting off, the search will have to be carefully timed and coordinated to prevent Burrow from doubling back. We will flush him here, to tunnel one at the back of the facility. We will enter here, at adit A. All the remaining adits and potential exit points have been sealed or have units assigned to them. Mind you, radio and cellular communications are limited in the tunnels, especially in the deeper areas where Ops teams will have to operate using voice and hand signals, so all teams will have to maintain strict visual contact.

"Each unit is to sweep their grid and wait at the checkpoint for the all clear, then proceed through their next assignment until reaching the next checkpoint. If at any point an unknown room, tunnel, or person is encountered, all units will stop at the closest checkpoint and await the all-clear. If at any point Burrow is spotted, all units will converge on that location, blocking him in.

"In case anyone needs reminding, the suspect is Timothy Burrow." Harris held up an enlarged mug shot. "32 years old, seven foot one, approximately 320 pounds. His employment records show he had previously worked in Drakelow, so he knows these tunnels. And as we have no evidence to the contrary, we must assume he is armed."

Oliver stepped in. "I'm not going to sugarcoat the situation. This will not be easy. Stick to your pairs and groups, watch each other's backs. There are thousands of places he could be holed up in these tunnels. Check and double check every nook and cranny before clearing it and moving on."

One of the other superintendents spoke up. "Why not leave the power off and follow standard procedure?"

"Normally that would be advisable," replied Oliver. "But the sheer size of Drakelow and the complexity of the search grid changes several factors. First, with the high number of teams coordinating and crisscrossing paths, a well-lit environment will reduce potential friendly fire scenarios. Second, the sheer number of officers needed to search the facility leaves us shorthanded on tactical vision devices. Each team will be issued one to two pairs for an emergency situation, but not enough for everyone. Third, Burrow disabled the power. This leads us to believe that the dark is an advantage to him for whatever reason. So restoring the power will give us both a tactical and psychological upper hand. Any other questions?" he added. The other superintendents shook their heads no and gathered their maps and packets for their units. "Alright, get your men organized and suited up. We breach in sixty minutes at fourteen-hundred hours."

Everyone dispersed to prepare their groups while Harris and Oliver continued their tactical discussion over the map. In the corner of the tent next to the communications center, Emma paced helplessly, unsure what value she'd bring to the search. She wouldn't be assigned a team—naturally so—and that left her anxious. Twice she had encountered Burrow at a disadvantage and twice he had wrought destruction. Emma didn't want a third.

The waiting game, which she had become an unwilling participant of, commenced. The tactical team to restore power breached the rusty steel doors of adit A first while a queue of assault teams followed suit tightly behind, disappearing into the dark void like a snake slithering into a hole. Emma's chest

pounded as she stood with a handful of communications officers waiting for a hint of light to glimmer out the doors, indicating the tactical team had achieved its mission.

A single, external light over the doors to adit A flickered
and snapped as it came on. Objective A complete.

Her imagination ran wild with scenarios the teams inside
were encountering. The twists and turns and seemingly in-
finite number of corners they would have to peek around, unaware of what dangers each one could reveal.

A few officers had remained outside. Harris and Oliver
loomed over the communications center where three techs
monitored radio channels. Two armed officers remained at the
entrance of adit A, both poised to apprehend Burrow should
he emerge. McArthur, along with two other PCs, buzzed
about acting as gofers for Oliver and Harris. And then there
was Emma—sticking out like a sore thumb.

The tactical team hadn't returned yet, which, based on
Harris and Oliver's furled brows, indicated a kink had been
encountered. Several minutes passed and Harris had checked
his watch as many times as the hands had ticked.

Taking his radio out and walking toward the adit, Harris
called the team. "Tac Team Alpha, this is Command. Over."
Harris waited, but there was no response. "Tac Team Alpha,
this is Command. Report your status. Over." Again, no reply.
Harris looked back at Oliver and the other communications
officers and snapped his fingers. "Tac Team Alpha, this is
Command. State immediate status. Over." Harris stood with
one hand on his hip as he impatiently waited for a response
that never came.

"All units, this is Command. I need a status report for
Alpha Team. Over." Before any of the teams responded, a

concussive *boom* rippled down the corridors, sending a plume of dust and debris out of the adit. The light over the entrance flashed out. Harris and Oliver held their arms over their faces as they ran toward the door. "All units, this is Command! Report status! Over!"

"Command... Bravo... checkpoint... Clear. O—," said Bravo Team leader amidst the static. One by one, each Ops team reported back.

"All teams, this is Command. Hold position at checkpoint two. Over."

Oliver and Harris conferred, looking over their shoulders back at the command tent, before they called for everyone's attention. "We need volunteers. Who is firearm certified?" asked Oliver.

McArthur raised his hand. "I think I'm the only one here, sir." The other communication officers and PCs shook their heads and looked around, wondering if anyone else volunteered. Every available officer was already engaged in the tunnels—no one remained.

Before Emma realized what she was doing, she raised her hand. "I'll go."

Harris' mouth hung agape.

"Hear me out," said Emma. "If anyone is injured, I'm more qualified than anyone else to give aid. And I'm more likely to be able to restore the power. I can do this."

"No," replied Harris.

"Who else are you going to send? Everyone qualified is already in the tunnels. Oliver is injured. I'm just as much of a liability as anyone else here except I have the medical and technical know-how they don't." Emma locked eyes with Harris as he scratched the back of his head thinking.

"Then suit up," he said without further hesitation. Harris turned and strutted back toward the adit, shaking his head, but not overruling Oliver.

As McArthur and Emma donned their Kevlar, the full weight of Emma's impetuous decision came crashing down on her. Had she really just thrown herself back into Burrow's path? She drew deep and puffed her cheeks as she exhaled.

"Don't worry. As always, I got your back, Emma. It's gonna be in and out," said McArthur. The fact that McArthur loaded up extra magazines made her think otherwise. She feigned a confident smile and checked the straps on her vest a third time.

Debris lingered in the air as Emma stared into the darkness that laid beyond the entrance of adit A. She would soon come face to face with the reality of what she imagined only moments earlier when the Ops teams breached the door. One non-negotiable fact surfaced amongst the others: somewhere, down in the tunnels, Burrow awaited her.

"You ready? Remember, due to renovations, you can't go straight to the old Rover offices and the technical room from here. You'll have to go around. Have you got the route memorized?" asked Oliver.

Emma fidgeted with her vest. "Yes. First left. End of the hall, small jog to the left, and straight again. Second right. Second right again. Second left. Right. Seventh right. End of the hall."

Harris butted in. "Repeat that one more time." When she finished, she unstrapped and re-strapped her vest tighter.

Oliver stood in front of her and tugged on her Kevlar. "Your vest is fine. Stay on McArthur's six, move quick. All you need to do is get in, assess the situation, restore power, and get out."

Harris made sure Emma looked him straight in the eyes. He wore concern like a father. "Repeat those directions just *one* more time." Emma complied and gave him a reassuring smile as she slung a medical bag over her shoulder.

Dust danced in the soft beams of light emanating from their torches and shining into the tunnels. Cold air of the adit wrapped tightly around them as they left the hot afternoon sunlight outside. Their torch beams fell dead only a few feet before them, forcing them to move slower across the gravelly sandstone floor. They came to the first turn and waited as McArthur peered around. He signaled the all clear, and they plunged deeper into the tunnels. On either side, as they crept along, other corridors branched off into the unknown; darkness obscuring their secrets.

Though Emma counted each turn and followed McArthur's path, keeping up with their map location became increasingly difficult. Emma kept her eyes on McArthur, refusing to let herself lose sight of him, least she wander off in the wrong direction.

As they came to the final turn, heading directly toward the technical room, smoke billowed across the ceiling and out the adjacent tunnel. Its soot fluttered down and choked both her and McArthur. Once around the corner, sparks flashed out of a doorway, subtly lightening one of the Alpha team members laying halfway into the corridor.

McArthur and Emma rushed down the hall and slid next to the officer, still gasping for air. Emma pulled out gauze from her bag and crammed it up under his vest. She couldn't find the source until her hand nudged the metal rod jutting out from between his ribs, just under the Kevlar strap. McArthur disappeared into the technical room to determine the status of the rest of the team. Within a few moments, he returned.

"Where is everyone else?" asked Emma, sweat dripping from her nose as she snatched more gauze from the bag. Electricity snapped and buzzed from the technical room, sending a rain of sparks over them.

"Inside. They're gone."

Emma glanced over her shoulder and through the smoke. Their silhouettes were illuminated by the small electrical fire. Light glistened off the pool of blood collecting around each of them. Beyond the bodies on the far wall, twisted metal and cabling flashed as they collided. There would be no restoring power—there was nothing left to mend.

"Command, this is McArthur. Over." He waited a few seconds and tried again. "Command, this is McArthur. We need immediate medical assistance. Over." Silence. "We're gonna have to take him with us," he said to Emma.

"We can't move him. Not without a stretcher, at least. You're gonna have to go get help."

"I'm not leaving you here alone. Not with Burrow possibly nearby." McArthur removed the side arm from the injured officer and handed it to her. "Do you know how to use this?" He didn't wait for her to answer. "Go, run, backtrack the route and get help!"

Emma looked at him, eyes wide and body stiff.

"Go!" He pointed down the corridor in the direction they came.

She stumbled to her feet and ran back to the last intersection, remembering to reverse the turns in her head. Her torch light flew from side to side as she ran, revealing the white sandstone walls. She neared the next intersection and dashed into the corridor. She counted the turns and came to the next one. This time when she came around the corner, she was confronted with a dead end.

Where was she? Emma reached for her map and realized she had set it down with the medical bag. She was running blind. She backtracked her last two turns, hoping to find the old Rover offices, but she only found more corridors leading in different directions. Emma tried going back to the dead end to repeat it, but now, it was nowhere to be found.

The labyrinth of Drakelow had found a victim.

Chapter 28
Lost in the Dark

Emma pulled out her radio and called, but as before, no one answered except static. Her pulse quickened as she looked down the dark corridor flanking her, stutter stepping as she struggled to choose which tunnel to take. The Ops teams, with their mapped assignments, had already delved deep into Drakelow, far from where she assumed she was. She had now become the liability she convinced Oliver and Harris she wouldn't be. The best thing she could do, much like getting lost in the forest, was to hold tight and wait it out.

She crouched down on the floor, sitting cross legged, and leaned against the wall with her torch lighting the sandstone opposite her, illuminating the cracks and the patchwork of mold littering the stone. Every few minutes she tried the radio, to no avail.

Emma... whispered down the corridor from a voice she didn't recognize. She flashed the light toward the source. There had been a voice, right? She uncrossed her legs and tucked them to her chest, continuing her inspection of the wall across from her, dismissing the voice as her imagination.

Emma... fluttered in the air, from the opposite direction this time. She swung around, only to see the vast emptiness of Drakelow staring back at her, the light of the torch dying a few yards from her. She flicked the torch along the ceiling and walls, tracing the edges of a few abandoned machines. If there had indeed been a voice, it came from much deeper within Drakelow. Emma squeezed her knees tighter, pulling her feet snug against her buttocks. Her fingers white-knuckled the torch and her pant leg.

Emma... This time, the cold whisper trickled over her ear and down the flesh of her neck. Goose-pimples pricked up and ran the length of her arm; hairs standing on end. She swatted as if a fly had buzzed too closely, interested in crawling into her ear. She dropped her torch on the floor; its glass cracking against the stone, its light flickering out. "Bollocks!" Emma groped the floor, slicing a finger on a shard of glass, and picked up the busted light, banging it on the heel of her hand in hopes it would light up. She reached for her glow sticks but stopped. They would be useless for anything other than marking a path. She had no choice but to sit in the black of Drakelow.

Darkness slithered and mingled with the cold, stale air of the tunnels. Emma, devoid of sight, became aware of every sound around her. Far away, down some unknown tunnel passage, water plunked as it dripped from a pipe, an animal scurried over gravel, and a wisp of air hummed through ventilation. None of them stole her thoughts more than the whisper of her name that floated maliciously in the shadows. *Emma,* it called again.

She jumped to her feet and pulled the 9mm from her waistline, clicking off the safety and indexing her trigger finger on the slide. She held it downward and took a deep breath, gathering what courage the voice hadn't robbed. "Hello? Is someone there?"

With a sense of futility, she blindly looked in either direction down the tunnel. Her eyes had adjusted, but all ambient light had been swallowed in the depths of Drakelow. Catching her eye, just to her right, a sliver of light glowed dimly underneath something large, something hidden in the void. Emma shuffled across the corridor to discover a large machine tucked against the wall, hiding the faint light amidst its rusted gears and worn levers. Had her torch not gone out, she never would have seen the soft rays emanating from behind.

Emma searched around the machine to locate the light source. As she leaned over one side, the machine, which had to weigh several hundred pounds, slid effortlessly away from the wall, exposing the dim light source behind. She peeked in the gap to discover another tunnel, almost the same size as the machine, plunging deep into the sandstone.

She unhooked her radio and called again. "Command, this is Lloyd. I've discovered a tunnel hidden behind a machine, somewhere near the Rover offices. Over." As she expected, there was no reply. She tried again with the same results. Emma removed several glow sticks from her vest and snapped them, tossing one in either direction down the tunnel and then two more on the ground in front of the machine. She tugged on the machine, pulling it outward, and exposed the hand-hewn sandstone steps leading downward.

Emma paused in front of the opening. The choice between waiting on the Ops team to arrive, assuming they received her call, or go down in search of Burrow gnawed on her mind. Oliver's voice rose in her imagination: "Stay and wait", but her legs chose differently and she descended into the stairwell.

The opening forced her to crouch in order to fit into the tunnel, but after a couple of steps the ceiling rose high enough for her to stand. The dim light from the tunnel below illuminated the sandstone as she descended. On both sides of the wall, scribbled in chalk, *those words* stared at her, begging to be read. Burrow had surely been here.

The tunnels on the lower level were less refined, unfinished, and roughly hewn. The ceiling, while tall enough for Emma to stand up in, hung considerably lower than the tunnels above. The corridors were far too large for one person like Burrow to carve out himself, but clearly not intended to be a part of the original shadow factory.

The fairy lights at the bottom of the steps led in one direction—to Emma's left. It would be as good a direction as any to start with. She checked behind her for any signs of the Ops teams and then tentatively proceeded, hugging closely along the sandstone. Emma held the gun close to her chest, elbows bent, and pointing the barrel forward, still indexing her finger on the slide.

Emma... the voice whispered again, but much louder, as if just down the corridor. Her thoughts wandered back to that night at the Evans' cottage. It was the same voice that had answered *yes* all those months ago. The hairs on her neck stood on end as she swiveled around in the direction it had come. Her palms sweaty, she gripped the Glock tighter. Emma cautiously followed the lights to the first juncture where they ended. Shadowed tunnels led in either direction. Her chest pounded, her heartbeat consuming all other sounds save the whisper which faded in and out.

Emma cracked another glow stick and tossed it into the

passage to her right. It landed on the gravel several yards ahead of her and rolled to the side. Its light, faint and dull, revealed and empty corridor. She followed its green glow and checked for any path or clue that might hint to Burrow's location.

Picking up the glow stick, Emma squinted as she scanned the corridor and tossed it again. It flipped end over end before bouncing off the chest of a brute standing in the middle of the tunnel. The glow stick fell to the ground and landed propped up on a worn out pair of dust covered Doc Martins. Burrow. He laughed like a small child playing a game and then ran away from her, disappearing into the darkness of the tunnel behind him. Emma flinched and jerked her gun up, struggling to move her finger over the trigger.

Where did he go? Had he ducked into another corridor? Emma stepped forward, fighting her panicked breath as she crept, picking up the glow stick in the process. She tossed it a little further down the corridor where Burrow had run to discover a T-junction.

Laughter echoed behind her and she swung round. As she did, her ears began to ring, as if standing inside a klaxon, sending her mind reeling and knocking her off balance. Cold fingers brushed the hair away from her ear as it whispered the question she had come to despise.

Recoiling from the figure which had materialized beside her, she fell into Burrow. His burly arms wrapped around her—his hands locking tight across her chest. She stomped her foot and thrust her head back, splitting his chin—and her scalp—open in the process. Her head rung, but he loosened his grip enough to wrestle free. She scurried along the floor several yards and then twisted around, pointing the gun at thin air.

Emma panted—her arms burned from extending the gun out for so long. After a few moments, she stood back up and checked either direction for Burrow but failed to see him in the dark. Deep in another passageway, he spoke. "Emma, do you know who did it?" His voice reverberated off the walls, mixing with the woman's whisper as if they spoke as one.

"Burrow! This whole place is surrounded. There are assault teams en route from the tunnels above. Give up. Turn yourself in."

They spoke in unison.

Who put me in the wych elm?

"Who put her in the wych elm?"

"I know you know!" His voice had changed from that day in the interrogation room. It seethed with malice.

"Burrow, let's end this peacefully. Turn yourself in!" Emma yelled in both directions, as she didn't know where he hid.

The air grew frigid, prickling Emma's skin down her back. Behind her, down one of the other tunnels where the colder draft blew, a faint sound drifted in the air.

Thump-shush… thump-shush.

Emma adjusted the grip on her gun and backed tighter against the wall. Her heart raced, pumping adrenaline through her veins. She shuffled to the right, toward the voice of Burrow.

His laughter turned sinister. "You hear her, don't you?"

Emma ignored him, but there was no denying she knew who Burrow spoke of.

"Just answer our question and it'll all end, Emma."

Despite her slow drudge toward Burrow, the *thump-shush* crept closer. Bella's shuffling steps gained as Emma began to run. Icy fingers reached out and grasped at her. Emma's mind spun as nails scratched and tore through her clothes. Throwing herself forward, she broke free from Bella's grip.

Up ahead, the fairy lights shone around the corner. Bella growled at Emma's desperation. Darting around the corner, the lights flickered out. Emma froze and slid on the loose gravel beneath her feet.

Drakelow fell quiet. Even Emma's heart and breathing were muffled and miles away. The shuffling stopped, the air still hung cold—Bella was near. Emma needed to leave; she never should have come down.

Before she could take a step forward, ghostly fingers gripped her feet and yanked them out from under her. The coarse sandstone gravel bit and scraped as Bella dragged her deeper into the tunnels, away from the stairs and toward Burrow. The sandstone dust covering the floors caked into her bloody scalp as she was dragged. Emma kicked and thrashed. She snatched hold of the fairy lights and reeled the cord around her hand, feeling it snap taunt and then rip from the wall.

Bella halted as Emma pulled on the fairy lights, still fighting to free herself. A hand released her ankle and reached up, taking hold of her trouser leg. Emma's heart stopped. Her arms, weighted down by fear, froze as Bella's apparition crawled over the top of her.

The stench of putrid flesh and rotten wood engulfed Emma as Bella inched up her body. Gaining her senses, Emma brought the full force of the gun's grip down on what she hoped was Bella's head, passing straight through. Bella wisped away, hissing *those words*.

Down the tunnel, heavy footsteps pounded the floor, running toward her. Burrow huffed as he charged, raspy and hoarse. The ghost of Bella lunged at her again, nails digging deep in her side. Emma aimed the gun in the direction of the footsteps and squeezed the trigger, sending three rounds into the black of Drakelow. The muzzle flash lit up the corridor, revealing Bella crouched atop Emma and Burrow bearing down on both.

Burrow collapsed with a thud, and the cold grip of Bella released. Behind her, voices yelled out: "Shots fired, shots fired!"

Chapter 29
Webster's Journal

Thursday, 6ᵗʰ July, 1944

Morale at the station regarding the Hagley Wood murder, or the Bella Murder, as some have come to call it, has taken a turn for the worse. All leads have been exhausted, and no new evidence has surfaced in months. With the anniversary of her discovery come and gone, most at the station believe her murder will never be solved—a sentiment I share.

Several missing person cases provided hope for a short time, but they too dried up as they either didn't match an appropriate time frame or the individual in question had been located—oft deceased. I fear, and Insp. Inight shares this notion, that without a confessor, her death will remain a mystery.

One point of curiosity, only felt by me as the others thought it mundane to the point of boredom, was the discovery of several tineid moths in the morgue today. When I tracked down the source, I found a small infestation on Bella. This is nothing unusual as they are often found on corpses. Both *La Faune des Cadavres: Application de l'Entomologie à la*

Médecine Légale by Jean Pierre Mégnin and *Die Fliegen als Gerichtszeugen* by Reinhard Buchholz, written in 1894 and 1921 respectively, discuss at length the feasting patterns of insects at different stages of decomposition. The tineid moth, or in this case the Tinea pellionella or common clothes moth, often feeds on hair during their larval stage. That's not what piqued my curiosity insomuch as the fact Bella had been devoid of any such biological material for an extended period of time. Why would they now suddenly find an interest in her?

Saturday, 8th July, 1944

Today, I temporarily took great personal and professional satisfaction at solving the tineid moth quandary. After a detailed inspection of Bella, I found minute traces of organic material which would have attracted the moths. After feeling momentarily vindicated, the realisation settled in that I had previously missed this biological material in the original autopsy. Perhaps I should review my processes. While the error has been corrected, this lack of attention to detail is unbecoming of my professionalism, of which I have always taken much pride therein.

Friday, 14th July, 1944

My self-doubt has now turned into self-loathing. More biological material has been discovered on Bella's remains. Not only did I miss this material originally, but also just the prior week. To make this more complicated, this material is quite copious in some areas, making my oversights all the more glaring.

Thursday, 27th July, 1944

After my previous revelations with Bella, I have taken it upon myself to review several of my more recent cases. In each, my work maintained an impeccable example of detail oriented notations during the autopsy. No such errors, as found on Bella, have been detected in my other cases. Which leaves me with one hypothesis that is quite puzzling: if it is not my work, then clearly it is something about her remains.

Thursday, 3rd August, 1944

I have now reached the point of ceasing any further hypotheses regarding Bella, as there is nothing I can conceive to explain the events unfolding before my eyes. Each week, nay each day, I make another discovery which completely baffles me. As such, I will keep track of the events in a separate log that I can amend without any disconnecting entries between and then insert the logs as an attachment when completed. At that time, I will return here to give an overall summary. When that might be, only time will tell, but the most unfathomable, impossible hypothesis—of which I hope is not true—could be in circa 3 months' time if correct.

Thursday, 19th October, 1944

What has transpired over the last 77 days has been nothing short of astounding. For me, it began as a journey of curiosity, full of wondrous new scientific discoveries. However, as the reality of my observations took hold, the full ramifications of what was potentially happening transformed my curiosity into terror.

The events I describe herein transpired over an 82-day period as predicted, but to any reader, these phenomena will feel as if they took place in a single moment. Like a time-lapse reel played on the silver screen.

As I mentioned in previous entries, small tineid moths had chosen to complete their life cycle on remnants of tissue I had missed in my original autopsy. What I didn't realise was my original assessment, Bella's skeletal remains were void of any tissue, was correct. What I had actually witnessed was new organic material growing on Bella's remains.

Multiple hypotheses ran through my mind explaining the scenario, the most improbable theory being the one in which ended up being true. Confirmation didn't reveal itself immediately, as several more data sets were required to prove a definitive answer. The new data and events were as follows:

After the appearance of the tineid moths and trace amounts of new organic material, mold began to grow on portions of Bella's remains, eventually covering whole swaths of her skeleton. When the mold receded, it left behind copious amounts of material. Hints of fingernails, hair, and desiccated flesh. At this juncture, in what I have begun to call the Bella singularity, beetles arrived, exhibiting their normal behaviour during their life cycle on a skeletal corpse.

However, in that regard I was very wrong. On the surface, with only brief observation, it would be easy to make that mistake. After a deeper investigation, using the strongest magnifying glass available, I didn't observe the beetles *consuming* biological material on Bella, but instead they were *regurgitating* organic material. They were not aiding in decomposition but aiding in reconstitution. As I continued my detailed observation of the beetles, I was dumbfounded when I witnessed a small beetle enter its pupa, absorb it, and emerge as larvae. While that alone is worthy of its own study, it is more likely to be symptomatic of the overall Bella singularity than its own anomaly.

As copious amounts of organic material *collected* on Bella, gasses associated with decomposition also formed. I could not have predicted the foul stench that would consume the morgue. It was even beyond my level of tolerance and I could only spend a few moments at a time inspecting Bella. In my ignorance, I attempted to ventilate the morgue. To my dismay, this only exacerbated the situation. By reversing the flow *towards* Bella, the odor in the air lessened. I can only assume the flesh is absorbing the gases and converting the molecules into useful material.

At this point, around the start of October, nearly 60 days in, the appearance of flies and maggots came as no shock and was completely expected.

Obviously, morgues and forensic laboratories are designed to slow down decomposition by removing insect life and controlling the environment. This is in order to preserve the body in as pristine condition as possible for the sake of evidence collection. As I soon discovered, due to the nature of the Bella singularity, this was counterproductive. One needs to allow *nature*—or whatever force this is—to run its course. The end result: a lab and police station infested with all these critters.

Therefore, the events taking place in the morgue had become common knowledge amongst those in the station. While they have all sworn secrecy, they will not approach the morgue for any reason, mostly out of fear. My religious colleagues speak openly of eschatological resurrections in Revelations and of the Saints during Christ's crucifixion. While I do not share these beliefs, I do not fault their convictions as even I do not have a sufficient answer.

As the singularity reached its end course, which in essence is reverse decomposition, several fascinating, if not morbid, events had been witnessed. In particular, I had misplaced the T11 and T12 vertebrae in my initial skeletal reconstruction. To my amazement, over a period of two days, the respective sinews and tissue around these two vertebrae, flipped and re-aligned them into proper order. This brought my attention to the missing tibia and right hand. What would the body do with these missing parts?

It is important to note neither the tibia nor the missing hand are present. There is a clear indentation on the leg where the tibia should be, but the leg *developed* around it normally. The missing right hand and excision site on the wrist, how-ever, is a different mystery.

Chapter 30
The Suspension

Emma stared at the slide bite on her right hand; the skin ripped just between the webbing of her thumb and hand. It had already started to turn black and blue. She traced the injury with her left thumb, at the same time noticing she had missed some blood from the downed officer on the inside of her ring finger. Emma rubbed at it, leaving a dark red abrasion mark in its place.

Across the room, Chief Constable Harris' secretary clacked away on her keyboard. Occasionally, she glanced up at Emma as if she were perturbed she were here again. It wasn't like Emma wanted to be there either. She'd much rather change from this oversized, police issued PT sweatsuit and slip into a hot bath. Forensics confiscated her clothes after the injured officer nearly bled out on her trousers and Burrow's blood splattered her shirt when she shot him. Both were alive and in a critical condition, but Emma only cared if one pulled through.

Any minute, Noah Harris would come bursting through

the door to give her a thorough reaming. She had broken at least half a dozen procedures, not including unauthorized use of deadly force. Burrow had a nice sized hole in his gut because of her. Emma considered it justice for Oliver.

As she fidgeted with her hand and waited for Harris, her ear buzzed. A familiar ring that had grown all too common lately. Emma shook it off and blamed exhaustion, but something inside her knew otherwise. She didn't want to confront it yet—there was too much at stake, especially with Harris—but her awareness of the inevitable confrontation with the truth bore down on her like a freight train. The ring pulsed in her ear and consumed her thoughts until her vision blurred black.

*

She jolted to as Harris slammed the outer office door shut and belted at her, "My office, now!" She shifted her weight in her chair and sat up all the way. She blinked her eyes and looked at Harris, waiting for her vision to fully return. Where had she been?

"You just gonna sit there or get your arse moving?"

She jumped up, still wobbly from the blackout, and followed Harris into his office.

"Damn it, Lloyd," he yelled as he slammed the door behind her. "You have me in a real bind here."

Emma kept her mouth shut. Anything she had to say would either incriminate her or further infuriate Harris.

"No one in the department wants this. They all see you as the *hero of Drakelow*." Harris raised his hands and scoffed as he gestured air quotes. "But IOPC is all over this. What the hell were you thinking?"

Emma kept her head down. Her only thought was to plead the 5th. *How un-British of me...*

"That wasn't a rhetorical question, *Lloyd!* I want an answer."

She raised her head to meet his gaze. Tears welled up behind his bloodshot eyes and replaced his typical stoic demeanor.

"He could have killed you, Emma. He *wanted* to kill you! If Liam were here—"

Harris crossed a line. Fire flared up in Emma's gut and her teeth gnashed tight before he could finish his sentence. "Well, Liam isn't here, is he?" She leaned forward, digging her fingers into the arms of the chair. "Let's just get this out of the way, shall we? Liam is *dead*. And for whatever reason—only God knows why—you blame *me* for it."

Harris sat back in his chair, eyes wide. "I don't blame you for any—"

"No, no! You don't have the right to play that card now. I *needed* you when Liam was sick. I *needed* you when Liam died." Tears rolled down her face. "And whatever grievance you had with us getting married in the first place should have died with him. But it didn't, did it? You just let that fester and you pushed me away!"

"I didn't push you aw—"

"Shut your bloody mouth, right now, or I swear to God I'll shut it for you! I planned that entire funeral and wake by myself. You didn't lift a bloody finger, you arrogant ass! I came to you, *begging* for help, and all you gave me was a business card to a funeral home! A funeral home!"

Harris asserted himself enough to answer. "Emma! I didn't push you away! I didn't know what to do. I had just lost my brother—my only family. I was grieving. He was the world to me!"

Emma crossed her arms and slunk back into her chair, hot tears still trickling down. It didn't change how hurt she had been, knowing Noah had left her alone to deal with everything. But he wasn't wrong, either. After they lost their parents as children, they clung to one another as they drifted through the foster system.

"I *know* I could have done better; I *know* I can be a better brother-in-law. I just—I couldn't bury him, Emmy. I couldn't do it." A hollow shell had replaced the man she knew. Emma didn't recognize the person sitting across from her, face buried in his burly hands, weeping, slumping forward with his elbows on the desk. The stout *man's man* was now reduced to blubbering tears. Perhaps this was the first time he allowed himself to grieve.

Emma recalled that same moment for her in therapy. She spent months blaming the doctors, blaming the nurses, blaming God. The moment she realized there was no one left to blame—including herself—the floodgates of grief finally gave. Was this *his* moment? Had he been holding it in all this time?

Minutes passed like waves on a shore, unaware of how many, just letting them crash on the sand as one sits in the moment, taking it in for all it's worth. Before either of them could speak, the intercom buzzed. Harris pried his face from his hands and quickly composed himself before answering, "Yes, Maggie. What is it?"

"It's Insp. Hall from IOPC on line 1, inquiring about… Dr Lloyd."

"Tell him I'll call back shortly. Thank you."

Harris flipped the tears away with his thumb before continuing. "You're right... I shouldn't have brought Liam into this. As much as I hate to admit it, and though you might not believe me, you are all I have left of him." Emma brooded in silence, digesting his apology.

Clearing his voice and rubbing his hands on his face, Harris picked up the file in front of him. "Emmy, there's no way around it. Bryant Jones is all over this like a fly on shit. He's screaming scandal to anyone who will listen and unfortunately, he has the ear of the IOPC. The woman who was first attacked by the assailant, who was then present during his escape, was the same woman who used an unauthorized weapon against the same individual. To make it worse, she just so happens to be the sister-in-law of the Chief Constable. And the unusual circumstances of your hire are not making anything easier. My hands are tied here."

"What are you saying? I'm fired?" Emma scowled at Noah.

"No. No one in the department wants to see that, but the IOPC needs to see a proper, hands-off investigation at my end. For your sake, and mine, I can't be anywhere near this. I have to hand it over. However, placing you on administrative leave, pending the investigation, is the last thing in my ability to protect you. Please, don't feel singled out, this is standard procedure for any officer involved in a shooting."

Emma swallowed hard, knowing it was the fair thing to do. She had screwed up—there was no question.

"You can thank Supt. Bennett for putting in a good word on your behalf. He spoke very highly of you. So, along with Charlie Team's statements and McArthur's report, they all afforded me a little wiggle room. If there is anything you need from Hagley, you have till morning to pick it up. Any questions?"

Emma quietly shook her head no and wiped a few straggling tears from her face. She left without saying another word.

Her mind swirled with *what if's* and hypotheticals as she drove back to Hagley from Hindlip. How long would the investigation take? Where should she stay in the meantime? The thought of being pent up in that dank hotel room for God knows how long reeked of torture. She couldn't exactly go home—everything was boxed up, packed, and prepared for the move. *Ugh—do I even keep looking at this point?* she thought.

Penelope would take her back in, but was that what she wanted to do? Crawl back to her friends and give up? No. She couldn't do that—Emma refused to. Taylor, Evans, and Edwards deserved to have this finished. And Bella wouldn't allow her to walk away even if she tried.

Pulling into the car park of Hagley station and feeling Bella's incessant beckoning reminded her of that fact. Bella would never let go.

The bullpen bustled with activity, exactly what she wanted to avoid—other people. Over the ringing of phones and officers' chatter, one lone voice could be heard: Bella's. She called with such urgency that it pulled on Emma's bowels, as if they would rupture from the inside out. Emma winced as she closed the gate to Otis. When she came into the lab, Bella's drawer swung back and forth, clanging against the metal behind it. She marched over, grabbed a padlock from a drawer, and bolted it shut. She didn't know if she had the key—she didn't care.

Emma packed her things; her spiraled pocket notebook, her laptop, a few personal items, and inadvertently—unaware of her actions—Bella's files. She slung her bag over her shoulder and ignored Bella's pleas to let her out. The other three morgue doors burst open and swung as Bella's door rattled in place. Emma clenched her eyes shut as she bolted for the door. Amidst the chaos, her phone buzzed.

She rushed out of the lab and slammed the doors behind her, taking two giant steps to reach the perilous comforts of Otis. Emma, still panting from her sprint, closed the cage doors. Curiously, a tineid moth fluttered in and alighted upon on her sleeve. She brushed it away and leaned her head against the wall of the lift as she pushed the button for the ground floor. Otis jerked as it carried its passenger upwards. Relieved to be free of Bella—if even for a moment—Emma sighed and ran her hands through her hair and then checked the notification screen on her smartwatch. One new email:

Ancestry: Your results are Ready!
You have 1 family member in the area.

Chapter 31

The Granddaughter

Steam billowed out of the blue and white floral kettle as the hot water poured into the matching teacup placed before Emma. The aroma of the tea enveloped her, calming her for the first time in weeks, though she feared it wouldn't last long. The whole flat, in fact, gave Emma a sense of peace. A traditional, yet modern, compact sitting room, light and airy and full of all the little things that make a house a home.

The host, Sarah Hawkins, had spent her whole life in that flat, inheriting it from her father in the late 70s and then raising three children of her own there. Over the years, her life had further been blessed with five grandchildren, all of whom had at least half a dozen pictures displayed in prominent locations around the sitting room and the rest of the home. Toys and children's books peeked out from the bottom bookshelf next to the sofa where they had been tucked away—sweet reminders of how often they came to visit their granny.

It was the type of life people dreamed of—a simple, but happy life full of love and family. Something Bella had been deprived of, though in a way, lived on here.

"So you found me on the interwebs?" asked Sarah. Her voice was sweet and gentle, still youthful, not at all showing her age of a woman at almost 80. Her gray hair was trimmed short, much like the fashion of many in her generation, though the photo of her on the table stand—without question from many years past—revealed long, black hair, cascading down her shoulders.

"Sort of," replied Emma. "I found you via a service called Ancestry. It's a DNA company."

"Oh yes, I remember that now! My little Danny, who isn't so little now with two munchkins of his own, got me that for my 65th birthday. It was fascinating to see all those charts showing where your ancestors were from. I have loads from here in England and Wales. Got some French, a little Dutch and Scandinavian. Oh, and some Greek, too. I love Greece. The food is just divine. You ever been?"

"No, I haven't had the pleasure," Emma said.

"You must go, dearie. They make these hors d'oeuvres from feta cheese, dipped in a sweet batter, deep fried, and then served with drizzled honey and sprinkles of sesame seeds on top. Sweet meets salty. What I wouldn't give for one right now!"

"That does sound delicious."

Sarah clasped her hands together and smiled giddily. "I can't believe I'm sitting here with my great-grand niece. You are literally the only relative I have ever met on my father's side. When Danny said you'd reached out to him via the website, I nearly dropped dead from excitement."

Emma loathed herself for not correcting the lie. After all, it wasn't *her* great-aunt who graciously welcomed her into her home, but *Bella's* granddaughter. The resemblance was uncanny—the same pudgy nose and eyes. Emma imagined if Bella were here sitting with them, they'd easily pass as sisters. The immediate thought of Bella in the room twisted her stomach.

"All this from that little swab from my cheek," Sarah continued. "Isn't science brilliant?"

"It absolutely is. It's why I teach science." The hole just kept getting deeper and deeper. Emma had to cut to the chase, or she'd never remember the tale she'd weaved. "So, tell me about your father. What does he know of his parents? I'm completely baffled anytime I try to go past my granny on the family tree."

"My father, Charles, was an amazing man." Sarah's face beamed with pride. "He came from nothing and built quite a life with my mother. After he returned from the war, he worked the coal mines for Hamstead Colliery right up until they closed in 1965."

Emma's head grew light as Sarah spoke of her father. The teacup, its contents of which she had almost finished, rattled in her hand as her fingers twitched. She sensed the darkness closing in on her; the small dots forming on the edge of her vision like droplets of mist preceding a downpour.

Her mind blanked, falling dead to everything around her despite Emma's efforts to remain focused. A small black void, no larger than a letterbox, opened up over Sarah's shoulder, near the bookshelf. Inching outward from the void, tendrils of tree branches crept around the room like ivy. Before long, its boughs had twisted amongst the lamp and curtains, reaching across the breadth of the room and devouring everything in sight. All that remained were Emma, Sarah, and that God forsaken wych elm with its hollow, bereft of life, stealing away the warmth of the room. The void pulled on Emma's gaze, forcing her to be drawn deeper and deeper into its emptiness. But it wasn't empty. Malice bled forth like ink from a quill held on paper for too long. Emma's heart fell cold as she sank into its despair.

The boughs creaked and snapped as its branches crept under the sofa and wrapped around Sarah's ankles. The words from Sarah's lips fell muffled in Emma's ears, jumbled under the buzzing sound in her ear. Tendrils of the wych elm weaved over the sofa and traced their way up the sleeve of the unaware host. Amidst her story, the black and gnarled twigs twisted around her throat. Emma dropped her tea and lunged forward to free Sarah, but the tendrils had already ensnarled Emma's wrists. The hollow swelled and the tree pulled everything in its reach toward it—toward the void. First Sarah, swallowed by the darkness, then Emma, enveloped by the wych elm's hollow.

"Dearie, are you okay?" asked Sarah, reaching out and steadying Emma's hand.

Snapping to, Emma feigned a smile. "Yes, I'm sorry. I'm fine. Just exhaustion—long week and all." Emma glanced over Sarah's shoulder at the bookshelf, lit by the afternoon sun peeking through the curtains.

"We can stop and continue another day. It's no problem." Sarah offered Emma a sweet, reassuring smile. "Or perhaps you'd just like another cuppa?"

"Yes, thank you. That'd be great."

Sarah poured another piping hot cup and continued on with her story—how much of it Emma had missed she could only guess. "My father worked long, tiring hours during those years, but that never kept him from spending every waking moment with me as a child. What he couldn't lavish me with in wealth, he bestowed in love." A sick feeling lingered behind in Emma's gut, but she couldn't place why—just a faint feeling of something dark. "Perhaps my father just wanted to give me what he was deprived of all those years growing up in a Wolverhampton orphanage."

"Wolverhampton? Really? That's unusual for an orphan not from the upper class."

"Oh yes, my dear. That's one of the little mysteries he always ran into when he attempted to trace his heritage. You had to have been from wealth to be there as an orphan. Even more so after it converted into a boarding school for the rich several years after he left."

"So he's never been able to track down any information about his parents? Nothing from Wolverhampton?"

"He hit a roadblock—the headmaster at the time cited privacy laws or some nonsense. But I can't say he doesn't know anything." Sarah lifted up a ragged shoe box from the floor next to her feet and placed it on the coffee table, sliding the Gardener's World and children's CBeebies Magazines to the side. When she removed the lid, faded photos from her parents' youth burst the corners of the box open, revealing a handful of documents lining the bottom. She carefully pulled a letter from the bundle and held it reverently in her hand. "Just before his 18th birthday, his mother came to visit him at the orphanage."

Emma's jaw dropped. "He met his mother?"

"Yes, just the once. At the time, he wanted nothing to do with her. Bitterness ran pretty deep in him in those early years. Mother said the war beat that out of him. While many men came home broken, he came home thankful to be alive and well, having escaped the 'depths of hell to live another day'."

"What happened when they met?" asked Emma.

"Nothing, unfortunately. Said he wanted nothing to do with the woman who left him there all alone. A pity, really. A choice he grew to regret in later years." Sarah grew sullen for a moment before she continued. "Anyway, the next day, the headmaster delivered this letter to him. It's the only memento he has of her. No picture—save his memory—just this letter."

Sarah tenderly opened the envelope and slid it out, tearfully re-reading it for the umpteenth time. "There were nights I'd wake up and head down for a glass of water to find my father sitting at the table, weeping over this letter. It was his greatest treasure. While many would have spoken ill of their parents if they were in his shoes, my father, on the other hand, never once said a bad word about her. In the end, he loved her and missed her."

She handed Emma the letter, its edges torn and wrinkled in places. The creases ran deep across the width of the yellowed paper, splitting it into perfect thirds and allowing it to be comfortably tucked away in its worn envelope. The ink was still readable, but it had clearly faded over the years. Emma gave it a quick glance, speed-reading parts of it. A chill brushed across her shoulders, sweeping the words on the paper to the side and replacing them with the eerie reminder of her true quest. Emma shrugged it off the best she could before returning to her inquiry.

"Is this the original envelope?"

"Yes, love. Why?"

"I was hoping for a return address or something."

"No, sadly enough. She must have hand delivered it or

left it after her initial meeting, knowing he might reject her."

Emma flipped the envelope around in her hands and in-spected the edges. "Was it just the letter? It looks like some-thing else was in here, too."

"You have keen eyes, my dear. She left him 500 pounds. A lot of money for an orphan back then. I did the maths once. It's about ten thousand quid today."

"Did he say where she got the money?"

"No. And that's what always confused him. He said her clothes were clearly second-hand. Dirt up underneath her nails and scuffed shoes. Her face was worn, as she appeared much older than she probably really was, like she had been in manual labor her whole life. I imagine she looked much like my father did when he passed. In the end, the money, like his enrollment at Wolverhampton, were a complete enigma."

"May I take a photo of the letter? Is that alright? Perhaps there's something I could find later on down the road."

"Of course, be my guest!"

Emma unfolded the letter and laid it flat on the table, plac-ing a book and paperweight on the corners to keep it open. She focused her phone's camera and snapped a couple of pic-tures. She inspected them to ensure the quality was useable and got distracted analyzing the letter. It was the handwriting. Something about it looked familiar.

Chapter 32
A Mother's Love

My dearest Charles,

Despite my dashed dreams, I respect your wishes to be left alone, though I hope one day that will change. For now, I'll leave you this sole letter as my one and only explanation as to why I left you all those years ago. I pray you at least give me this opportunity.

Your father and I were very much in love. He was a very handsome man and I see him in you. Your birth, while un-planned, was something we very much looked forward to. In our hearts, the world was our oyster, and you were the pearl.

But life had other plans. Your father left for the great war and didn't return the same, if he returned at all. After years of complications from the Sulphur mustard scaring his lungs, I was left widowed and with child, surrounded by a family which had rejected me for what they saw as a reckless tryst. My hand was forced. I wept endlessly after you were sent away and you have never departed from my hopes and dreams a single day since.

I know you are almost a man and about to enter this frightening world, but my prayer was that we could do that together. My family has all but turned their back on me and my only wish is to start anew somewhere else. I had hoped with you.

I have enclosed what little I have for you to begin your life, perhaps make a home somewhere and maybe even start a family. I would love to know you have lived the life that your father and I dreamt of for you.

I love you with all my heart, dear son. I forever pray for blessings upon you.

Love,
Your mother

Chapter 33
Prison Interview

If Phillip's knee didn't stop bouncing, Bryant Jones was going to slap the nervousness out of him. The IOPC had assigned this plonker to Bryant to assist in the investigation into CSI Emma Lloyd despite Bryant's objections. Sure, he understood the importance of accountability and he appreciated the help, but at least assign someone competent enough not to piss himself while conducting an interview. Even if the interviewee *was* a hulking multi-murderer known for targeting police.

Bryant put his laptop and files onto the cold metal table in the prison consultation room while they waited for Timothy Burrow and his barrister. "Have you seen the CCTV footage of the shooting?"

"Yes," replied Phillip. "The whole thing creeps me out. The static that *moves* with Burrow through the station—nope, no thank you. Have you heard what people say?"

"Meh, it's nonsense. People let their imagination run wild and create all kinds of idiotic fantasies. It's all poppycock."

"I don't know. A part of me thinks it's true."

"Which part? You mean where the ghosts of his murder victims try to warn others away?"

"Okay, so it sounds weird when you say it out loud like that, but you have to admit that weird follows this guy everywhere he goes."

The door behind them opened, and Bryant quickly closed the video. Burrow's chains rattled as he shuffled around the table and took a seat across Bryant and next to his barrister, Reginald Smythe QC, a mouse of a man compared to his client.

"Good morning, gentlemen," said Smythe. "I've agreed to this interview with the explicit condition that the focus of your inquiry remains on the actions of West Mercia Police Authority and Dr Emma Lloyd. If, at any time, I feel the focus has shifted to my client, I will terminate the interview post haste. Understood?"

"Absolutely," replied Bryant. "Our goal is purely to investigate the conduct of Ms Lloyd." Phillip sheepishly agreed.

"If all parties are in agreement, then you may begin." Smythe turned to Burrow. "Only answer the questions you feel comfortable answering. Okay? And remember, we can stop at any time."

Timothy nodded.

Bryant opened another video file and spun his computer around so he could play it for Burrow and Smythe. "I need your help filling in the blanks—adding a little context here. The original video file has some... *imperfections* shall we say. What pictures did Ms Lloyd show you here?"

Bryant pressed the space bar and played the file. The audio clicked and popped as Emma interrogated Burrow—every other word missing or distorted. As she set the photos in front of Burrow, static streaked across the screen and obscured them from view.

Burrow scrunched his brows and chewed his lip as he thought back. "The first one was the graffiti on the station. Yes, that's right. She asked if I wrote it."

"And these others? Especially the last three."

"The first few… they were also graffiti in Hagley. She wanted to know if I did them, too."

"Yes, but these last three specifically. I can make out the first ones—I need to know what these last three were." Bryant zoomed in and paused the video on the distorted pictures in question.

"I don't remember. I thought they were all photos of graffiti in Hagley." Burrow looked around the table as if someone would tell him how to respond.

"Yes, I believe they are," Bryant said. "But can you tell me any specifics about these photos? Where were they taken? Outdoors, indoors, on brick, on concrete, et cetera."

"No, I don't remember. I just remember they were graffiti," replied Burrow.

Bryant took a deep breath and exhaled slowly, rolling his neck and massaging one shoulder. Completely useless interview. "Okay, okay, no problem. Let's move to another section here." He scrubbed the video forward to another sequence. "Who did she show you here? It looks like a portrait of some kind."

"It was just some woman. I don't know who she was. Never seen her before."

"It looks like there is a sticker in the lower corner here. Something is written on it. Do you remember what it said?"

Timothy squinted at the screen as he leaned in to look closer and then shook his head no.

"I really need you to try, Timothy. It's very important."

"I'm sorry. I only looked at the face and I only saw it for a second."

"I understand. There was a lot of pressure on you that day. Easy to forget details on a first glance. Just close your eyes and try to recall the moment. Trace the image in your mind. Don't think about the whole picture but scan it to see if any details stick out. Eye color, piercings, scars. Things that might trigger other details. It might help you remember other parts of the photo, like the label."

Burrow did as instructed, but after a few seconds his brows furrowed and he shook his head again. "I'm sorry, mister. I just can't remember anything."

"Please, I need you to try harder."

Smythe held his hand up and stopped Burrow. "My client says he doesn't remember."

"Okay, okay," replied Bryant. "How about this photo? This one invoked quite the reaction from you. I'm sure you'd have to remember it." Bryant moved the timeline forward a few frames.

Burrow shifted his weight in his seat, causing the metal to creak. Bryant thought it would snap under his weight if he kept jostling about.

"I-I-I don't remember."

"How can you not remember? You freaked out and fell to the floor at the sight of that photo! I mean, if something terrifies me that much, I remember it. I think we all would. Things like that have a tendency to stick with you."

Clearly agitated, Burrow answered, "I'm sorry... I don't

remember anything that happened after this. I get blackouts sometimes, sometimes for hours on end, and I can't remember anything that happens."

"Blackouts, uh-huh, right. So you had *one of these* blackouts during the interrogation?"

"Yes. I remember Ms Lloyd coming in and asking about Stacey and the graffiti. But as she started asking about the woman, it all got jumbled and dark in my head."

"So this second picture, the one that frightened you, was also a picture of a woman? The same woman?"

"Erm, yeah? I think so?"

"You think or you know? Please be clear."

"I think so? I can't really recall. It made me dark inside—like now. I really don't want to talk about it anymore. I don't feel well."

Phillip slid a bottle of water across the table.

Timothy, both hands shackled together, grasped the bottle and chugged its contents, water dripping from the corners of his mouth and drizzling his ragged beard.

"I know this is difficult for you," Bryant began, "but it's very important we know the details so we can prosecute Ms Lloyd and prevent anyone from having to suffer as you have."

Phillip side eyed Bryant and cleared his throat.

"Do you have something you want to add, Phillip? " asked Bryant.

"M-maybe we should move on?"

"Yes, I think that's a good idea," said Smythe.

"Okay, fine. Let's go to the day they raided Drakelow; the second time you were apprehended. Do you remember that day more clearly? Or did you have any more blackouts?" Bryant didn't even attempt to mask his inconsiderate tone.

Timothy slunk in his chair and tried to make himself smaller, as if someone his size could actually do so. "I can't control them—they just happen." His eyes dropped to the floor and he shifted his weight again, stressing the chair's joints and bending the frame.

"Listen, you are clearly upsetting my client. This is a debilitating medical condition which he has suffered from for several years."

"I hear you, but his inability to remember hampers my investigation." Bryant turned to Burrow. "Which, need I remind you, helps your case, Mr Burrow." Bryant's teeth ground between words; he'd have his answers one way or another. "So, moving on to that day in the tunnels. Why did you attack Ms Lloyd?"

"Timothy, don't answer that. This interview is over. Guards!" Smythe motioned to the window and waved for them to come in. Timothy lumbered to his feet—his fetters rattling like a children's ghost story. Smythe straightened his suit coat and stuffed his notes into his briefcase.

Bryant reared back and crossed his arms, huffing in response. Neither Bryant nor Phillip spoke until the pair left the room. "Why did you have to push so hard?" asked Phillip.

"Why did you have to sit there like a useless dimwit?" Bryant retorted.

"I just think we could have been a little more sympathetic to him—to get what we needed."

"Yeah, well, that would have been easier if King Kong hadn't hidden behind his *condition*. He knows more than he's letting on. I can tell."

"If he does, we'll never get it out of him now. You've made sure of that. Burrow's barrister will never allow us to speak with him again."

Bryant scoffed and rolled his eyes. "He'll come round. Once he realizes he can get a shorter sentence, he'll become much more compliant." He packed up his computer and files and left Phillip in the room. Bryant had other angles to pursue which required returning to Hagley.

He followed the yellow guidelines painted on the floor, leading him to the exit. A series of security doors separated him from the outside. He waited as each one slid open and closed in sequence before navigating through them. The air was no less stale on the outside than behind bars, but the sight of freedom made the air sweeter nonetheless. Bryant returned his visitor's ID to the guard desk and spun round toward the exit, meeting a surprise in the process—Oliver Bennett.

"Good afternoon, Superintendent," said Bryant wearing a smug grin.

"Afternoon, Jones. What trouble are you up to today?"

"Oh, I just had a glorious conversation with our resident giant. He had some interesting things to say."

"Did he tell you why he killed eight of our men?"

"Don't be sexist, Bennett. He killed Officer Brown and tried to kill Lloyd. He was an equal opportunist."

Oliver scowled. "Your depravity really has no boundaries, does it? Do you actually care about anyone?"

"Yes, of course. There are three very important people in my life. Thank you very much. Me, Myself, and I." Bryant snickered at his own joke.

"I hope the three of you have a long, wonderful relationship." Oliver shook his head and turned to walk away.

"It's more than what I can say about you and your unhinged Dr Lloyd once I get finished with her—"

Oliver lunged back and pinned him against the wall, jamming his left elbow under Bryant's chin. "I never want to hear her name come out of your mouth again." Oliver's fist clenched tight, but it remained steadfast at his side.

"Hey, hey, relax… it's not my fault." Bryant popped his hands up and feigned innocence. "She got herself into this all on her own. I'm just following facts."

"Be careful with that. One day that *fact following* is gonna get you into a heap of trouble. And no one but *You, Yourself, and Bryant* will be there to get you out." Oliver gave him a shove and let go. The guards behind the visitor's window pretended not to notice the altercation.

Bryant responded with his patent smile, straightening his wrinkled shirt and tucking it back in. "And you be careful of that temper. It's unbecoming of a superintendent."

Chapter 34
Webster's Journal

Thursday, 19ᵗʰ October, 1944

All eyes fell upon me as I arrived at the station today—the visceral tension was palpable. I entered the morgue and placed my things upon my table as I am wont to do, and then pulled the sheet back from Bella to discover the smell of decomposition had dissipated. Pressing into her upper thigh and torso, I tested for stiffness to which I discovered had begun to set in.

The clock had now started, though I could not say specifically when. Since rigor normally sets in the face first and progresses downward into the larger muscle groups and then wanes in the same order, it is only logical the legs would be 'first'. I promptly checked the jaw and eyes for any signs of stiffness, indicators of full rigor.

To my relief, the muscles of the face were still supple. I made my way down her body, checking her muscles and joints, and found that rigor only presented in the larger muscle groups. I had discovered it at the 'beginning'. The approximate clock of T-Minus 36 hours had now begun, give or take a few hours.

As expected, it was near full twelve hours for full rigor to set in, reversing from the lower extremities towards her face and fingers. At that point, the clock was confirmed around 24 hours remaining.

While one could have been caught enthralled by the unique event, the singularity provided opportunities that never would have been available in a case as far removed from the time of death, assumed to be 18-plus months to April 1943. We could now observe her condition as they were after her demise.

I chose to start with her excised right hand. The flesh and bone showed clear signs of tool markings. Not from a saw type instrument that could cut through bone, but something sharp enough to cut the flesh and sinews and manoeuvre between the carpal bones and the ulna and radius. More than likely, a sharp knife due to the clean lacerations in the skin and musculature. Naturally I questioned if the hand was removed postmortem or perimortem.

I attempted to biopsy a small portion of tissue around the wound to test for any inflammation, a typical sign of an ante-mortem injury. However, after excising a sample of muscular tissue, I immediately observed it growing back at an astounding rate. Likewise, the tissue in my sample dish rotted away and was no longer viable. All in all, par for the course for the singularity. I had to perform the test a second time, bearing in mind I had but moments to examine the tissue.

The wound, clearly inflamed, had been antemortem or perimortem, perhaps within minutes to an hour before her death. There is no telling how much she suffered during that time.

As I inspected the rest of her body, there was a noticeable

indentation around her midsection. A deep, six-inch incision extended from the right side across her midsection, stopping near the navel. Inside the wound, copious amounts of subcutaneous adipose tissue that would normally be present were missing. This wound, unlike her hand, occurred postmortem. The directionality of the incision indicated a left-handed motion.

While exsanguination from the excised hand presents itself as the most probable cause of death, there were two other visible and plausible wounds on her body that needed consideration: a large laceration in the occipital region of the victim's head and extensive bruising around her neck.

The laceration is approximately one inch in length and appears to be caused by blunt force trauma. Like her hand, the laceration was perimortem. The extent of the wound does not appear severe enough to be the cause of death, but perhaps incidental during a struggle or inflicted to incapacitate the victim.

The pattern of the ligature mark on her neck, V-shaped and angling upwards, as well as the width and pattern of the bruising, clearly indicates a rope or noose-like instrument was used. Upon observing her eyes and detecting petechial hemorrhaging, it confirms, with a significant degree of accuracy, strangulation as the cause of death. What cannot be determined at this time is if she was hanged or if an individual stood above her at a significant height and strangled her with a rope-like garrote.

Unfortunately, being that the victim is a woman, there was one extremely private examination remaining; one that is never pleasant, especially if confirmed. For simplicity's sake, I shall spare the details and simply state that a crime of a sexual nature had *not* been committed prior to or after death. In this regard, she was spared one terrible fate.

My observations indicated that the general chronological sequence of events were as such:

1. Initial attack (antemortem, non-sexual in nature)
2. Gag (piece of taffeta) inserted into mouth (antemortem, timeline uncertain)
3. Incapacitation from the head wound (perimortem)
4. Removal of the hand (perimortem)
5. Hanging or strangulation causing death
6. Excision of the subcutaneous adipose tissue from the abdomen (postmortem)
7. Insertion into the Hollow (postmortem)

I then checked the clock and noted another approximate three hours remaining in full rigor state, leaving around twelve hours remaining before the 'time of death'. It was now just a waiting game.

Chapter 35
The Headmaster

The aroma of rich mahogany and antique books filled the headmaster's office of The Royal School of Wolverhampton, exactly what one would expect in a bicentennial school building. Behind the headmaster's grand desk an antique hutch rested against the wall, packed with works from literary greats of British literature: Shakespeare, William Blake, T. S. Eliot, Charles Dickens, Jane Austen, Lord Tennyson, and Emily Brontë among the many neatly lining the shelves. Some of the bindings were so worn that Emma couldn't read the spines as she awaited the headmaster to arrive.

Her attention quickly shifted to the beautiful view out of the headmaster's window overlooking the quad where she imagined, all those years ago, Bella stood begging the young Charles to listen to her plea. The other children gawking at the awkward sight—some jealous that Charles had a family and equally confused why he'd push them away.

The shadows outside stretched long across the quad indicating late afternoon and Emma wondered if the headmaster would see her at this hour. His secretary, who had seated her in the office, assured her he'd arrive promptly to assist her query.

Emma hadn't thought through how to play this yet. Fooling an elderly woman into thinking you're long lost family in order to gather information was far easier than tricking a school administrator who was accustomed to the fibs of school children and had learned to see through them. Perhaps, considering her skills of deception were lacking, playing this straight from the hip and being honest was the best approach.

The door swung open and a distinguished gentleman, wearing a blue blazer with an embroidered school crest, barged in and offered his hand. "Good afternoon. I'm terribly sorry for the delay. I had a few students that needed attending to. It's summer, but we do run several end-of-holidays activities each year. I'm Dr Williams, Headmaster of The Royal School. Pleased to meet you."

"Very pleased to meet you as well," Emma replied as she decided at the last second her angle: honesty. "I'm CSI Emma Lloyd from the Hagley police station of West Mercia Police."

"Officer Lloyd, I hope this isn't pertaining to any of my students. I would hope none of them have wandered so far as Hagley to make trouble." He leaned back in his plush leather office chair and crossed his arms.

"I'm a crime scene investigator, I'm not an officer. And to answer your question, much to your relief I'm sure, my query has nothing to do with any current pupil nor staff. So please, don't worry."

"That is a relief! As headmaster, you always fear getting blindsided by some scandal from your students or staff. My next assumption is a child you wish to enroll? I must tell you in advance, we do have a strict policy about accepting new students after the spring deadline. Exceptions can be made in extenuating circumstances, of course."

"No, no, it's not that either. It is a police related matter, but it's involving a cold case I have inherited from my predecessor."

"A cold case?" Dr Williams' eyes lit up with excitement as he leaned forward. "There's nothing quite like an unsolved quandary to get the neurons firing. I'm not sure how I can help, but I'm always keen on brushing up my armchair sleuthing skills. What's the case? A thief? A missing person? A murder, perhaps? And how is it that The Royal School can assist?"

Emma was encouraged that she had piqued his interest. Perhaps she'd played the right card after all. "It's a murder case, actually. Unknown victim, Jane Doe scenario. We were able to perform some DNA testing and determined that a family member, most likely their child, was a student here. Somewhere around 1921 and finishing circa 1939."

"Fascinating—that certainly is a cold case. What type of information are you seeking?"

"Anything really, a birth certificate, adoption or enrollment papers, payment receipts, et cetera. Whatever would allow us to identify the family of the student, specifically the mother."

Dr Williams furled his brows and sat back in his chair contemplatively. "1921 to 1939. That's going to be a challenge. There was a small fire back in the 60s—nothing major—but it did affect the records room and some of our oldest files. Quite unfortunate, really. But not all is lost! It only affected a limited portion of our archive."

"Is there a way to check? If the individual's records are still intact?"

"Yes! And quickly, I might add. A couple of years ago, one of our classes undertook a project to create a queryable database of all our students, past and present. It was quite the endeavor. The teacher, Professor Anderson, really pushed…"

Emma feigned interest in his little tangent, only in hopes that she'd easily get the information she sought. He chatted on for several minutes about the project and all the hurdles and obstacles involved. Slowly, she couldn't keep focus and her attention drifted to the window again.

A gentle summer breeze ruffled the trees in the courtyard. Their branches swayed back and forth, ebbing with the wind. Almost out of view from the window, Emma saw a figure standing in the shade of a little cherry tree. The figure, a woman to Emma's best guess, appeared to be staring back at her. Chills rolled down her skin.

"Name? Ms Lloyd? The name of the individual you are inquiring about?"

Emma snapped out of it and quickly replied, "I'm sorry—yes, um, Roberts, Charles Roberts." She looked back out the window—the woman was gone.

"Looks like we have a few possible hits. You said it would have been around 1921-1939? Can you narrow those dates to his enrollment years?"

"As far as I know, he was enrolled shortly after birth," replied Emma.

"Well, Wolverhampton orphanage enrollment, much like The Royal School today, didn't accept anyone prior to their seventh year. It's highly doubtful he would have been taken in as an infant. Let's narrow it down to, say, 1927 to 1930?"

Emma nodded. "Your guess is as good as mine."

"There we go, 1928-1939, Charles Roberts. Born 1921. Not all his records are digitized. A few will be stored in our archives in the administration wing. I can send someone to fetch the files and or print out what we have in the system now."

"That would be fantastic, thank you."

"But," he interjected.

"I was waiting for the but…"

"His enrollment is 1928. So, I'm assuming you have a court order for these documents?"

"It's a cold case—everything is basically off the books or has zero priority," replied Emma.

"That puts us at a roadblock. However, you're in a bit of luck. Since it is a very old cold case, meaning time is not of the essence—I'm assuming—you can come back in five years and you can get his documents, no problem. National law declares any personal data over 100 years as *free domain* so to speak. No court order needed."

"Ugh—five years? There isn't anything you can do? I'm so close to confirming the victim's identity. Giving this poor woman a name for the first time in 80 years."

"I wish I could help, I really do. When you first said 1921, I was quite hopeful, but you know as well as I do, the law is the law."

Emma wanted to reach across the desk and give him a smack in the head. "No, I get it. I do. Just frustrating to be this close and to walk away empty-handed."

Dr Williams tapped his fingers on his desk and then gave a little grin. "I tell you what." He wore the devious smile well. "I'll take a look at the records myself. If I see a name of any family members attached to the file, say a mother's name,

I'll—accidentally leave it scribbled on a piece of paper on my desk. Give me twenty minutes?"

"Yes! Thank you so much!"

Dr Williams pushed back from the desk and headed toward the archives. Emma couldn't contain her eagerness. Had the key to Bella been here all the time, sitting in a filing cabinet waiting to be discovered? Her eyes once again drew to the window to see the woman standing by the tree. Emma studied her, feeling as if she knew her from somewhere. The deeper she gazed, the deeper her mind fell to darkness.

A memory, not her own, surfaced from the recesses of her mind, swirling in the blackness of her thoughts. The grass swarmed around as she was raked over the roots and stones of the forest floor. Emma's hair pulled on her scalp, yanking and tearing the flesh; a trickle of blood formed on her brow. She reached up and felt a hand gripping tight, twisting her hair around its tense fingers. Emma clawed, ripping deep gashes into the flesh of the arm and hand, leaving chunks of skin under her nails. Her shoe flung across the grove as she kicked to free herself. Her heart raced as a fist slammed down upon her several times and then bashed her skull on a rock. Her head reeled as she tried to gain control of her senses. Crashing down upon her like a wave upon rock, pain seized her senses before Emma could come to. *Schhht, schhht, schhht* pulsed as the last feeling of a warm wet substance drenched her hand before changing to an intense prickling and pings of pain radiating up the nerves of her arm. Emma attempted to scream but was thwarted by a strip of cloth shoved into her mouth. A rope was slung over her head and cinched tight around her neck. Little by little, rhythmic tugs hoisted her off the ground, leaving her to swing as she choked. She strove to reach the ground, but her toes just grazed the grass below. Her lungs burned as she gasped; her bloody stump and fingers scratched at the rope around her throat. Then she fell still. Emma's limp body squirmed as wet metal pierced her stomach, gutting and excising flesh. After her disemboweling, she fell back to earth. The leaves rustled around her as a shadowy figure dragged her body to a tree and lifted her up. Her joints snapped and popped from the contortions of her lifeless corpse being stuffed in the hollow of the tree. Emma's mind, separated from her body, glared at the man, seeking out the face of her tormentor. She could not as the shadows of the woods obscured the man's features. She screamed into the nothingness. *Who put me in the wych elm?!*

The door to the headmaster's office flew open and smashed into the cabinet behind, startling Emma. Dr Williams and his secretary froze in place as she crouched on his desk. "What in God's name are you doing?" he yelled.

Coming to, Emma looked down at her bleeding hand, still clenching a letter opener. The leather desk pad had been thrown from the desktop and its papers were now scattered all along the floor. On the desk, below Emma, deep gashes carved out the words *who put Bella in the wych elm?* Blood trickled from her hand onto the wood, flowing into the crevices and tracing the words in a deep crimson. Emma's face flushed hot with terror and embarrassment; she dropped the opener and crawled down from the desk, unable to utter any kind of apology.

"Get out! Get out of my office!"

Chapter 36
Breaking & Entering

The sun set late, well past 9pm, and then it was another thirty minutes before it got truly dark. Emma laid her seat back in her car, closed her eyes, and did her best not to dwell on the events of the day. The embarrassment was still fresh and stung deep—she could scarcely believe it had happened. When her blackouts first appeared, they were innocuous, even if they were unusual. But this, this was far from harmless; this was downright frightening. Had this been Timothy's experience? Stacey's experience? Emma shuttered at the thought—she knew full well the path they took.

Dr Evans didn't fare any better in the end, either. Even if she couldn't decipher his mad ramblings, it had become abundantly clear after today's episode that their paths were on a collision course. Solving Bella's case was no longer about bringing justice to a wrong, long overdue, it was about self-preservation. Dr Evans suffered for years more than likely; Timothy at least two; Stacey unknown. How much could Emma take? She didn't want to find out.

Which was exactly why she had camped out in her car a few blocks from The Royal School. She wouldn't leave without answers. There would be no more petitioning The Royal School after today, so if Emma wanted answers it would fall on her to get them.

She rolled on her side toward the passenger seat and stared at the brown B&Q hardware bag. Knowing what supplies she needed came with her job; knowing how to use them was a different question. Breaking and entering hadn't exactly made the syllabi in uni. Emma checked her phone and read midnight. How much longer should she wait? How long would it take to sneak in and find the archives?

Scaffolding from a summer reconstruction project on the exterior of the school limited her options. They dashed any hopes of a quick entrance near the admin wing. Emma's only choice fell on entering from the far side of the complex—a wing which extended outward from the main building. As she made her hasty exit following her episode earlier in the day, Emma glimpsed the school orientation map hanging on the wall next to the main doors. The Administration wing, where Dr Williams said the archives were situated, laid on the northeast corner. Where exactly, Emma didn't know—she was wading into uncharted waters and that didn't sit well with her. Emma's eyes grew heavy as she schemed.

When she jolted to, she glanced down at her watch: three in the morning. She'd dozed longer than she had planned. If Emma wanted to do this, now was the time. She pulled a dark navy cap over her head and tucked her hair up underneath. Throwing her supplies in her rucksack, she slung it over her shoulder as she rushed out the car toward the school.

A new moon obscured her movements through the neighborhood as she approached the southern entrance. A six-foot stone wall surrounded the school, but Emma had found some trash bins from an adjacent home pushed up against it. She scurried up the containers and threw herself over the ledge, dangling by her fingertips for a moment before releasing and landing sure footed on the other side. Construction supplies littered the rear courtyard, which would aid her escape in the same manner once she completed her task.

Some of the windows on the lower floors had been bricked up, restricting her point of entry. Emma spotted several un-bricked, wooden framed windows and peered in, finding one unlocked after checking a few. Letting her eyes adjust as she cupped her hands over them and pressed her face to the win-dow, she spied what lay on the other side of the glass pane. A classroom—perfect, as it'd be the least likely occupied room this early in the morning.

She rummaged around the bottom of her rucksack for the industrial magnets and duct tape she'd purchased earlier in the evening. Old wooden window frames disrupted the magnets the least, allowing Emma to slide it down the frame slowly until she felt the magnet drag heavy against the wood indi-cating she found the magnetic sensor on the other side. Care-fully, she taped the magnet in place and then used two large suction cups to grab the glass, giving her leverage to push the window up. The magnet fooled the system into thinking the window was still closed. No alarms, no lights, no nothing. Emma crawled into the opening and over the radiator to find herself in a Maths classroom.

Not wanting to waste any time, Emma rushed to the door, only to have the lights of the room flicker on. She froze. No sounds of shoes thumping down the hall or voices yelling out instructions. Just silence. After a few moments, the lights clicked off—motion sensored. Relieved, Emma stepped forward again, triggering the lights, and looked out of the door's port window either way down the hall. Again, no lights, no movement, no sound. She twisted the doorknob and crept out into the hall, which no doubt would also have motion sensors. Potted plants and narrow tables lined the hall on either side. Noticeboards and children's pictures hung between the classrooms, proudly displaying the works of students' summer projects. Emma clung against the wall, shuffling her feet, and inched her way down the long corridor to the first intersection of several before reaching the administration wing.

She had a difficult choice to make at the first junction. The next corridor had three smaller hallways splintering off to the right before she'd make the turn into the main corridor, which ran the length of the central wing. If she hugged the left wall, she'd avoid any light sensors, but she'd be more exposed to any night owl or security guard wandering around the building. If she hugged the right wall, she'd more easily peer around corners undetected, but would trigger the motion-sensored lights as she crossed to the other side. Both posed risks.

Emma imagined how the students, seeking a night of revelry, would navigate these passageways. Her mind conjured up four boys sneaking along, avoiding the lights, muffling their laughter as they shared swigs of contraband gin. Each turn, avoiding the sensors and checking for clumsy night guards traipsing the halls, triggering the motion lights as they strolled the school. *What if a student sees me? Will they mistake me for another student or security?* she thought. The more pertinent question was if security saw her.

She stood at the first juncture, checking around the corner.

The darkness of the new moon outside obscured the hall. Only the dim red lights of occasional exit signs offered any illumination. Emma took a deep breath and hightailed it to the far right wall across the intersection. She heard the click of the light before it flashed on, revealing everything in her section. The entire corridor wasn't triggered, just the light directly above her and closest to the sensor—a relief to her stealth. When it finally clicked off a minute later, her eyes—newly adjusted to the light—were blinded. She couldn't see more than a few inches from her face.

Her feet quietly shuffled over the checkered floor as she made the short scurry to the first hall on the right. She peered around the corner into the black. A faint red glow pierced the veil of darkness at the end of the hall. All was clear. Emma held her hand over her eyes to block out the light and darted across. Again, she heard a click, followed by the light directly above her gleaming between her fingers.

As she crept past the next two passageways, she scanned the corridors for any cameras. There were none that she noticed, giving her ease of mind that she was moving undetected despite triggering the motion sensors. It felt too easy.

The next corridor housed the central wing, which lead to the administration rooms on the other side of the building. Emma peered around the corner. The stained glass windows, which adorned the front façade along the left, cast odd shadows down the corridor—their colors diminished by the new moon and only detectable from the security lights out front.

She scurried along until she came to the grand foyer. To the left, large ornate iron doors stood sentry from the world outside; to the right, the dual wooden staircase whose twin-flights curved along the foyer's outer walls and met in a center landing framing the top of two large wooden doors below—they were both closed and seemingly guarding another corridor disappearing into the back of the complex. The foyer's silence echoed reassurance to Emma that it was now or never to cut across to the far side.

The building map near the entrance revealed a semi-symmetrical, mirrored floor plan in the administrative wing which laid opposite the foyer. *But which of the three hallways held the archives?* thought Emma. She dashed across, setting off the lights as before, and then hugged the wall on the other side, awaiting the security lights to disengage. One by one, she checked each hallway and their corresponding directory. Coming to the last hall, she spied the notice: Bursar's Office, Registrar's Office, and Archives. Bingo.

Emma managed to pick the lock, something she'd only done once or twice before. She just might be able to get in and out without incident. She opened the door and slid in, closing and locking it behind her. The archives room was cramped and lined with dated metal filing cabinets against the wall and in the center of the room, forming small aisles barely large enough for a person to walk between, certainly not enough for two people to pass one another.

Thankfully, Dr Williams had given her one piece of the puzzle to work with—Charles' enrollment year. 1928. Being in a small room with the door closed and locked, Emma risked a little light from her torch. She flashed its beam across the front labels as she walked from cabinet to cabinet until she found it: 1928 Q-T.

She thumbed through the file folders. And there it was, right in front of her.

Roberts, Charles 1928-1939

She held the torch between her teeth and retrieved the file. Emma furiously flipped through the pages, past his medical and academic reports. She wanted a birth certificate, something, anything, with parental records. One file caught her eye. A letter from Viscount Cobham of Hagley Hall. It contained a request for the orphanage to accept Charles into the institution—with a sizable donation pending approval. Why would he sponsor him? She took a photo and then continued her search. Glued by years of humidity and tight storage, several pages stuck to the back of the letter. Emma peeled them apart to find his admittance papers and a birth certificate. She slid down to the floor as she read it out loud.

> *Name & Surname of Child:*
>   *Roberts, Charles Nathaniel*
> *Sex:*
>   *Boy*
> *Date of Birth:*
>   *18 July, 1921*
> *Name & Surname of Father:*
>   *Roberts, Nathaniel*
> *Name & Maiden Surname of Mother:*
>   *Roberts, née Davies, Isabella*

Emma gasped, dropping the torch as she held her hand over her mouth. "Bella—" Her hands shook as she snapped a photo of the certificate and then put everything back in the drawer. Emma knew the possibility of finding Bella's identity, but the realization was both overwhelming and surreal. *Isabella Davies*, she thought in disbelief.

Emma locked the door behind her and made her way to the foyer with the grand staircase. She was about to manoeuvre across to the other side when she noticed the wooden doors under the landing were now open. She leapt back against the wall, but not before triggering the motion sensor. This time, the light malfunctioned. As it clicked and flashed on, it flickered out and back on again. The light got stuck in a strobe effect, flashing in and out and clicking with each cycle.

She hugged the wall and looked through the opened doors down the hall. At the far end, visible only for an instant as the light strobed, stood a female silhouette. She pulled back and clenched her eyes shut, cursing under her breath. Assuming it might be a student, Emma knew that if they freaked out, they might call security. She needed to get out and get out fast before the student saw her. She peeked around the corner again, but this time, the hall was empty. Perhaps they got scared and hid, thinking Emma was security. She could only hope.

Taking advantage of the *all clear*, Emma ran across the foyer to the other side, glancing down the hall once more to check if it were empty. It wasn't. The girl had come all the way down the hall and crossed the threshold into the foyer as Emma ran. If they hadn't seen Emma before, they had now. Emma tucked herself behind a trophy case and waited to see what the student would do.

Amongst the clicking of the light, Emma heard the girl's steps grow louder. But she ambled slowly and in such a peculiar manner that Emma couldn't help but peer out from behind the wooden case and catch a glimpse of her. And then it became clear, the sound of her steps, even before she saw her, she knew who it was by the *thump-shush*.

Emma screwed her eyes shut and crammed herself between the wall and the trophy case.

Thump-shush.

Thump-shush.

Bella had moved into the middle of the foyer. Emma saw her through the panels of the glass case, flashing in and out amongst the strobe. She didn't move, and neither did Emma. Her heart pounded so loudly in her chest, she swore Bella could hear it. Emma held her hand over her mouth and muffled her breathing.

The *click, click, click, click* of the lights raced in sync with Emma's pulse. The strobe sent Emma's head reeling—a headache rose up from behind her eyes and moved backward. Then the strobe stopped. Everything fell quiet and darkness returned. Emma was all alone, or so she thought.

Emma, a voice whispered.

Before Emma realized it, she was running down the hall, triggering all the lights as she sprinted until she got to the corner and ducked behind to catch her breath. She peeked around the corner to see if Bella had followed. One by one, the lights shut off with no sign of her.

The voice whispered from the darkness again. *Emma...*

She didn't wait to see her. Emma darted back down the hallway, triggering all the lights as she went. Each time she passed one of the smaller hallways now on her left, she glanced to see if Bella was there.

Emma came to the final corner. The Maths room where she entered was halfway down the corridor on the left. Before she rounded the corner, a light down past the classroom flicked on and in the still air Emma could hear the *thump-shush* nearing.

If she waited any longer, Bella would block her exit. She had no choice. Emma screwed her eyes shut and ran as fast as she could to the classroom, sliding into the door and ricocheting into a table and knocking it over. She didn't look down the hall, but out the corner of her eye she saw the motion-sensored lights click on closer and closer as the *thump-shush* grew.

She tried the knob—locked. Emma fumbled in her bag for the lock pick. Sweat dripped into her eyes as she fiddled with the pins. The tumblers popped, but the core didn't turn.

Thump-shush.

Another light, this time just two doors down, clicked on.

Thump-shush.

Emma twisted it again, but this time the pick slipped and fell to the floor with a *ting*.

Emma, Bella whispered over Emma's shoulder. Rotten wood and putrid flesh hung in the air. *Who put me in the wych elm?*

She snatched up the pick again and tried one last time. The lock released, and the door gave under Emma's weight. She threw herself in and slammed the door shut, bolting it behind her. Light streamed into the room from the door window, casting a shadow from the other side.

Emma… Fingers scraped against the frosted glass as Bella pleaded again. Emma didn't wait. She pushed herself up off the floor and leapt out the window, ripping her trousers in the process. She didn't bother closing the window or removing the magnets. She only cared about scurrying over the wall and driving as fast as she could away from the school.

Chapter 37
The Repair Job

Oliver Bennett retched back when he buzzed open the doors to Emma's laboratory. The stench stole his breath away as he threw his arm up and over his nose to hold it at bay. His gag reflexes kicked in and his stomach lurched—the sour taste of bile sat on the back of his throat. The technician, Barry Kemble, a short and stout fellow, who had followed Oliver out of Otis and through the lab doors didn't fare as well. He just plain threw up in the wastebasket next to Emma's desk.

"Dear God, who died in here?" said Kemble.

Oliver appreciated a good sense of dark humor, but he wasn't sure if Kemble was being serious or making a joke. It didn't matter much really, all Oliver cared about was dealing with these broken morgue refrigerators so everyone upstairs could get back to work without feeling nauseous anytime they neared Otis. Hell, on hot days, you could smell the putrid decay from the lobby.

They inched over to the drawers, Kemble with a handkerchief over his mouth and Oliver still with his face in the nook of his elbow, and inspected the units. "Well, just by looking at 'em, I can tell you the first thing that's wrong," said Kemble. "All four handles are busted. The locking mechanisms won't even latch. Even with a properly working unit, if the doors won't stay shut, the unit won't remain cool." Kemble slammed one door shut several times to force the latch to catch, illustrating its malfunction to Oliver as it bounced back open each time. "Why this hasn't been fixed before is beyond me. It looks like it's been broken for some time and has just been Jerry-rigged over and over."

Oliver shook his head and shrugged. "I'm new as Station Superintendent and the lab technician is also new. We, uh, both inherited our jobs recently after the sudden passing of our predecessors. This is all new to me."

"My condolences," replied Barry. "I understand how these things can happen during a rough transition." Barry inspected inside, wincing from the odor bellowing out. Despite trying to assess the refrigerator units, Oliver could see Barry's eye stray toward the corpse just inches away from him. Oliver sympathized. It was hard not to look, regardless how gruesome.

"Per your request, the shop-vac and step ladder are there in the corner. Is there anything else you need from me or shall I just leave you be so you can get to work?" asked Oliver.

"I think I have everything I need. I'll holler if I don't," replied Barry.

Oliver walked to the doors, checked the exhaust vent in the room, and proceeded to turn it on. Couldn't hurt, after all. He shut the doors behind him and took Otis back to the bullpen.

Barry Kemble leaned back on the autopsy table and mentally assessed his first steps. Being his first repair on a centennial unit, especially one in this condition, Barry needed to change up his normal approach. The locks and seals only? That'd be the easiest and most obvious solution. That'd be five, ten minutes tops for each of the four morgue drawers. If he didn't hear the refrigeration unit kick in after a few minutes, he'd do a check of the fan, exhaust, and condensation drain—oh, and the circulation system leading to each drawer. All easy tasks, especially if they just needed cleaning. Another twenty minutes. *But*, if the compressor, evaporator coil, or condenser coil were shot, then he'd be stuck in here with that foul odor for much longer than he wanted.

He slapped his hands together and rubbed them around, ready to put his plan into action. But first, he needed to deal with the smell. His mind kept wandering back to that movie with Jodie Foster, where she worked for the FBI. *What movie was that?* She kept putting Vick's Vapor Rub under her nose. Barry scanned the room, but didn't see anything sitting out. He did, however, find some N95 masks. He spritzed a little of his cologne on the inside and fixed the straps over his ears. Perfect. Task one complete.

Next up, the locks. Barry slipped off a broken padlock and removed the malfunctioning parts of the latches from the drawers and tossed them to the side. Not all of them were broken in the same manner. Some had their drop pins torn away, others had malfunctioning latching mechanisms. Unfortunately, the doors were so old he didn't have the right replacement parts, so he took all the working parts of the four locks and frankensteined them into one working unit. The morgue only needed one working lock for now. Barry made note to ask Superintendent Bennett if he wanted him to return later and upgrade the whole refrigeration unit to something more modern, with key locks or an electronic system. His boss would be happy with the up-sale.

The seals on each door made clean connections, which meant he could skip their replacements and check the cooling unit above. He grabbed his small stepladder and shimmied up, removing the access panel in the process. He flashed his light into the fan and then waited for it to kick on. Dust particles, from years of use and neglect, caked the blower and evaporator coils. Somewhat more than usual, but not unheard of. The wiring in the back shared the same condition. Nothing a little compressed air and a shop vac couldn't deal with.

He stepped down to fetch the shop vac and noticed a woman standing in the corner wearing a mustard yellow skirt and striped blue cardigan. "Sorry, miss. I didn't hear you come in."

Barry continued going about his business and blasted the blower fan and coils with the can of compressed air. More dust particles flew about the insides and fluttered out of the unit before being gobbled up by the vacuum nozzle he frantically waved around. After a few minutes, he felt guilty for not talking with the woman.

"I don't see how you could be in here with this stench. Of course, if this is your job and all, you must be used to it. Can't imagine how, though."

Barry hopped down and waited for the unit to kick in. He glanced over his shoulder at the woman, still wearing the same blank stare. He didn't give it much thought, as he was so pleased to see the unit finally spin up. He popped open the first unoccupied drawer and crawled near the back to inspect the circulation duct.

"You're a quiet one, aren't you?" he said to the woman.

"No matter. My wife always says I'm a complete chatterbox and she can't get a word in edgeways. So, if you just wanna watch, that's fine by me. No harm in a little curiosity. Well, the proverbial cat might not agree with me on that, but that's his problem and not mine." Barry chuckled a little at his own joke. He knew the woman wouldn't—his wife wouldn't have either.

He reached for his screwdriver on his belt, but it must have fallen out when he crawled in. "Excuse me, miss." He blindly held his hand out of the opening. "Do you see a screwdriver on the floor? Could you—oh, thanks. Much appreciated." He wrapped his fingers around the screwdriver and pulled himself back in, then loosened the vent cover to the duct and checked for obstructions. Clean as a whistle.

Pulling himself out, he dropped down to the lower drawer and repeated the same inspection. As Barry flashed his torch into the duct, his ears started to tingle. Within a minute or two, a full-on ring clanged in his head like church bells on a wedding day. He wiggled his pinky finger in his ear to make it stop.

"You ever get a wicked case of tinnitus? Man oh man, did one just spin up. My doctor tells me it was down to too many years as a roadie for the Stones. Probably shot my hearing for good. Hell, you could be talking to me right now and I might not even know it. But it was worth it. I saw some amazing performances over the years. Yet, my wife got me to settle down and take a real nine-to-five job instead—been at it twenty years now. Got me three more before I retire. I'd never admit this to her, but she was *right* and she was *worth* it."

Again, he switched drawers, moving to the one below the corpse. Before he could finish his inspection, the ringing doubled in intensity, spinning his head all around. He pulled himself out of the drawer and grimaced. He forced a yawn and wiggled his fingers in his ear. It was then that he noticed the woman had left the room.

"Huh, wonder how long I've been talking to myself. No matter." He reached in his bag and fiddled around until he retrieved his medication and dry swallowed two pills. He wiggled his fingers in his ears once more and then finished up in the bottom drawer.

Barry slid the drawer out which contained the corpse. The white sheet over the body, drenched in decomposition fluids, triggered his gag reflex again. The grayish ooze ran along the edge of the steel body tray and encircled the corpse in the drip drain. A hand fell out from underneath the sheet as the drawer popped into its fully extended position. The flesh, a putrid splotch of green and purple, sloughed off and exposed bone underneath. Barry adverted his eyes, but he couldn't look away for long. He retched up a mouth full of bile and then spit it out in the waste bin.

Normally, he never needed to handle a corpse, but with the lab tech gone and the other woman no longer present, he had no choice. Barry wheeled the body hoist over to the drawer, cranked it up, and gently rolled the tray onto the hoist. He didn't want anything to do with it, so he quickly transferred the rotting corpse to the autopsy table and secured it.

Even with the cadaver removed, the drawer in question reeked. Regardless, Barry had to climb inside and check the circulation vent and duct. If it were clear and cold air flowed, he'd be done and out of here. He stuck his head in, grabbed a hold of the railing mechanism, and pulled himself under the vent cover. Placing his hand over the slats, he sensed restricted air flow. He unscrewed the brackets and popped off the cover, revealing the thickest spider's web cluster he'd ever seen. There had to be dozens, each teeming with hundreds of desiccated insects. Barry flinched and hit his head against the steel partition, adding to the headache already developing from the tinnitus.

He smashed a dozen of the juicy, hairy, little critters, and then scanned the vent for any more live ones. He reached in with his gloved hand and swirled it around, grabbing the sticky threads with his fingers. Bits and pieces of dead things dropped onto his mask and goggles. Barry shook his head to knock them away.

As he worked, something crept up his leg and lit on his knee. Thinking it was his imagination, he brushed it with his hand and continued cleaning the duct. Whatever it was returned a few moments later. It better not be rats; Barry hated rats. Spiders he could deal with, maybe even cockroaches, but rats—that was a hard *no*. This time, he glanced down to see what had crawled on him. His vision blurred from the cobwebs sticking to his goggles, but it was clear something was there. He brushed away the webs from his face and saw a woman's hand on his leg, inching its way like a spider up his thigh.

Barry cursed and kicked his legs to rid himself of it. When he looked back down, it had disappeared. He chuckled a sigh of relief and blamed it on an overactive imagination because of the corpse on the autopsy table. He laughed again as he replaced the vent cover and secured it in place. "Barry, you old codger, you're such a fool."

Barry... Barry...

His imagination it was not.

"Who's there? Is this some type of prank? I'll tell you right now, I have no patience for niggling behavior. I'll come out and wallop you a good one, if you don't stop."

Barry... the voice called with more urgency.

He slid his fat little frame out of the drawer. "Listen here, you bloody shi—"

Standing toe-to-toe with Barry, just to his chest height, was the woman in the mustard skirt. Her face, beaten and bloodied, stared Barry down with her ashen, dead eyes. He struggled to look away and when he finally did, his eyes dropped to her neck, covered in deep black bruises which wrapped all the way around. She ran her fingers across his face and then traced her fingertips over his mouth. The veins in his neck swelled and thumped, sending heavy pulses of hot blood up his scalp.

Her black lips, dried and cracked, pulled back in a crooked grin, revealing her rancid teeth. *Barry...*

Barry couldn't speak, his chest frozen in fear. His knees buckled and his back pounded against the morgue drawers as he slid to the ground. She followed him downward, crouching over the top of him, her soiled hair falling over her face as she hissed her eternal question.

Barry stammered. "I, I, I—"

Her gaunt fingers—nails split and torn back with dirt underneath—wrapped around his shirt collar as she pulled him in face-to-face. Something warm and wet ran down his leg and pooled under him. The smell of his urine mixed with the putrid odor of the woman's breath, cold and lifeless, fell on his cheeks. Her eyes turned black and her grip tightened as her whole body tensed up in rage.

WHO PUT ME IN THE WYCH ELM, BARRY?!

Barry finally cried in response. "I don't know, dear God, I swear, I don't know." In a flash of composure, he snatched his bag of tools lying next to him and swung them at the woman. He stumbled to his feet, slipping in his own piss, and ran out the door to Otis. As he slammed the gate shut and pounded repeatedly the ground floor button, the woman, still crouched in front of the morgue drawers, turned and whispered again. *Barry...*

His white knuckles clenched his bag tightly, his nails digging into his palms. When the lift finally stopped on the ground floor, he swung open the gate and bolted, ignoring the calls of Bennett floating from across the bullpen. He threw his bag in his van, sending tools all over the floor. Fidgeting in his pocket, while still wearing his work gloves, he fetched his keys and started it up. His only thought was to get away as fast as possible. He threw the van in first and floored it out of the car park, swerving around traffic and driving the wrong way down the road.

Barry... The voice returned. He looked in the rearview mirror to see the *woman* directly behind him. Barry jerked the wheel and sent the van careening off the road and into a tree. His body burst through the window and flew some twenty feet until he struck a stone wall. He gasped for air as his lungs filled with blood. The last sight before his eyes turned black was the *woman* crawling over the top of him, still asking her plea.

*

Oliver and McArthur watched as the technician burst from Otis and sprinted through the bullpen. Papers flew off the desks in his wake.

"Hey, wait! Is it done? Is it fixed?" asked Oliver.

"What's that all about?" said McArthur.

"I don't rightly know. Maybe the stench got to him? I guess I'm gonna have to go down and check if the work is done."

Oliver got up and took Otis to the lab. When he entered through the doors, he heard the gentle hum of the refrigerator unit running. In the center of the room laid the corpse on the autopsy table. "Ah, for Pete's sake. You could have at least put it back."

He stood there, blankly staring at the corpse, and couldn't for the life of him recall the case for the cadaver. He pulled out his phone and called Emma. "Emmy, hey, we just had one of the morgue refrigerator units bust. Had to call a tech to come and repair it. Unfortunately, the cadaver inside suffered some damage and really started to stink up the place. Anyway, I can't recall the case file for this. What case does this cadaver pertain to? Who is in there?"

Emma paused for a few seconds before replying, "There's no one in my lab, Ollie. Well, no one but Bella."

"Then who is rotting away on your autopsy table?"

Chapter 38
Full Disclosure

Oliver waited at the back entrance with his foot propping open the rear emergency door—the only way into the cellar except for Otis. Emma hopped out of her car and casually snuck in behind him.

"If Harris catches wind I'm here, we're in for a world of hurt."

"Yeah, well, we better make sure he doesn't find out," replied Oliver. "Besides, I think we have bigger fish to fry than what Harris is going to do."

Oliver led Emma down the stairs and through a door that came out next to the evidence room, just down the hall from the lab. Immediately, the stench hit Emma. "Oh God, you weren't kidding. That's horrendous."

"It's been like that all week since the refrigeration unit went out. It doesn't help that some idiot mis-wired the exhaust hood—it's set to reverse."

"What? Are you kidding me? How did Dr Evans and Taylor not notice that?"

Oliver scoffed. "It's hardly even the most difficult question at this point, if what you said is correct." He buzzed the two of them in and opened the doors. They were greeted by a swarm of flesh flies. "That's just lovely. Looks like we have a party in here."

Emma's eyes flicked up at the HVAC vent above the autopsy table—flies crawling out the vent hood. Since her last visit, the crack in the ceiling had expanded all the way from the green subway tiles and to the edge of the vent, spanning half the arch. *Why hasn't maintenance repaired it yet?*

"I'm not surprised if the exhaust hood was left in reverse for a period of time," replied Emma. "These guys will come right through it." Emma walked over to her desk and grabbed a pair of nitrile gloves, snapping them over her fingers as she approached the corpse.

Oliver stood back a way, holding his hand over his nose and mouth. "Well, what do you think? Who is it?"

"I believe we are beyond rational thinking—at least if you want a rational answer."

"How so?"

"Here, let me show you." She pulled the white sheet from the body. Flies buzzed away, leaving behind maggots writhing in the exposed, rotting flesh. "First observations: female, approximately 5 foot, right hand missing—" Emma rolled back the raw tissue serving as lips to examine the dental structure. "Excessive overlap of left central incisor—first right molar missing." She then moved down toward the lower left leg and felt around the shin. "Missing the left tibia." Emma slid the sheet back over the corpse.

"Okay, what does that mean?"

"Either someone snuck in a decomposing corpse with the

exact same physical traits as Bella, or this *is* Bella."

Oliver shook his head in disbelief and stepped forward. "What do you mean, this is Bella?"

"Everything matches, Ollie. Without comparing a DNA profile to the one I submitted to Ancestry, it's a guessing game. But if I had to put money on it, my money is on Bella."

"I'm gonna put a pin in that Ancestry comment for now. That's the least of my worries. How in God's name is this Bella?"

Emma shook her head. "Outside of God—or the other guy—there's no science to explain it. I'm as lost as you are. But I have a feeling that Dr Evans and Taylor knew, or at least had a theory."

"What makes you think that?"

"There was a lot of secrecy surrounding Bella from day one. It wasn't like any of the other cold cases I was assigned. Every time I tried asking a question, Taylor clammed up and got defensive. He kept going on about some special protocol that Evans had for Bella, but he could never find it."

"Okay, well, that explains something else I've been curious about and couldn't solve."

"Explains what?"

"Shortly after Taylor's funeral and after I was officially announced as his replacement, Taylor's solicitor showed up in my hospital room. He said that Taylor had bequeathed his successor something of importance. Then he handed me a safety deposit box key."

"Interesting. What was in the box?"

"Just a letter. Very cryptic. He said that I would need to meet with Dr Evans asap as he had an important protocol that I would need—that Dr Evans would explain everything to me.

He went on to say that reading it in a letter wouldn't be *believable*. That was it."

"Looks to me like he didn't get a chance to update the letter after Evans died. Now we're flying blind."

"So you have nothing?" asked Oliver.

"Not exactly. I have Dr Evans' old journal, but I wouldn't call it useful. Most of it contains insane ramblings, all about Bella, of course. There were a few intriguing tidbits in it, but this?" Emma pointed at Bella. "This was definitely not a part of his journal that I could decipher."

"So, what do you have?"

"I have a name. Her real name, that is: Isabella Davies."

"Okay..." Oliver shifted his weight. "Her identity has been a mystery for 80 years and now you show up with her real name? You're gonna have to do better than that."

"Then let's take that pin out of my Ancestry comment. I was given *strict* orders that nothing about Bella would ever leave this lab. Taylor was adamant about it, and even threatened to fire me if I did. Well, I did it anyway. I sent a bone scraping to Ancestry to see if I could locate any relatives."

"I'm assuming you did."

"Yes, Sarah Hawkins from Birmingham. Bella's granddaughter. Bella had always been rumored to have had a child based on her pelvic bone. Looks like that was true. Anyway, I was able to track down Bella's identity at the orphanage where Hawkins' father, Bella's son, grew up."

"I don't like where this fishing expedition is going. Should we just leave the details to plausible deniability?"

"Yeah, that might be best. So the gist means, I have the names of the parents. Nathaniel Roberts and Isabella Davies. I'm stuck after that."

"It's further than Evans and Taylor ever got, further than anyone ever got for that matter. Why do you think they never did a DNA test before?"

"Do you remember the day Taylor died? Not what happened to him, but what happened before that, with Burrow's interrogation?"

"I heard rumors from other officers that visited the hospital about you interrupting the questioning, but it obviously became second page news at the water cooler pretty fast."

Emma nodded. "So, I confronted Burrow about some pictures Evans had of Bella. I wanted to see his reaction to them—never mind why. That's a whole other story. Anyway, afterwards, Taylor tore into me for showing Burrow the photos. Not just because it threatened his secrecy over Bella by putting them on public record in the interrogation, which I still can't suss out, but because he believed that physically taking anything—DNA, evidence, photos, et cetera—out of this lab was going to have some *effect* on the situation. He was genuinely terrified."

"What kind of affect?"

"I don't know. We got interrupted by the transfer of Burrow. He said we'd talk when he got back." Emma looked down at her feet; her throat tightened as she spoke. "I left something out of my incident report following Burrow's escape, something I wasn't sure how people would take. When I came into the van, he was still alive. I held his hand in his last moments. He didn't say *Tell my wife I love her* or anything you'd expect. He said one word, a name: Bella. Why would she be so important for her to be his last words?"

Oliver studied Bella lying on the autopsy table and pointed. "If he knew about this, then I could see why. There's definitely more going on here. Do you have all your notes on Bella? On you right now, that is?"

"No, everything is at the hotel."

"Where's that pocket notebook of yours? It's always attached to your hip."

"Trust me... there's too much to keep in a small notepad."

Oliver looked at his watch. "I have a meeting at Kidderminster in thirty minutes to discuss the yearly budget—which, by the way, includes a hefty annual donation from Viscount Cobham to run your division here in Hagley. Then I have to run to Hindlip to meet with Harris—don't worry, unrelated to you. Go back, grab everything you've got and come to my place. Say eight? Plausible deniability be damned... we need to suss this out."

Emma rolled Bella back onto the body hoist and then returned her to the cadaver drawer, dropping the new security pin into the lock. On the way out, she turned off the exhaust hood and flipped off the lights. Oliver gave Emma a nod as he got in Otis and she headed out the fire exit. She feigned a reassuring smile, as this recent discovery had her on her heels.

When the doors to the lab clicked shut, the latch on Bella's drawer rattled and shook until the metal pin snapped. Then the door swung open.

Chapter 39
Death Week

Emma dragged herself into Hagley station after three straight days of overtime—processing no less than seven different crime scenes. That was on top of all the other scenes the previous three weeks since she returned to active duty. She now had a mountain of evidence to process and even more paperwork. October was shattering all records for cases. Death Week had come early; Death Week had become Death *Month*.

"Emma, perfect timing." PC Louis McArthur, eyes swollen and dark, looked exactly how Emma felt. "Kidderminster wants to know where you want Mr and Mrs Perkins at? Their morgue is at capacity."

"Remind me, which case is that?" asked Emma.

"The one with the butter knife."

"Oh God, yes. Eww." Emma shrugged off the chills. "Umm, what about Stourbridge?"

"Nope, they're at capacity, too."

"Damn, try Rubery."

"Same. And don't suggest Halesowen, either," said McArthur.

"Are you kidding me? Try Brierley Hill then."

"All the way up there?"

"Do you have a better suggestion?"

"Brierley Hill it is." McArthur removed his hand from the phone receiver and relayed the message. Emma heard the moaning of the coroners from the earpiece as she walked away.

She needed a Red Bull and headed toward the break room. That was until she saw Bryant Jones walking from that direction. She turned her face away from him and made a B-line to Otis. It was too late.

"Ms Emma Lloyd—the prodigal daughter returns." Bryant's voice oozed with sarcasm.

"It's been three weeks already, not that accuracy and truth actually matters to you."

"I'm hurt you'd say that. I'm your biggest fan after all. You are the *hero of Drakelow*. I'm sure I'm just one of many in this station who *adore* you. After all, you've got everyone here wrapped around your little finger—not wanting to give up any dirt on you."

"They're just looking out for their own, I guess." Emma wanted to punch him square between the eyes.

"Their *own*? You really think they see you as an *equal*? A *CSI tech* granted a position because their brother-in-law is the Chief Constable? Someone who hasn't put in the time yet? Don't fool yourself."

That *want* slowly manifested into a *fantasy*—the sweet sensation of knuckles to nose. "I'll take nepotism over sleazy reporter any day of the week."

"I'm glad we're feeling honest with each other," Bryant

continued. "Let's just dispatch all pretense and get down to business, shall we?"

"Sure, why not? Let's have it." Emma's face flushed hot as she stood hip out, arms crossed.

"Don't think I don't know there's more to Burrow's story than a mentally ill individual. You put that poor kid in a coma unjustly. You and Superintendent Bennett can try to hide the truth of your corruption behind a person suffering from mental disease all you want. It won't stay hidden forever. Your pet project is bound to surface and expose you all."

"I look forward to it. Now, if you don't mind, I have work to do. If you haven't noticed, we're a little busy around here." Emma ignored his snide response and walked away.

As she neared Otis, Emma traded one nuisance for another—Bryant's inquisition for Bella's plea. Her nagging worsened as the floor indicator arrow moved closer to the cellar.

Emma buzzed herself in to find Oliver already in her office chair, feet propped up on her desk as if he owned the place. She didn't mind in the end—he always brought a little comfort to the chaos, which she needed after that conversation with Bryant and Bella's swelling plea.

Oliver didn't budge when Emma came over, so she slid herself onto the edge of her desk and let her feet dangle freely. She huffed and blew a strand of hair out of her face before venting. "I thought the dust men took out the rubbish on Friday mornings?" She wiggled her finger in her ear to block out Bella.

"Good morning to you too, Emmy." Oliver smiled and gave her a wink. "And yes, the rubbish is always taken out on Fridays."

"Well, they forgot that piece of trash, Bryant Jones lurking around upstairs on another one of his fishing expeditions."

"Ignore him. He's just bitter because I got his boss to shut down his story on you after Drakelow. Even his editor didn't want to slam the police with all the public support we got."

"Well, someone needs to notify his *face* the story is dead before I notify it for him." The thumbing blood coursing through the vein in her temple matched Bella's wailing in Emma's ear, driving a headache deep behind her eyes.

Oliver dropped his feet to the floor and leaned forward. "Listen, you have nothing to worry about with him. Even the IOPC has had enough of his nonsense. Apparently, he was the lone dissenter in the vote to clear you for duty. Rumor has it he's made a lot of enemies at the IOPC and his obsession with you hasn't helped him much. He's on a short leash."

"Short leash or not, he's clearly not letting go," replied Emma, as she reached up and discreetly rubbed her temple.

"If he doesn't, he's gonna hang himself one day on a story he should have dropped and end up like that." Oliver thumbed in the direction of a corpse under a white sheet on the autopsy table.

Emma hopped off the desk, strolled over to the table, and pulled back the sheet to reveal Bella fully reconstituted and in the midst of rigor. How Bella's corpse could be so removed from the voice in her ear baffled Emma. "I don't quite think anyone could end up like this, but I get your point." She snapped on a pair of nitrile gloves and tested Bella's joints and tissue, fighting off the burning question still ringing in her head. "I say she has another six, eight hours of rigor remaining."

"And then what?"

"You've read all my notes; you know as much as I do.

There's no precedence for this unless you count Lazarus. But I doubt J. C. stood at the hollow in Hagley Wood saying, 'Bella, come out'. In short, here's what we have—" Emma slipped off her gloves and leaned against the table, denying Bella the satisfaction of acknowledging her plea. "Complete reverse decomposition. As far as I can tell, everything has progressed in exact reverse order up to rigor. To make it worse, there is nothing that gives any indication that the process will stop after rigor mortis finishes."

"I don't like the way that sounds."

"I don't either. But let's face it, *this* shouldn't be happening, so whatever comes next, regardless of how outlandish it might seem, is within the realm of possibilities. It does at least answer my question why there's a folder with dozens of photos of Bella in this state." Black speckles swirled in her vision as she pinched herself to stave it off.

"Let me get this straight—and I can't believe I'm going to say this out loud—you think she's going to come back to life?"

"I don't know what to tell you, Ollie. Do I think it sounds insane? Most definitely, yes. If you had told me this six months ago, I'd have thought you had lost your marbles. Which makes Taylor's hesitancy to tell me everything from the onset understandable in hindsight." Emma's head grew light as darkness crept around her.

"Okay, so… she comes back to life? Like every year since, what, 1943? Is there a random farm somewhere that Taylor and Evans have absconded away 80-something one-handed *Bellas* to live out their lives in secrecy?"

"I mean, I don't know." Emma bit her lower lip as she shrugged her shoulders and fought the impending blackout.

"That seems wildly too difficult to cover up. Maybe she doesn't resuscitate. Maybe this is it, and they just quietly cremated her at the end of every cycle. But—"

"But, what?" asked Oliver.

Emma stared blankly across the room before snapping to and answering. "When I *see* Bella here, on this table, she's this benign, yet enigmatic *science project* —inanimate and harmless. However, when I *feel* Bella, it's different. She's angry, full of malice, incessantly demanding an answer to that frigging question. It's what drove Evans mad; it's what drove Burrow mad." Tears welled up behind Emma's eyes—what would Oliver say if she mentioned everything including seeing Bella?

Oliver walked over and wrapped his arms around her, embracing her tightly. She buried her face in his chest and let the tears trickle down her cheeks. "That's not going to happen to you. I promise. We're going to figure this out. We have so much more to go on. We know her name because of you. *You* found her family. No one else has ever got this close."

"No one that we know of. What if they knew all this and we just don't know it?"

"You have to think positive. If you let yourself go down that path, you *will* end up like Evans." As Oliver spoke, his phone buzzed in his pocket. "Huh, that's odd. It's Hagley Hall calling on my personal line."

Oliver, baffled and unsure, answered the phone. "Superintendent Oliver Bennett." He listened intently for a few moments and then checked his watch before replying. "Yes, I totally understand. I'm currently at Hagley station now and I'm with our in-house CSI. We can be there in fifteen minutes, give or take." Oliver tapped *end* and just blankly stared at the phone for a moment.

"Well," inquired Emma, still teary-eyed. "What was that all about?"

"We have another case—at Hagley Hall."

Chapter 40
Hagley Hall Tragedy

Oliver and Emma pulled up to the opulent 18th century Gregorian country home, not far from, and once purveyor of Hagley Wood. Hagley Hall's front portico entrance, flanked by stone columns, towered over its split red stone staircase. While small in stature compared to other mansions littering the British countryside, it didn't lack any grandeur or beauty.

Emma, minus her typical crime scene coveralls, carried a discreet bag of supplies and her camera up to the rear, staff only entrance. Oliver, likewise in street clothes, also carried an additional kit for Emma. They were both greeted by a young man, barely in his twenties, wearing a sharp, dark blue suit and tie.

"Thank you for coming post haste as well as for your discretion. I'm Samuel Hatfield, designate to the Personal Secretary of Lord Cobham, the Viscount of Hagley Hall. Well, I suppose *I'm* the Personal Secretary now, considering the recent events."

Oliver extended his hand and shook Mr Hatfield's. "Good morning, I'm Superintendent Oliver Bennett and this is CSI Emma Lloyd. Sorry to meet under such circumstances."

"Please, come in. I'll fill you in on the way to the library." Oliver and Emma followed Hatfield inside and wound through the kitchen. "Around nine this morning, one of our cleaning staff, Miss Winters, entered the library as part of her daily duties. When she encountered Mr Brighton, the Personal Secretary, he was in a catatonic state, sitting at the reading desk with several books open in what looked like some sort of display. She promptly alerted myself and when I entered he—" Hatfield paused to compose himself. "He had the letter opener to his throat. Before any of us could react, he… he took his own life."

"Was anyone else in the residence during the incident?" asked Oliver.

"Yes, Mr Cunningham. He oversees the house staff. He was meeting with me at the time of Miss Winters' notification, thus he came with us to the library."

"Has anyone other than you three entered the room or touched the body?"

"No, Mr Cunningham closed and locked the library doors immediately following our phone call. He's been standing outside ever since. I'm the only one to touch Mr Brighton. We had just entered the room when he committed the act. By the time I could run to him, he had already perished. Full disclosure. I checked for a pulse, but I panicked and did not administer CPR." Hatfield swallowed hard. Guilt hung heavy on his face.

"It's doubtful CPR would have helped," replied Emma. "Especially if both the carotid and jugular were equally severed. I'll know more after I inspect the body."

"I appreciate the words of reassurance, Ms Lloyd. However, it will not absolve me of my ineptitude in that moment."

"And where was the Viscount during the incident?"

"Thankfully, in London fulfilling parliamentary duties. Has been all week. We know this will eventually make the papers, so this isn't about a coverup. We just want to get ahead of it and avoid any potential scandals," replied Hatfield.

The three of them navigated the grand hallways until they reached the library, currently guarded by Mr Cunningham, a gray-haired portly fellow whose skin hadn't seen the sun for ages.

"Mr Cunningham, this is Superintendent Bennett and CSI Lloyd. They are here to conduct the investigation," said Hatfield.

"I'll need to ask you and Miss Winters a few questions. Is she available?" asked Oliver.

"She has retired to my private quarters for the time being. Understandably, she's feeling quite unwell."

"That's no problem," replied Oliver. "I'll finish with Mr Hatfield and I can wait and interview Miss Winters afterwards. Emma, you can start processing evidence unless you have any questions."

"No, I'll start with the scene," said Emma. "Mr Cunningham, if you don't mind."

As Emma pulled up her coveralls and donned her goggles and mask, Cunningham took a large, overflowing keyring from his waistcoat and unlocked the door to the library. The windows, which faced southwest, blocked the morning sun and obscured the room, rendering the antique furniture, a reading table, and thousands of leather-bound books as shadows of their existence. The furnishings and inset bookshelves, which wrapped around the room, centered on a cold fireplace opposite the windows. The floral wallpaper and furniture came alive against the bright red carpet, which ran wall to wall.

It didn't take long for Emma to locate Brighton seated in a chair behind the reading table, slumped over the desk and sprawled out. The red carpet darkened underneath the chair where he had exsanguinated—the letter opener still dangling in his fingertips.

"Thank you, Mr Cunningham. If you wouldn't mind, please remain outside as I document the scene. Thank you." He nodded and shut the door behind him as he left.

Emma began with photo documentation, covering every angle and item related to Brighton's death. The arterial spray reached as far as the floral sofas and armchairs flanking the fireplace, at least six to seven feet away. The patterns and colors made it difficult to locate splatter, so Emma closed the ornate curtains and applied luminol to suspected areas. The excessive arterial spray and blood pooling underneath the body and on the desk confirmed her initial statement to Hatfield—death would have been quick, under a minute, easy.

After assessing the area around the body, which included several books laid out on display across the reading table, Emma progressed to the body. Without touching him, she studied the wound to his neck—a single, deep laceration across the throat, opening the carotid, jugular, and trachea. No jagged edges; no tears; nothing indicating hesitation—a singular determined motion. Not an easy task using a letter opener.

Within a few minutes, Oliver returned with Hatfield in

tow, continuing his line of questioning from the hallway.

"Yes, as Miss Winters stated, several of the staff had noticed a distinct change in his behavior over the last two to three weeks. On more than one occasion, he had been found blankly staring at this bookcase here. I myself had walked in on him doing the same on at least two separate occasions."

"Which bookcase?" asked Oliver.

"This one, on the far wall next to the entrance to the old dressing room." Hatfield led Oliver over and placed his hand on the shelf.

"What books are these? Any in particular he expressed an interest in?"

"Most of these are historical financial records or journals of the previous Lords documenting their service." Hatfield scanned the shelves and ran his fingers over their spines. "That's odd, several are missing."

Emma butted in. "Would it be these? Over here on the desk? The ones he had displayed?"

Hatfield timidly walked over, his eyes avoiding Brighton. "Yes, I believe they are."

"Do they hold any significance? Something that might shed some light on his train of thought?" asked Oliver.

"No, I couldn't imagine they would. They all predate his time as Personal Secretary by at least 50 years, give or take. The last journals we house here are dated just after World War II. Everything else is stored in the business offices."

"And just for clarity, what do these books contain?"

"Employment records, financial statements, endowments, and other various records. Except that one. That's an old photo album. One of the previous staff of Lord Cobham, either the 9th or 10th Viscount—I can't recall at the moment—was an avid photographer. He documented much of the life at Hagley Hall, from the lavish parties to the mundane daily work of the groundskeepers."

Emma, leaving the book where it laid, cracked it open and thumbed through its pages, casually spying the photographs. "There's a photo missing here. Would you happen to know which one or where it is?"

Hatfield drew closer and inspected the photos over Emma's shoulder. "I can't say for sure. I've only perused the album once before, though it looks to be a series of the grounds staff during that period. It wouldn't have any intrinsic historical value, so why that particular photo is missing is beyond me," replied Hatfield.

"Thank you for your time," said Oliver. "Please let Mr Cunningham and Miss Winters know to stay in town for a few days, in case we have any follow-up questions. We'll let you know when we finish up here."

When Hatfield left the room, Oliver turned to Emma. "Okay, time to be honest with me—no more avoiding the subject cause we both know you've been having blackouts just like this."

Emma's eyes widened. "How did—"

"I'm not blind, and neither is McArthur. You do this exact same thing in the station, especially around Bella. Not to mention all the reports you have submitted with doodles of the hollow on them, just like Evans. Does Hatfield's description of Brighton sound like your experience?"

Emma's cheeks flushed red as she hung her head. "Yes."

"With Hagley Wood being so close and the journals in question all pertaining to the period of time leading up to Bella's death, I can't help but think it's related," said Oliver.

"It's possible." Emma shrugged and gestured aimlessly at the books.

Oliver's brows scrunched as his voice fell soft. "My next question is, why haven't you noticed Brighton's left hand?"

But Emma had noticed. She knew it the moment she examined the gaping wound across his throat. How could anyone *not* see his bloodied finger resting on one of the books, marked with bloodied fingerprints. Clearly, this book held significance in his last breaths. Yet, every time Emma had thought to examine the book, a fog clouded her mind, distracting her. Before she'd realized it, she had moved on to another piece of evidence.

"I'll take that look as a *yes*," said Oliver.

Emma snapped several photos of the book's placement on the table and under his finger before sliding it out and inspecting closer. Immediately, the pages, bookmarked by a photo, opened up to a ledger. Oliver began reading the list out loud; Emma, on the other hand, picked up the photo.

"It's a list of endowments. September 8th, 1939–5,000 pounds, British Red Cross. September 20th, 1939–1,000 pounds, The Royal Society for the Protection of Birds. October 11th, 1939—5,000 pounds, Save the Children Fund. October 18th, 1939—500 pounds—"

Emma held the photo up to Oliver and pointed to a woman in the middle, finishing his sentence. "Isabella Davies."

He stopped reading and snagged the photo from Emma. "There's no question. That's Bella."

"Do you think the previous Viscount was involved?"

"If he was, it would be strange to leave a paper trail leading right back to him. Although, Hagley Wood used to be a part of the grounds here at Hagley Hall. He would have been uniquely familiar with the woods."

"It doesn't feel right. I still feel like we're missing a piece of the puzzle." Emma laid the photo on the table and took an enlarged snapshot with both her camera and her iPhone.

"I agree."

For the next few hours amidst the conundrum of Brighton's cryptic message, Emma and Oliver processed the scene before finally calling it into the station. As Emma awaited the coroners to come and collect the body, Oliver notified Hatfield. "We've completed everything, as much as we can, without undue compromise. Whether the media wants to make this into more than it is, that's on them. But we don't see any reason this should come back on the Viscount."

"Again, your discretion is much appreciated. If there is anything we can ever do to pay it forward, just let me know."

"I believe your annual donation to Hagley police station is more than enough," replied Oliver.

"I'm sorry, the what?"

"The annual donation the Viscount makes to Hagley police. It's quite substantial from my understanding."

"You must be mistaken. The Viscount has never made a donation to Hagley police. Matter of fact, he's never donated to any police fundraiser."

Oliver looked at Hatfield, unsure how to reply. "It must be my misunderstanding then. My apologies."

*

That missing piece of the puzzle nagged Emma as they drove back to the station, almost as much as Bella's incessant plea. She pulled out her phone and opened the picture of Bella they discovered in the ledger, studying every face and shadow down to the pixel. Bella leaned affectionately against a young man wearing a flat cap and dirty trousers and shirt. Emma assumed it was Nathaniel Roberts, the father.

In the foreground, not far from Bella, a young gypsy girl, maybe two or three years old, played with a doll. Around Bella stood others, dressed in typical gypsy garb. One woman, a little older than Bella, looked as if she could be Bella's sister, especially in the eyes. Next to her stood another gypsy male, approximately the same age, dark and brooding.

Something kept drawing Emma back to him, something familiar. She zoomed in and isolated his face. What was it? Why did she know him? From where?

Oliver glanced over at Emma as he drove, spying her phone until he finally butted in. "What's with the old creepy photo of Councilman Parry?"

The revelation came crashing down on her. Yes, it *was* Otto Parry.

Chapter 41
October 20th, 1944

Prof. James Webster jerked up from his desk, awoken by a peculiar *sloshing* sound behind him. Still groggy, he wiped the sleep from his eye and checked the clock: 10:05pm. The unexpected sound of slicing flesh and cartilage drew James' attention to the autopsy table where Bella crouched overtop the recently deceased Mrs Sellers.

His chest tightened as blood dropped from his face to his gut. Horror filled James' eyes as Bella sawed through sinew and tissue, scraping bone as she butchered the corpse. Gristle crunched and tendons snapped under the pressure of the blade until she fully excised the hand. Bella regarded the freshly amputated appendage for a moment, and then affixed it to her open stump.

The gray flesh of Mrs Sellers' hand faded as tendrils of Bella's flesh crept and subsumed it, filling it with a pink tone. Bella wiggled and flexed her new fingers, acclimating herself with her new body part. James froze in his chair. For a moment, while still perched on top of Mrs Sellers, Bella admired her new appendage, that is, until James flinched and knocked over a pencil holder. Pencils fell to the floor and rolled along the ground as Bella's gaze shifted from her hand to her companion in the room, the bones of her neck cracking as she turned.

The corners of her blackened mouth curled upward, compressing the extensive bruising on her cheeks into deep, black splotches. James pushed himself away from her, but his chair caught the desk, turning its wheels up and sending him crashing to the floor. Bella inched like a spider over the autopsy tables and onto the floor, ever closer to James. His heart pumped ice through his veins.

As she neared, her putrid breath gave life to *those words* which had haunted Hagley for months, *"Who put me in the wych elm?"* James just didn't hear them, he felt them in his heart, it reverberated in his mind amongst his thoughts. Her fingernails, black and cracking, tore into his thigh as she crawled under the desk with him.

She repeated her query as she pressed her body against his. Her skin, cool as fresh death, robbed him of warmth. The hair on his arms and neck stood on end as her lips met his ears. Her breath, shallow and raspy, full of tree rot, rolled down his neck as she whispered once more, *"James, give me my answer…"*

He didn't know. Nor did he know how she'd react to his ignorance. Bella's hands clenched tight around his arms as she awaited his response. James swallowed the dry lump that had formed in his throat before mustering the strength to speak. "I—I don't know."

Eyes bleeding to black as her skin rippled ashen, Bella recoiled and hissed before screaming, *"WHO PUT ME IN THE*

WYCH ELM?!"

James foundered a second time, frantically shaking his head side to side.

Unsatiated, she backed away and arose, leaving James to peer out from under the desk—her leg sans tibia collapsing under the weight of her body, limping as she dragged her foot forward.

Thump-shush.

As she exited the morgue and made her way upstairs, *those words* merged into the wails of the police officers, exuding her wrath as she limped along. James, still holding his knees tightly to his chest under the desk, couldn't move. Minutes passed and the roaring cries upstairs drowned into moans.

Pulling himself together, James staggered and hobbled past the lift to the stairs where he found PC Durst weeping in a fetal position. James snapped his fingers in his face and gave him a slap, but he was met with blank stares in return. Screams fluttered down the stairwell. James rallied his courage and ran up to the hallway leading to the bullpen. At the top of the landing DC Whyte banged his head against the wall, mumbling *those words* over and over again. James pulled him back and cleaned up the blood dripping from his forehead. As with Durst, no consolation breached his madness.

Those in the bullpen fared far worse. Several were left screaming bloody murder and clawing at their own skin. Inspector Smith took out his sidearm and dispatched himself, leaving a spray of blood over the wall. PC Richards ran to Smith's side, but not to give aid. He grabbed Smith by the shoulders, shaking him to and fro, pleading for an answer to *those words*.

Inspector Inight had run from his office, having missed

the trail of terror Bella had wrought, and attempted to help the others. James rushed to his side. "Where did she go?"

"Where did who go? What the hell is going on?"

"It's Bella—she's awake."

Inight's eyes widened and his pupils narrowed as he processed what James had said. "Dear God, the town, she'll tear them to shreds."

They sprinted outside in hopes of locating Bella—no sign, no trail of destruction to indicate her whereabouts. "Where the hell did she go?" asked Inight.

James' heart pounded and raced as he fathomed where Bella would go—fearing a labyrinthine search of the parish. "Hagley Wood?" he replied in a panic.

Inight ran to his Morris 8 squad-car and motioned for James to follow. They ripped out of the car park toward the tree. James looked for carnage along the way; relieved to find a peaceful city sleeping, unaware of the menace afoot. As they sped through the streets, James scanned every shadow, every movement of tree and leaf for a victim fallen prey.

They ran through the woods, both stumbling several times before arriving at the clearing where the wych elm stood. Inight spun around, looking out of the meadow and into the darkness of the woods in hopes of spotting her. James took the defeatist approach and fell to his knees. For the first time in his adult life, he prayed.

Minutes passed before they both heard the rustling of leaves coming from the silver birch grove just outside the glade. What they expected, Bella limping in bringing wrath and terror in her wake, was not what they beheld.

Instead, to their shock and horror, they witnessed an invisible force dragging Bella through the woods and into the clearing. Instinctively, they both rushed to help her, but were thwarted by a force preventing their interaction. They had become involuntary bystanders in the moments to follow.

James dropped to his knees once more; the grass and fallen leaves beneath Bella ran red as her beating, mutilation, hanging, and disembowelment stained the woodland floor.

Bella's end neared.

Her limp body was dragged to the tree and hoisted feet first into the hollow of the wych elm. Without any hesitancy, the force crammed her lifeless flesh into the tree with ease. Afterwards, her hand and flesh were lifted from the ground and disappeared into the woods.

Inight ran after the force, but there was nothing to chase once it passed the tree line of the small clearing. All signs of it had vanished. James beheld a different concern: that of the woman who had spent over a year on his morgue table. He trudged to the tree and peered inside. She was already gone.

Chapter 42
Guilt and Family

Oliver knocked on the door to the Parry residence, a modern mansion juxtaposed by the ageing brick homes on either side. Emma had heard the Parry's made their money via various businesses, but no one ever said exactly what those *businesses* were. She never gave it much thought until now, seeing their home in all its grandeur.

After a few more tries, at last a frail, elderly woman came to the door. The moment she swung the door open and greeted them, something was off—like presque vu or something. Emma desperately tried to place it.

"Good evening, madam. I'm Superintendent Oliver Bennett. This is my colleague, CSI Emma Lloyd. I work with Councilman Parry and have some urgent business to discuss. Is he home?"

The woman chewed on her lower lip as her eyes flicked about, checking over their shoulders as if she expected someone else with them. "My husband isn't here."

She went to close the door in their face, but Oliver threw

his hand up and held it open. "It's very important that we speak with him this evening."

The gray-haired lady, who Emma recognized as Parry's wife from the vigil, hesitated and continued to look over their shoulders, spying for someone or something else. "What day is it?"

Oliver, confused by the question, answered, "It's Friday, the twentieth of October."

Mrs Parry scoffed. "Then he'd be at the cottage. He's always at the cottage on this night."

"And where might that be? As I mentioned, it's urgent business and we must speak to him. I've made a terrible mess of the budget he was helping me with and it gets ratified tomorrow, so I need him to help me sort it out before then. I hope you understand, Mrs Parry."

Mrs Parry pursed her lips before finally answering. "It's just off Hagley Causeway. At the roundabout before Halesowen, take Hagley Wood lane. Only house out there. You can't miss it."

Then, for a split second, her scowl softened and her eyes relaxed—and the dots in Emma's mind finally connected, revealing what was so uncanny about Mrs Parry when the door first opened. The eyes. They reminded her of Sarah Hawkins. The same haunting eyes staring back at her from the photo this morning at Hagley Hall—Bella's eyes.

Oliver went to say thank you and goodbye, but Emma interjected. "Mrs Parry, I'm sorry to be so intrusive, but what is your maiden name?"

Mrs Parry's mouth hung agape, bewildered at the question, as was Oliver. Emma pressed on. "It wouldn't happen to be *Davies*, would it?" Mrs Parry's face changed from bewilderment to dismissive.

"Your name again, what was it lassie?" Mrs Parry asked.

"I'm CSI Emma Lloyd."

"The new CSI at Hagley?" Her dismissive demeanor changed, replaced by a curious, mischievous look.

"Yes, that's right."

Mrs Parry's eyes narrowed as she grinned. "Then you are not where you should be this evening, especially at this hour. My husband has spoken quite a bit about you—since you replaced Dr Evans—and I can see why you've been a thorn in his flesh. I like that about you. Perhaps you two should come in," replied Mrs Parry. "Would you like an after-dinner cuppa?"

Oliver, who had no idea what was happening, agreed. "A cup of tea sounds great, thank you." When Mrs Parry turned her back to lead them in, Oliver elbowed Emma and mouthed, "What are we doing?"

Emma flashed an impatient scowl and shushed him, gesturing to follow into the house. The interior design bore witness to both their affluence and gypsy heritage. Opulent furnishings and decor festooned the hall and sitting room, yet beneath the surface, a subtle dissonance unfolded. The rich colors and eclectic styles wrestled against their roots, creating tension in both air and ethos. When Emma first entered Ethelinda's humble home, the style and colors portrayed harmony; here, it expressed conflict.

"Please, have a seat." Mrs Parry gestured to the sofa, more expensive than Emma's monthly salary, and disappeared down the hall to prepare the tea.

"What are we doing?" whispered Oliver.

"I have no idea… just roll with it," replied Emma.

"You seemed to have a pretty good idea when you were talking to her at the door."

"Well, I did when I asked the question, but I didn't know she'd invite us in."

Mrs Parry returned with a beautiful porcelain tea set. Her hands shook and rattled the tray as she placed it down on the coffee table in front of them, promptly serving Oliver, Emma, and then herself, before reclining in an armchair adjacent to them.

"Thank you, Mrs Parry," said Oliver.

"Please, call me Ada. Now, before we get started, first and foremost, something needs to be known. My husband had me committed in the 50s for *trying* to tell Prof. Webster what I know. When I approached Dr Evans years later, I was dismissed by Supt. Burton as a mad hatter. So you have a choice before you: dismiss me as a loon like everyone else and go about your business tonight at the morgue as you should, or listen to what I have to say."

"We're all ears… er… Ada," replied Oliver. "If you feel we need to know something, then we are here to listen."

"Where to start then—I loved my sister very much. I wanted no ill will to befall her." She sipped her tea, long and slow, and shuttered ever so slightly. Oliver lifted his cup and flinched, hesitating before setting it back on his lap.

"We appreciate your candor, Ada. We don't doubt your love for your family one iota. Please continue," replied Oliver.

Emma raised her teacup for a cursory sip just as Ada took her second gulp. Oliver subtly held his hand over Emma's to stay her. As he did, the aroma of Earl Grey with a hint of almonds filled Emma's nostrils. Unsure why, she casually complied and placed her teacup back in her lap.

"You see, we come from a *very* traditional family. If you can't tell already, we are both Romani—*Gypsy* to you gadje folk. Times have changed, of course, and that's the irony of it all." She shook her head in disbelief as she finished her first cup of tea and poured another. "Back then, it was just unheard of in our culture. You see, *she* broke all the rules. You can't blame us after all. It was *her* who violated family honor. So, I pleaded her case to Otto."

Ada sliced the cake and offered it to Oliver and Emma, who both declined. "Suit yourself. Where was I? Oh, yes, I told my Otto to leave it be. *Don't get involved.* Those were my words to him, *Don't get involved, Otto.*" She wagged her finger as if he were in the room with them. "But Otto viewed honor of the community to be of the highest importance. So when my sister first told our parents she had fallen in love with Nathaniel, I was happy for her, but our parents didn't share that same enthusiasm, and neither did my Otto. Otto grew angry, especially after it was revealed she and the *gorgio* were with child out of wedlock. They wed several weeks later against the wishes of the family."

"If you don't mind, can you identify the individuals in this photo?" Emma pulled out her phone and showed her the picture from Hagley Hall.

Ada lifted her reading glasses, which hung around her neck, and put them on the end of her nose before taking the phone and studying it. The corners of her mouth curled into a smile before falling somber again.

"Yes, this was taken about a year earlier, if I recall correctly. There's Isabella and Nathaniel in the front. Myself and Otto are in the back here along with my parents and his sister and brother-in-law, right there. They have all since passed.

But here, in the front, playing with the dolly, that's Otto's niece, Ethelinda. Last I heard, she's still around." She handed the phone back to Emma and took another draft of tea.

"Not long after that was taken, Nathaniel went off in the final year of the great war, the first one I mean. My dear sister Isabella waited all those long months for him to return. But, like so many boys who had come home in those days, Nathaniel wasn't the same afterwards. Although he survived the trenches, the mustard gas had inflicted its damage nonetheless. He died from pneumonia complications a year later, but not before secretly eloping and planting his seed in Isabella first." Ada shook her head in disapproval. "Isabella was devastated; Otto saw it as a righteous punishment deserving of a *gorger*. His words, not mine, mind you." Ada again swigged her tea, finishing off the cup and serving another.

As Ada spoke, Emma's hand quivered, rattling the cup on its saucer. Behind Ada, in the darkness of the hallway that led to the kitchen, a shadow swelled, blacker than the darkness surrounding it. As Ada continued, it crept nearer.

"Now, before I go further, I want it on record that I didn't know the full breadth of what had happened until all that damned graffiti started popping up around town. I had nothing to do with it."

The shadow drifted over the threshold and into the room; its tendrils fingering along the wall, down the floor, and lurking under Ada's armchair.

"Eventually, my sister came back to the fold on the condition she disavowed her marriage—which she did, though she kept the ring. The bastard child was placed in a home to be raised outside our community, since he'd never be accepted with us. Isabella, on the other hand, did her best, but it was never the same. Otto made sure of it. She was shunned by almost everyone outside our immediate family."

Emma's attention locked onto the shadow. Slowly, it materialized and revealed itself as Bella. Emma gripped Oliver's hand and squeezed. "Ow, Emma…"

She looked at Oliver, glanced at Bella, and then back at Oliver, hoping he saw her too. Oliver just shrugged and mouthed, "What?"

"She came to me one night, years later," Ada continued. "She confided that she was leaving the next morning. She had acquired some money and intended to run away with her boy, who was about to turn of age. She made me promise not to tell anyone." Ada pulled her tea in and took a deep whiff of its fragrance before gulping it down. She promptly filled her fourth cup. "However, that night, I told Otto. He was livid. He tore the house apart, yelling and screaming about betrayal. I thought he was going to kill me at one point. I believed that it would end there." Ada wheezed as she spoke, holding her hand over her chest.

Bella prowled behind her as she tearfully spoke. She leaned over, wrapping her fingers around Ada's shoulder, and whispered into her ear. Ada flinched, screwing tight her eyes, and shifted her weight in the chair away from Bella. Even if Emma hadn't heard it, Ada had.

Sobbing, Ada continued. "However, the next day, Bella came home—without her son. I asked her what had happened, and she refused to talk about it. When Otto saw she had returned, he confronted her. They had an argument, most of which I was unable to hear." She cleared her throat and continued to grasp her chest.

Yanking back Ada's hair over her ear, Bella pressed her

foul lips to Ada and audibly hissed, *Who put me in the wych elm?*

Tears streamed down Ada's face. Oliver had to have noticed Bella, but he gave no indication; he just sat enthralled by Ada's confession.

"I never saw Isabella after that. It wasn't until years later, when those four boys found her body in the glade where Otto and I would picnic during our courtship, then I finally figured it out. I never forgave myself."

Bella whelmed up in fury, her face filling with blackness, and her fingers digging into the chair, puncturing the fabric. Wrath consumed her as she wailed, *WHO PUT ME IN THE WYCH ELM?!* Emma jumped back in her seat, fearful of Bella's intentions.

Ada trembled and hyperventilated, struggling to draw air. She dropped her cup and saucer to the floor, spilling the last of its contents. "I'm sorry, Bella." Ada seized and vomited, her eyes rolling back into her head.

*

Emma's consciousness slipped into the crevices of the sofa as the CSI agents from Hindlip processed the scene. A surreal sensation crashed over her as everyone, including Oliver, buzzed about the sitting room and kitchen. While Mr Brighton's suicide had national implications, due to his connection to a Lord, it would fall to the wayside as news of a Councilman's wife committed suicide in the presence of two members of the local police and attempted to poison them in the process.

She understood the importance of dealing with the scene

before Councilman Parry found out, but the reality of what had taken place—what was unfolding before her—exceeded Emma's scope of comprehension. She had always seen Bella when alone, or near Burrow. But now—now Bella manifested in a room full of people going about their business, everyone oblivious to her presence.

Bella's shrieking drowned out the voices of everyone in the room. Her sole focus laid on the corpse of her sister. Bella crawled about like a roach over the top of Ada, who remained in the armchair under a white sheet. As she screamed *those words*, her eyes bled black while her skin faded in and out from pale to translucent. She gripped tight against Ada, pouring out all her vile wrath onto her, but something pulled back on Bella, something not in Bella's control. The more she resisted, the harder the pull wisped away at her presence. Before long, Bella disappeared and only the echoes of her plea remained.

Emma didn't snap to until McArthur tapped her on her shoulder. "Emma, here, drink some water. You'll feel better." He was right. The cool draft running down her throat and swirling in her empty stomach revived her. "Do you want to give me your statement now or later?"

Oliver butted in. "Later, Emma and I need to pay Mr Parry a visit."

"Oh, don't worry about giving him notification, sir. I can do that once we finish up here."

Emma knew even before Oliver spoke that he would tell McArthur no. This responsibility fell on the two of them. "No, thank you, McArthur. Emma and I will give *notice*."

Chapter 43
What They Say about Curiosity…

That smug bitch was gonna get what she had coming to her. Bryant had never failed to get his story and he refused to allow Lloyd to be the first one to get away. Screw his boss. That useless fool gave in to the court of public opinion after Drakelow and let Bennett talk him out of the piece. If Bryant had to go elsewhere to get his story out, he would—even if it meant launching his own news blog or going independent on social media.

He just needed a little more dirt, something to tie it all together and expose her as a fraud. And with everyone preoccupied at the councilman's house, he had his final opportunity. This time, the lock on that drawer wouldn't fool him. There would be no more hiding his tracks after using a crowbar to rip it out. Bryant didn't care if he lost his IOPC credentials for it, either. They were just as incompetent as his editor.

Bryant's only concern remained on the validity of the temporary keycard he lifted months ago. The buzz of the door lock gave a satisfying confirmation.

The last time he broke into the lab, he had collected enough tissue for a DNA test, leading him to a Sarah Hawkins of Birmingham and The Royal School of Wolverhampton—unfortunately behind Lloyd both times. While the school ended up in a dead end due to privacy laws, he did discover a very perturbed headmaster. More evidence of an unhinged CSI technician conducting unethical investigations.

The cadaver on the autopsy table failed his expectations as it was neither Stacey Inight nor Bella. Bryant checked the morgue drawers for the skeletal remains—all four empty. Perhaps Lloyd had moved the bones elsewhere? He went back to the autopsy table to see what dirt could be dug up with the body—any case Lloyd worked could be potential for a scandal. To his surprise, the toe tag read Bella. But *this* Bella was *fresh*. He checked for a missing right hand and crooked teeth, which sent butterflies tumbling in his stomach. "Oh, please tell me you are mutilating fresh corpses to look like Bella." He laughed deeply and took some photos. "That's pure gold right here. Grade-A front page train-wreck!"

But he needed more—more to tie it together. The story was moving away from nepotism, though it would play a role, and was shaping up to be about an obsessive and corrupt CSI tech. Identity fraud, vandalism (the headmaster's desk was irreparably damaged), harassment, breach of multiple protocols (many illegal), and now defilement of a corpse. This exposé could write itself.

Bryant checked his watch: 9:50pm. He needed to work fast. First up, clone the laptop. He inserted the thumb drive with a key generator and started copying all the files. They'd be read-only, but that didn't matter. While the files were copying, he turned his attention to that damned drawer that wouldn't unlock during his last visit.

The crowbar drove deep into the space between the latch and the locking mechanism, folding the metal backwards and dislodging the bolt, causing the drawer to roll out. Most of the files he saw were recent and unrelated to Bella. Nothing of use. However, one file looked promising as it was marked: Bella Facial Reconstructions.

As he perused the file, something drew his attention. All the photos looked like the woman on the autopsy table behind him. And why so many over the years? Bryant spun around and did a quick comparison. Interesting, the face is the same—right down to the bruising. What sick game is Lloyd playing at? As Bryant returned to the cabinet, the cadaver's foot hung out from under the sheet and over the edge. Had it been like that before? He shrugged it off and continued his search.

Bryant put the file with the reconstructions to the side and checked the computer's file copy progress. Ten more minutes to go. He checked his watch again: 9:58. "Hurry up, let's go," he said, while snapping his fingers.

The remainder of the files in the drawer ended up being a dead end. When he slid the drawer back in, its twisted drawer frame—caused by the crowbar—caught the cabinet and pulled way, revealing a hidden compartment at the bottom. He yanked the drawer's face off to access its contents. He discovered a protocol list, a letter from a Prof. Webster, and a leather-bound journal belonging to the same person.

Bryant started reading:

> *Those who cannot remember the past are condemned to repeat it. ~ George Santayana, 1905*

While our great statesman Winston Churchill immor-
talised his rendering of this truth in the annals of his-
tory only a few short years ago...

"Blah blah blah..." he said. "Where's the good stuff?" He placed the letter down with the protocol and started flipping through the pages.

Early in this AM, Inspector Inight... Bryant thumbed to another entry, *More biological material has been discovered...* Again he skipped to another page, *As the singularity reached its end course, which in essence is reverse decomposition...*

"Wait, what?"

Bryant returned to and studied the corpse again. "It's not just Lloyd... it's like everyone here is obsessed to the point of insanity with this case!" Bryant reached over to another table and grabbed a scalpel. He poked the corpse with the blunt end first to see a reaction. Nothing, just a dead piece of flesh. Next, he flipped the scalpel around and sliced deep into her face. No response. He sliced two more times across the cheek. Nothing. Bryant drew close and opened her eyes with his fingers to find a fogged over glare gazing toward the ceiling. The dead eyes gave him the chills. He shuttered before setting the scalpel down on the autopsy table and returning to the desk to finish reading the journal. Enough of that tom-foolery.

He checked at his watch, 10:05, and then checked the remaining time of the transfers. Three more minutes. He picked up the journal and then felt a sharp, tingling pain in his back rippling upwards. Bryant cursed and reached around, but couldn't lift his arm, like he had suddenly become paretic. Before he knew it, his whole body tingled numbly, and he slumped off the chair to the ground.

Bryant found himself laying on the floor, stomach down, twitching like a fish out of water. He flipped his head in either direction to see what had happened. "Hey! Is anyone here? I need help! Hello?"

No one answered, but the shuffling in the room meant someone had to be here. "Hello? Who is that? I need help. Can you call 999?"

A hand snatched his foot and started dragging him across the floor toward the autopsy table. He flopped his head around again and caught his distorted reflection in a steel cabinet across the room. Something metal, long and slender, jutted out from between his shoulder blades. Bryant flinched as his cheek grated across a floor drain. There, at the edge of the cabinet reflection, his eye caught the woman from the autopsy table, dragging him by his leg.

Mustering all his strength, he fought to free himself. He grabbed for the leg of the autopsy table, but his enfeebled grip failed him and the table leg slipped out of his grasp as easily as water through a sieve.

"Hey, what do you want? I can help you! I have money! Did Lloyd do something to you? If so, I'm on your side. I can help!" But the woman ignored his pleas.

The woman wrapped her arm under Bryant's torso and lifted him in one swoop onto the autopsy table. Bryant hunched over the edge, unable to move his legs more than a twitch. Using his left arm, he swatted futilely at the woman, who proceeded to swing his legs onto the table and then slam him down face up. The scalpel, which had been lodged in his back, thrusted the rest of the way through his rib cage; the blade tip piercing the flesh of his chest.

The swinging pendulum light overhead obscured his vision

until the woman mounted the autopsy table and crouched over him as an eclipsing shadow. She leaned in tight, face to face with Bryant, so close her putrid breath flooded his nostrils. The three scalpel slashes he had inflicted on her earlier healed, yet the black bruises littering her face and neck remained—as did her dead eyes. Fingers groped the raw flesh around the exposed scalpel blade as she whispered her enduring question.

Bella drew the scalpel from his flesh. Searing pain radiated down his spine and to his legs as a warm sensation flowed over his shoulder and across his neck. Bryant's chest grew heavy, shortening his breath. Again, he feebly swatted at her, but there was no use trying to overcome her strength. A new sensation gripped him, one he was aware of, but dulled as if numbed by lidocaine. A tingling, prickly sensation raised the hairs of his right arm. Then he heard it—the sawing and slicing of flesh. His flesh. There was no pain, just the absolute terror of his inability to escape the woman and the mutilation she inflicted.

*

The slushing stopped with a tug and snap of his wrist. Bella admired the severed hand, holding it close to her face, caressing it against her cheek, before she affixed it to the end of her stump. Bryant's oversized, tattooed hand meshed with her wrist, their flesh joining in gruesome matrimony. She wiggled the fingers of her new appendage and turned to him as she placed the scalpel down on the autopsy table. Her dead eyes locked with his as she spoke. *"Bryant, who put me in the wych elm?"*

Not waiting for an answer, she crawled off the table and

disappeared, leaving behind the sounds of shuffling feet as the doors swung open and slammed. Bryant's eyes focused on the pendant light above, still swaying, as his body fell frigid and lifeless.

Chapter 44
The Cottage near the Woods

How appropriate, thought Emma as they pulled up to the rundown cottage that sat opposite Hagley Wood, not far from the trailhead leading toward the wych elm. It's easy to return to the scene of the crime when it's directly next door.

To the left of the gravel driveway sat a junk yard that ran the length of the property. On the right, next to the cottage, stood a dilapidated wooden shack that tilted over to the point that the next stiff breeze blowing by could render it a pile of sticks. Such a contrast to their palatial estate house in town.

All the lights were off, save the one over the front door, giving Emma the impression no one was home and that perhaps Ada Parry had sent them astray, except for the fact her husband's car was parked there. Oliver stepped to the door and rang the bell; Councilman Parry answered. "Superintendent Bennett, Dr Lloyd, to what do I owe the pleasure this late in the evening?"

"We have an urgent issue that we need to discuss. May we come in?" asked Oliver.

"Absolutely, come in. Make yourself at home."

The inside of the cottage wasn't much to look at, but at least in better condition than the exterior. Clean, with dated furniture sparsely arranged in the room. It shared the same homage to their gypsy past as their mansion had, sans the glamour and conflict of style. This felt *real*, like the honest version of the Parry's. To the left was the sitting room, and to the right was a small den with a narrow staircase leading upwards. Straight ahead, leading toward the back of the house, Emma spotted what looked like the kitchen, with a second set of stairs leading up.

"It's a little late for a cuppa, but perhaps a night cap? I was just about to open a nice bottle of port wine, if you're interested."

"No thank you," answered Emma.

"Suit yourselves. You can have a seat and I'll get me my wine." He smiled in excitement and headed toward the back as Emma and Oliver took a seat on an old, worn out sofa whose springs were about to punch through the cushions. Councilman Parry yelled from the back. "I am curious. What type of urgent business would bring you out to my cottage late on a Friday night?"

Oliver motioned to Emma to let him do the talking. "It's in regard to the budget meeting tomorrow. I know we'd planned to have it Saturday to avoid any daily work distractions, but I really think we need to postpone till Monday."

Parry stuck his head into the room, still trying to yank the cork from the bottle. "That's the urgent message?" He laughed, strolling back into the kitchen. "If this is your definition of urgent, then you are in for a shock as superintendent. It's going to get a lot worse, my friend."

"Normally I would agree with you, but Emma and I had a visit at Hagley Hall today and their annual donation came up in conversation."

"Oh, it did, huh? What did the Viscount have to say about it?"

"He didn't," replied Oliver. "The Viscount is currently in London. We spoke to his Personal Secretary."

"Mr Brighton, what a jovial chap. I'm sure he tried to charm you, Dr Lloyd. He has a way with the ladies, even for his age. Say, what business brought you out to Hagley Hall?" Parry sauntered out from the kitchen with a brimming glass of port and plopped himself down in a weathered chair opposite them.

"A case. Mr Brighton's unfortunately. He chose an *early exit* with a letter opener."

Parry winced and then tsked. "What a shame. I always liked the bloke. So, you must have spoken with Mr Hatfield then, no?"

"Yes, and as we were wrapping up the scene, I casually dropped a *thank you* for the donation. He seemed quite taken aback as he stated the Viscount had never made a donation to Hagley police before."

Parry contorted his mouth as he contemplated his reply. He motioned to Emma with his glass. "You know, it's a sizable donation he makes every year. That annual donation keeps your lab open and funds your salary."

"I'm very appreciative, that's for sure," replied Emma, trying to hide her contempt.

Oliver butted back in, "Yes, the station is very appreciative about it as well—"

Parry tipped his head back and finished off his glass of

wine. "Looks like I need a refill. Are you sure you don't want any?" Oliver and Emma declined again. Parry jumped up from his seat and headed toward the back once again. From the hallway, he spoke up, "Please continue. What did Mr Hatfield have to say?"

"When I pressed the issue, Mr Hatfield was very confident that there were no donations made from the Viscount's estate, this year or any year, for that matter."

"Well, I'm not surprised by that," yelled Parry from the kitchen. "Mr Hatfield, though a competent fellow in my experience, isn't privy to the *personal* finances of the Viscount. If I recall correctly, that is where the donations come from." Parry rustled around for a few moments before replying, "At least, that's what I was always told. Mr Hatfield might not even be aware of the contribution."

"Be as it may, I just want to do my due diligence, cross all my t's and dot all my i's, since it is my first budget meeting at all. I just don't want to be blindsided by anything."

Parry returned with another sizable glass of port. "Well, since that's settled, I don't see why we can't move the meeting to Monday. I'm sure the council will understand. I'll get everything sorted out for you, don't you worry. Your lab stipend will go unaffected, I'm sure of it." He winked at Emma.

When she first met Parry, she'd dismissed the quirks of his facial features, in particular his eyes, as random, unusual idiosyncrasies. Now she just saw them as unnatural. She thought back to her interview with Ethelinda, who spoke of the Hand's mystical properties, specifically the extension of life. *How old was he, really?* Emma set the question aside—it was moot at this point. All that mattered was Parry was evil hiding behind flesh.

"Again, much appreciated," replied Oliver. "Unfortunately, there is one more delicate matter that we need to discuss. I'm not quite sure how to broach the topic."

"Shoot straight from the hip, Bennett. Honesty is the best policy, after all."

"In our attempt to locate you, we paid your house a visit and ended up having tea with your wife." Emma knew the conversation was about to get very intense; her heart thumped hard in her chest.

"Really? I'm quite shocked. She's such a wallflower." Parry shifted uncomfortably in his chair. "I hope she didn't bore you with any of her fanciful gossips."

"Oh no, nothing like that. But her maiden name *Davies* did come up."

Parry swallowed down the wrong pipe and coughed up his wine, spilling a little on his shirt. "Blimey, please excuse me as I go clean up." Parry started patting his shirt with a handkerchief as he made his way back to the kitchen for a third time. "That's a random topic, how did that come up?" he asked, followed by some more sounds that were not at all related to *cleaning his shirt.* Emma was on edge; Oliver unclipped the holster strap to his firearm under his jacket.

"We recognized her from an old photo we found at Hagley Hall in the midst of the suicide investigation. We didn't talk about it for very long as the conversation devolved into the disappearance of her sister... Isabella—"

All movement in the kitchen ceased.

"—which also came to an abrupt end after she poisoned herself with cyanide over the guilt of what you had done."

Silence swelled in the cottage for what felt like ages until a shotgun blast boomed from the hallway, spraying pellets across the room. Most of it hit the wall between Oliver and Emma, but both were struck on their shoulders. One grazed the top of Emma's head, sending a trickle of blood down her temple. Emma dove for the floor and crawled behind the coffee table; Oliver rolled off the sofa and onto a knee, returning fire in the process.

The house fell silent.

Oliver pulled out a second, smaller sidearm and slid it to Emma. "The safety is off. Shoot to kill." Emma held it in her hand and wondered if she could pull the trigger again.

He motioned to the study where a set of stairs ascended upwards. "Wait there. You have a perfect angle on both the stairs and the hallway if he decides to make his way out the front." Emma nodded and then followed Oliver's lead to the hallway. Once cleared, she bolted for the den and Oliver made his way toward the kitchen.

The waiting was unbearable. It had only been a few minutes, but it felt like an eternity. She had no idea where Oliver was at this point—only sparse creaks indicated they might be in the house. Had he followed Parry out of a back entrance? Had he pursued him upstairs? The cottage was so silent, there was no telling where either Oliver or Parry were.

Emma adjusted her stance, trying to keep her leg from falling asleep. She couldn't just wait there in hopes that Parry would come running through first and not Oliver. She'd never forgive herself if she shot Oliver.

Creak.

It came from upstairs somewhere. Suddenly, a volley of fire rang out. Several shotgun blasts with intermittent pistol fire between.

"Emma, quick, come up!"

Oliver? She pushed herself up from her stance and raced up the stairs, looking down the hall for Oliver or Parry. The smell of gunpowder lingered in the empty hall.

Several rooms lined both sides of the narrow corridor of the first floor. Only a faint glimmer of the waxing moon shone into the hall from the windows tucked away in the rooms, making it difficult to discern anything with clarity. Emma reached for a light switch and stopped, realizing she'd announce her presence—if her stomping up the stairs hadn't already.

She slowed her breathing and listened for any movement that might tell her where either Oliver or Parry were. The house had fallen silent once again. Only the thumping of her heart echoed in her ear.

She adjusted the grip of the gun, remembering the feel of the kick when she fired on Burrow, and slid her thumb further down the backstrap to prevent slide bite. She stepped toward the first room and peeked in. A single bed sat comfortably in the middle of the room, flanked by bedside tables and a chest of drawers at the foot. Empty. In the hall, old photos—hung by wires—leaned outward, pushing Emma away from the wall as she crept.

The next room shared the same decor and layout; it was equally as empty. Emma started to doubt anyone was upstairs but her. She came to the third room and tucked tightly against the doorjamb to peer in, when she kicked something with her foot. She stepped back to find a hand laying on the threshold, swimming in a small pool of blood, and then leapt into the room, clearing it before assessing Oliver.

Oliver laid sprawled out on the floor with a shotgun blast to the torso and leg. It had ripped the shirt wide open and penetrated his stab vest underneath. Blood drizzled out from his rib cage, his arm, as well as his leg. Emma removed her belt and used it as a tourniquet on his thigh. She then ripped the bed sheets behind her and used them as a bandage on his arm—there was no telling the severity of his wounds. Oliver took shallow breaths, slowing with each one. "Stay with me, Ollie! I'm calling for help!"

Behind her, the floor creaked again. She swung around and before she could take aim out the door, the butt of a shotgun crashed down on her skull.

Chapter 45

The Confessor

Emma's eyes peeled open to see a faint light floating before her. Her head rang. This time not from tinnitus, but from the stock of Parry's shotgun. She swung her head around to assess the room and look for Oliver. However, she couldn't see anything except a languid glow in the middle of the room.

"I've been meaning to ask you," said a voice from across the room, "are you and *Ollie* an item? Did you finally put Liam behind you and move on? Wait, don't answer that. It's too personal, and frankly, I don't care. And considering you will neither live through to the morning, it won't matter."

Parry's voice eked through the shadows, but the darkness held him from Emma's sight. The pale light in the room failed to reveal any secrets save itself—and her. She struggled to move and looked where and how she was restrained, but there were no ropes, no duct tape, no zip ties holding her in place. Instead, her muscles simply refused to comply, as if something heavy laid upon her and held her still. "Did you drug me?"

"Drug you? No, no, no. There's no need for that. Besides,

I need you coherent, so I can determine if anyone else knows besides you. Taylor, Edwards, and Evans—God rest their souls—kept their mouths shut. Sheer terror stayed their curiosity, and I never had to worry about them. You, on the other hand, kept breaking the rules, regardless of how much *she* punished you and everyone else for it."

Emma jostled about, trying to free herself.

"I can't believe it was the budget that became my downfall. I blackmailed the previous personal secretaries to go along with it, convincing them of a tax scheme. Mr Brighton even wanted in on the action—cheeky bugger cost me a pretty penny to keep up the rouse. Burton and Evans were much more easily persuadable. I pretended to have caught them in the act of covering up Bella's body one October and revealed that the previous mayors all knew—which was clearly a lie—and that my predecessor dreamt up this donation to help keep it all under wraps. Honestly, I couldn't let word of Bella get out, and creating this elaborate scheme aided that endeavor—quite effectively I might add. Only error—not foreseeing the death of Evans, Taylor, and Brighton in the same cycle. No worries, a problem I will suss out this year. With that said, I only need to know who you told, besides Oliver, who, by the way, bled out on my parquet flooring."

Emma squeezed her eyes and shook her head to clear her vision, so she could see through this veil that had befallen her. Eventually, the dim light came into focus, revealing a tiny, flickering flame held aloft from a desiccated hand gripping a rudimentary candle whose wax had melted and sloughed down around its fingers over the years. The flame called to her, seeking to pull all volition from Emma, mesmerizing both her mind and body into submission. The candle cast as much shadow as it did light which held Parry and everything else in the room at bay. Only the candle and herself were visible.

"Tell who what?" replied Emma.

"About our friend laying on your morgue table. Well, maybe not now. She's probably already started her little *stroll* through Hagley at this point, wreaking havoc on anyone unlucky enough to get close to her. You clearly didn't follow the protocol very well."

How does he know of the protocol?

"Yes, yes… I'm well aware of the protocol. Have been since about the '50s. Prof. Webster and Inight were not as *discreet* as some of their successors, though much better at following instructions than you. Now, let me return to my line of questioning, and don't make me use the hand on you any more than I already have. I hear it's quite unpleasant. Who else knows of Bella?"

"The whole station," answered Emma.

Parry laughed. "Ha, if that were true, you two would not have come alone or, at the very least, would not have been allowed to remain here for the last few hours unassisted. I'm going to assume your brother-in-law doesn't know. For the same reason the station doesn't. But, PC McArthur or DI Wright? Am I getting warm? I just need to know who to blackmail, who to bribe, and who to train."

Emma wiggled to free herself, but she couldn't budge a single muscle more than a twitch, as if she were paralyzed. "They don't know. Only Oliver and I do." Emma told the truth, unsure if Parry would believe it.

"I hope you are being honest with me. I really do. None of this is pleasant for me either. It's bad enough I have to start over with a new superintendent, CSI technician, and personal secretary to the Viscount—don't want to bring in more people than I have to. The cover up just gets messy when they ask too many questions. I had really hoped you were going to work it out... I did. I was rooting for you and Oliver. But alas."

Mocking her, Parry broke into a diatribe about honor and family—something she couldn't possibly understand according to him. Emma didn't care to listen, her attention now lay on the flaying knife that appeared next to the candle. Her chest pounded as the thought of the knife's purpose raced in her head. She *knew* what he had hinted at, but hope kept driving her mind to conjure up other uses. Hope failed.

In between Parry's narcissistic rantings and excuses, Emma caught a faint sound of rustling behind her. A chill rushed up her spine as cold filled the surrounding air. A plodding drudge of *thump-shush* plunged her into fear as she helplessly fought to free herself from the *thing* behind her who she knew all too well. It crept inch by inch, remaining in the shadows of the candle as it edged toward Emma. A faint whisper fluttered in the air, familiar in its pain, but somehow less ethereal and more tangible. *Emma.*

The knife lifted up and stabbed into the tabletop as Parry angrily continued to speak. Emma jerked back in her seat, now reminded that two terrors in the room had been set against her.

Cold fingers ran up under her hair and tightly gripped. Bella's nails dug into her scalp as she pulled her head back, stealing away Emma's attention. A tepid face pressed tightly to Emma's as it forced her to look away from the candle and into the darkness beyond. A form appeared and Emma could just make out the outline of a man standing on the other side of a table—it was Parry.

Parry's arrogance blinded him, or something else had, for

he was completely unaware of a resurrected Bella who had now ensnared Emma. "I know you will fit nicely in the wych elm where I once put *Bella*, but your cohort in my house will be far more difficult to dispose of." His confession came as easily as his wife's, but carried none of the remorse.

Bella tensed at the hearing of Parry's admission. Her nails dug deeper under Emma's scalp. A palpable anger rose in the room. The leg of Emma's chair snapped; the table banged violently; glass shattered somewhere unknown across the room as unseen items whizzed about in the air. The whole building shook like an earthquake rolling underfoot. Bella's other hand reached up and took hold of Emma's chin, her fingers gouging deeply into her cheeks.

The whisper that came forth from Bella dripped with such malice that it stole away Emma's breath and plunged her heart into her gut. *"He put me in the wych elm."* The whisper metastasized each time she spoke, growing in wrath and sending the whole room into chaos. *"HE put me in the wych elm!"*

In a wisp of vengeance, the flicker quenched, finally revealing the whirlwind of chaos and the room around Emma. Parry stood in the eye of the maelstrom, mouth agape and eyes wide, gripping the cabinet behind him. His nails ripped from their beds as he clenched in terror. With the candle extinguished, it released Emma from its hold.

Bella, still holding on to Emma, threw her across the room and into a work bench full of tools. Her back crashed into the table, folding her backwards, and sending everything from atop the table—screws, nails, hammers, and wrenches—on top of her or into the cyclone still swirling around Bella and Parry. The bench's legs snapped as the table crashed down on her leg; her knee painfully popped.

Parry groped for the knife as Bella limped toward the table and crawled atop. He furiously slashed at her as she inched toward him. Each cut of the blade faded within moments, disappearing with no sign of blood or scar. Parry fell to the floor and pushed himself up against the cabinet; a trail of piss left in his wake as Bella slithered toward him. He threw his arm up and drove the knife down behind Bella's collarbone up to its handle.

Bella didn't break her gaze upon Parry and continued to perch on his chest. He pulled the knife out and drove it into her chest three or four times before she grabbed his wrist and snapped it, forcing him to drop the blade. Bella pulled him to her and wailed, her black spittle flying as she screamed, *"YOU put me in the wych elm!"* With that, she backhanded him, sending him crashing into the wall.

She pulled the knife out of her rib cage and inspected its edge. Bella regarded the tattooed hand affixed to her wrist and then looked at the mummified candle holder on the table. She placed her surrogate hand on the table and slipped the knife under the fleshly seam. Once amputated, it fell to the floor and tumbled near Emma—she immediately recognized the tattoos as Bryant's.

Bella picked up the desiccated hand and placed it on her wrist. The candle and melted wax crumbled and fell away as she wiggled her fingers about. No sooner had the blood rushed into her veins, the cyclone ceased and the items suspended in the air as if the world stood still. For the first time in 80 years, Bella and her hand had been reunited. Bella picked up the knife and limped toward Parry. Still unconscious, Bella slid the knife behind his collarbone. Parry moaned in pain, but hardly stirred.

Grabbing Parry by his arm, Bella dragged him around the room, searching for something. Emma helplessly tried to free herself from the table, but couldn't lift it in her condition. A chill swept over her as the gaze of Bella fell on her. She limped over to the table and crouched down to retrieve a rope that had entangled itself around Emma. Bella lifted the table and pulled on the rope, inadvertently freeing Emma from the table's trap. The rope twisted around Emma's waist and leg, entwined around her from the maelstrom moments earlier.

Bella flung Parry over her shoulder and yanked on the rope, dragging Emma along with it. The three exited the shack and headed in the direction of the tree.

Chapter 46
The Wych Elm

Oliver stirred, pain throbbing in his arm, leg, and back of his head. He pulled himself up against the wall to assess his injuries. His gun just peeked out from under the bed, so he reached for it and in doing so realized he already had a tourniquet on his leg and a bandage on his arm. Someone had attended to him and disappeared. On the floor, not far from his feet, laid the sidearm that he had given Emma.

"Emma? Emma?" There was no response from either her or Parry. Oliver reached in his pocket for his phone, but all he pulled out were shards of glass and metal riddled with pellets.

Blood pooled around him, causing him to wonder if it were all his. Reaching with his right hand, he checked the inside of his thigh for any pellets that may have nicked his femoral artery. Pain shot up his leg and hip, but his pulse was good and there were no entry points on his inner thigh. He loosened the tourniquet and replaced it with scraps of bed linen over his open wounds. When he checked his brachial artery in his arm, he wasn't so lucky—pellets had ripped dangerously close. Oliver wrapped the belt around, just under his armpit, and fastened it tight, and then replaced the soaked bandages with fresh linen.

He needed immediate help.

Oliver holstered his firearms and stumbled to his feet, slipping twice on the blood soaked floor. He staggered through the doorway and checked both directions for Parry and Emma. The house was quiet except for the rain pattering on the windows and roof. "Emma?"

Easing himself down the stairs, he checked for a landline on the ground floor and found nothing. He'd have to drive somewhere, unless he found Emma soon. But where was she? Had she gone for help? Did Parry have her? Questions raced in his mind, but that didn't change the fact that he needed to act, one way or another. Hagley was a three-minute drive—he could hit up another residence and call for backup and help would arrive in five. In his condition, that would be the best option.

But what of Emma? What if *she* needs immediate help? Oliver had no idea where she was or where to even begin searching—but in the cottage, she was not. He exited the front door to a swelling drizzle and found that both his car and Parry's were still parked in the driveway. Clearly they were here somewhere, which was a good sign—or so he hoped. Fumbling for his keys, he pulled them out of his pocket, un-locked the car, and got in.

Oliver threw the car in reverse, looked over his shoulder to pull out of the driveway, and through the rain splattering on the rear window saw someone or *something* crossing the street toward the woods. He slammed the car in park, opened the door, and got out to take a better look. Through the downpour, he saw someone dragging a body into Hagley Wood. Was it Emma? He hobbled down the gravel; his panicked breath floating in the air. It was Bella—and Emma was in tow.

*

When they reached the glade just past the silver birch trees, Emma hadn't yet regained all her strength. Though the candle's flame had long been extinguished, its effects lingered, bringing all of Emma's motor functions to a crawl. Her knee painfully popping with every jostling movement, compounding her predicament.

Bella dropped Parry to the rain drenched ground with a thud and released Emma's leash from her hand. Emma untangled herself from the rope and pulled herself up to escape, but Bella quickly turned to her and screamed like a wild beast. Despite subduing Parry and redeeming her hand, Bella was no less filled with rage. In fact, she felt more dangerous than before—unhinged, feral, and unpredictable. *What does she want with me?* thought Emma.

Parry laid helpless in the middle of the clearing, not far from the wych elm. He moaned and reached up to touch the knife still embedded in his shoulder, using him like a sheath. Bella limped back to Parry and straddled him, pinning him to the ground. She wrapped her fingers around the knife's handle and pulled Parry up toward her so they were face to face. *"You put me in the wych elm… now join me in the wych elm,"* she said.

Emma had no choice but to watch in horror as Bella met out, with unfettered vengeance, all the vile evil Parry had enacted on her. She pounded ruthlessly on his face with her bare fists, sending splatters of blood into the rain, and knocking several of his teeth out in the process. Bella rolled her fingers around his hair, tightly gripping his head, and then bashed downward on a stone protruding from the mud.

The crack of his skull echoed in the rain, rivaling the thunder of the storm. Emma couldn't bear to watch what came next, she knew all too well what followed. She screwed up her eyes and turned away.

Bella hissed at Emma. *"Watch."*

Emma gave Bella and Parry a side glance, peeking with one eye only, but it didn't satisfy Bella as she wailed again. *"I... said... watch!"*

Turning her face square to them, she opened her eyes as Bella withdrew the knife from behind Parry's clavicle and severed his right hand. Bella never broke eye contact with Parry; she savored every wince and tear he shed.

Parry's amputated hand twitched in the mud as Bella snatched the rope from the weeds around Emma's feet and clenched it around his throat—the noose cutting into the supple flesh of his neck as it tightened. While Parry choked and gasped for air, Bella threw the rope over a bough above her and hoisted Parry upward like a deer carcass. She knelt and took the knife resting next to his hand and then thrust it into his gut, twisting it around, ripping it out, flinging bits of tissue and organ into the air. Bella again drove the knife deep, contorting its blade around and around until the bough holding Parry up snapped—sending him into the mud once more.

Before pulling the blade out, Bella leaned in tight overtop Parry and whispered, her black lips brushing his face, *"Not... yet."* She stood up and dragged him by the noose to the tree.

Parry, eyes barely visible from the swelling, looked over

at Emma. She wasn't quite sure, but she thought he mouthed the words. "Help me—"

Bella raised his limp, dying body and began cramming him into the small hollow. From across the glade, Emma could hear his tendons and ligaments snapping. Soon enough, the last of Parry's bloodied scalp disappeared into the tree. Bella stared into the void of the wych elm for several moments. Emma pondered if her vengeance had finally been satisfied.

"Emma…" Bella said, *"join me in the wych elm…"* When Bella turned around and gazed at Emma, she saw that Bella's eyes had lost none of their malice. Her vengeance, raw and unsatiated, burned on her face.

Emma scurried to her feet as best she could, but her footing gave way under the mud and her busted knee. She slipped about and then stumbled as she limped toward the silver birch grove.

Rain and wind beat down on her as she lifted her failing legs up with each stride. Then a blow came crashing down on her and sent her tumbling into the grass. Emma groped the forest floor for anything she could and fingered the fallen branch that Parry had hanged by. She swung it furiously at Bella, who had already grabbed her leg and begun dragging her toward the wych elm.

With each strike of the bough upon Bella, they neared the hollow of the wych elm. Emma reared back and swung with all her might upon Bella's leg with the missing tibia. The fibula snapped on contact, sending Bella to her knees. It didn't deter Bella as she clawed at the mud and continued to drag them both to the tree.

The wych elm loomed over the pair as Bella reached the tree and pulled herself up, straightening her leg and setting her bone. Emma kicked with all her might, but Bella's strength couldn't be matched. Bella's gnarled fingers snatched Emma by the shoulders and attempted to lift her up to the hollow when several shots rang out and pelted Bella with lead.

Emma seized the moment and scrambled on all fours toward the gunfire. Oliver, soaked in rain and his own blood, stumbled out into the middle of the glade and emptied his magazine into Bella, now slumped over amongst the twisted roots. He helped Emma to her feet when a voiced called out: *"Emma... Emma."*

Oliver reloaded and took aim once more, but before he could fire, Bella lurched and tackled him. Emma snatched the tree branch again and swung, knocking Bella off balance, giving Oliver the opportunity to crawl out from underneath her. Bella stood, back handed Emma, and sent her into the rain.

Unable to stand, Oliver crawled away. Bella reached down into the mud and pulled out the rock that still had Parry's blood on it, and lifted it overhead to strike Oliver. Emma, aching from every joint and muscle, flung herself forward, not at Bella, but over Oliver, protecting him from the blow. In a moment of raw, selfless desperation, she prayed, *God, not Oliver...*

Out of breath, Emma panted, awaiting the pain of the rock crushing her skull. Seconds passed, and it never came. She rolled over, still protecting Oliver, and found Bella trapped in conflict. Flashes of sorrow eked from behind her wrath as her natures fought with one another. Emma knew not where her words flowed from, as if something ethereal interceded the groans of her heart and gifted her grace. "I found your son... I found Charles."

The internal struggle manifested visibly on Bella as tears

mixed with vengeful screams belted forth. She dropped the stone, letting it sink back into the mud, yet still grasped violently at the air toward Emma. Her whole body trembled and twitched as each movement to mete out her vengeance was countered by an act of compassion. Her eyes, still black with fury, glistened in regret. Bella gnashed her teeth, spittle mixing with rain, as her shrieks mingled with mournful wails and echoed amongst the thunder.

The words still flowed from somewhere Emma couldn't comprehend. "He lived a long happy life, Isabella… you gave him that. You gave him that the day you delivered your letter. He never forgot you, and, in the end, cherished every little memory he had of you. He got married, had a daughter—Sarah—and loved her as you loved him. She has her own family now, with beautiful grandchildren. That's your family, your bloodline, your legacy… your love."

What Bella didn't find in killing Parry, she found in Emma's words.

"Please, don't take that from me," Emma pleaded one last time, still praying to God for mercy. Bella stumbled as she backed away, fighting the rage she cultivated all those years. She turned and limped toward the tree. She beheld the hollow one last time before she crawled in and disappeared into its void.

Emma and Oliver laid amongst the muck and dead leaves, beaten, broken, and bleeding, in the sideways rain pelting Hagley Wood. Gathering what strength she had, Emma stood in the downpour and stumbled toward the wych elm. She peered into the hollow that had ensnared Bella for all those years and found it as empty as the tomb.

Chapter 47
The Protocol

As I close out this letter, I must reiterate to you one more time of the utmost importance of the protocol (attached to the end of this journal). Do not modify or deviate from it one iota. It has served me well over the last nine years to mitigate the incidental hardships of dealing with Bella's vengeance. The alternative, ignoring the expectations of Bella, God, or whatever force is behind this, is a scenario of the most unpleasant and destructive nature. It will strike you, the station, and Hagley without consideration of innocence to her plight. This I have learned the hard way.

As you read through my diary, you will notice one entry absent—the day of her awakening. That day, and the events that transpired, are too painful to relive even all these years later. I cannot bring myself to speak of it nor to recount it in ink. With that said, I will highlight the most significant instructions in the protocol missing from the journal. Far more important than anything, are these two instructions for the 20th of October, not later than 9.30 pm:

1.   Take Bella, clothed in her garments, and place her in repose near the wych elm's clearing in Hagley Wood (map enclosed)

2.   Leave with Bella a severed right hand. The hand can be from a male or female cadaver. All that matters is that it is:

     a.   a right hand and,

     b.   fairly recent and in good condition.

My last advice I will impart to you is more wisdom than instruction, though I do pray that you take it to heart. After completing the tasks for the 20th, depart immediately. Do not linger; do not stay. I know the temptation will be great, but suppress this; stay your curiosity. For your own sake, do not give in. Depart and know you have done the best you possibly could until the day you can unequivocally answer her query. Until that day comes, savor your moments of peace between the 20th of October and the 18th of April every year. They are the only respite you will have. Nurture your body, mind, and soul in those days—you will need the rest.

May God bless you and give you strength during your trials until the time you see fit to pass on this mantle.

Whisper carefully,
~ Prof. James M. Webster

Epilogue

Timothy shuffled down the cold cinder-block hallway; his undersized shackles causing him to hunch over as he walked. Two guards escorted him through a series of security doors and finally into a corridor with numbered visitor rooms on both sides.

The last time he came here, his guest had come unannounced. Timothy knew it wouldn't be him again, for he had lost his hand and life to *that woman*. In the end, he couldn't fathom who had requested a meeting with him, nor why. Yet, his barrister seemed well aware and concerned, judging from the nervous pacing in front of room number three.

Stepping toward Timothy in a panic, Reginald Smythe QC held his hand up and shook his head. "Listen, I advise you not to do this. This is a trap, I feel it." His voice oozed with the same sleaze as the gel in his hair. "I'm telling you now, we shouldn't go in there."

"Who is it?" asked Timothy, as he peered through the reinforced glass window. Sitting in a chair with her back to the door was a woman Timothy recognized, even without seeing-her face. "I want to talk to her alone."

Waving his hands adamantly, he said, "No, no, no... I cannot, in good faith, allow you to speak to that woman with-out me, your barrister, being present."

"Fine, you're fired." Turning to the guards, Timothy nod-ded to be let in the room. Reginald stood in shock, blubbering like an idiot. Timothy didn't care.

Shuffling around the table, the guards pushed him down into his seat and secured his restraints to the steel table bolted to the floor.

Emma smiled and spoke to the guards, "Please, that isn't necessary. You can remove his restraints."

"Madam," replied a guard, "you of all people should know the danger this man poses."

"Timothy and I have faced worse, trust me. I'll be okay." The guards shook their heads in disagreement, but complied and left the room.

The two sat in silence for a few minutes before Timothy finally broke. "What do you want?"

"How are they treating you here? Okay? I see your wound has healed well."

"You shot me in the gut. I nearly died. What makes me think you care one bit about how they are treating me?"

"Because I of all people know what *she* did to you; what *she* did to me; to everyone. What happened to you all those months ago was *not* your fault."

"You sure had a funny way of showing that," muttered Timothy.

"It's not like you were all sugar and spice at Hagley or Drakelow," said Emma. "People died. But I know, out of everyone here or in that courtroom, it wasn't really you. I'm sorry. I truly am. I wish I would have known it all earlier. I could have helped you and saved others."

Her eyes teared up as she spoke. Timothy tried to assess if she was being honest. "It wouldn't have mattered. There was nothing you could have done," he said.

"That doesn't mean I couldn't have tried." Emma hung her head and then winced, holding her hand to her lower back. She took a deep breath and sighed. "But it's done. It's all over. You deserve to know that, and I needed to be the one to tell you."

"You think, just because she got her vengeance, it's some-how over? It'll never be over."

Emma slid today's newspaper onto the table. The front page article caught Burrow's attention: *Missing Council Chair caught up in embezzlement scheme wanted for questioning related to murder and mutilation of local journalist.* "Timothy, it's April 19th. She didn't come back. I went back to the tree. She's not there. She found her peace." Emma stood, using the table to awkwardly balance herself. When she stepped out from behind the table, Timothy saw it—the sparkling diamond on her left hand supporting underneath her protruding belly.

"Boy or girl?" he asked.

Smiling with a hint of a tear in her eye, she answered, "A boy." She walked to the door and knocked for the guards to escort her out. Before exiting, she spoke to Timothy one last time. "If you need anything, let me know. And please, rest assured, she's gone. Our nightmare is over."

Timothy waited for the guards to secure him in his restraints before ushering him to his cell. The walk back was lonely, despite the chaperones. The last two years replayed in his mind. His choices; his actions; his regret. None of it mattered anymore. He couldn't change any of it after all. Nothing he could do would bring back Stacey nor the lives he took.

The door to his cell shut and locked behind him, leaving him to his true hell. Perhaps it was a taste of what Bella experienced—no way out, just his thoughts and a tiny window above his sink that mocked him with the light from the outside.

Sketches of the wych elm festooned his cell walls, the one thing from the outside he could remember with any clarity. Ironically, something he never saw with his own eyes. It didn't matter what he tried to draw from memory, everything turned into that bloody tree.

Timothy sat on the edge of his bed, sullen and alone. His eyes lost in the blank nothingness of his cell. Behind him, hewn into the stone and tinted crimson by his own blood, the wych elm's hollow spiraled outward and consumed the wall. It stole away all warmth and hope from the room, leaving Timothy empty. Deep from within its blackness, floating on the chill of his living coffin, a voice drifted and rested on his ear: *Timothy, join me in the wych elm.*

Afterword

This novel began mundanely—me casually delving into the black hole of YouTube videos and watching whatever the algorithm served up. That day in 2022, the servers saw fit to queue 'Top 10 Unsolved British Mysteries'. I expected Jack the Ripper would make the list, probably at No.1. However, I was curious about the other nine mysteries, so I let autoplay do its thing.

And that's when, halfway through the list, the next mystery presented caught my attention. It was labeled with the same haunting question that graces the cover of this book: No.5: ***Who Put Bella in the Wych Elm?***

I was sold. The banner hadn't moved off screen, and the narrator hadn't begun to tell Bella's tale before I knew ***this*** was my story.

I didn't even play the final four mysteries. I immediately opened Wikipedia, read the whole entry on Bella, and followed all the citation links to the source material. I then Googled Bella and read a multitude of blog entries and listened to several podcasts as well. That still wasn't enough; I wanted to know more.

Not long afterward, I discovered a book co-written by a father and son duo specifically dedicated to her historical murder. I ordered the book as well as its companion follow-up and read them both in a day.

I wanted to bring her story to life, but not as a non-fiction novel or blog post. I wanted something more. Something no one had done before; something that would grab people's attention and force them to confront her mystery. And it hit me: what if her ghost was the reason for all the graffiti over the years? The whole book was written in my head before I finished asking myself that question.

That brings us to the first fact.

Fact 1: The graffiti

The graffiti is legitimate. All the years and locations mentioned in the book are also real, leading up to the 1994 vandalism of the Wychbury Obelisk. The one fact I changed is the supposed identity of one of the 'artists', Mr Bailey, and the car crash with the fictional PC Ward. Mr Bailey and PC Ward are products of my imagination, though graffiti did appear that day, but I changed the street name and the text.

So if Bailey and Ward are fictional, who is historical?

Fact 2: The People involved

The two most prominent characters from the 1940s timeline, Professor James Webster and Inspector Sidney Inight, are real and truly did lead the investigation into Bella's murder.

In a few places, other factual police officers were woven into Sidney Inight's character for simplicity's sake. Another liberty taken for the story was regarding Inight's son and great-granddaughter, Stacey. To the best of my knowledge, he didn't have any children.

Regarding Professor Webster, his journal is fictional. He may have kept one in real life, but the one I created is pure fantasy. Factually, he was a forefather to modern forensics and paved the way for police forensics both in the UK and abroad. And yes, he really did have one eye and wore a monocle.

Other historical individuals were the four boys—Robert Hart, Tom Willetts, Fred Payne, and Bob Farmer—and their story surrounding the discovery. Their whole account is factual, down to the police officer who interviewed them, PC Jack Pound.

Outside of these aforementioned individuals, and Bella, of course, all other characters from the 1940s timeline and the 2023 timeline are fictional—except for one person, forensic anthropologist Caroline Wilkinson. Her work with the very real Face Lab of Liverpool John Moores University has indeed given us a face for our dear Bella.

Is anything else from 2023 real?

Fact 3: Drakelow, Hagley Hall, Hindlip, Hagley Station, and The Royal School

While Stacey is fictional, her account of Drakelow during Timothy's tour is 100% accurate, down to the marijuana farm (which was shut down in 2013). The name of Stacey's boss has been changed. Along with the history of Drakelow and the farm, regular public events did take place there, such as paranormal night tours and Airsoft tournaments. Although part of the tunnels is closed today for security reasons related to a wine import/export business, portions of Drakelow remain open for tours. One item I fabricated about the tunnels is the lower level. While the description of the tunnels in my novel are accurate (with the exception of the technical room location), there is no lower level.

Hagley Hall is accurate down to the description of the Library, but I took liberties with Hindlip and Hagley Station. Hindlip is the current headquarters for West Mercia police, so its floor plan is confidential for security reasons. Harris' office and the archives are fictional.

Hagley Station, where much of the story takes place, is also changed from historical fact. While the station's location and exterior are accurate, it no longer houses Hagley Police. It was closed and sold to a preschool in 2014. Hagley station has since merged with Rubery a few kilometers away. What Hagley station previously looked like internally, and if it ever had a cellar, is a mystery to me. No floor plans were publicly available.

Finally, there is The Royal School, which is indeed a boarding school that formerly operated as an orphanage. The general layout of the school and its description are accurate, but since it's a school, I changed some locations and internal descriptions to maintain student safety. One other accurate detail is that during the summer of 2023, the school was undergoing external reconstruction, as presented in the novel.

And Hagley Wood and the tree? How about those?

Fact 4: Hagley Wood and the Wych Elm

All real. The only things made up were the wych elm's location and the silver birch grove. The real tree is lost to history. No one knows its location or if it's still standing. There is an extant photo of the tree and the hollow where Bella was found, but the location's descriptions in the police records are so vague that no one has relocated it in the last 80 years. It's important to note, if you do your own research, that a picture of the wrong tree was printed in a local newspaper back in the 50s. The real tree from the police files is below.

Side note: there really is a house with a junkyard sitting on Hagley Wood Lane, next to one of the supposed locations of the wych elm. I have no idea who lives there, as it's privately owned.

Anywhere else that's real?

Fact 5: The Badgers Sett and Premier Inn Hagley

The Badger's Sett is a restaurant near Hagley Wood and it really does have some Bella hauntings attached to it. However, to my knowledge, there isn't a room to rent on the first floor. The Premier Inn next door does have rooms available if you want to visit Hagley for yourself.

So, now that those facts are out of the way,
what about Bella?

Fact 6: Bella

The truth of Bella in actuality is just as mysterious as portrayed in my novel. We have no idea who she was. Everything we know about her, we learned in the weeks following her discovery on April 18th, 1943. And yes, we don't even know if her name is Bella. That identity is ascribed to her from the mysterious graffiti found in and around Hagley (she is often called Lubella).

Much of her description is accurate: her clothes, the wedding ring, the shoes, the last remaining patch of hair on her skull, her teeth, and the signs on her pelvic bone indicating childbirth. Her left tibia was never located, nor was her right hand. Though none of the police records I uncovered specifically state it was her right hand, the photos of her skeletal reconstruction clearly show a significant number of smaller bones missing. The reality is she's missing more than just her hand, as some bones in her feet are also missing.

That does pose the question of what happened to the hand. The Hand of Glory and the theory of witchcraft are one of three prominent theories floated in the earlier years. The Nazi spy ring theory and domestic abuse theories presented in the novel are also true. The legend surrounding the Hand of Glory and its occultic abilities are all historical, except for the granting of long life—sorry, I needed it for the story.

Early in the novel, there are two news clippings from 1943 discussing the nature of Bella's murder. They are, in essence, real. I rewrote them to avoid copyright issues, but for all intents and purposes, they are accurate. I found about 15 articles from the 40s, all covering her death, and I merged them into what you read.

Conclusion

I struggled with how to present Bella. I needed an antagonist ghost, but that was difficult to write, knowing in my heart she's an innocent victim—which is why I settled on a vengeful spirit seeking retribution. I felt that was something we all might want if we were in her shoes.

And that is where I'd like to conclude this. Bella, whoever she really was, like so many people throughout history, is a nameless victim who fell prey to circumstances outside of her control and, unfortunately, outside of our knowledge.

Her bones were lost sometime in the 1950s, meaning

we'll never be able to perform any modern analysis to uncover her identity and, with it, perhaps how she came to be in that hollow. Bella will forever be an enigma. A victim who will never find her justice, especially since her case was officially closed in 2005.

While I wove a tale of wrath, vengeance, and ultimately resolution, her real story is far from that. Somewhere in the UK in 1943, there was a grieving husband. Somewhere there was a child missing their mother. Somewhere there was a murderer who escaped justice, which means the question that started it all will go unanswered: *Who put Bella in the wych elm?*

Acknowledgements

For my first novel—and hopefully not my last—I have many people to thank wholeheartedly.

First and foremost, my wife, Linda. She put up with long hours writing and editing on a hope and a prayer that this project might actually come to fruition. She's been nothing but supportive along the way and I am forever grateful. Next, my parents, Daniel and Jana Myers, for their unwavering support, despite their possible preference for other genres. Then, my sister, Holly Folk. Definitely my biggest cheerleader. She was my alpha reader and provided constant, valuable feedback. She was a great ear to bounce ideas off and to check if the artistic direction was smart or chaotic. My family let me explore this wild dream, and I will never be able to thank them enough for it.

Thank you to my beta readers for their honest and positive feedback on my story and characters: Michael Madigan, Marc Felton, Ben Hilton, Bethany Dryer, and my online friends who I know best by their gamer handles, Lathra, RachelDeDragon, aSirKnight (plus his father), and Jawzz.

I also want to thank my editor, Kathryn Hall, who helped me make some tough choices and guided me (and this novel) in the best possible direction.

Lastly, my heartfelt thanks goes to my financial supporters: lifelong friends, former students, their parents, and even strangers who took a risk on my Kickstarter. In no particular order, thank you to Adam, Jeremy Appelt, DarkStar's Book Cavern, Susan Edwards, Vannessa Goodwin, The Leibold Family, Rachel Lucas, Jaime Mckie, Joshua McGraw, Sherry Mock, Thomas & Erica, and Wendy & Gene Tolly.

Again, thank you all!

Book Club Questions

1. The story opens with a mercy killing. Was Thomas's decision to end Pearl's suffering justifiable? How does this act set the tone and raise ethical questions for the rest of the novel?

2. The narrative is presented from multiple viewpoints, including Timothy, Emma, Professor Webster, and Bryant. Which perspective did you find most compelling, and how does this multi-layered narration enrich the storytelling?

3. The characters grapple with intense emotions like grief, guilt, and obsession. Are their responses to these emotions relatable and realistic? How do these emotions propel the narrative?

4. The "Bella in the Wych Elm" case casts a long, dark shadow over generations. How does this inherited burden shape the lives and choices of those it touches?

5. The novel weaves together elements of mystery, horror, and the supernatural. Discuss the balance of these genres and how they contribute to your reading experience

6. The characters in the story grapple with grief, guilt, and trauma. How do these emotions shape their actions and decisions? Are their responses to these emotions realistic and relatable?

7. The story raises questions about the nature of truth and the power of belief. How do the characters' beliefs about the Bella case and the supernatural influence their actions and perceptions?

8. The ending leaves some questions unanswered. Share your interpretation of the final scene. Do you believe Bella found peace, or will the curse of Hagley endure?

9. The novel delves into themes of mental illness and the blurred lines between sanity and madness. How does the story portray

mental illness, and how does it impact the characters and their actions?

10. Emma Lloyd, the CSI, approaches the case with a scientific mindset. How does Emma, as a CSI, reconcile her scientific approach with the unexplained phenomena she encounters?

11. The pursuit of vengeance is a central theme. Is Bella's quest for retribution justified? What are the consequences of her actions, and does she ultimately find solace?

12. The novel raises questions about the nature of evil. Are the antagonists inherently evil, or are their actions influenced by external factors or circumstances? Is there a clear distinction between good and evil in this story?

13. Were there any plot twists or turns that caught you off guard? Did the ending of the novel align with your expectations, or did it leave you wanting more?

14. The novel touches on the theme of family and the complexities of familial relationships. How do the relationships between parents and children, siblings, and spouses affect the characters' choices and actions?

15. The legacy of trauma echoes through generations in the novel (ie. The Inight Family). How does the trauma of Bella's murder affect her descendants and those connected to the case? How do they cope with this inherited trauma?

16. The story features a strong female protagonist in Emma Lloyd. How does her gender influence her experiences and interactions within the predominantly male-dominated world of the narrative?

17. The characters experience varying degrees of isolation and loneliness. How do these feelings contribute to their actions and decisions throughout the novel, and are there any characters who find solace in their isolation?

18. The concept of reality is questioned in the story. Are the supernatural occurrences genuine, or are they manifestations of the characters' fears and anxieties? How does the novel challenge our perceptions of what is real and what is not?

19. Can redemption and forgiveness be attained by the characters who have committed wrongdoings? Is it possible for the victims of Bella's murder to find peace and closure, and what does that look like in the context of the story?

20. The pursuit of power is a recurring motif. How does the desire for power corrupt the characters, particularly Otto Parry, and what are the consequences of their relentless pursuit?

21. Fear plays a significant role in the story. How does fear manipulate the characters' behavior and perpetuate the curse that haunts Hagley? Does anyone overcome their fear, and if so, how?

22. The story features a blend of historical and contemporary settings. How does the author use these settings to create a sense of continuity and contrast between the past and the present?

23. The characters cope with loss and grief in diverse ways. How do their experiences with loss shape their lives and choices? Are there any healthy or unhealthy coping mechanisms depicted in the novel?

24. The story blends realistic and fantastical elements. In your opinion, does the author strike a successful balance between these two aspects, and how does this blend contribute to the overall atmosphere of the novel?